THE MERCY OF GOD

THE MERCY

TRANSLATED FROM THE FRENCH BY RICHARD HOWARD

1963 NEW YORK

OF GOD

JEAN CAU

ATHENEUM

THE MERCY OF GOD

WHITE EYEBALLS IN A WHITE FACE. At times like these the Doctor's whole face would come apart. He looked like a man who has been tied to the rails and sees the train bearing down on him. The skin would turn papery, stretched on bones that looked as if they were going to stick through it; the lips would go a very faint blue, just bordering on white; the ridge of the nose would grow sharper and the Doctor's head take on the kind of beauty skulls have.

"Do you want me to have a fit?" he murmured.

"I don't think you're ready yet," Match said.

Match had a strange way of talking. He dictated what he said to a shadow, and his remarks were entered somewhere in the cell, as though in an invisible ledger. You could see quotation marks, italics, underlined words. For instance, he underlined the word "ready." The Doctor took off his heavy canvas shirt, revealing a milky torso, repulsively white and bristling with bones, which he caressed. He recited: " 'O beloved, through your flesh I shall finger your bones, the better to recognize you on Resurrection Day!' "

"Those," he said, "are the most beautiful lines I know. The author was an eleventh-century Jewish poet from Toledo."

"Oh!" Alex said.

The Doctor squeezed his skinny chest with both hands. "The eyes," he said, pointing his forefingers at the two gum-pink nipples; "the mouth," he said, thrusting his finger into his navel.

Alex said the nose was missing.

"Here," the Doctor said, rubbing his chest, "lives a spider. I like her so much I've given her a home, but when I wake her, she stretches her legs, one after the other, until she feels like walking around. Then I suffer. This poet from Toledo was named Juda Halevi."

The Doctor told us more about his spider, whose legs are legion. (Spider or octopus? As a matter of fact, it could easily have been an octopus, voluptuously uncoiling its tentacles.) With his index finger, as if he were giving an anatomy lesson, the Doctor described the routes of the tentacles. One of them unfurls, slides across his belly, and rummages around in his head, hesitating; two others grope down his ribs and embrace his stomach; at his navel one branches across to his left side and fastens its warm suckers there; the other rises so far up into his throat that it penetrates his mouth and the Doctor thinks he might slice off its tip by gnashing his teeth; and a third, last of all, gently squeezes his heart. If the embrace is too strong, the Doctor's fit would be upon him.

"Some day," Eugène said, "you'll throw up and get rid of it once and for all."

"If I vomit the octopus, everything else will go with it: heart, liver, spleen, brains—everything it's holding on to."

"In that case . . ." Eugène said.

Sometimes, this "thing" is not an octopus but a flower, a deep-sea flower that breathes, lazily opening and closing its broad, fleshy petals. The sensation affords a certain pleasure. When the petals shudder with the currents that pass through the Doctor's body at night, it is even hideously agreeable. In fact, if it weren't for the flower-octopus-thing's fits of rage, the Doctor wouldn't have minded being lived in, being haunted by it.

The guard brought the coffee and black bread for our breakfast. "Enjoy it." The noise of jaws. Slitherings. Gurgles. Tinkle of spoons against steel mugs. Alex burped (and excused himself). We ate and drank in silence, like animals, but neatly, like men. Alex has given up swallowing fish heads, when fish is on our menu, the way he used to; Eugène no longer whistles between his teeth to expel the food particles that stick there, nor does he spit apple seeds all over the cell with a farting noise; Match has stopped sniffing the soup and commenting on its odor; the Doctor no longer looks for hairs in it. Every morning we leave a little coffee at the bottom of our cups and are careful not to eat all our bread, some of us leaving a crust, some half a piece, some a few big crumbs. One day last year, Alex protested this decision—though it had been taken unanimously—to leave something after each meal. He said "leftovers" was "really too much"! We reminded him of the meaning of our decision. Since that incident, none of us has dreamed of contesting the appropriateness of our behavior on this point. In this connection, we had a new morning guard three years ago. There was his expected amazement, that first day, when we all stood up together, the moment he opened the door, and greeted him: "Good morning, monsieur!"

He stared at us, and his round, rooster eyes filled with shrill poultry anger. But what could he do? We were polite, and anger doesn't work against extremely polite people, even when they're prisoners. He grumbled. A shudder ran across his shoulders. He looked like a giant who had been slapped by an invisible man. When he left, he slammed the heavy steel door and all its bars shook. Match smiled.

"He'll get used to it," Eugène said.

Half an hour later, he came back to take away the dishes. His amazement when he saw coffee at the bottom of the cups and the crusts on the wooden tray!

"Sick?" he asked.

"No, why?" Match said.

"Leaving coffee? Bread?"

The guard, like many of his colleagues—in order to accelerate conversation or to show that a jailer should economize something as precious as language if he must employ it at all—practiced the ablation of personal pronouns. He repeated: "Leaving food?"

With a broad gesture he pointed to the cups, the crumbs. We looked at him with surprise.

"Trying to get me?"

We didn't answer. If this jailer had the stupidity of a rooster, it was from some bird of prey that he inherited his greedy malice. Gradually, in the days that followed, he diminished our daily ration of coffee and bread. We held out, for honor's sake, but in fifteen days our rations had diminished by three quarters. Soon by nine tenths. Then they went back to what they had been.

Apparently the Doctor's fit was a false alarm. But it gave him a scare. Drops of sweat stood on his brow, and the blue of his eyes turned violet every once in a while. He rolled up his trouser legs, like an old-time shrimp fisherman, and nervously scratched his knees. In a very gentle voice, he explained that his fear was now in retreat. "Before, I was afraid of the fit; now I'm afraid of *nothing*. I once knew an epileptic who sat on a stool and watched an invisible hand draw a hieroglyphic whose meaning grew more and more complex. Concentrating with all his might, eyes glued to the wall, he followed the hand's movements with mounting anxiety, for he knew that the moment was coming when the hieroglyphic would be incomprehensible to him, and that just when the sense of its thousand curlicues disappeared, his fit would come. Then, hiccuping, racked with sobs, he walked toward the wall and rubbed the stone so furiously that he tore the skin off his hands." The Doctor mimed the gesture. He added that this man was his friend. The Doctor had prescribed a cure. "You watch the drawing take shape and then, just as its meaning is about to escape you, you close your eyes." His friend explained that this solution was impossible. "I keep hoping that some day I'll understand it all the way to the end; on that day, I'll be saved." "No, you'll be tired of trying to understand before the hand gets tired of drawing." "If I closed my eyes, I'd lose all hope of being saved." "You wouldn't have any more fits." "I'd be a stone, a piece of rind, a louse."

"I was seven years old," the Doctor said, "when I discovered what absolute intelligence was, in the huge glassy eyes of a mad horse. Tethered, he trembled in every limb, while a reddish foam frothed over his chest. The carter kept trying to relax the paralyzed animal by making strange noises full of gutturals and rolled *r*'s that sounded like some new language of love. That day, when I saw the naked terror rising out of the ground like electricity, running up the horse's legs and breaking in tiny waves over his rump, that day I finally realized I was a horse."

He burst out laughing. We all laughed with him. The Doctor happens to have a child's contagious laugh. How many times he's apologized for his behavior by explaining that he was a horse! "If Christ came back to earth, he'd deliver me not from a raging swine, but from a horse whose mouth, when the bit forced it open, would show long, yellow teeth." Helène, Helène didn't laugh. She didn't think "that" was funny. But who's talking about being funny? "I'm ready to present myself at the door of a slaughterhouse and formally declare that I'm a horse. I agree to walk on all fours, to eat grass, to till the soil. Provided I'm addressed in a new language full of gutturals and rolled r's whose strange music will teach me peace." To be friendly, Eugène, who said he had "served in the cavalry," offered to treat the Doctor like a horse.

"Thank you, Monsieur Eugène, but it's too late now. It should have been done early, very early, the minute I was born. I call myself a horse in fun; in reality, I know I'm a man."

While waiting for Match to announce the news bulletins, Alex began doing his calisthenics, as he does every morning.

"I can't live without pectorals," he said. "Soon as I wake up, soon as I open my eyes, I feel them and I'm happy. They're good, but they've been better. They've been great! Round as plates—personally I don't like square pectorals—and full and hard as tires. And a belly! Oh you should have seen my belly, my 'abdominal belt,' Monsieur Siméon used to call it! If I didn't keep in shape,

I think I'd die. I've always been happy just being in shape!
It was enough for me. Being in shape, that's all that matters in life . . . you walk down the street and you say to
yourself: 'I'm in shape!' You pick up a girl and you say
to yourself: 'I'm in shape!' When you're in shape, you're
not afraid of anything. I can't explain it . . . it's like living in a town where everyone else is dying of some disease and saying to yourself: 'I don't give a damn! I've
been vaccinated!' When you're in shape, it's like you're
at the movies; you feel good, you stretch your legs, you've
paid for your seat. No one has the right to kick you out.
Skinny guys, weaklings, they look as if they haven't paid
for their seats. Someone ought to strip them right down
and get rid of them. All right, knock-knees, line up in
front of that trench! You too, chicken-breast. Over here,
potbelly! This way, limp-wrist! . . . When I stepped
into the ring and took off my robe, I was king. Everyone
stared at my chest, my back, my legs, my belly, and their
eyes were warmer than the floodlights. I felt they were
kissing my skin, licking me . . . when I think about
that! . . . Yeeow!"

Alex made a fist with his right hand and delivered a
ringing "punch" into his half-open left palm.

This is one of the key gestures of American movies.
The director uses it to show that the hero is in a difficult
situation. Usually, in American movies, the hero, after
having made this gesture, reaches a decision. Almost all
of Alex's gestures were borrowed from Westerns. But no
one had written Alex's role, so he wasn't sure he knew it,
and he stuttered; no one had arranged his life, so he never
knew how to deal with it. His life was behind him, a
huge shapeless block which some accident had reduced

to smithereens. Alex swore. How could he glue it all back together? Out of the rosary of insults, one sentence finally emerged: "That trouble with Khadi wasn't my fault." Afterward, there was a silence—a heavy silence —from Alex. Then he would say: "There was a scooter accident ten days before the bout, and he went into training with his head all taped up. His manager was a bastard, like all managers. He told the sparring partners: 'Don't hit him on the right side,' but he went on training Khadi. The night of the bout, Khadi looked all right— he wasn't wearing any tapes, of course—but something was loose inside. I didn't know anything about it. Bong! Everything starts. And I punch, I punch like crazy. I was having a ball—it was like sponge cake. I noticed Khadi's face each time I gave him a jab on the right side, and I could tell that was the place to aim for. Every once in a while the guy fought back, he had guts all right, no doubt about that. It was a great fight. I never felt so good punching. At the bell for the end of the second round, all of a sudden Khadi missed his corner and started for mine. He'd lost his sense of direction and didn't even recognize his trainers any more. Still, he looked all right; I'd hit him a lot but he was fresh as a daisy. So I think: 'Baby, you're making a mistake if you get in the wrong corner. You want more candy; okay I'll give it to you.' In the third round it wasn't sponge cake any more, it was butter. I gave him two hooks strong enough to knock over a street lamp—a tall one; then a third hook hard as I could on the right side. He staggered a little. I stood him up straight with an uppercut, and then he fell on his belly, kayo. The referee began counting . . . at nine they carried him out, limp as a puppet. I helped, even though my gloves got in my way. The crowd likes that: it looks good to pick up your opponent when he's down. I felt great. A kayo's the prettiest thing there is, a kayo that really knocks the guy out cold . . . that's just plain beautiful. And it's great for publicity. They carried Khadi out on a stretcher . . . two hours later he died in the dressing room: cerebral hemorrhage. Yes, that's what happened. I got myself known as a killer, and they started canceling contracts. Afterward there was the two-ten."

"Oh, the two-ten," Eugène said, as if he knew what Alex was talking about.

"An idiot doctor—sorry, Doctor, I don't mean all doctors, just that one—an idiot doctor noticed I had only two-ten vision in my right eye. So all of a sudden the Commission took away my license. He also said I was getting encephalopathia, and that I was already past the first stage."

"Oh, encephalopathia," Eugène said.

"It's supposed to be when a boxer's always happy and keeps laughing without any reason and swears he's going to kill everybody in sight. When a boxer starts thinking he's the champ, he's in the last stage of encephalopathia. I wasn't that far along yet. I was just having a good time. The next stage is sadness—'the desire for solitude'—that's what this doctor said; and then comes the last stage, loss of memory and collapse. All the same, you should have seen that fight with Khadi . . . and the ref counting: one, two, three, four . . . it would have been good if he never stopped: nine, ten, eleven, twelve . . ."

"I like that referee counting for eternity," the Doctor said. "As a matter of fact, he hasn't stopped, Monsieur

Alex, he's still counting . . . listen hard and I'm sure you'll hear him."

The Doctor laughed in that irresistible way of his, and we all laughed with him. Alex stopped first and suddenly stared blankly at the Doctor. As if he were either going to ask him a question or jump him. In his bewilderment, Alex was like a sulky child hesitating between sobs and rage. But he didn't say what he was thinking, just shook himself the way a dog does.

"The point is," he said, "you always go in where the opponent's weakest: 'Give him some lefts to the right temple,' that's what Monsieur Siméon told me. So that's where I hit the bastard, on the right side of the head."

"That's always where you should hit him," the Doctor said, rubbing his hands together. "On the right side, the right side! Hee! Hee! Monsieur Alex, on that right temple softer than a baby's skull and throbbing like a frog's throat, that's it, hee! hee! That's it . . . hee! hee!"

This morning Alex did seventy push-ups, from the floor. Then he stood up, red all over and covered with sweat. His eyes filled with blood and a huge violet vein ran straight across the middle of his forehead. I don't like that vein that always appears on Alex's forehead like some explosion of brutality, a vein that swells up not just from effort but from rage too. Even so, Alex has a kind of beauty at these moments, with his vein standing up like a crest, like Pharaoh's pschent, a sign of royalty. It was the last thing they saw when he came toward them, swollen with rage, his hands open. To die staring at a vein . . . sometimes I think it's just a huge, violent

worm stuck there right in the middle of Alex's forehead
and eating away his brain. Alex is nice, nice and gentle,
but then that worm wakes up, swells with blood, and
drains our friend's brain, in spite of all his kindness.
That's when he used to kill. The Doctor has his octopus
in his chest; Alex has his worm in his head. All four of
us are inhabited by terrible little animals that have af-
forded us many cares and many joys.

Now Alex was skipping rope, using an imaginary cord
that strikes the floor with an imaginary and obsessive
rhythm. Five minutes of rope-skipping, then three rounds
of shadow-boxing. Eugène counted the seconds, only his
lips moving, his eyes fixed on his wrist as if a real chro-
nometer were strapped there. At 180 he went: "Ding!"
and Alex did deep breathing for a minute, under the
tiny barred skylight of our cell. At 60 Eugène went
"Ding!" again, and Alex resumed shadow-boxing with
extraordinary energy. He was preparing for the world
championship. It was training Alex that made Eugène
despair.

"It's all a waste," he said, "keeping in shape like that
and not being able to do anything with it! . . . a
waste!"

Match agreed.

"We should organize a world-championship bout for
three months from now," he exclaimed one day, inspired.

"Against who?" Alex asked. His vein swelled up.

"Against Robinson, the title-holder," Match said.
"You'll be the challenger."

No sooner said than done. Alex would face Robinson
in exactly twenty-seven days, and with this prospect his
training morale rose.

As the date of the fight approached, he perfected his form and made great efforts not to let himself get too nervous. We all hoped Alex would win the title.

Our friend has just finished his daily training session. His head wrapped up in a shirt, he stretched out on his mattress to "recuperate." We were waiting for the news. The Doctor was massaging the back of his neck. "Who can do this?" he suddenly exclaimed, striking his forehead with one hand and rubbing his stomach with the other. No one answered. Alex, his eyes closed, was busy breathing. Eugène was tormenting his joints to make them crack. "That means you have arthritis," Alex said. Match was preparing his broadcast. Planted under the skylight, legs wide, he stared at the unchanging square of sky where a bird's always-anticipated passage is an event. This spot was the source of the news which he would recite in a singsong voice twice a day and which we would listen to with passion or boredom, depending on our mood. His nose to the wall, his hands behind his back, Match announced the news.

"And now the late news; as a result of the flooding of the Rhône and Saône, all the low-lying districts of Lyon are under water. More than three hundred victims are feared lost. The government is sending emergency first aid. Helicopters are flying low over the housetops and parachuting in supplies and medicine to the unfortunate inhabitants who, paralyzed with terror and cold and often clinging to the chimneys, are waiting for rescue boats. The Soviet ultimatum to Finland expires tonight. The United States announces that if the Soviet troops cross the Finnish border, such action will be regarded as of the highest seriousness. The health of the Holy Father continues to inspire grave anxiety. According to word received from Rome last night, His Holiness has received extreme unction for the third time. On the local and national scene, nine crimes have reportedly been committed throughout the national territory. The victims include two employees of the Hôpital Saint-Louis, which brings to seven the number of nurses murdered this week by the mysterious sex fiend sought by the nation's police. Finally, the government announces that during the preceding month forty-nine thousand persons of both sexes have been arrested and interned on various charges. This figure will probably be exceeded during the course of the month since, in a single week, twenty-four thousand individuals have already been placed under lock and key. This concludes our broadcast. Next news bulletins tonight at eight o'clock."

Match turned around and we commented on the news. The floods at Lyon scarcely concerned us, and we didn't believe that America and Russia would go to war over Finland. The Doctor felt that the Russians would lose face if they were to retreat at this point. Although uncertain of the Soviet intentions, Match was sure there would be a war because the recent positions adopted by the United States were categorical. Alex, who is vaguely Catholic, was interested in the Pope's health.

"Four popes dying in three months is a lot," he said.

"I can't help it . . ." Match answered.

"I know, I know . . ."

"I'm a journalist, I report the news, I do my job."

"Four popes dying in three months, no one ever heard

of anything like that before," Alex said.

"They're old," Eugène said.

"The most interesting news," Match said, "is that they keep arresting more and more people in this country. Each week sets a new record. If it goes on like this, half the country will be in prison pretty soon; and after half, three quarters, and then soon . . ."

"You don't know a thing about it, Monsieur Match," Alex said calmly. "Suppose the government decides to let everyone go?"

"Of course . . ." Match said, crestfallen, for Alex cut him short, and all his energy seemed to have vanished.

The conversation broke off. We seldom argued long about the news. Hopes fade, wars break out, floods flood, murderers murder, rapists rape. Every verb has its subject. The Doctor, leaning against the wall, fell into a stupefied contemplation of the void. His expression slowly drained away, his eyes dimmed and filled with dust. Then they turned blank, swimming with tears as if he had been staring at the sun too long. Sometimes the Doctor would stay like that, without moving, for hours at a time. If we asked him what he was thinking about, he would answer that he wasn't thinking. He was sleeping, eyes open, a dreamless sleep.

"Were you asleep, Doctor?"

"No."

Was he awake? No, not awake either.

I'm absent. Neither awake nor asleep—absent. I don't fall asleep, I empty myself, I take leave of this skin (he pulls up his shirt, pinches his belly and pulls up a fold of skin). One day, I won't come back. I'll exile myself for good. (He releases the fold of skin that gradually slides out of sight.) In museums I've seen paintings of martyrs whose bodies stick out of a ring of flames. Their eyes are raised to heaven, and a dove flies up from their head. Maybe I'll decide to leave my body to you like that some-day. You can do whatever you want with it.

He walked toward his mattress, arms dangling, hands limp, face grim, and lay down.

"All right, what'll we do?" Alex asked.

"We could talk," Match said.

"Let's talk," Eugène said.

Today, Eugène has murdered his foreman. Today, Eugène was an excellent construction worker. His job was to run a giant crane, a delicate piece of machinery that requires skill, a cool head, and constant attention. The giant crane costs a lot of money and only big firms can own them.

"They're worth millions, those things. I was an ace with the crane. You know, I used to work cranes on trucks, tractors. For two years, I was in charge of a float-ing crane, on pontoons, two hundred fifty tons of power . . . Cranes know me, I know cranes, everyone could see that . . . besides, that's why I was suspected right away. Me, Eugène, be absent-minded like that? Impos-sible . . . Everyone knew I could pick up a butterfly with a fifty-tonner . . . It was impossible, all right!"

Today, Eugène was jealous. Every day his wife came to bring him his lunch while it was still hot, wrapped in a checked napkin. She was blonde with bright blue eyes, his wife. Provocative, like those young waitresses in work-men's restaurants who roll their hips between the tables and hand out smiles and cold hard-boiled eggs. Who sleeps with her? Each man wants to try his luck, since no one's talked about getting in yet. If love is measured by jealousy, everyone would agree that Eugène was wildly in love with his wife.

"Perched up there in my cab, just before noon, I was starting to glance down the road."

Perched up there in his cab, he saw her coming down the shed-lined dirt road that led to the construction site. He remembered exactly: a July noon . . . she was wearing a lemon-yellow dress. The road that the trucks, tractors, and bulldozers used was reddish-yellow. The walls of the new building were ocher. The planks of the sheds where the workmen slept were yellowish-brown. Over all this, a yellow and white sun made the colors flare like torches. There are moments of happiness when everything is just right . . . Noon, July, the sun, the cranes, the scuttles, the new carcass of the building, all colors one color now, the noises of the hammers, the screeching of the electric saws breaking off, the stubborn, irregular hum of the bulldozers interrupted by sudden coughs, the hissing of the steam machines, and Jeanne, queen of that empire, walking under that sun and in the middle of that order.

"And me perched up there in my cab like I was sister Ann, but I saw her coming and my heart started pounding, and I made my crane maneuver in her honor."

He manipulated his crane the way a captain runs the colors up the mainmast when the flagship passes. It was his own way of loving Jeanne, offering her this power, the salute of this steel monster.

"When I think of her, it's always that day I live over

again. In her yellow dress . . ."

In her yellow dress, with her pink complexion and the
helmet of her golden hair that the July sun touched with
a thousand diamonds. Never would he love Jeanne the
way he had loved her that day, at that minute, on the
path where the trucks raised the fire-colored dust and he
had realized that the pale blur in the distance was his
wife.

"She told me: 'Tomorrow I'll wear my lemon-yellow
dress, and you'll see me coming.' "

*This afternoon at exactly five I'll think of you very
hard.* A quick kiss on the tip of her nose, and he answered: "All right, me too, I'll think of you too." *At exactly five I'll close my eyes, I'll clasp my hands like this—*
and she playfully assumed the attitude of a Madonna, but
a gleam of eager malice sparkled between her half-
closed lashes—*and I'll think of you as hard as I can.*
That's what love's first seasons are like. You eat out of
the same plate, you say: "Quick, make a wish!" when a
falling star scrapes across the night's black diamond, you
doze off in each other's arms until sleep disentangles
your bodies and restores them to the indifference of
turned backs. You don't mention your headache or the
pain in your shoulder. If you're hungry, it's with her—
and I'm so hungry I could eat her—and your appetite is a
kind of homage paid to the casserole she's made. You
play, you tease each other, you caress each other, you
laugh; you take a kiss with the gumdrop she pinches between her lips. You don't mind a laugh that's too shrill,
you don't fuss over a steak that's burned. You forgive
each other everything: faults are adorable failings, moods
adorable whims. Soon the time will come when the plate

is pushed away, silences are filled up by the radio and *that smell of tobacco on your breath keeps me from kissing you.*

She loved him. That dress had been put on for him. It was the sign and proof of her love. As if she had written on a poster—"I love Eugène, my husband"—to inform all the inhabitants of the earth of the fact. How brazen her love was! How she'd have liked to load herself up with necklaces and bracelets and rings, so many chains and fetters, and proclaim in a challenging voice that she was Eugène's slave! How could she show the world she was in love?

She walked, her hips rolling because she was short, well built, and plump. They say that women who are short, well built, and plump can't help rolling their hips.

"It's a question of physique. Which didn't stop the guys from watching her go by, and they were pretty interested in what they saw. They used to say: 'It must be around noon, there's Eugène's wife coming with his lunch.' "

The saws stopped screeching. One man stood with his hammer in the air; the other opened his mouth, out of which dropped three nails he had been holding tight between his lips; another raised the isinglass visor of his helmet; another stuck his head out the window of his Dodge and whistled. She smiled at all of them, joked, held up the lunch box and the big bottle—a "super-Thermos" in which the cold wine sloshed. She was nice to them all, but once in a while she looked up, and then, even though she couldn't see Eugène inside the cab, it was to him she sent her broadest smiles and it was toward him she was walking.

"The guys envied me. They used to say: 'Which do you prefer, the crane or your wife?' Or else: 'If you had your choice between a sixty-ton diesel crane with two beams and a cab with a dentist's chair where you could sit in a white labcoat—between that and your wife, which would you choose?' And they said: 'You want to lend her to me Sunday? I have a night off.' And: 'If you plan to sell her, let me know first, I'll pay cash.' "

He was proud then and he laughed, the slightly embarrassed laugh of a man whose friends tease him about a man's weaknesses. Eugène in love, of course, was a good excuse for kidding. He laughed.

"I wasn't jealous."

Today, Eugène wasn't jealous.

"You couldn't stop the guys from laughing."

At the first blast of the siren, Eugène, with two sharp clicks, pulled the levers and immediately the crane immobilized its gigantic crab claws. All over the construction site, the monsters stopped living: the red blobs of the tractors bled wherever they happened to be; the drivers jumped out of the trucks without slamming the doors, the bulldozers stopped short just as their blades were about to swallow up a clay slope; the men climbed down from the scaffolding, rushed toward the corrugated tin tubs of warm water, and plunged their arms in up to the elbows. Like children, they sprinkled their faces, and often those who weren't wearing any helmets, their hair white with plaster-dust and lime, stuck their whole heads under water. In three strides, Eugène would be standing next to Jeanne. His neck shiny with sweat, his legs wide, laughing and showing all his teeth and his bright-red gums, he looked like an animal.

"Don't kiss me, you're sweating too much," Jeanne said.

She saw the sweat trickling in two silver threads across the wrinkles of his face. A man's wrinkles. And the two half-moons of perspiration under his arms. And the black hair that his khaki cap—the kind the American soldiers used to wear—had pasted flat on his forehead but that the July sun would soon crinkle up again. Did she love him? She laughed, and the sound was as clear and cool as an icicle melting in your mouth.

"If you touch me with your big paws, you'll get my dress dirty. You should wear gloves."

Tonight, he wouldn't be wearing gloves when he seized that warm body and kneaded it under his fingers. She loved him.

"Gloves? In this heat? You're crazy!"

Flirtatiously, she answered: "You should."

The men started laughing.

"She's right, Gégène, you'd better put on pigskin gloves and a tuxedo . . ." one of them said.

"And a pleated shirt and a bow tie . . ." another said.

"And those spit-soaked butts of yours stink. We ought to all chip in and buy Eugène a holder."

"And install air-conditioning up there in his crane . . ."

"Stick in a television set."

"And don't forget the flowers, flowers are important!"

Eugène's smile spread to a grin. He untied the pink-and-white checked napkin, missed a knot, forced it, grew impatient. Jeanne watched the grease-spotted hands with their flat nails covered with black stains. Eugène's face was calm: all his rage was in the hands trembling over the pink-and-white checked napkin. Does she love me? Tonight she'll love me. Tonight I'll ask her: "Do you love me? Say it. Say it. Do you love me?" And when she's naked and helpless under me, then I'll say: "Say you love me now, swear it!"

"I wasn't jealous. It's crazy to be jealous. Stupid. Once you start that it's never over. You begin suspecting your own shadow."

He concealed his jealousy clumsily, like a child hiding a stolen apple. The boys weren't fooled. When someone would look at his wife, Eugène lowered his eyes like a priest witnessing a scene of wild debauchery. It's not always so much fun to have a pretty wife and love her. There was a time when Eugène didn't love anyone— they loved *him*. He didn't think about anyone while he maneuvered his crane; he sang songs he'd heard on the radio, and when he didn't know the words he whistled. That was why they used to call him the warbler. He was happy up there in his steel cage, and on Monday mornings he told the boys about his "pickups."

"Naturally," he used to say, with a glint of cunning in his eyes, "if you work a crane it'd be too bad if you didn't know how to pick up something."

"How much did yesterday's weigh?"

"Five tons!"

They used to laugh all the time.

Eugène stopped his story there. Match was beginning to yawn. We were just talking to make noise, and if certain meanings rose out of our words—and if we called that "telling the story of our lives"—it wasn't really our fault. We weren't responsible for our "stories": they would come to our lips like our bad breath. Prisoners, we have neither present nor future, nothing but pasts that we contemplate from these heights. From so high up, from so far away, we contemplate the cities of our lives, playthings now!

His thick canvas shirt outside his trousers, the Doctor, awake now, walked back and forth, grumbling. He said that once, in a train, he stared at the other passengers with the greatest attention and wondered why he didn't love *everybody*. Why love this person more than that one? If you thought about it, there was no valid answer to this question. "Why shouldn't I love—even passionately —these people reading or dozing in my compartment? That's the kind of question that stirs you to the depths of your soul! Anyone is worth as much as anyone else, and what's always astonished me is that you decided to love *this* person rather than that one. What I've concluded is that you didn't love *this* person at all."

"Then who is it you love?"

"Your own infamous person, Monsieur Match! Love is just training someone to love you, the way you train a dog to retrieve a slipper."

"Still," Match said, "sometimes you really do fall in love with someone who doesn't love you back."

"Oh, no!" the Doctor said, "that person loves you in his own way, which might be to hate you, for instance . . ."

"Or with someone who's indifferent."

"Well that's because you've secretly trained that person to hate you or to be indifferent to you."

"If we went on with this discussion, Doctor, would

you have an answer for everything?"

"Absolutely everything. So if you don't agree with me you'd better stop asking me questions, since you won't change your opinions."

"And if I did change my opinion?"

"Impossible, Monsieur Match. If one person existed on this earth who could convince another person, all the mysteries of the world would be solved."

Now Eugène was thinking. He was terribly happy but he was thinking. He wasn't singing, he wasn't whistling any more. He was thinking about Jeanne. I love her. Once he didn't "believe in love." A man who was in love really disgusted him. Besides, he was good-looking, with his brilliant eyes that went white with anger, as if he had suddenly gone blind, and his long, almost girlish eyelashes that sometimes veiled the harsh violence of his stare, and his black hair that glinted blue at night when he put lotion on it. He knew he was good-looking because he would hear girls whispering to each other in the dance halls, or in a café, or in a movie line: "Look at that dark boy over there. Did you see his eyes?"

He had all the girls he wanted, because of his eyes. "Girls," he said, "all you have to do is look at them and they come and eat out of your hand." The guys envied him, and Monday noons they clustered around to hear about his easy victories. Both bard and warrior, Eugène claimed he didn't want to give away any secrets, and each time they would beg him, the way the couples in a dance hall beg the orchestra for their favorite song. Finally he would accept, and do his number. The theme was always the same: a story about a girl he had met, picked up, slept with. The variations were the personality of the girl. Short, tall, thin, plump, blonde, dark, rich, poor, young, mature . . . She had said to him . . . Then he had said . . . then she had said to him . . . and he had answered . . . and he had . . . and then she had . . . It was a tapestry Eugène began over and over again for the guys, a Penelope's web unraveled during the week but by Monday just the same, only woven with new colors. Eugène gave details, quoted phrases and intimate words, displayed his betrayals with all the more pride since it seemed to do him no harm with the girls. And in his friends' eyes, it was the plume that gleamed above the helmet of this invulnerable amatory Achilles. On one side, there were the girls you hunted, captured, then abandoned, obliterating the footprints of your flight. On the other, there were the men, the boys, the accomplices, the brothers at whose feet, like trophies, you laid the confession of all your adventures. Never had Eugène said: "I love you" to a woman. These words had never passed his lips, and to speak them seemed an obscenity. He gave nothing but his caresses, his eyes, and the warmth of his enormous hands between which so many bodies surrendered their secrets.

"It's sautéed rabbit," she said. "And I brought you some peaches for dessert."

"Great, great!" Eugène said, sniffing the golden rabbit leg before he bit into it.

"All right, I'm going now," Jeanne said, standing up and smoothing her dress.

"Already? Don't you want to stay a little longer?"

"To watch you eat? No. . . . Do you think I have

nothing better to do? I have three blouses to finish before tomorrow."

Does she love me? What was her tone when she said: "to watch you eat?" I'd be glad to watch her eat, to watch her sleep—for hours. I love her gestures, all I hear is her voice. Once she asked if he'd still love her when she was ugly. He answered with something sweet he's forgotten.

"You're like a baby that only eats if he has his mama with him."

Eugène shrugged. The guys winked at each other.

"See you tonight, darling."

"Yes," Eugène said, his mouth full.

They always told me I'd get caught some day. You're right, Monsieur Alex. The boxer who's never been knocked out thinks he can't be. At a hundred miles an hour, a wheel comes off and the car smashes into the wall of the track. You're walking along in the country and you step on a snake's tail. Just one banana peel on the widest sidewalk in the biggest city, and that's the one you slip on. Where does it come from, that one direct hit that gets you when a thousand others scarcely shook you up at all? Why *that* wall? *That* snake? *That* banana peel? Why *that* woman?

"Because everything is written!" Alex said in the voice of a preacher during Lent.

"No!" the Doctor exclaimed.

"What do you know about it?" Alex asked.

"I'll prove it to you," the Doctor said.

In the beginning, there was no difference between her and the others. Everything was just as easy, and taken care of just as fast. He took her out two Sundays in a row, then, as usual, he dropped her. Forgot about her.

Hung her up in Bluebeard's closet. Deader than dead, because nothing's more out of sight than someone you've forgotten about. A few months later, he met her at the Tourbillon. Christ, I know that girl! He'd even forgotten her name. What are you looking at? He was with a friend. The one in the red dress? Yes. You know her? Christ, she's stacked! Yes, I know her, I had her about three months ago. "Go on! . . ." his friend sighed. "If you hang yourself someday I'll take a piece of the rope for luck." She was dancing with a boy who had a band-aid on his neck; a kid still at the pimple stage. She was dancing, waltzing, with that serious look, a little stiff, a little angry, the look of "girls who like to waltz." She was turning, her head held high and staring over her partner's shoulder, each movement pulling her away or flattening her against him. Queen of the ball. The starched and radiant angel of this low-ceilinged dance hall where a colored ball revolving on the ceiling spattered the whole half-darkened room with light. Does she recognize me? He was trying to catch her attention, to hold her captive, for a quarter of a second, in the frozen lake of his eyes, but she kept turning, turning, turning, and her eyes sparkled over her partner's shoulder, as though on a pinnacle, her gaze intoxicated by the gravity and the vertigo of the waltz. Maybe she recognized him, but she was pretending not to. . . . Are you going to ask her to dance? She'll probably freeze me out, I dropped her pretty hard. We'll see. Unless that pimply-faced kid is with her. Why did you drop a piece like that? And why did your sister join the Foreign Legion? He severed the rabbit leg in one bite, like a mad dog. Pretty good, this rabbit. She loves me. The waltz was over. Pimply-

face was walking back to her table, talking to her, probably trying to fill up her card for the whole night. She
smiled, she didn't say yes, she didn't say no . . . she
was drinking a crème de menthe, her lips pursed around
a long straw. She raised her eyes as if she were waiting—
for whom?—wiped her mouth with a crumpled handkerchief, and leaned back in her chair.

That's when he loved her. No, not right away. He
wanted her, that was all, but with a total desire that
scorched him all the way down. Not one of the usual de-
sires, ruled like music paper, well regulated in his head,
and cold between his hands. He had pepper in his throat.
He hated her because she was intact. Because at that
precise moment she was incredibly free of all desire for
Eugène. She was nibbling at the straw, and Eugène had
no more importance for her than any of those other men
whose eyes were roving all over the room. Maybe some
people commit murder just to attract attention.

"Very true," the Doctor said. "The last look in the
eyes of someone you strangle . . ." He stopped, then
added: "I mean, it's a look of crucial importance." (Another silence, then): "Twice I've been of crucial importance that way. Have you ever noticed that animals are
incapable of sustaining the human gaze? There's a terrifying mystery about it. When I was a child I used to like
to stare into the eyes of all the cats and dogs I could find.
For a whole summer, that was all I did . . . it was a
craze, a mania . . . I crossed the street whenever I saw
a cat crouching on a window sill. I went over to it and
imprisoned its eyes in mine. Soon the cat closed its eyes or
got up and went away. I've seen some run away with their
tails straight out behind them. And each time I won-

dered: 'Why?' without finding any answer, and with a
kind of melancholy fear."

"How old were you?" Match asked.

"Seven. I asked my mother: 'Why don't cats want to
look me in the eye?' 'They've probably got something
better to do.' 'No, they're just sitting there on the window
sill, so why?' One day I began crying, and my father
found me in tears, my eyes all red and my cheeks stained
with despair: 'That boy is crazy,' my mother said, 'he's
crying because cats don't want to look him in the eye. He
spends hours standing in front of all the cats in the neighborhood. Yesterday he stopped ten times in front of
Madame Saint-Roman's window, you know, she has a
Siamese that's always sitting there, behind the glass. Finally Madame Saint-Roman had to go out and she said
to him: Go on inside if you want to play with Pasha. So
he screamed no! and ran away.' I went on sobbing. My
father took a handkerchief out of his pocket and asked
me to wet it with saliva and wiped off my cheeks. 'Tell
me about it!' My father looked at me very gently, kissed
me on my forehead at the roots of my hair, and said:
'We'll go to the zoo and ask the big tiger to tell us, all
right?' I swallowed my tears! 'Yes.' My mother made a
gesture of irritation."

"He took you to the zoo?" Match asked.

"Later."

"What did the big tiger say?"

"Oh, I didn't care any more, my mania had gone. I
had another one."

"What was it?"

"Another one!" the Doctor said dryly.

Using a spoon whose handle he had sharpened, Alex

was carving a heart inside a wooden clog. He stuck his tongue out as he worked. In the cell, all you could hear was the scraping of the spoon punctuated by Alex's sighs. We admired his work.

"In this one I'm carving a heart," Alex said.

"And in the other?"

"Guess . . ."

We guessed. Only two subjects nourish our friend's artistic imagination: the heart and the phallus. The only art exhibitions he had ever seen were the *graffiti* drawn or carved in public toilets. To these small tasks he brought a fanatical attention, and anyone trying to snatch the clog out of his hand would die with a spoon handle down his throat.

"And inside the heart I'm going to engrave a motto."

"What?"

"I haven't decided yet. I can't make up my mind between 'Bravo boxing' and 'Souvenir of Guitare.'"

"Your friend?"

"That's right, my friend Guitare d'Amour."

Match sat down on the mattress. He held his head between his long hands. Dry white hands, with pale pink nails. All the beauty of his swarthy, awkward body full of nerves and agonies had taken refuge in these splendid hands. In the workshops of the Renaissance, the Master occasionally painted some detail of a painting. The Master walked over to the portrait of Match his students had botched. You could scarcely discern a livid face emerging from the gloom of the canvas, corroded by the night. It looked like an apparition, and when you blinked, the whole canvas seemed black. You had to get very close to it, and then you saw Match's bulging forehead and the ridge of his hooked nose emerging from the darkness, trying to focus the light; but from deep in the painting rose a flood of shadows that drew his body backward toward darkness. There was one special thing about Match: he disgorged darkness through every one of his pores, he secreted darkness like the squid that hides itself in clouds of ink. His presence on top of an Acropolis would darken the sky of any Greece. Match was a *funereal* individual. Then the Master, out of this black mud, brought forth these hands, illuminated with milk, that were given to Match to cling to the world with, the way a drowning man clings to the ropes that are thrown to him.

Match believed he was an artist on account of these hands, which early in his life he held before him, like the two luminous vessels in which the holy oils gleam. Hands, you were my one hope, and I raised you to heaven. You were the monstrance of my pain when I celebrated my ugliness and my solitude. You were my sole treasure. So beautiful that they've proved to be useless . . . No piano has sung beneath their caress, no poem has sprung up at the penpoint they clasped. They were stupid, with that stupidity of overbred animals, and Match still bore them before him, useless and deceptive as to his genius and his glory. The day he took his First Communion, a man photographed him carrying his candle high. Match was so moved that his hands trembled. Don't tremble. Hold the candle in both hands. Yes, monsieur. Click, click, click, click, the photographer prowled around Match; his camera glued to his eye, he crouched, stood up again, put one knee on the ground, all very fast. It was as if he were dancing, as if he dared not come closer. Fine. Higher. It'll come out in *La Semaine Catholique*. Match clenched his teeth, looked up, looked down, sniffed and tried to give his face that grave and relaxed expression he had admired in all the photographs of First Communicants. Thank you, my boy. Yes, monsieur. His parents smiled as they watched the photographer at work, and their hearts were filled with pride. Perhaps my mother even wiped away a tear, I don't remember. The Friday after, she bought *La Semaine Catholique*. Where's my picture? Wait, let's see, let me find it, sit still. Isn't it there? Yes, it was there: two beautiful hands clasping a huge candle. That was all. Mother, all they photographed was my hands and the candle! It's a beautiful photograph. Mother patted my head: "It's pretty, isn't it?" They cut me out . . . I wanted to be in the picture, all of me. Match felt a ball swelling in the pit of his stomach, like the balloons you blow up until they burst. Why did the balloon burst? Why didn't they photograph me? "That's enough!" his father shouted, but the wild bells of a thousand "why's" rang in Match's head. "Because you're too ugly, you dummy!" "Shut up!" his mother said. Match rushed to his mother and hugged her legs and cried, butting his head into her belly the way he might have knocked on a door, but his mother said nothing and remembered how he had butted against the walls of that same belly, but from inside, when Match lived there. Then he tore *La Semaine Catholique* into a thousand pieces and in the years that followed, when people asked him if he had made his First Communion, he always answered no, he wasn't the sort of person who ever set foot in a church.

Every evening, though, before going to sleep he would cross himself, furtively, without moving his lips. It was a habit: if he didn't cross himself, he might not fall asleep.

"In fact," he told the Doctor, "I had another eccentricity. Between the ages of eleven and sixteen I couldn't go into a church. It was as if the threshold were barred against me by a wall of flames."

"You lost your faith?"

"Yes . . ."

"Why?"

"I don't know."

"Did you find it again?"

Match examined his hands carefully:

"Do you think it's like a pair of keys that you lose and find again?"

"Yes," the Doctor said.

"Personally," Alex said from the other side of the cell, "I believe in God."

Match suddenly turned toward him.

"Why?"

"Because you never know."

Match began to laugh, but almost immediately forced himself to stop. He had forgotten that he crossed himself each night, his nose turned to the wall, when the cell's blue light began to shine. It was a habit.

Match's parents were very surprised. His mother was very devout, her infinitely gentle piety never drawing on the treasury of her indulgences. She had that rather stupid, rather irritating kindness of people who are unaware of the existence of evil. She surrounded herself with images, statuettes, and pious medals of an absolute ugliness. Very good people, of course, have no esthetic sense.

"Don't say esthetic sense," the Doctor said.

Match said nothing, abashed.

"What you should say is, they have no sense of beauty," the Doctor added.

"Whatever you say . . ." For her, Chartres or an ugly pseudo-Gothic reinforced-concrete church was the same thing. Her God was everywhere. A God of dreadful bad taste, statuefied in Saint Sulpice images of faded pink plaster with visible hearts pasted on the breast, ugly as the rear end of a cynocephalus. Not having any sense of sin, she forgave everything. 'That poor man's drinking himself to death,' she said of the concierge. And if you added: 'He also beats his wife,' she would sigh: 'Poor woman!' only pitying this 'poor man' or that 'poor woman' all the more. The existence of unhappy people didn't scandalize her, indeed seemed *natural* to her, since God had provided for it in his organization of this world. She lived in a universe where each thing was in its place. There were the rich, the poor, children, 'grownups,' women, men, thoroughbreds, mongrels . . . she walked calmly through God's order. Evil? She never saw it. She never suffered it, and to her confessor she confided a little girl's sins. Her faith wasn't militant, for she couldn't conceive of pride—even the pride of persuading a soul in order to lead it to God. Match fell into a writhing fit in front of the church door.

"No, no!" he screeched.

"What's the matter with you?"

"I don't want to go in!"

"Why?"

"Because."

"The Good Lord won't be happy if you refuse to go into His house."

I'm ugly because of the Good Lord. If I go into the church, I'll become uglier still. He had nightmares. Masked men, often priests, came toward him and fell into murmured councils. "Let's cut off his hands," they said. Match couldn't hear them, but he guessed the meaning of their buzzing speeches. "Let's cut off his hands, the rest is worthless." Then they took out huge knives which shone like the photographer's flash bulbs, and Match woke up. "I don't want to, I don't want to." "The boy's going crazy," his father said. "That's all we needed." "Please, Abel, don't say such things!" Abel never used physical violence, but his words hurt more than slaps. "Are you going in, yes or no?" "No!" It would look even worse to drag a screaming child inside the church. "Go back home." His mother wanted to consult an exorcist, but Match hid on the day of the appointment; and when the priest came to the house on a surprise visit, Match locked himself in the bathroom and refused to come out. The priest shouted through the door. To keep from hearing him, Match flushed the toilet and rustled paper the whole time that he stayed inside.

"Perhaps the influence of certain school friends," the priest said.

"He doesn't have any," his mother said. "The strangest thing, Father, is that he doesn't refuse to say his prayers and still crosses himself before meals. He's always very good and obedient."

"I see," the priest said.

From then on, each Sunday, Match watched his parents get ready to leave for High Mass at eleven. Until twelve-thirty, he remained alone in the house and walked through the empty rooms, parading his idleness and his anguish. Certain Sundays, he would actually celebrate this Mass he wasn't attending. He stood up, knelt, stood again, prayed in front of the cast-iron stove which he had promoted to the status of altar. The upper oven, where the Sunday chicken was roasting, was the tabernacle which he opened and closed with unctuous gestures. He blessed the faithful, presented the roast chicken, chanted in a tremulous voice, rebuked a choir boy. His father's footsteps outside interrupted the celebration of the sacrifice.

"My mother never knew I had lost my faith."

"Had you lost it?" the Doctor asked.

Match didn't know. He hesitated . . . he shook himself like an empty purse, and nothing clinked inside. Or had he heard a noise?

"My mother died without my ever telling her . . ."

"What?"

"Well, you know—about my doubt, my unbelief."

"And your father?"

"It doesn't matter about him."

And now, this month, Match told us he hadn't killed his father. That severe old man, his white hair carefully divided by a part on the left side, his face brick-red—he looked like a noble old Indian—tall and well built till the end (you couldn't say this child resembles his father), today, Match hadn't killed him. "Once he took me to the Luxembourg because I was dying to sail a boat someone had given me on the pond there. For two hours, without saying a word, my impassive father walked slowly around the pond that was quivering under dozens of white sails. From time to time, while supervising the maneuvers of my boat, I glanced at him anxiously. His indifference to my games was so complete that it made them . . . well . . . silly for me. The wind swept my boat under the fountain, which drenched the sail; unbalanced, the little boat capsized, keel in the air. All the children laughed, and I didn't dare say that it was my beautiful sailboat that had been shipwrecked. Nor did I dare disturb my father, walking around the pond as steady and meditative as a circling donkey. At five, the guards' whistles filled my heart with panic: we had to leave the park. 'Where's your boat?' 'Under the fountain, against the pillar; it turned over!' 'Come on, we're going home.' 'And my boat?' 'It's lost.' 'I want it.' 'Come on, now! And I forbid you to cry.'

"He dragged me away. My heart, my head were aching with hatred. Listen, do you know what a child's hatred is? That total longing to kill, to see the object of affliction disappear! My God, little Jesus, Holy Virgin, kill my father! Kill him! Hurt him! My God, little Jesus and Holy Mother and all the blessed saints of paradise, make him catch fire, make a car knock him down and run over him, make people throw stones at him, make him be sick and make the doctor say that he's going to die right away!"

"Then you hadn't yet lost your faith?"

"Oh! Anyway I always believe in God on important occasions." But Heaven didn't help me so I gave my father a tremendous kick in the shins. He let go of my hand, stared at me for a few seconds with an expression in which I read exactly the same hatred that I felt for him. Can you understand how a grownup can hate a child so fiercely? Isn't it strange? But he controlled himself. "Come on, we're going back to the house." After about twenty yards, he stopped, looked me straight in the eyes, but this time without hatred and without anger. "Never ever kick me again." "Does it hurt you?" "No, but you don't have the right to do it."

I didn't kill him. I was just angry. My mother had been dead for over a year and yet he couldn't bring himself to let me have the apartment. Every time I visited him, we began quarreling. "I'm master here, and if I choose to stay, then here I'll stay! And if I choose to rent a house in the country, I'll rent a house in the country. And you're not going to make me change my mind!" His stubborn will exasperated me. "It's expensive for you at the hotel? Well at least that's something that will make a good-for-nothing like you work a little."

Until that day when he wanted to get rid of me. "That's enough talk; I've seen enough of you! Never set foot around here again!" He was red with anger, and his head shook so violently that the part dividing his white hair was spoiled. "You're a no-good loafer . . . get out!" He came toward me, grabbed my arm, pushed me. I shook myself loose and I could see his red face a couple of inches from mine. I saw its swollen pores, the pouches under his eyes that were purple now, and the yellow threads in the whites of his eyes. A spectrum of colors, grimaces . . . I don't like angry old men: their fragility frightens me; I always feel they're going to explode and die. Their anger looks so much like a death agony. He grabbed my arm again, spattered my face with drops of saliva and shrieked hideously. I made him let go, but he raised a clenched fist: "You know what you are? Do you know? You want me to tell you?" I grabbed him by the shoulders and I think I was shouting louder than he was then, and I pushed him back with all my strength. He fell down like a puppet, sitting at the foot of the wall he had fallen against. He was bleeding and he had fainted. I didn't kill him. I pushed him to avoid the blow he was going to give me. Besides, he didn't die of it, and except for that damn woman next door who swore in court six months later that she'd heard him call "Help, help!" during the fight, I wouldn't be here.

Match recalled his kindness to the senile, mute invalid. Every Sunday he went to see him at the Old Folks Home, brought him oranges, and cookies with powdered sugar on them. On days when the weather was good, he pushed the wheel chair in the garden under the tall linden trees. "A good son," the nurses said. Ten times, slowly, he walked around the garden, pushing the wheel chair in which his father sat, stiff as a wax mannequin. Then he sat down on the mossy bench and peeled the oranges, which the old man ate gluttonously. The juice trickled down his chin, stained his vest. Some days, he would refuse to eat. On those days, as Match held the sections of orange to his lips, he stared at his son and refused to open his mouth. Then Match stood up, pushed the wheel chair, and went on walking around the garden.

"I'm not guilty. The sign of guilt is remorse, isn't it? Well I don't feel any."

"But if . . ." the Doctor said.

"Listen, I tell you I didn't kill that man!" Match said, holding out his hands to prove they weren't covered with blood.

"No, of course not, my friend," the Doctor said. "That's not the point."

"Then what is?"

Since the Doctor didn't answer, Match began day-dreaming.

"Funny, all the same," Eugène said, "someone who kills only nurses . . ."

"Oh, girls . . ." Alex said. "Kill them all. Like Eugène killed his. . . ."

Strangely enough, Eugène didn't protest, and Alex continued: "You, Doctor, you strangled a couple of them, and I smothered one—that makes four or five, at least."

"I killed my mother," Match said.

We turned toward him, a little surprised, but Match went on:

"Yes, you can count her too."

"Good," Alex said, "let's say that makes five. At least five. If they hadn't taken my license away I'd never have had anything to do with girls in the first place."

It was Guitare d'Amour's fault; he lived in an attic room covered with sports photographs. There was even one in a frame—and dedicated!—from Marcel Cerdan, and another from Fausto Coppi. He was ugly, he looked like a grasshopper, but he was a champ, that Fausto. Guitare spent most of his time sprawled out on the bed, staring at his photographs and plucking at the strings of his black guitar. His favorite song was "Guitare d'Amour," and one day this bartender from Martinique decided to nickname him that. What do you want me to play? "Sole Mio"? Guitare sang songs in Italian or Spanish even though he didn't know one damn word of either language. "Beautiful, isn't it?" he would say at the end, caressing his instrument. "I tell you, nothing's as beautiful as a guitar." And his fingers slid over the varnished wood. . . .

I never saw anything as beautiful as that, except for a little Negro from Abidjan who was training with Monsieur Siméon. What happened to him? You'll find out. . . . That Negro, it was like it made him angry to have the most beautiful face on earth, like he was actually trying to get himself knocked around and spoil his looks. "Be careful," Monsieur Siméon used to say to Big Alfred, "don't spoil his face too much."

"That's all right, Monsieur Siméon, that's all right, let him alone," the Negro would say. I swear, he'd say: "That's all right!" You want me to play "Sole Mio"? When you went into his bedroom, the perfume almost knocked you down, it smelled like a big hot cat. You stepped back. "Are you coming in, yes or no? What's the matter with you?" "It's the perfume, Guitare, it's like getting into a bed after a houseful of whores slept in it." Guitare chuckled. "I wonder if I shouldn't have Robinson framed, too, he's cute, isn't he?" For five minutes or so he would examine Robinson's photograph from every angle, moving it close, holding it away, squinting like he was painting his first portrait. "I wonder . . . what do you think? I'll buy a bronze-plated frame. Or maybe white with gilding. I'll see. I have to think it over." Soon you got used to the smell. Like you get used to the water in a bath when it's too hot. Sometimes it came back, by surprise. In drafts. As if the room was crossed by heavy, sticky currents, stagnant at floor level,

roused by a sudden movement. "Why do you use perfume, Guitare?" "I don't know—maybe because it's no
good wrestling with someone and giving him your own
smell. You feel like you're fighting yourself. Besides, you
should see how surprised the other guy gets: he thinks
you're a fairy. And while he's wondering what a queen
is doing on the mat, you have time to get a couple of
holds that'll stay with him till the end of the fight. You
know?" Every day at five, Guitare put on his black pants,
his white turtle-neck sweater and his checked jacket, and
after pouring a last douse of perfume over his head,
said: "All right, let's go to work." The gym was sacred
and Monsieur Siméon was not just anyone: he was Monsieur Siméon. Alex and Guitare went down the street,
leaving a wake of perfume behind them that stopped the
startled pedestrians short. "It really bugs them to see guys
like us wearing perfume." "Yes." "You're too much, Guitare. You wear enough to smother a police dog . . ."
"It may come in handy." Laughter. "Good morning,
Monsieur Siméon." "Good morning, Guitare, good
morning, Alex. Everything all right?" I put on my gloves,
and the helmet and did a few rounds with the boys, but I
worked out so hard that one day Monsieur Siméon said
to me: "Alex, I can't let you go on. If you get in trouble
with your two-ten, I'll get the blame . . . If you want
to come in and skip rope or work out on the bag, okay,
whenever you feel like it, but I don't want you working
with the boys, not any more!" For weeks after that my
morale was down to zero, because of that conversation.
I kept coming to the gym, I came with Guitare d'Amour,
and I'd sit on a medicine ball and watch him work out.
"Why don't you start wrestling?" "No, I couldn't stand

it." You know, a boxer who starts wrestling is like a watch-maker turning into a blacksmith, right?

"I know," Eugène said, "it's like someone told me: you can't work the crane any more, from now on you run the concrete mixer."

"Exactly," Alex said.

"Boxing is to wrestling what the crane is to the concrete mixer . . ." the Doctor said.

"Right!" Alex said. "Monsieur Siméon's a great guy. He treats all the guys that go to his gym sort of like his kids. 'Don't drink, don't smoke, don't fuck around with girls, kid; go to bed early.' And he was always saying: Pastis, Gauloises, and vamps are the enemies of champs."

"That rhymes," Eugène said.

"On purpose," Alex said. "Monsieur Siméon used to say it all day long so we'd get it through our heads. When some guy asked him what about Al Brown, having a time didn't keep *him* from becoming a champ, Monsieur Siméon went into a fury: 'Listen, I don't like freaks, get it? Work, that's all that means anything. I say work and I mean work!' What he liked to do most was to work up a champ starting with a bum. He was actually suspicious of anyone with talent. 'They burn bright for a few minutes and then they go out.' He used to like me, so when he had to see me sitting there on the medicine ball, my arms between my legs—I'm sure that hurt him a lot . . . I was sort of his model pupil. 'Don't drink, don't smoke, go to bed early, and above all don't fuck around with girls. Girls are a man's real enemy.' 'Bravo, Monsieur Siméon!' Guitare d'Amour used to shout back, skipping rope in a cloud of perfume. And Monsieur Siméon would say: 'Because that's the way it is: if you start with girls you end up with all the other problems on your back. You make dates in a bar, so you drink. You get nervous because they're always late, so you smoke. You run around with them and all the rest of it, so you go to bed late. Right or wrong?' And the guys always shouted back: 'Right, Monsieur Siméon: Pastis, Gauloises, and vamps are the enemies of champs!' "

"It rhymes," Eugène repeated, amazed.

One day Alex went back into training. For the hell of it. And he had to eat, pay his rent and his gym expenses. Oh, if it hadn't been for those two-ten's! Actually, that wasn't all; there was that business with Khadi too . . . I was the boxer who'd killed a man. Still, it wasn't my fault. It was really Monsieur Siméon's fault.

"You said all managers were bastards, didn't you?" the Doctor asked.

"What I mean is . . ." Alex said, "Monsieur Siméon knew Khadi had had a scooter accident, but he didn't tell me about it."

"So you didn't know about it, did you?"

"Monsieur Siméon hadn't *told* me about it. God, what that poor Ayrab took!"

Remembering, Alex smiled like a connoisseur. His fist scythed the air. The worm swelled in the middle of his forehead.

"Anyway," he said, "if you really think about it, the real bastard was Lucienne, Khadi's manager."

"A woman?" Match asked.

"His name's Lucien, Monsieur Lucien. We call him Lucienne because he's queer. Lucienne wanted Khadi to box all the same . . . whether he had had an accident or not. After all, it wasn't Monsieur Siméon's business to know about it, was it? And it wasn't any of mine, either."

"But you did know?" Match asked.

"Know, know . . . what does that mean . . . a guy who was training with Lucienne told me the fight would go like a dream."

"He told you about the accident?"

"No. And even if he had, so what?"

Alex would have *known* if Monsieur Siméon had *told* him: "Alex, Khadi's had an accident." Otherwise he couldn't *know*. Even if Monsieur Lucien had taken him aside, in a corner of the dressing room, before the match: "You know, Alex, I'm letting you have Khadi tonight because I'm a good guy, but don't give him the works, because I'm making you a present, it's all sewed up . . ." Even if Khadi had told him when they left the scales: "I'm boxing for the money, not for the title, I'm hurt and the bout's yours, I'm counting on you, all right?" Even if Alex had answered yes and only hit him on the shoulders without saying anything, he wouldn't have known anything. Those "yeses," those knowing smiles, those slaps on the shoulder didn't mean anything, once Monsieur Siméon said nothing, once Alex warmed up in the dressing room, skipping up and down and doing a few knee bends. I'm not thinking about anything, I don't know anything, I fight Khadi the best I can with all my strength, and that's all and that's enough.

"Tttt . . . Tttt . . ." Match said, persisting, "but did you *know* or didn't you . . ."

Alex said nothing and made a tremendous effort to remember. Did he know: *yes* or *no?* Or maybe between yes and no there was a kind of dust of ignorance, thousands of yeses and nos ground up together, a soft paste with hard veins running through it that sloshed around in his head. In life, is there always a red light when you have to stop, and a green light when you can go ahead? Christ, are things always white and it's *yes,* or black and it's *no?* Did he know he was going to kill Khadi and win a bout easier than anything in the world? "It's all lined up," Monsieur Siméon had said. Alex smiled and winked. Well? What was all lined up? Khadi's death? Victory? Both together? Nothing at all? Why did he work so hard, why did he punch like a madman when he knew it was all sewed up? Why did he deliberately work around to get at Khadi's right temple? To kill him? To win? For *something* that exists between killing and winning and which has no name? I thought about it for whole nights at a time. Why hadn't Monsieur Siméon told him, at the end of the second round: "Go a little easy, kid, don't kill him. Don't *kill him!*" Monsieur Siméon hadn't said a word. We didn't look at each other, we didn't say a word to each other. As if we had a terrible and inadmissible secret in common, as if something were going to happen of which we were both ashamed . . . and fat Lucienne with that green sweater and his round, pink face—he shouldn't have worn those green sweaters: his face always looked like a pig's head resting on a bed of parsley—why didn't he stop the fight when he saw Khadi going into the wrong corner, half out? He looked at me, that pig, with his pink toad's blue eyes, and there was hate in his eyes. What did he say? Besides, it wasn't me he was looking at, I'm sure of that, it was Monsieur Siméon. What did that look say? Siméon, you're a bastard but I'll be an even worse bastard than you, just to get you. Siméon, it'll be all your fault. And what did Monsieur Siméon's eyes answer? Lucienne, you're the queen of bastards, all right, sacrificing your kid just to get me, but I'm not going to give in, and so it'll be you, you big fairy, you'll be the one who's to blame for what's going to happen. So the real fight was the one between Monsieur Siméon and fat Lucienne. And Khadi? Oh, Khadi didn't even know what his name was, or if he was born in Oran or Bougival, or if he was in a ring or walking around on a cloud. Ten seconds after the fight started, he was up on a cloud, like an alcoholic after his first glass . . . Khadi didn't count . . . Alex hadn't killed anyone. Monsieur Siméon and fat Lucienne fought it out through intermediaries, that's all. That's all, is it? That's what I think, anyway.

"That's what you think," the Doctor concluded.

Alex was prowling around like a lost soul. After that, Monsieur Siméon was still nice to him, but it wasn't the same any more. There was a kind of embarrassment between them. Monsieur Siméon shook the hand Alex held out a little faster now. O.K.? Fine. You? A slap on the shoulder; but quick, absent-minded, and still watching what was happening in the gym. Alex kept coming back, the way a lover knocks on the door of a mistress he knows will leave him, knowing she's already left him in her heart. And just as all the lover asks is permission to sit down and watch this woman he loves spreading her presence in the apartment with futile tiny gestures, so Alex watched Monsieur Siméon give advice, scold, laugh, congratulate his boys without paying any attention to his old favorite sitting on the bar of a dumbbell that cut his ass in half. And good-by bread! In the old days, Monsieur Siméon kept the cash box and advanced money on the take from the fight. That was over now! So then Guitare d'Amour, lying sprawled as usual on his bed and nestling in the deepest part of his perfumed trench, set down his guitar, looked at Alex with his soft eyes and said in that tiny voice of his that sounded so funny coming out of a body as big as his: "You go on like this, you'll end up nuts, you better pick up some bread somewhere." Where? Guitare wedged a pillow behind his head, clasped his priest's hands and said in his tiny voice: "Where you find it, where else? Under a horse's tail? No, *chéri,* in a broad's bed." "You mean . . ." "That's exactly what I mean, you guessed it!" And Guitare d'Amour explained that he had two girls who "worked" for him, and he did pretty well. Very well, in fact "Two nice, hard-working little cunts trained to drop it in the cash box regularly, without me even having to whistle. I'm like their father, their big brother. They even call me 'Papa' or 'Junior' . . . sometimes I'm their big strong husband, too, but only when I can't help it: I don't like that stuff. I'm only their big strong husband once in a while, on very important occasions. Christmas, New Year's, Bastille Day . . . Oh I love my little girls all right, I don't want anyone hurting them. I buy them earrings, lace blouses, the latest junk for their skin, flowers, compacts. These days you don't find nice papas like me growing on trees, you know? I've seen some poor little kids completely lost in the shuffle and sniffing everybody's pants to find their daddy. That's the kind of thing that breaks my heart, but I can't worry about them all, you know? Two kids are fine, but if you really take care of them, that's enough. You get it?" "Yes, but I was wondering . . ." "Listen, I just close my eyes, I forget they're broads, and then I give them a couple of good whacks, after, just to keep things running all right." "Oh you do?" "Yes, sure. You know?" "I guess." "When I have a match, I get them seats, not together of course, so they'll be proud of their papa. Now if I say I have this kid brother who needs help, they'll hustle up a friend for you, and then you'll see for yourself how good you can do. I don't want to spread out too thin, you know? Later on, you can always see. You know?" "Yes . . ."

"In other words," the Doctor said, "it's because of your friend Guitare d'Amour that you became a pimp."

"Yes, it's thanks to him."

"Excuse me," the Doctor said.

"What for?"

"That's what I meant to say, too: it's *thanks* to your friend Guitare . . ."

"And what was it you did say?"

"I said: *because of* . . . but it comes down to the same thing, doesn't it?"

Alex shrugged.

"Sure . . ."

"What happened then?" Eugène asked, his eyes shining like a child listening to a fairy tale.

"In a sense," the Doctor said, "you could also say that it's because of . . . no . . . *thanks to* Monsieur Siméon. And even, if you go one step further: thanks to Khadi, or even further, thanks to Monsieur Lucien. Or going one step further still . . ."

"So then?" Eugène repreated, irritated by the Doctor's chatter and turning to Alex.

"Then Maridge . . . her real name was Julienne but Guitare said that for work 'Maridge' was better . . . then Maridge started working for me."

"At first . . ." Alex suddenly stopped talking. He made the gesture of someone who's very tired gently massaging his face. A dark girl with a pointed nose, an enormous fleshy mouth with sharply outlined lips and good teeth under them. Eyes loaded, overloaded, with dark cream and endless lashes, tiny fringes that revealed an empty gaze. Her legs were a little skinny, but her breasts were high and firm. She had been a salesgirl in a fancy men's shop. Not only had she been paid miserably, but every now and then, when it came over him, the shopkeeper had locked the door, drawn the curtains between the shop from the back room, and gave it to her for as long as his interest lasted. That's when she began to learn something about men. The customers asked her to go out with them. A free dinner. And then, gradually, one guy offered her money, then another, a third . . . I'm sick of selling your ties. I'm cutting out. From that day on you can bet he sold less ties. At first, Alex was intimidated by this beautiful, silent creature. Luckily, Guitare d'Amour was keeping an eye on this new couple, and Maridge knew he was around, in the shadows, ready to restore order and impose the eternal and magnificent law that states that whores must be eternally crushed under the heels of pimps. Up till then, you know, it was only sports I cared about. Girls, never. I used to listen to Monsieur Siméon: "Pastis, Gauloises, and vamps are the enemies of champs!" It was sacred, you know, carved in bronze or reinforced concrete, sacred and hard as my fist, my belly, my steel head. "You're Alex the boxer?" "Yes." She was actually proud of me. I showed her the posters with my name in great big letters and the programs with my victories written up in them and the photos in *Miroir-*

Sprint and *Ring* and the articles in all the papers. Especially lately, when the reporters started calling me "The Killer," "The Terror," "Double Thunderbolt". . . Why "Double Thunderbolt"? Because I had a thunderbolt in each fist and I hit as hard with my left as my right.

That's how it happened . . . that idle, useless violence . . . that boredom in his hands, hands with hairy joints and broad palms; that boredom in his shoulders . . . Maridge was there with Alex, obeying his mysterious orders that came from the dark abyss of time; Maridge loved him; Maridge gave him her money. She was serious, too, and punctual. For all eternity. Because it's called fate. Maridge called it "destiny." Soon she found out he never went into the ring any more. For reasons which seemed to upset him. Talk, Alex, talk. I don't want to talk. Talk, talk. She was there, that whore, ready to understand everything, because that was her "destiny," to understand everything; because, when a man talks, a whore has to understand. Talk to me. I don't have anything to say. The useless violence sweated through all his pores, made him clench his fists . . . he sat in the back of a bar for hours, staring at his glass of beer, watching the froth dry on the rim. When he wet his lips, it tasted lukewarm and bitter. Or else he watched all the men who came into the bar. He was looking for a fight, but no one would provoke the colossus squatting in his corner, a vein squirming across his forehead. That boredom he dragged along the street with him . . . some gooks stick swords down their throats, others eat fire, twist iron bars, break chains, lift weights; others sell stockings or little gadgets that peel everything—potatoes, carrots, turnips, celery—and make them into flowers. Others shoot popguns at little bits of paper; others go to the tent where Arab dancers are squirming around. Before, he used to like carnivals. Now they didn't mean a thing.

That anger when he dreamed, eyes glued to the ceiling, all his useless muscles flattened on the bed whose springs groaned at every movement he made. He felt like hitting something, someone. Yesterday, he gave that flea-bitten concierge a good punch in the mouth and laid him out across a garbage can in the courtyard. With the back of his hand he swept off all the jars and perfume bottles Maridge had arranged on the shelf over the sink. Legs wide, his vein pulsing, he admired this absurd little disaster. What's the matter? What's wrong with those bottles? . . . Shut up! You're the one who broke . . . Yes, that's right! Why! . . . Shit! Maridge sniffed, cried, slammed a door. With Alex's permission she had bought the large-size bottle of "Femme" that cost her twelve thousand francs, and it had been three quarters full.

The wreckage covered the bathroom tiles. The mingled perfumes swirled around the room and added to Maridge's dizziness as she sat sighing and sobbing on the bidet. "Why did you break everything?" "I have my reasons, leave me alone!" Alex turned his nose to the wall. Maridge undressed, turned out the light and lay down beside him, her body not touching his. In the darkness of a Paris bedroom, a whore and a boxer lay sleepless, side by side. Eyes open, silent, they thought of things they wouldn't know how to say. Two giant thumbs were pressing Alex's temples as if, in a chaotic scream, the words that might comfort him were about to spring out and explain everything. But they didn't come; his temples hurt, but the pus that was rotting his brain didn't spurt

out between his teeth—words, cries, obscenities. Maridge
didn't move either; she was a tomb figure petrified with
hate. "You're just a coward." She felt Alex's body turn
rigid. The sentence had been said very calmly. Unmodu-
lated. Had Alex heard that anonymous voice? He
stretched his arm toward the light, turned it on, sat up.
He was calm, gentle. "I'm a coward?" She didn't answer.
"I'm a coward?" She didn't answer. I'm a coward . . .
He's knocking my head off, he's knocking . . . he's
knock . . . he's knocking . . . her head turned as if it
were on a pivot . . . ; it snapped back and forth, depending on the direction the slaps were coming from. He
would unscrew it. Alex stood up, got dressed, drank a
mouthful of water from the faucet and walked out.
Maridge slid from unconsciousness to sleep. Alex went
for a walk and breathed deeply, slowly—an old habit
from his fighting days, taking plenty of time inhaling and
exhaling—breathing the cool night air. From that night
on she got herself hit a lot. In a way, I didn't start it . . .

"You found a way of training for free," Eugène said.

"That little sentence of hers burned me up and I didn't
know what else to do. How could I get rid of it? Forget
it? A sentence doesn't really exist. 'You're just a coward,'
it's just noise, isn't it? Wind? Air? A lot I care about
what a whore says. A whore's nothing but a garbage can.
Well then, there it was, a talking garbage can; what difference could it make? The crowd must have called me a
coward a hundred times, a thousand times, and I didn't
give one fuck. Listen, Doctor, can you explain that one?"

"None of it matters very much, Monsieur Alex."

"Except that she decided to commit suicide, and slit

her wrists."

"No . . ." Match said.

Yes! Today, Alex saw the bed full of blood, Maridge stretched out, dead. The police investigated, interrogated Alex, discovered that he was her pimp, arrested him. That's why he was in jail.

"And the business about the cellar?" Eugène asked.

"What cellar?"

"The one where you locked Maridge up so you could knock her around in peace?"

"Me?" Alex asked.

"I must be mixing you up with someone else . . ." Eugène said.

The peephole slides open sideways. We could see our guard's eyes and thick lashes. Then his lips, nothing but his lips whispering: "In five minutes I'm turning out the lights. All right, boys, get to bed now. Sleep tight. And cut that chatter."

Alex quickly pulled off his shirt and did some thirty push-ups. Then, standing with his nose toward the skylight, he inhaled deeply, and in the sudden darkness all you could hear was the gentle sighing of his lungs. All you could see was his profile faintly etched against the moonlit skylight. He looked like a saint oppressed by the visitation that precedes his ecstasy, a saint for whom the prayer's words lose their meaning and fill up with nothing but happiness. Yet Alex wasn't praying. He was breathing.

Eugène was still jealous. He had married Jeanne. He could take care of the boys. They kidded him, but he wasn't ashamed. Jeanne's beauty was a guarantee that he knew his way around with women and that he could always find his way back again if he wanted to. In Jeanne, his incomparable wife, all the women of the world were seduced, ravished, and chained to their conqueror. This marriage that might have been Eugène's defeat as a man was actually his victory. Don Juan's secret temptation is to seduce God. I won't be damned. On Judgment Day, I'll seduce God himself, and the long line of the dead will see me passing through the gates of paradise. Eugène has seduced God on earth. He decided Jeanne was worthy of him, of what he was, he chose her above all others and made her sacred: "Yes, but do you know his wife? . . ." Eugène hasn't put himself on the shelf: Jeanne would give him the love of all women. She would walk down the yellow dirt road to the construction side. She would walk in the sun and participate in the light. From high up in his crane, Eugène followed her with his eyes. He saw the foreman's jeep . . . that thirty-year-old dope thought he was in the Wild West. He wore khaki shirts and trousers covered with countless pockets; he jumped into his jeep as though he were mounting a bronco and drove as fast as he could, raising clouds of dust that drowned the road in their reddish haze; he wore a canvas cap with a tiny visor, and dark glasses. His brakes screeched. From high up in the crane Eugène watched a scene from a movie. The foreman talking to Jeanne. She answered. He said something, a long sentence. She answered with two or three words. This time, the foreman said only a few words and she answered at some length:

at least five or six sentences. Then he answered, laughing, it looked like. From far away Eugène couldn't see very clearly, but the foreman's shoulders seemed to be shaking, as though he had burst out laughing. Yes, he was laughing, because Jeanne was laughing too. Jeanne looked as if she were saying good-by now, she was walking away, but the jeep moved along beside her, very slowly. They stopped again. Jeanne held her basket in both hands, like a monstrance. Her feet were set a little apart. Firmly planted on the ground. Solid. They were far away and he could scarcely see them at all now. Luckily there was the bright spot of her dress. There . . . that was it . . . the bright spot moved toward the jeep, melted into it, disappeared. A cloud. The jeep drove away. Jeanne had gotten in. I'll take you home, the foreman must have said. No, I can walk. Of course you can walk, you've got legs, haven't you? But I've got four wheels, here, come on, get in! . . . No, thank you. All right now, don't make me beg you, is that what you want? No, my husband's jealous, you know . . . If I were in his place, I'd be jealous too. You see . . . Come on, get in anyway; my jeep isn't like other cars, it's really a kind of wheel chair, you know? The foreman was thirty; he had wide eyes in a sun-tanned face, and his eyes were laughing. He had the assurance of a man getting ready to steal another man's wife. No matter how hard he looked, no matter how hard he questioned himself, he just couldn't manage to discover the slightest trace of a scruple in his conscience. In front of him: a woman. Between her and himself: nothing. Neither God nor Devil nor husband, only a void that swallowed them up. And all the instincts of rapine suddenly awakened, and dreams of piracy, and plunder carried off on shipboard, on horseback or in a jeep. Eugène's chest hurt, and he grew very pale. But he didn't get angry; instead he was flooded with an enormous calm that made him maneuver his crane all the more precisely—with the maniacal precision of men devoured by rage who take tremendous pains to execute some complicated manual labor. Eugène's mother behaved in exactly the same way. After a violent quarrel with his father, the dishes were never so meticulously washed, the copper pans never shone so brightly, the kitchen was never so well swept. There was something that terrified the child about this rage for order. He would have liked it better if she had exploded. As if it were a deliverance, he waited for a plate to be broken, for a corner of the kitchen to escape the furious broom. But no, every crumb, every shred of dust, every cigarette butt was quickly swept up and carried to the garbage can like a treasure. That was the definition of ferocity, of cruelty: that stony attention to everything, that precision, that gentleness . . . the cat crouching in front of the mousehole. The mouse sees the dilated eyes, the ivory fangs, the pink mouth; it hears the monster's growl of victorious delight. For a fraction of a second, it will *see* what it has always dreamed of seeing . . . there comes a moment when, for the space of a second, life collapses into death; when all the dikes burst; when the *flesh* knows the dread feeling of life being torn from it; when strange fluxes of clarity, whirlwinds of fireflies, devastate it like radium. And all the earth and everything that should be *known* is illuminated in that flash. Then everything falls away to darkness and death. The pink mouth, the ivory fangs, the dilated eyes, and facing them a tiny gray ball of paralyzed flesh; . . . in that moment, mouse, you understand everything. You are all knowledge, and all ignorance. And except that His is renewed perpetually; something like the dazzling totality—of God.

"God," the Doctor added, "God is always what is on the point of dying, what will die, what nothing separates from death and what—O terrible joy—doesn't die. God is the eternal life whose death is always im-mi-nent!"

"You think so?" Alex asked, stupidity suddenly crumpling his face like the blow of a fist as he turned to stare at the Doctor.

"I'm convinced of it," the Doctor said.

He diligently gnawed his left thumbnail, stared back at Alex, and Alex, under that gaze, was nothing. Nothing. The Doctor stared at him pitilessly and said:

"One of these days, I'll tell you about fear."

Eugène went back to work. Later, when he came down again, the guys asked him: "What's the matter, warbler, aren't you singing any more? Did you swallow your whistle?" He'd choke back his anger: "With all the racket around here, how can you tell if I'm whistling or not, you idiots?" "Oh we can tell, we can't hear but we can tell." "Christ you guys are creeps." And Eugène made an obscene gesture.

He straddled his bike, a racing bike, a marvel: tubes thin as cigarettes, extralight aluminum rims, and a five-speed shift. Years ago, long before he had married Jeanne, Eugène used to dream of being a bicycle racer. He had saved up for all the ritual instruments: canteens, sweater, shoes, helmet and—sacred above all other objects of the cult—the bike itself. At night, before falling asleep, he would select a dream; sometimes he was struggling up a mountain path, five minutes ahead of the pack at his heels while thousands of spectators shouted: "Go, Gégène, go!"; sometimes he would outdistance all his adversaries on a sunbaked flat stretch: the spectators sprinkled him with hoses and threw buckets of water on him to whip up his exhausted, overheated muscles; the press cars would ride along with him, pass him in a cloud of dust in order to telephone from all four corners of France: "Eugène the superchamp is way out ahead at Montpellier"; the concession carts, streaming paper hats and many-colored butterflies, rolled behind him in a royal procession. Stretched out on a hotel bed while his masseur worked on his legs, he held a press conference on the day before a crucial lap. Reporters overwhelmed him with questions, trying to find out the secrets of his training, wanting to know what he thought of his opponents. Eugène would answer nothing but sibylline remarks that the reporters feverishly transcribed. Over everything floated a smell of eau de Cologne and liniment. Sometimes Eugène would doze off without breaking the thread of the dream, and without jolts, without starts, the dream would resume the follies of the day before.

Eugène, smiling at glory, would continue to be the invincible champion, the idol of the crowds, the phenomenon of the race, the cycling God. In his sleep, he would stretch out his legs in sudden jerks, like an animal shaken by the last spasms of life; he would groan, clutch the handlebars; in the morning, when the shrill bell of the alarm clock went off, he would stagger across the room, the dream shattered, wondering why in hell he slept so badly. Now, since he's been married to Jeanne, he'd bought an English motorcycle, too. Jeanne would have preferred a Citroen. "Why not armchairs on wheels?" "Listen, when it rains, a car's practical. With your motorcycle I get all dirty, my hair comes undone, it shakes me up, and it hurts my stomach." "No, it's good for you; you get a lot of fresh air, you can sneak in anywhere and pass everybody on the road." "Passing, passing . . . that's all you think of, what is it men all have about wanting to pass?" "Oh, just that it's fun to pass guys sitting there in their cars as if they were in front of their desks." "It's stupid, I tell you, that's what it is, it's stupid. What difference does it make whether you get there five minutes later or five minutes earlier?" Someday you'll kill yourself." Eugène shrugged. "A racing car, even a sports car . . . but otherwise I'd be ashamed to drive those snails, those two- and four-horsepower snails. And a Dauphine? That's even worse." "Don't you give a damn if I'm all shaken up? If it does something to my insides? It's going to make me sick, I can feel it, and then some day when we want to have a baby, that'll be that! Listen, if I get pregnant, you're not going to get me on your motorcycle." "We'll see, we'll see." "You don't give a damn, you couldn't care less, there's you and your motorcycle, so the hell with me and my son!" "Your son, where *is* he? . . ." Eugène burst out laughing. "That's right, my son! You'll have your motorcycle, and me, I'll have my son or my little daughter, so then if you want, you take your motorcycle on Sundays and pass everybody on earth. Without me. I'm warning you."

Eugène got off his bike five hundred yards before the house. He guided it with one hand as he walked, not hurrying, to have time to get his thoughts sorted out. They were all mixed up. He couldn't quite believe what he believed. This had been going on for over two weeks. There was something between Jeanne and him. But what? The other night . . . she said to him: "No, you're hurting me. . . . What's the matter with you? No . . ." He kneaded her shoulders, he crushed her as if he wanted the bed to swallow her, as if he wanted her to disappear. Then he would find himself alone, lying flat on his stomach on the warm sheet, and he could sob to his heart's content. He remembered flattening himself like that when he was fourteen years old, on spring days in the luxuriant alfalfa, or in the wheat fields. Like a dead soldier, forgotten. He would lie there for a long time, face against the ground, motionless, eyes closed, his member stiffened against the cool earth that drank in his warmth. Then he would stand up, staggering, and stare at the place where his body had been, its ghost still crushing the grass or the luxuriant alfalfa. I was lying there . . . That was me . . . I was alone . . . The emptiness, that phantom body inscribed on the green earth, would frighten him. He would be standing where he could see his solitude sculptured in the wheat or the alfalfa. He would feel like crying. Here lay a boy and a girl, actually dying. Look! In all the fields and all the grassy clearings of the world, yesterday—it was a Sunday in May—the same kind of tombs have been dug. Thousands of boys and girls lay there, and each of their embraces was the last they addressed to the unhappiness that would be their life. Try to understand. You too, some day, when the girl from the next farm was sweating underneath you, when her round stupid face turned red and she said: "I'm hot . . . the grass is scratching me . . . there are nasty bugs here . . ." you too, you were dying. Eugène was fourteen. His right cheek was red—it was the one that had been pressed against the ground—and the grass had traced its pink labyrinth there. He would look at the green velvet tomb where he had been lying. His heart . . . O my heart, speak to me, I'm fourteen years old and my name's Eugène . . . you tell me: dying with a girl is nothing, but you've just died alone. Look, just look! You're alone. This tomb's a lie. For a second, the illusion thrilled you when that warmth sprang out between your thighs, but no one returned that heat you gave the earth, no one gave it back to you, and already the grass is rising to efface your criminal solitude.

"A criminal," said the Doctor, who sometimes talked to himself, "is a man who realizes that love is impossible."

Match pricked up his ears. Yes, sometimes Match was a weasel, a rat, or a rabbit and—it was *visible*—he "pricked up his ears."

"Hey!" he said, as if the Doctor had suddenly extracted a terribly painful tooth, and as if he had been simultaneously illuminated by suffering and relief.

The Doctor went on: "That love is impossible or, if you prefer, that it's vile because no one has the right to involve anyone else in death. To die by twos . . . because you're afraid. Yes (the Doctor turned toward us), I'll have to tell you about fear. It's becoming urgent."

For two weeks, Eugène had been wondering if Jeanne was cheating on him. Now he wasn't even wondering about that any more. He wasn't wondering at all. He was jealous. Whether Jeanne was or had been sleeping with the foreman didn't matter much; he was jealous of every man. Jeanne was beginning to get scared. On Saturday they went to see a cowboy film. During the whole time, she felt Eugène stiff as a wooden doll beside her. Afterward, they went home and Eugène hadn't said a word about the movie. She took off her clothes, slipped into bed, and for the second time in two weeks, Eugène couldn't do it.

"Are you tired?"

"Leave me alone . . ."

"What's the matter? Are you sick?"

Eugène didn't answer, turned his back to her, and didn't move again.

"Shut up. Don't talk to me. I don't want to talk any more."

As long as they weren't talking, they didn't know anything. If they talked, they would find out and then they couldn't forget what they knew. At this moment, Eugène was thinking, but not in words. Waves washed over him; burning or icy currents enveloped him. It's only if you asked him what he was thinking about that he would find out, that he would know. He was thinking it wasn't his fault if he couldn't sleep with a woman any more, with a woman who had become a whore. Then why this rage, an hour later? Why did he throw himself on her with an incomprehensible violence, as if he wanted not just to make love to her but to pollute her?

"What's come over you all of a sudden?"

"Don't you want it?"

"Yes but . . ."

"And if you don't want it I couldn't care less, do you hear? I don't give a fuck! I'll do what I want! . . ."

He fell asleep immediately afterward and—in a nightmare—with a single blow of an ax, split Jeanne's skull, and inside discovered the foreman's body curled up like a fetus. He pulled it out with his fingers, with his nails, but Jeanne began screaming with pain. Then he closed up the split skull but Jeanne was dead.

"Was she cheating on you, yes or no?" Match asked.

Eugène didn't answer.

"Anyway, it's all the same thing," the Doctor said.

"No it isn't, no it isn't . . . it changes everything," Match said, staring at Eugène with a kind of disapproval.

The Doctor laughed. Eugène met his eyes, called for help.

"Do you believe in balance, Monsieur Match?"

"Do I believe in . . . ?"

"Yes, you put the fault in one pan and the punishment in the other and the scale no longer moves?"

"I put . . . ?"

"Yes, Eugène's wife cheats on him, Eugène kills her, and then that's that, right?"

"But," Eugène said, "I killed the foreman."

"Let's suppose," the Doctor interrupted, "that you killed your wife . . ."

"All right . . ." Eugène said, resigned.

The Doctor continued, still addressing Match.

"Crime against fault, and crime equals fault, isn't that fair?"

Match was cunning. His eyes glowed, deep in their sockets. He didn't answer because he knew that, whatever his answer, the Doctor had his own idea and would spring on his arguments and tear them to pieces. He immured himself in his silence, but his eyes were still alive, and they watched the Doctor. At this moment he looked exactly like some sort of "vermin"—rat, fox, badger, or bird. He wrapped himself up in darkness, at the bottom of which gleamed his coal-black eyes. He listened. He said nothing. A rat doesn't talk. That way the Doctor was cornered and either had to shut up or go on alone.

"Now look, Monsieur Match, how could you, a murderer, be unaware of the true motives of a crime?"

Match's face suddenly stiffened and he hid his hands. His eyes sank still deeper into their sockets. Two wild animals retreat deep into their dens. Alex, who had been asleep, mouth open, wakened just in time to hear this last remark. He sat on the edge of his mattress and listened. The Doctor would go on talking for about an hour. He would explain that criminals are always in a state of self-defense, and at the moment when they are preparing to commit their crime someone "necessarily" has to die. When a man murders, it's impossible for him *not* to murder, that's the truth. Alex yawned.

"You always murder for something," he said.

The Doctor is hard to figure out. It was always the stupidest remarks that pulled him up short and plunged him into interminable silences. Match, Alex, and Eugène watched him meditating like respectful interns waiting for a great doctor's diagnosis. Alex coughed; the Doctor shook himself awake: "You murder," he said slowly, "because somewhere in the world there is someone who must die. You or someone else . . . the victim is of no importance. It's a question of heads or tails."

"Which doesn't keep me from being alive and glad to

be alive," Alex said.

"I'll never forget your face, at night, when you breathe under the skylight and the moonlight falls on you . . ."

"I'm alive and I'm glad to be alive," Alex repeated.

"If you knew how little it mattered whether you're alive or dead . . ."

"It matters to me."

The Doctor rested his blank gaze on Alex.

"Yes, but who are you?"

This morning, under Eugène's direction, Alex went into training, for the world championship bout, which was to be fought in two months. Eugène, who used to read the sports pages, knew all the expressions he was supposed to use. Language, in matters of this kind, is very important. It is *crucial* to employ only certain words, to use only certain formulas, and to know the right moment to repeat certain phrases, even sentences, without changing a comma. Eugène chewed on his cigar (a piece of damp straw he pulled out of his mattress).

"You feel all right, kid?" (During the training sessions, Eugène must call Alex "kid." The latter, on the other hand, always refers to him as "Monsieur Eugène.")

Alex stopped jumping, gave the air a left and a right, the way a painter, before turning toward his visitors and laying down his brushes, might add, eyes half-closed, two more tiny strokes to his painting. Alex smiled stupidly:

"Sure, Monsieur Eugène."

"Sleep all right?"

"Like a top, Monsieur Eugène. Listen, Monsieur

Eugène, could I have a little advance on my next fight?"

"You need money? Listen, kid, there's no skirt mixed up in this, is there?"

Alex smiled even more stupidly:

"Oh, no, Monsieur Eugène!"

"I don't mind giving you a little advance, but watch out. There are plenty of champions around, even world champions. They get mass-produced these days. The carpenter makes tables, the baker makes cakes . . . and me, I make champions. I picked you because I liked you, but if you're no good . . ."

"I'm O.K., Monsieur Eugène . . ."

"All right, all right. I'll give you something. But watch it! No alcohol, no women, no night clubs, and no more than four cigarettes a day."

"I promise, Monsieur Eugène."

"It's not enough to promise, you have to keep your promise, right?" Eugène clapped Alex on the shoulder, and Alex blushed with pleasure. "And now let's see a little training around here, right? We'll work fifteen days, rest three, work two, rest three."

"But, Monsieur Eugène . . ."

"No arguments, kid, it's the only method that's right for you. It's the kind of metabolism you've got. For two days we turn it on, then we recharge the battery for three. Get it?"

"Yes, but Monsieur Sim—"

"—méon, I don't give a damn what Siméon did. You're in my gym. Did Siméon get you up to the championship? No. So no more arguments, kid! After the first fifteen-day period, we'll see how far you are."

This morning, Eugène and Alex went to the Bois for a

running session and a workout with the medicine ball. Alex trotted around the cell, skipped rope, threw and caught the imaginary leather ball filled with sand.

"Breathe, kid, breathe!" Eugène shouted. "Watch your breathing! Watch your breathing. All right, stop! Relax now, let your muscles go loose, that's right! Breathe! . . . All right, go on now! Deep knee bends, raising the ball over your head . . . One . . . Two . . . Three . . . Stop! Rest! Lie down in the grass, arms out, legs spread . . . *Rrilax!*"

Alex lay down on the cement floor of the cell, arms and legs spread wide. The Doctor and Match watched the session from their mattresses, very interested, very proud to have the privilege of observing a future world champion in training. Alex breathed deeply . . . eyes closed, nostrils dilated when he inhaled, pinched when he exhaled. He looked like a dying colossus swallowing oxygen in great mouthfuls and trying to put off the moment when death would squeeze his neck between its bony hands, forcing him to empty his lungs of the last bit of air.

The guard heard Alex jumping and Eugène shouting orders and counting: One . . . Two . . . Three . . . He slipped open the peephole and saw Alex lying flat on the floor.

"Sick?"

"Training session!" Eugène answered dryly.

"What?"

"I'm training my kid for the world championship."

"The boxer? But he's in for life! And you are, too!"

"I tell you, in two months we're fighting for the world championship."

"Yeah? Where?" the guard asked.

"In Madison Square Garden, New York."

The guard gave the crucified Alex a last glance, and slowly closed the peephole. First his left eye disappeared, then his right. The door which the Doctor, Match, and Eugène were staring at once again became smooth and silent. Alex hadn't moved. He was sweating. He was pale. He was breathing regularly.

"Who was older, your mother or your father?" the Doctor asked Match.

"Why ask me that?"

"Well, just to know . . . to talk . . ."

"You want to talk, Doctor?"

"My God . . . yes . . ."

Match didn't answer. My father, my mother . . . It wasn't the same thing, not at all, not at all. Father wasn't actually *old* . . . You see, (Match remained silent. The Doctor waited, rubbing his chin.) it was really that he thought that the good Lord . . . no, that God—neither good nor bad—was his equal. He prayed, his features rigid. In church, I spent all my time watching him, much more than the service; my father was my spectacle and my ceremony. Surreptitiously, I glanced up from my missal stuffed with pious pictures (which fell out each time and scattered on the stone floor. My mother helped me pick them up); then I looked along the narrow bench; I stretched out my neck; I slowly turned my head and finally managed to glimpse my father's profile. I see him that way forever. There was that smell of incense and melted wax, there was that chasuble with heavy embroidery, that chill paralyzing my skinny shoulders . . . that murmur, and that organ music rising behind me in a black wave that flung me to my knees. God, have pity on me! . . . God, don't have pity on me! Thy will be done! No! I stared at him; my eyes rolled in their sockets, they hurt me, but so what, I had to see, had to know. Over there, far away, the statue of gold and light proceeds to terrible things. The choir boy smothers a laugh. How can he laugh, so close? Will my father kneel like everyone else? Yes. Hail Mary, Mother of God . . . (Match lowered his head, stared at the toe of his shoe and still said nothing.) My mother . . . was pious in a brutally obvious way when my father said to me . . . Like the woman who was once, in her own eyes, a great sinner; like the woman who tries all her life to make up for an action whose shamefulness she had learned after committing it.

"My mother was convinced of the existence of evil," Match said.

"You said the opposite the other day, you said your mother was unaware of the existence of evil. I even think, if I remember correctly, that I heard you say that as a consequence she had no esthetic sense."

"Both are true," Match said. "She didn't believe in evil but my father did; and with him, but only with him, you understand, she felt guilty."

Match stopped talking. Out of my father's sight she was totally innocent of what his severity had made into a crime. Furthermore, my father *had made it his personal duty* to make up for *the act*. This act was me—the sickly, blackish, hunched, and secretive thing I am. I was never entitled to the qualities of a child: I will always regard myself as a duty or a crime; guilt or peevish pardon fallen

from on high like perpetual alms. Why am I ugly? I
didn't know, but all my being felt it in the anguish of my
solitudes, in my nightmares or when I walked along the
towpath. Even the water didn't want my reflection. Didn't
love me. How can you live when everything refuses you
life? When nothing loves you, and when you sit down
on a slope overhanging the path between a heap of rusty
tin cans and a few rotting sacks of jute? The part of the
slope I used to sit on was actually a kind of rubbish heap
. . . When nothing loves you, you can envy the grace of
a spot of oil dancing along the rippling water. I've been
jealous of a rusty tin can; I've been jealous of a rotten
sack of jute, of a puddle of oil. I've had moments of
absolute misery. Absolute! I'm the kind of child who suffers in silence. Speaks to no one. Has no friends. They say
I have a "taciturn temperament." I'm a secret, but a poor
secret that no one's interested in.

"Do you feel bad?" the Doctor asked.

"What?" Match said, suddenly raising his head.

"Your hands are trembling."

"Forgive me, I'm sorry," Match said, hiding his hands.

Where were my mirrors? All broken, all filthy. My
family broken and the canal water filthy. Why will nothing consent to resemble me? Because I'm evil!

I squeezed his shell between my thumb and forefinger.
At first I was afraid of him, but soon my passion got the
best of me. Back from school, I rushed to his cage, raised
the sliding door, and petted him. Or else I took him
out of his bed of grass and lettuce and watched him run
around in the hollow of my hand.

"He'll die," my mother said, "bugs don't live in cages."

I loved that June bug; it was the only *person* in the

world who would run around in the hollow of my hand, run up my arm . . . My face tipped back as if in ecstasy, I rested him on my mouth and the prickling of his little legs in the pink hollow between my lips gave me unmentionable pleasure. Then I would set him on a smooth green leaf, purse up my lips, and plant a delicate kiss on his reddish shell. Sometimes his wing cases hung out over his shell; then I was playing with a magic knight who wore precious lace under his armor. I, too, was black and hard, with my bulging forehead and my shoe-button eyes; I too, my June bug, was armored with ugliness, while my heart was a swarm of lace, and my soul—like your wing cases spread for the instant of short, heavy flight—gleamed with all the colors of the rainbow. Crouching in front of your cage (my first glance in the morning was for you; and my last in the evening), I would murmur for hours on end a language so secret it must have been the tongue of all untranslatable loves. June bug, June bug, why did you die, oh, why did you die?

"I think your bug died," my mother said. "It's not moving any more."

Tell me, is that what the Annunciation is like? A woman with a white porcelain face, perched on a chair (that day she was doing the windows) who turns around and casually remarks in a toneless voice: "I think your bug died. . . ." My mother, perched high, sovereign and terrible, that day you were the Annunciatrix. Your voice made a hideous noise and filled my head with a pain of unknown limits. I felt that everything was dying in me and around me, and that the disorder of eternal pain would bury my soul in its ruins. It was, oh how well I

understood it! . . . irrefutable . . . Stupidly, I stood
nailed to the spot, my schoolboy satchel in my hand, and
if you had turned your face toward me once again,
Mother, isn't it true that you would have given me death's
bony grin? I took the corpse between my fingers. Light,
light, so light . . . what difference is there between a
living June bug and a dead June bug? None, except that
the word has been spoken, and my mother said . . .
What difference is there between me and me? None, except that I'm dead. I open my bed and I put you on the
immaculate pillow. Nearby, my mother breathed on the
windows of the old-fashioned living room. Then she
rubbed, rubbed. God! How stupid it is, how meaningless
it is to rub the windows of a place where death is! Why is
my mother so cruel? Why doesn't she get off her chair and
help me die, or die with me? Standing there, I stared at
you, and all the life slipped out of my body. All my life
slipped down my chest, down my hips and thighs to
spread out around my feet like a tangle of clothes fet-
tering my ankles. I was drained. I had it later, that sense
that everything was rushing out of me in a heap, everything: life, will, pride, sadness, goodness . . . yes, I
felt it later—how much less strongly!—at the gambling
tables, on nights when luck roared past me like a train
roaring through a station. I had to do something, the
pain was unbearable. You can't be both living and dead.
Do what? Say my prayers? Kneel down at the foot of the
bed and murmur a litany of love? But there's rebellion:
life is tremendous, and the fragment of it enclosed under
that shell and beating beneath that lace was so infinitely
tiny . . . why was it taken away? Such a little scrap of
life, the merest drop . . . why was it extinguished? Kneel

down, pray, light a candle, set a flower on the pillow beside its head; but where is a June bug's head? Close its
eyes the way they do in books; but where are a June bug's
eyes? You were nothing, nothing . . . I was crying
over nothing. I was crying for all you weren't and for all
I loved.

I decided on a solemn funeral. The following Sunday, I
slipped you into my jacket pocket and I took you to
Mass. Organ music, gold leaf, songs, and prayers; the
holy ceremony was dedicated to you, curled up in the bottom of my pocket. . . . For a month you went to every
Mass, and Our Lord died and was crucified—for a June
bug. My next idea was to give you a sepulcher worthy of
our love. To lay you, swathed in tissue paper, in the
tabernacle when the church was empty. . . .

"The bigger I grew," Match said, "the guiltier I got. A
child is like a June bug, he hides . . ."

"Why like a June bug?" the Doctor asked.

"Like a June bug, like a cockroach, an ant, a cricket
. . . like a tiny black insect the color of night, the color
of darkness, something that hides . . . so you can
scarcely hear more than a scratching, a timid song . . ."

"Ants, cockroaches, and June bugs don't sing."

"Crickets do! You come close and they suddenly stop
scraping their little fiddles . . . You have to be patient
then, hold your breath and stand perfectly still, or crouch,
more humble and hidden than the insect in his hole . . .
One scrape, then two . . . A pause . . . And then
the song rises again, reassured. Then you're the one
who sings, you're the cricket. As soon as my father came
into the house, I grew smaller, I fell silent, I made myself
even smaller and blacker, and plunged my nose—that's

what caused my myopia—into my books. But I couldn't help growing bigger, despite all my efforts."

Match stopped talking.

"Now come on, eat!" his mother said to him. "Little boys who don't eat their soup never grow up."

I wouldn't eat my soup because I didn't want to grow up. On the door of an old abandoned shed I had drawn a yardstick with a piece of crumbling plaster. I went there to measure myself in secret, and despair filled my heart when I realized I had grown a centimeter or two. Baffled, I sat down on a huge rusty saw-toothed wheel (the shed had once been a machine shop) and my eyes filled with tears as I stared at the accusing mark. I was growing up. Often I ran to the shed twice a day to make sure I hadn't grown between eight in the morning (before going to school) and four in the afternoon (when classes were over). I took a ruler which I tried to hold perfectly horizontal; slowly I slid it down until it made contact with the top of my skull and then, suddenly wheeling around and still holding the tip of the ruler pressed against the door, I read the dreadful news. Sometimes, to my surprise and joy, I managed to lose a centimeter in a day, and rather than impute this diminution to a slant of the ruler, I calculated—at the rate of one centimeter a day—the exact date of my disappearance from the earth.

"Mother?"

"Yes, baby?"

She used to call me "baby." I asked again to hear the marvelous word once more.

"Mother?"

"Yes, baby."

"Could it happen that instead of growing up someone grows down?"

"No, a little boy grows up. He has to. Afterward, he becomes a man."

"No one ever grows smaller?"

"Yes, when you get very old. You know, they always say 'little old men' . . ."

"Mother?"

"Yes . . ."

"I'm growing smaller!"

My mother burst out laughing. I laughed too. Sometimes I made myself wait and managed not to measure myself for several weeks at a time. Finally, the date I had set to end my impatience arrived, and I headed for the shed, as agonized as a criminal facing his judge. Deliberately—for my calm was often only my anguish—I took off my shoes, smoothed my hair (I used to think that only bald men knew their exact height) and pressed my back up against the old door. Two centimeters! I had grown two centimeters! Impossible. I started over again. No, a centimeter and a half. I tried again! Just one centimeter! One, or one and a half, or two? It didn't matter, for whatever the "height" of the disaster, disaster it was.

"Eat!"

"I'm not hungry."

"Do you want a glass of milk?"

"I'm not thirsty."

"But milk's good for you."

I looked at the glass of white liquid in horror. *That—* that nasty white thing, foamy and warm—*that* was good for you. I clenched my teeth: not a drop of "that" would run down my throat.

"If you don't eat, you'll never grow up."

I didn't eat. I got dizzy spells, and at night I had bad dreams: I grew up, I became a giant. . . . So tall, so tall I didn't dare look to see what was happening where my feet were. My mother no longer recognized me; my head was so far away she could no longer make out my features. I was all alone with my head lost in the clouds; I was crying and talking in a void; no one could hear me. I woke up. It was dawn. In pajamas, I cautiously opened the door of my room, crossed the hall, opened the house door, crossed the deserted street and rushed toward the shed. Panting, barefoot, I measured myself. If I grew up, "he" would eventually notice it. I never called him "Papa"; the two syllables never passed my lips. In the parks, I listened to children my age shrilling their dreadful "Papa, why? . . ." How could they? How could they dare? I would be walking along in silence beside my father and we happened to run into an acquaintance we hadn't seen for two or three years: "Is that your son? How he's grown!" my Father didn't answer. I would hang my head, bend my knees, pull my neck down between my shoulders. "Stand up straight!" "He doesn't stand straight? That's bad, very bad!" joked the wretched "friend" we hadn't seen for years.

The bigger I grew, the uglier I got. It's a terrible thing, I think, not to love your own physique . . .

"Don't say 'physique,'" the Doctor said, "say 'body.'"

"It's terrible not to love your body. This head that swells like a pumpkin so that only old berets will fit it, these arms that get covered with hair, this nose that

hooks and grows longer . . . I didn't want my mother
to buy me a new beret; that would have meant accepting a
fact. I wore the old one that had turned gray and looked
more like a skull cap, perched on top of my head. They
say that there are madmen in asylums who can only be
happy when they're wearing little sailor suits and blue
berets with red pompoms."

"They act even in their coffins," the Doctor said.

"They're lucky," Match said.

"Yes, but they drool all the time," the Doctor said,
"and sometimes they scream."

Match repeated that they were lucky. One day, everything was over for him. He had his definitive body and
he neither drooled nor screamed.

"Besides," the Doctor added, "it's not a question of
your body."

"In my opinion," Alex said, "the Doctor's right: it's
not your body that's wrong, it's your morale."

"Yes indeed," the Doctor said, "that's it: your morale."

It doesn't keep me from having an ugly physique . . .
I mean an ugly "body." Nasty ideas in a nasty head . . .
Garbage in a rotten can . . . What counts is the envelope. If it's good-looking, nothing else matters . . . I
could have camouflaged myself behind beauty; behind
my ugliness, everyone can tell who I am. My father used
to say: "Look at me!" and I didn't dare show him my eyes
full of garbage.

"What garbage?" Alex asked.

Calmly, the Doctor explained to Alex that he asked
stupid questions and deplored the absence of mirrors in
the cell.

"I'd hold one up so you could look at yourself straight in the eyes for five minutes, and then we could discuss this further."

Alex claimed that he'd already tried, but that this exercise made his eyes fill with tears. He was lying.

"Besides, there were lots of mirrors, even as high as this, at Monsieur Siméon's, like in every gym. To correct faults: bad defense, right elbow too high, head not covered, chest exposed. You know, I spent hours and hours correcting this, that and the other thing in front of those mirrors and looking at myself. In boxing, a good defense is half the battle, Monsieur Siméon used to say. I'm used to mirrors, all right . . ."

He used to plant himself—once inside the hotel room, the key turned in the lock—in front of the one on the wardrobe. He was tired of roaming the streets and playing the slot machines in the *Khédive* or the *Soleil levant,* tired of arguing with pimps chewing gum and wearing silk handkerchiefs in their pockets.

"It was different for me. Actually, I never was a pimp. Profession? I always answered: boxer! A lot of cops had seen me fight. One even asked for my autograph . . . for his son. I always gave people the address of the gym, and Monsieur Siméon would say: 'Yes, that's right, he boxes here' . . . With real pimps, you know, I didn't feel right. After all, I *am* a boxer. The guy I never really understood, I mean, really, was Guitare. You know; a guy who doesn't like to do anything but sleep all the time, play his guitar, sing, wear perfume, and polish his nails sounds like a queer. All right. But this guy runs two girls, and when he hits them he makes them cough up plenty. Doesn't that sound more like a pimp than a fairy?

All right! Then you go to the gym and watch him jump around, sweating buckets, picking up weights heavy enough to kill a man, pedaling with five kilograms on his legs and taking kicks strong enough to knock over a gorilla. Sounds more like a wrestler. All right! So who is Guitare anyway?"

Who was Guitare? Alex admired the ease with which his friend shifted from one character to another, the way an actor changes role and costume. Guitare was nothing. One June night, in front of a bar, he was arguing with a man of about fifty. This man had heavy-lidded, shiny eyes and blotchy cheeks. He was smiling all the time he was talking to Guitare, and with his lips all pursed up, every word that fell out had the roundness and the obscene warmth of a fresh-laid egg. Guitare stood there listening, shifting from one leg to the other and rolling his shoulders as if the sidewalk was the deck of a ship on a high sea. He didn't say anything, but he was smiling, too, with that exasperating smile he has when he's sprawled out on his bed in a cloud of perfume, listening to "romantic" records. The other man kept laying more and more words and getting redder and redder under his shiny laughing eyes. Suddenly the man's hand sprang out and came to rest on Guitare's forearm, hesitated—and the gesture died in a timid caress. The first punch knocked him off balance; the second knocked him back again, his shiny little eyes turned into two big diamonds . . . tears . . . he walked away without even bothering to pick up his hat that was hanging on a hook inside the bar. A whore burst out laughing, throwing back her head.

"Can't stand fairies," Guitare said. "That queen had the nerve to lay his hands on me."

"Then why did you talk to him so long? He thought he had it made . . ."

"That's just it. It wasn't made."

"Then why did you stand there with him for almost half an hour?"

"Because it got him all excited, the bastard."

There was Guitare, the slot machines, the conversations with night-club doormen. Alex walked back to his hotel, took the key off the rack, walked up the three flights, went into his room, took off his shirt and pants, and stood in front of the mirror. He inhaled, jumped up and down, twisted his neck in order to glance at the state of his back muscles, shadow-boxed a little, read old clippings of his fights that he kept in a satchel with rusty clasps—I was someone!—stood in front of the mirror again, inhaled, measured his biceps using a tape measure with the first three figures missing, sucked in his belly . . . still all right. Sometimes, when he was on display like that, Maridge walked into the room. There had been some arrests in the neighborhood and she came in to wait until the mess was over before going back to work.

"I was working out," Alex would say.

"Go on with it, don't bother about me," Maridge answered, sitting on the edge of the bed with her high-heeled shoes off, rubbing her toes.

"No, I have time."

"You planning a fight soon?" she asked in a level voice, without raising her head.

"No, but it's coming. I know it."

"Fine, that's great . . ."

"What I need is to get some money. Then we can go to South America. Down there I'll get another name, a false identity card, false papers, everything, clean! Nothing easier. And I'll start fighting again. In less than six months, I won't have any more opponents . . . Then the U.S.A. . . . New York, Chicago . . . 'Unknown six months ago, this boxer has scored a triumph in South America before arriving in Chicago for a crucial fight. . . .' That's what the papers will say. And wait till you see Monsieur Siméon's face when he looks at *Miroir-Sprint* and sees me right there in the middle! Hey, that's Alex! Listen, that big Pancho Perez is Alex!"

"You're calling yourself Pancho Perez?"

"Yes, that's the name I think I'll use. Pancho Perez! Pancho Perez! It's a great name for a boxer. Can you think of anything better?"

"No, it sounds great," Maridge said, putting her red shoes back on. "All right, I'm going downstairs. I've got someone waiting for me at the Bagdad . . . Unless the bastard's run away . . ."

She kissed Alex on the forehead.

"Later, champ! I'm leaving. You know, I hear it costs a thousand francs a mile to go to America. And it's a long, long way. I better get moving. Be good, Pancho!"

He listened to the clatter of her heels fading down the staircase. He opened the window, leaned out to see two buttocks rolling under the much too narrow skirt before she turned the corner. In front of the mirror, Alex spat on a corner of his handkerchief and erased the tiny red wound Maridge's kiss had made on his forehead. "You understand, Doctor, it couldn't go on like that."

Today, Maridge committed suicide. "Guitare could serve as a witness," Alex said. He was with the perfumed wrestler listening to records when a friend of Maridge's

named Stella came to tell him. "Come quick, Alex, something's happened to Maridge." "What?" "Come right
away." "Was she picked up by the cops?" "No, come
on, she's sick, very sick. Come on, now, right away, for
God's sake! Hurry up!" Guitare can be my witness, I
swear.

"Oh, well, if you swear . . ." the Doctor said, rubbing
his chin.

And then Guitare even said: there's no fire, is there?
What's the hurry? Then Stella screamed: Listen, I tell you
she's dead. Dead, dead, dead! She repeated "dead!" about
ten times more, at least, and each time Maridge got a little
more dead. And Guitare even said: then why get so excited, it won't bring her back to life. And Stella screamed:
don't you understand, you idiot? Don't you understand
what it means to be dead? Sure, you cunt, Guitare said, it
means being tired and not feeling your feet hurt anymore.
Then Stella sobbed three times, three big sobs that puffed
out her cheeks. There she blows! Christ, Guitare said,
raising his eyes to the ceiling, as if there were any short-
age of whores around here! Come on, stop sprinkling my
rug, enough's enough. Alex said he sat there nailed to the
bed and turned back and forth to look at Guitare, then at
Stella, who was sopping up a handkerchief now. It was
no business of his. Maridge? Never heard of her! He
spat on the page and erased it from his memory; the
paper was blank again, he couldn't see a thing. No one
would decipher that ridiculous nickname "Maridge" on
his white memory. He hated trouble, cops, blood . . .
He had no desire to see the stretcher come down the stairs
and then be pushed into the police truck like a long loaf of
bread. Then he'd have to answer questions, put his finger-

prints on record, go to the church, the cemetery, stumble, get his shoes all muddy if it was raining and it was always raining on days like that, knot his tie. He hated ties too. Nobody knew if she committed suicide or . . . Stella said. They telephoned the cops, who should be there by now. "Fine," Alex said, "you go ahead, I'll come later."

"Did you knock her off?" Guitare asked, as if he were saying: "Want to go have a drink?"

Alex said he answered no.

"You going?"

"No, I'm keeping down. The whole bit wears me out."

"You'll be a suspect. . . . More than a suspect, and if the cops pick you up . . ."

"If I don't keep down I'll have to go to the funeral, and I can't stand all that crap."

"It's a drag."

"Ties, flowers, the hole . . . when my old man died, my mother borrowed a tie from a neighbor. It was the first time in my life I ever put one on, and I can tell you I had a time . . . you don't forget things like that."

"I'll say . . ." Guitare sighed, curling back his lips in front of a pocket mirror to check the whiteness of his teeth.

Guitare loaned him some money and Alex managed to get as far as Nice. From there, he wanted to get to Italy and take a boat for South America from Genoa.

"The police are looking for a former boxer, a friend of the slain prostitute and her presumed murderer . . ." the newspapers wrote, ". . . his arrest is imminent." Alex couldn't have cared less. The meshes of the web gradually closed around him, but he preferred to be suspected, arrested, tried, condemned, and even executed rather than have to go up those stairs. He would have had to climb those three flights, bend over Maridge, her neck mottled with blue blotches, see the bed all red with the blood that had flowed out of her open veins, say something, go to the funeral, put on a tie. Faced with so many gestures to make, so many things to do, Alex was overcome by a terrible sloth. At least with the cops, it would be easier: they would arrest him, tell him Maridge had been killed and that he was the murderer; they would prove it to him, throw him in prison, try him, and send him up. Then he wouldn't have to bother about anything, the cops would do all the work and it would be like with Monsieur Siméon, when all he had to do was sign the contracts and fight.

They claimed that Maridge had been strangled and that her lover, the boxer Alex, had cut her wrists with a razor to plant an unlikely suspicion of suicide.

"I'm completely innocent," Alex said.

"Didn't they believe you?" Match asked.

"No."

"They never believe anyone," the Doctor said.

"It sure wasn't pretty to see," Alex said.

That girl with yellow hair, the roots growing out black . . . it had been fifteen days since she'd had it dyed . . . all that blood on the sheets . . . "Even the mattress was ruined," the hotel manager had said . . . Her eyes staring at what? . . . Once I heard someone say that your eyes were just like cameras and that the retina, I think that's what he said, is exactly like a film. So I thought it would be easy to pinch the murderers—stranglers, for instance. All you had to do—you know, those guys can do anything now, they know everything—was take the eye

out of the socket and then with special machinery and
equipment, just develop the retina. Then you'd have the
picture of the guy who strangled her. It still surprises me
they haven't thought of that, those guys are so sharp.
When you strangle someone, in any case, be sure to do it
from behind! Her mouth was open too. She was completely naked. A naked body is more than a corpse, an
animal. You see the cunt, the feet with the nails overlap-
ping because the shoes were too tight, the belly and
its blind eye, the breasts. Raw meat. When you see that,
you understand why guys cut them up and put them inside
a trunk. It's natural. Besides, they cut you up with the
guillotine, too. Only in two pieces, but they still cut you
up. And blue marks all around her neck.

"You saw her?" Match asked.

"I read about it in *Detective*."

"And then they arrested you? You confessed?"

"I said I was innocent!"

"But the blue marks around her neck?"

"There are a lot of funny customers in a job like hers
. . . Maridge always had marks on her somewhere.
When it wasn't her neck, it was her shoulders, her ass,
her thighs . . . once, an officer beat her on the soles of
her feet with his riding whip. . . . Some guys, just to be
sure they've really had a girl, have to . . ."

"Maridge! What a name!" the Doctor said. "Whoever
thought of calling a girl like that Maridge!"

"Her real name was Julienne."

The Doctor almost shouted: "Then why did she call
herself Maridge? Why?"

"Because, it's better for her work. It sounds English."

"No, no! No!" the Doctor shouted.

Alex looked at the Doctor, who was standing up and pounding one clog on the floor of the cell. He stopped and sat down on his mattress.

"Listen, I know."

"Then don't get so excited, Doctor."

"It's because she was . . . dead! For so long, so long, Monsieur Alex! She was as dead as you were stupid! Did you never realize that Maridge was the name of a dead woman?"

Alex's face turned white, then red. The caterpillar swelled under the smooth skin of his forehead.

"All right, all right," the Doctor said, "Don't get excited. I just meant you haven't done much studying."

"With you, Doctor, it's easy: everyone's dead. All the same, though, some people *are* still alive, aren't they?"

The Doctor burst out laughing. His nose turned red, his eyes streamed with tears, his shoulders jerked. He had two fingers stuck in an electric plug, and the current of laughter almost broke him apart. Finally he sat down on the mattress and belched little crumbs of laughter, wiping his eyes with his cuff. "After all, some people are alive . . ." and his laughter started up again in broken-winded bursts which gradually died away.

Drawn by the Doctor's cries and by the noise of the clog beating on the floor, the guard pushed open the peephole. His eye. Then his voice: "If you want someone to calm you guys down, I know just the guy who can do it."

Silence.

"No one wants it?" the voice asked.

Silence. The peephole closed.

News time: "There will be no Sino-British conflict. In an announcement broadcast at nine last evening, the Prime Minister declared that Great Britain has decided to inaugurate the cession of Hong Kong to China. Peking then announced that the Emperor has ordered the Chinese troops to withdraw peacefully to their homes. In Rome, the obsequies of the Holy Father were followed by a crowd estimated at some million persons. In Baghdad, the world records for the high jump and hammer-throwing were broken by the Iraqi champion, Selim El Hafiz. The Soviet runner Voidine equaled the world record of two hundred meters in 18.7 seconds . . . (from Alex and Eugène, a brief whistle of admiration. His nose to the wall, Match continues:) The revolt of the Brazilian peasants has been put down at the gates of São Paulo. Impelled by famines due to an exceptional drought, great hordes of armed peasants from the interior had marched on the cities of the Brazilian coast. After devastating Bahia and Rio de Janeiro, two million fanatical peasants were preparing to attack São Paulo, solidly defended by the army. The latter initiated its first offensive against the Brazilian peasants last Tuesday night. More than a million peasants met their death during this engagement, which was a crucial one. General Franco, it is reported from Switzerland, has been declared undesirable on Swiss territory, which he has chosen as his place of exile. Upon announcement of this decision, the former chief of the Spanish government committed suicide. In the Southern states of the United States, the war between Negroes and whites is still raging. Premier Khrushchev has declared that the Finnish problem was invented by foreign agents. Lastly, and to conclude our bulletins, we wish to inform our listeners that 2,344,000 individuals have been arrested during the last month throughout the national territory. Which brings the total number of prisoners, as of today, to virtually nineteen million. This concludes our news bulletins."

Match turned around. He was exhausted.

"Terrific, today!"

"It's always like that," Alex said.

"Nineteen million, almost twenty . . . one out of every two people is in jail, right?" Eugène asks.

"More than that," Match said. "Because, after all, it would be pretty strange if they started arresting kids."

"In my opinion, they're arresting everyone," Alex said.

"Anyone!" the Doctor said.

"The most amazing thing of all," Alex said, with a yawn that split his face from ear to ear, "is the Ayrab who did two hundred in 18.7. I'll bet a record like that won't be broken for a long time."

The light went out. Time to sleep. Only the tiny night light burned in the cell, inside the big blue bulb protected by a metal grill.

"Good night!" Eugène said, stretching out on his mattress.

"Good night!" Match, the Doctor, and Alex answered together in chorus.

Today Eugène . . .

The Alex–Robinson world-championship bout was scheduled for six weeks from now, in Madison Square

Garden. The news, according to Eugène and Alex, was official. The contracts were signed. Alex would receive 14 per cent of the take; Robinson, 26 per cent.

"Listen, I'm the challenger," Alex said.

Eugène swore that the New York bookmakers offered him thirty-five million francs if Alex went down before the second round. He refused.

Today Eugène declared that the scenes between him and his wife grew more and more violent; she wanted a son or a daughter and he wanted a motorcycle.

Today the Doctor said he had an older brother. "He was very handsome. He died. My mother, for whom he was a God, bitterly reproached me for not dying in his place. Was it my fault? Yes, it probably was."

"Not the way I see it," Alex said.

The Doctor begged Alex not to interrupt him. "Monsieur Alex, I know what I'm saying, and I'm not speaking carelessly. When someone dies in the world, it's always in your place, don't you know that? And in my family, it was *obvious* my brother had to die, in the name of every grace, and I, in the name of every shame, I had to live. Don't forget, too, Monsieur Alex, that there's no use finding an answer to the questions I'm asking. Don't forget that I conduct my investigations by myself, with a few exceptions. You'll say that if I would listen to other people's answers, I'd have a better chance of getting through my fits. That may be true in part, but I'd rather die than *listen*. You'll understand why the day you know who I am. Besides, you won't ever find out. You'll make it up, which of course will come down to exactly the same thing. Can you doubt that all this has to end? All what? Aha! Monsieur Alex, you have no idea of the comedy brewing between these walls. A man who has any idea is . . . but I won't say another word! I've lived —I was saying in words everybody can understand—in place of my brother. Very badly, of course, for it's difficult to imitate, in this realm. I didn't know my role, and I committed innumerable errors. More exactly, my whole life was a mistake. My brother—the little devil— left like a king, like a God. Sovereign. Discreet. Elegant. Distinguished. Someone who made a marvelous appearance, was loved, spread a thousand lights and then just —disappeared. That's what being loved is: you strike, you pierce the other with a whizzing arrow that will sing for eternity and then you disappear forever. You strike, you open the door and walk out of the house. God knows; at Emmaus, or on the road to Damascus, He remained with his lovers only long enough to dazzle them. Clumsy as a peasant, I stay on and refuse to leave."

"So you believe in God, Doctor?"

"I have to. I'm certain my older brother was a fool, but I admit his beauty, and, therefore, he was very easy to love. We've already talked about that, haven't we, these last few days?"

"Yes," Match said.

"Well, so there's something interesting here! Clumsy as a peasant, I hang on, and I'm even very bright. That was inevitable. I couldn't do anything about it. The more I played the fool in order to resemble my brother, the more intelligent I became. Mouth open, snotty nose, stupid look in my eye . . . Of course, no one was fooled. Everyone guessed my hypocritical genius. I insulted my brother, I behaved as an impostor and a bastard. Was I ugly? No, no, you can see for yourselves that my face, although deteriorated by years in prison, still produces a nondisagreeable impression. Actually, I was even rather good-looking. A little more and I would have been almost as good-looking as my brother. All that was required, unfortunately, was a trifle, a mysterious detail, a touch. My mother looked at me with astonishment. Not only had I had the cruelty to kill my brother, but I even had the nerve to resemble him. To be *better*. Mother—yes, it even happened to her, sometimes had impulses of tenderness toward me. She made a mistake there, and afterward her sadness at having been so abused grew worse. When I was ten, a disease that almost killed me kept me in bed for over three months. Three months of happiness for my mother. I was sick like my brother, I was going to die the way he did. On this condition alone—that I should agree to resemble him even to the point of dying—my mother opened her enormous heart to me. They moved me, like an Egyptian mummy, stiff with a fever that had already exhausted my poor body, into my brother's room, which had been 'condemned' since his departure. 'He'll have more air in here,' my mother claimed, 'and the windows get the sun all day long.' They took the dust covers off the chairs, propped up the bed, wound up the clock that had stopped at the very moment my brother had departed this life, so that it could accompany my agony. I was again the child-king, come back to die in state in the room of the palace reserved for this event. My faithless subjects remembered that the blood of Saint Louis flowed in my veins, and prepared to mourn the prince they had pushed into the tomb. Mother was so happy! And *I* was so happy when I raised my grayish, leaden eyelids and saw her beautiful, tragic face, roughed by grief, leaning over my bed. 'You're going to die, aren't you, darling? You're going to go away to be nice to Mama, aren't you, my love? Your mama will be so sad, you know, and maybe she'll die, too. You won't get well like a bad little boy. . . .'

"Without a word, she stared at me for hours at a time, pulling the sheets up under my chin, planting on my wet forehead a kiss which my motionlessness and my pallor often led her to believe would be the last. I was going to die. Around this death, the celebration was organized. Mother took out long black dresses which she unfolded and sprinkled with tears; and hats, from which fell long veils behind which she hid her face, black leather gloves to hide away the white hands that had murdered me. Imagine my happiness! I closed my eyes and the fever taught me that my mother, standing in front of a high three-paneled mirror, was rehearsing the gestures of her imminent desolation. She walked toward the mirror, withdrew, turned around, raised and lowered her little veil that was embroidered with great black dots. She arranged her feet in black, pointed slippers the way the mannequins in dress shops do, or like the characters of *Commedia dell' Arte*. I even suspect that she had a certain flirtatiousness about her.

"I lay dying. My sweat was a wax, melted by fear. Sometimes I suffered a shameless impulse, the kind desire causes. . . . Under the skin of my torso, the ribs grew sharper. Everywhere, the bones rose to the surface, stretching the skin which they would pierce. A miniaturist would have had his work cut out for him: all my veins were visible, my bones that were once scattered to the four corners of my body drew together into this skeleton. Mother left the room, my dear mother who loved me. . . . The house was full of muffled noises I heard through a cotton helmet: footsteps, plates clattering . . . Who was eating? Who was hungry? Mother, no doubt, whom I saw sitting at a table and devouring an enormous calf . . . Doors opened and closed, voices whispered incredible secrets, and that, that—didn't it sound like music? It was summer outside. A black spot concealed the light from me for a long time. I know that Abbé Rolland had called. My brother died very quickly, almost by surprise, leaving my mother no time to sink slowly into her despair. And now I was dying like him, or rather the way my mother had hoped he would die. If I disappointed her, it would be terrible."

Eugène said that bicycling is hard but that it gives a lot of satisfaction.

The Doctor stopped. He was jammed, the way you say a car or a locomotive is jammed. His silence lasted over three hours. No one in the cell moved, and you could hear a fly buzz. Unfortunately, the cell was regularly disinfected as well as fumigated with smelly liquids, and the flies that visited us were rare. Whenever one of these dipterous Muscidae happened to wander into our environs, Alex immediately gave chase. Alex said that the day he went to see Guitare on his death bed . . . Guitare's parents asked for the body of their son who had been murdered, stabbed through the heart. The police granted them this favor, and Guitare didn't even have an autopsy: of course it was a crime, it was all too obvious. Christ, Guitare looked handsome, lying there on his child's bed! He had left his father's house when he was fourteen and had never returned. At fourteen, of course, he was no more than maybe five feet tall, and he didn't weigh anything like his full weight. He was gaining weight and growing taller all the time, and his parents were planning to buy him a new bed, a grownup bed, when all of a sudden he ran away. His mother cried, his father went to the police. Guitare, in those days . . . But that's *his* story and not much of one. We were talking about the bed, or rather about the business with the fly. Christ! How pale Guitare was on his child's bed! He just barely fit onto it. There was a branch of cypress, and four candles burning in broad daylight. I wonder why. Also a chromo painted on a kind of bark or a piece of wood, showing the city of Lourdes. Lourdes, a general view. Even though they had rummaged through the whole of his wardrobe, they hadn't found one dark suit in which to dress him up as a corpse. The least peculiar of his clothes—a purple suit—clung to the outlines of his body. He was wearing a narrow green bow tie, white shoes, and a pink shirt. I never saw a dead man dressed so beautifully. It's true that this dead man was called Guitare d'Amour. Under the pink shirt, under the jacket of the purple suit, I imagined the wound with its lips closed, brown now. A quiet wound, not even a hole. Unless the lips were gaping: a corpse didn't form a scab easily. So right in the middle of the chest, on the skin, Guitare was wearing a shiner. He really looked great. You think of such stupid things when you're standing by a dead man. And Alex, who had come to "pay his call," thought of stupid things. How long were you supposed to stand there staring? Alex didn't know. A corpse was relaxing. It never moved, never talked. They said some people keep them around and don't even register the deaths. I could understand that. But they'd start to stink. Believe me, I could have had Guitare stuffed and kept him in my room all my life. I'd have put him on the cushions the way he liked, his guitar on his knees, and I'd have sprayed him with perfume morning and night. Maybe Alex should have left long since; but he was all alone. Madame Guitare . . . the mother . . . what was her name? . . . was sniveling in the kitchen.

That's when Alex saw a fly land on the lapel of the purple jacket. It landed there, wandered around on its mechanical legs; it stopped, trembled; gave a little leap, and then it flew over to Guitare's right hand and stopped. Fascinated, Alex stared at it. It had no respect for Guitare: to the fly, he was just somebody dead, a corpse, meat . . . Alex's open hand advanced slowly, then swept the air over Guitare's face. Missed! Alex was filled with a cold rage. The fly grew suspicious and walked across the ceiling, then came back and landed on the dead man's chin. Motionless. There! Got it! Alex crushed it with all his might, squeezed, squeezed . . . a drop of pulp in the hollow of his hand.

"So you kill flies, too?" Out on the sidewalk two policemen took Alex's arms, one on each side.

"They were hiding in the room and saw me kill the fly.

That confirmed their suspicions. You don't catch flies in a dead friend's bedroom. I was the murderer. They were sure of it: according to them, Guitare was living with me, but afterward I met Maridge and so I could take her to South America with me I killed him and stole his money. According to them . . . but Maridge was my witness . . . she told the judges . . ."

For us, the appearance of a fly in the cell constituted an event. By tacit agreement, the creature would be handed over to Alex, whose predatory instincts awakened immediately. Instead of killing the animal, Alex did his celebrated circus act for us, the one called "the calisthenic fly," which he claimed he learned in school. Let's describe it: the fly was delicately impaled, alive, on a thin splinter of wood, itself stuck into a miniature cork pedestal. Thus impaled, it nonetheless continued—what a resistant life these little creatures have!—frenziedly waving its tiny feet. Then all you had to do was hand it a dumbbell (that is, two tiny bits of cork stuck on each end of a splinter). Its legs, pedaling in the empty air, seized the dumbbell and since it had six very prehensile legs, the fly began a whole series of remarkable exercises. Alex would provide a commentary:

"One! Out! Two! Back! Three! Up! Bravo! Change hands! One! Out! Two!"

We would applaud these remarkable exercises, and when the insect—Christ, how long it took!—finally died, we commented on his performances like connoisseurs. Alex disimpaled the corpse and put the apparatus away in a hole in the wall, above his mattress. Sometimes he took the inert fly between his thumb and index finger, lay it on the tip of his tongue (which he stuck out as far as he could) and with a smack of his lips, swallowed it.

"I'm a snake," he said. "I feed on flies and I'm twelve yards long."

He smacked his clogs on the floor of the cell: "I'm a rattlesnake!"

The Doctor was jammed. For several days now, he had been preparing his next fit the way a chef prepares a meal for royalty. Everything in him was brewing, and this slow cooking decomposed him. "It's coming," he said, then he shook his head and frowned. "No . . ."

"Are you expecting a fit, Doctor?" Match asked him, in the tone of a man asking: "Are you getting off at the next stop?"

"Yes, I feel funny."

"Aha, you feel *terribly* funny?"

"Yes, yes, yes, *terribly*."

"And it's coming soon?"

"I think so . . . but not right away, because I'm still not happy yet. You're always happy before, just before. You feel you're being lifted up by an enormous wave, with infinite gentleness. Did you ever take the scenic railway? When the car goes down and your heart stops . . . just before? What happens afterward must be . . . there aren't any, there aren't, aren't, aren't (the Doctor is stammering) any words to describe it, to d-d-d-describe it. Do you watch me, all three of you, when it comes? Well, don't answer! The postman in our village used to fall down with his epilepsy. He would collapse all of a sudden, right there in the street, and all the letters would fly out of the bag and spread around him. People appeared at windows and doors, looking out to watch the mystery occur. The man would fall down, roll up in a ball and sink into the dirty water of the gutter. Slowly—then all the heads vanished at the windows and all the doors concealed the black and curious old women who crossed themselves—he would stand up again, dust off his blue uniform and wipe the spots with his handkerchief. Then he would carefully gather up all the letters, fling his bag over his shoulder again and continue on his rounds. I saw it happen another time, too, in a big city, in the middle of a crowd. Some women screamed. A policeman threw his cloak over the body, but I had time to see the plaster eyes, the pink foam on the lips, and the little trickle of urine that came out from under the cape."

"Doctor?"

"Yes?"

"Couldn't you . . . well, just . . . refuse to have the fit?"

"Monsieur Match! Monsieur Match! The fit is a train; I'm bound, gagged, lying on the rails. It's written somewhere—isn't it, Monsieur Match?—that the man whose faith is as big as a grain of mustard seed will move mountains. Exactly! Irrefutable! Well, a man who has faith stops the train. I don't have faith. So the train moves on. It appears on the horizon; at first there's only a certain faint difference in the gray color in the distance, very far away on the gray of the horizon; then a black spot; finally it bears down on me. Did you ever suspect the terrifying stupidity of a train?"

"Is it coming? Do you see the horizon darkening?"

"No, at first I hear the noise; if I listen, if I press my ear to the ground, I hear—or think I hear—the sound."

"The sound of a troop of riders? The sound of the sea breaking through dikes? The sound, the subtler sound, of the octopus uncoiling its tentacles?"

The Doctor laughed his kindly infectious laugh. "There is no octopus. That was a joke. There isn't any train, either. The horizon itself swallows me up."

"At this moment?"

"Soon. I don't have my exceptional memory yet. When only a few minutes separate me from the fit, if you knew what my memory is then! All my recollections are released in a sheaf, which explodes when my head's not big enough to contain them."

"What recollections, Doctor?"

"They spring out in jolts, in spatters. Sometimes one spreads like a sheet of calm water, but the explosions begin again right away. What recollections!" (The Doctor pursed his lips. Does Match think that recollections are coins or ribbons forgotten in a drawer?) "I remember extraordinary things. For instance, that man doesn't exist, and that we are all going to die, Monsieur Match. I remember what it is that we should know every moment of our lives. I also remember love. Of course, she was—as you would have suspected—a whore. Always whores . . . wait a minute, I must wail . . ." (He whimpered like a dog dreaming and pressed his closed eyes with his finger tips.) "It does me good. No choice; either you no longer believe in love, or you love a whore. Sorry, Monsieur Match, but my ideas are getting away from me. They're a herd of wild horses; of bullocks, that's it! Buffalo! They're grazing and then suddenly their bodies start trembling. 'Something' tells them that a brush fire is roaring toward them at unheard-of speed and will soon wrap its tentacles around the herd. And they go crazy, fight each other, lowing. I can't get them back together again; the herd goes wild. They stampede. I scream, I run, I wave my arms and snap my whip, but the animals rush over my body and trample me with their hoofs. What?"

"I'm listening to you, Doctor."

"Thank you. In a minute I'm going to ask a favor of you." (The Doctor pursed his lips. The hoofs of the herd are pounding through his skull.) "I'm convinced that the bullocks and horses know more about this than we do. The whores are everywhere. We don't have any choice. We have to love them. It's a duty! Hah! A sacred duty. But what can we do? How can we love such horror? How can we adore it? I've held out my hands, look, like this, open, and I've closed my eyes. They spat on them. Puah! The slime spread over my open palms. Fine. Since that's the way it is, I strangle people! . . . Unless you find a way of loving shit. We have corkscrews, bottle openers, jacks, punches . . . they should perfect some shit-lovers, some gadget to make us love whores. You could sell them in grocery stores. You understand that I'm not talking about women, don't you? If I strangled two of them, it was by accident; someplace in Africa I might just as easily have bandaged the running sores of lepers. The same, my friend, exactly the same! A question of loving. Now, I want you to understand that to bandage a wound and then contemplate the bloody, pus-soaked cotton and the tiny brown scabs gives me pleasure. It's a question of loving. What else can I do, I ask you?

There must be a trick, something very simple and very complicated at the same time. Wait! . . . Or first of all, of being loved?"

When she told him she loved him, he raised his faded eyes, gentle and harsh at the same time, like the eyes of certain sick people with their heads leaning against the white pillow, staring at their visitors as they act out the farce of cheerfulness.

"Tell me, since I love you?"

"If you love me, you disgust me. Besides, you don't have any right to. However, you have to love me. Without my authorization and without my joy. You have to bet all by yourself; you'll lose, but you have to play."

"Do you know any soul nobler than mine, Monsieur Alex?" The Doctor said to Match: "If you knew how I treated her! She went crazy, she no longer understood anything. Neither did I. I needed her to love me and then, once that was done, I needed her not to love me—or rather, not to be able to love me. Starting from there, I could swear she had never loved me. I had reached my beloved conclusion: you don't love when you can't love to the end; therefore, since it's impossible to love to the end, you never love. Hence, one is never loved. I've dreamed of demonstrating this mathematically, with figures, formulas, equations, graphs, etcetera, until the final "hence" which falls with the sound of a guillotine. Since I haven't managed it, I have my fits."

He began by having "absences." At home, in class, all of a sudden his eyes stopped focusing. . . . That's it, you follow me? A "lost" expression. I frightened my deskmate at school; he shook me to wake me up. I even managed to frighten my mother, eventually. One day, she slapped him—she said—so he'd stop being absent-minded, but he didn't stir, just went on staring at her. Why did you slap him? Because I don't like his funny way of always looking surprised. After a long time he woke up and said: "What's the matter, Mother?"

"Monsieur Match?"

"Yes, Doctor."

"When I couldn't stand any more surprise, I had my absences, and my friends told me my mother slapped me when they came on. But I didn't remember a thing. My cheeks were burning, yes . . . One day I read a book, a detective story full of corpses, where a gangster slaps a dead man. The scene was very carefully described: the slaps on the cold skin, the dead man's head snapping back and forth, the fury of the gangster gasping with impotence. I was about that high when this book fell into my hands. From that day on, I was afraid of my 'absences.' What was my mother doing when I wasn't there? What was she doing with me? Was she taking advantage of my little fits to beat me like the gangster in the book? Or to caress me, embrace me, kill me, tell me she loved me? 'He's had another absence,' she would tell my father, in an indifferent tone of voice at dinner that evening. I wouldn't say a thing. I lowered my nose over my plate, but all night long I wept with shame and disgust. Monsieur Match?"

"Yes . . ."

"You're listening to me?"

The Doctor laid his palm on the back of Match's hand; it was streaming with sweat.

"Yes," Match said, "I'm listening to you."

"But it's possible that I'm lying to you, that I'm telling you nothing but nonsense. It's even probable. Maybe I'm making up stories to amuse you?"

"Oh! That doesn't matter," Match said. "So long as we were talking anyway . . . it's interesting. It passes the time."

"Thank you, Monsieur Match. That's the way I like to be answered. We were just talking, isn't that right?"

"Yes, Doctor."

"All right then! I'll go on . . . So then the fear came. When was I going to be absent, or more important—because don't forget that I didn't remember anything—was that minute when the world was present for me going to be followed by an absence? Had an absence preceded it? Did I come out of a *blank?* Was a *blank* going to swallow me up? Since I had no memories of those 'blanks,' I could suppose I had just gone through one at any moment. I forced myself to watch for the times when I felt my attention diminishing, turning into some kind of astonishment. It was a waste of time. For then I learned that right in the middle of a careless burst of laughter my face had suddenly gone smooth, my eyes empty, and that I had gone away . . . It seems they expected me to get over it. For three months my mother assured me that my absences had vanished. But I didn't believe her, she was lying to me, the bitch!"

"She was lying to you?"

"I don't know. I decided to have fits."

"You decided? . . . Really!"

The Doctor's tone grew harsh: "You can decide anything, Monsieur Match, don't pretend to be innocent! Christ, how hot it is in this cell! . . . A fit, at least, that's a real horror, a solid one, the kind that resists when you bite into it! You bite your tongue, you drool, you piss, you roll around and all your bones crack, you groan on the ground in the dust, the mud, the shit . . . that way, at least you know you've been—for several minutes —a monster. During my first fit . . . Monsieur Alex, put your hand on my forehead. Am I sweating?

"One windy night . . . Monsieur Match, if you saw me for the first time, would you say I looked normal? Years and years ago, I was walking with a woman at night, on a deserted beach. The silence, the enormous expanse of the beach, the sea, and the night, everything was deep to the point of dizziness. Suddenly I stopped— but did the moonlight fall on my face?—and I said: 'What a beautiful night!' Do you know what that woman did? She screamed and ran away. I still see her running down the beach . . . here, hold my hand, Monsieur Eugène. I had gone to look for two bottles of wine in the cellar; I was coming back up, but no sooner had I closed the little door under the hall stairs than I let go of the bottles . . . that wine spreading the splinters of glass around me . . . I uttered a short animal scream and I fell . . . I pissed into the wine, I spattered the hall, I knocked over the table and the marble statues on top of it broke. When I came to my senses, I was in my bed, my arms and legs strained with exhaustion, a big cut across my forehead, my hands gashed by the splinters of glass. Happy! Happy! Happy like a saint dazed by the vision of his Lord and who now contemplates the bush where the ineffable face appeared to him. Now I know. It is impossible to be mistaken. From my absences, I would emerge bruised, wounded, filthy but at least I would know that I had been absent. And when I opened my eyes, my mother was there: I knew she hadn't touched me; that she hadn't even dared approach this child's body shaken with demoniacal convulsions; that she had trembled with horror before this possessed creature who crawled and groaned down the hallway. We stared at each other a long time. At the end, when she lowered her eyes and went out of the room, I realized my victory. I was saved! Delivered! I was the Master! Let me drool, let me shriek, let me be an animal, an animal! And the world prostrates itself at my feet. What happened to Helène?"

"I beg your pardon?" Match asked.

"I said: what happened to Helène?"

"She committed suicide."

"Exactly," the Doctor said. "You guess everything. You're very shrewd. And why did she commit suicide?"

"Because she couldn't prove to you that she loved you."

"Exactly! And what did I conclude from this suicide?"

"That only the dead love us."

"Yes . . . that's just about it."

The Doctor grew calm again. He breathed deeply and rubbed his hands with a look of satisfaction. As if, suddenly, he were receiving his patients—years and years ago—sitting behind his desk.

"Oh, oh! Apropos . . . I'd like" (he said in a happy, detached voice) "you to do me one little favor, dear friend."

"Gladly," Match answered in the same worldly tone.

"As you know, one of these days I have the intention of having a fit. Would you be kind enough, the minute it breaks out, to observe me with very close attention, and

note down everything you see, everything, *everything?*
Even the kind of details that seem insignificant to you.
Yes, note down everything in your memory . . . from
start to finish. Would you do that for me?"

"Certainly," Match answered.

"Then," the Doctor added, still agreeably, "you'll
tell me? You'll describe the scene to me without forgetting
a single detail?" (There was a flash of light in his eyes.)
All the details, even the most insignificant . . . give me
all of them? The most insignificant, the most . . . (He
snapped his fingers, once, twice, three times). Will you
give me your word?"

"You have it, Doctor."

Eugène kept swearing it was an accident. Why didn't
they let him go! Stop making trouble for him! Leave him
alone! He wasn't lying; couldn't they see for themselves—
Since he was swearing, pounding his chest, trembling with
rage, why didn't they believe him? The lever slipped out
of his hand; maybe because the leather glove was soaked
with oil; maybe because the safety catch slipped; maybe
. . . engineers, experts, have checked the mechanism of
the crane, questioned the witnesses who saw the jaws
opening and the three iron beams. On that day, the foreman was wearing riding boots. In accidents . . .

"Accidents?" the Doctor asked.

". . . In things that happen there are real master-
pieces of horror. One beam fell flat . . . just a minute,
I'll try to explain." (Eugène once more became very
precise, very technical.) "One beam knocks into the foreman's hips and he falls on his back, another beam a

quarter of a second later lands right on the poor guy and cuts his legs off just above the boots. But then something strange happens: when the edge of the beam cuts off his legs, those legs stand up again—probably the shock on the knees has functioned as a lever—and what do you see? A pair of boots standing straight up, and the guy's legs still in them; a pair of boots with two stumps of meat pissing blood that flows out all over the leather. You don't see things like that often."

I was arrested two days later. The experts rejected the possibility of an accident. I could have protested and been acquitted, but a neighbor and his wife testified they had heard Jeanne call me "monster" and "murderer" on the night of the accident. For a long time she sobbed and sobbed, sprawled out on the bed, her head buried under the pillows. "Don't touch me." If I had touched her, I think she would have gone crazy. She sobbed and sobbed, and her shoulders were shaken with nervous spasms. From time to time her legs kicked out as if her body were trying to get rid of the criminal weight that was crushing her. Murderer! Murderer! The neighbors had come out onto the landing and were listening. They testified that they heard me answer: "It's you. You're the one who asked for it. You knew I'd kill him. You knew the day would come when I couldn't stand any more of your bitchery, and you watched that day come without blinking an eye. You're the one who killed him, you're the one who's the murderer." They testified I'd said: "I'm innocent." I pushed the lever. If the guy was crushed by the beams, it's because he happened to be underneath them. And who put him under there? You, Jeanne! If not, why would the crane jaws have opened? Why would the beams have crushed him? For days and weeks you pushed that man toward the place where you knew he was going to die. Inch by inch. Patiently ("That's what's called *loving*," the Doctor said, so low that no one heard him). Jeanne screamed: No, no, I didn't know it, I didn't know anything! ("That, too, is what's called *loving*," the Doctor said.) She sat up on the bed, her hair wild, her dress above her knees, her features out of control. As if a drunken sculptor had ruined the soft paste of her face.

She stared at Eugène and a ridiculous thought went through her mind: he's handsome. He's a monster, but he's handsome. The thought was dissolved, pulverized by rage and disgust but, as though by electricity, Eugène— for a second—had been jolted by it. For a second, they made love over the body, and the foreman was murdered so that they could experience this brief moment of unique pleasure. For a second, Eugène and Jeanne were accomplices, murderers together, innocent and forgiving each other for the murder. For a second, Jeanne and Eugène defied the world and loved each other as they had never been able to love before. The earth turned in silence. Billions of men and women pronounced the simple words that ward off death. The sun stopped. Time was eternal and vanquished. Jeanne and Eugène were face to face, riveted forever to each other's eyes, beginning again the swaying waltz that first brought them together. And they fell, petrified, hieratic as two statues, each finally in possession of the secret of life. Jeanne screamed and the words exploded in stone and blood: "You're a monster!" She fell back on the bed, drained of her love for Eugène. Drained, nothing but a sack of skin filled with squirming bones and nerves.

"Afterward, she swore she had never slept with the foreman, so now I 'looked fine' with my crime on my hands. I had killed him for nothing. Out of stupidity, out of selfishness. She said that was the worst of all. 'You wanted to because you're crazy, you wanted to kill someone and you used me to do it.'"

"Ha, ha, hee, hee, hee!"

That was the Doctor's childish laugh. Eugène, nonplused, stared at him.

"Sorry. And then?"

Apparently the foreman was a ladies' man, a bachelor, and always spruced up like a freshly groomed horse. Why did he have to stamp and sniff around Jeanne? There was nothing more disgusting than a ladies' man. Guys like that made Eugène want to spit.

"You were one before you knew Jeanne."

"It's not the same. Guys like that don't love anyone."

"But you didn't love anyone when you were like them."

"I wasn't like them."

"Why?"

"Because I was going to love Jeanne."

"How did you know that? You didn't know that!"

"I did."

Match plunged an endless index finger into one of his nostrils and rummaged. A sign of meditation.

"He knew it," he said. "And Jeanne's love saved him."

"Ah! That's the whole question," the Doctor said.

Match and the Doctor began quibbling. The former asserted that Jeanne's love had saved Eugène, that Eugène squashed the foreman to get rid of a past symbolized by the future victim. The latter maintained that Jeanne's love had actually saved nothing, nothing at all, zero, and that in fact Eugène couldn't get over his failure. He had continued to resemble the foreman and had tried, by squashing him, to suppress himself. Listening closely, Eugène didn't miss a word of the argument. The Doctor supposed that if they were to ask Eugène a question—for instance: "Did you cheat on your wife?" —the answer—yes or no—would settle the argument in favor of one thesis or the other. But will they ask this question? No, they decided.

"I'm completely innocent," Eugène said, "but I've learned about neighbors that'll say anything."

"And girls, too," Alex said.

Eugène and Alex began a routine conversation about girls. The Doctor had fallen asleep, lying on his back, one arm folded over his face, like a child about to be slapped. Match was dozing, but the conversation reached him in snatches.

The Doctor was dreaming of Helène, to whom he was saying: "I'm lost." He was sitting in an armchair. Helène crouched at his feet, rested her head on his knees, and he, caressing her hair, kept repeating: "I'm lost." Why? Because there's something that's not working, it'll never work. What? I don't know. Between you and me? No, of course not, don't say things like that. Then explain it to me. It's you, Helène, you know everything; you should explain it to me. But I don't know anything. Yet you're on the side of people who know everything, Helène. She raised her head and saw something like tears in the Doctor's eyes. I know you, she said, you'll get over this and I'll go crazy listening to you and believing you. He told her: My little girl, I love you, you know that. I love you so much I could live with you, have children with you. We'll build a house, we'll have a boy and a girl, and I'll teach them to read and write. We'll quarrel over their education. When the boy does stupid things, you'll take his side. Behind my back. I'll potter around the house, I'll have tools. Your friends will come and visit you and you'll try on dresses in the bedroom, laughing and whispering while I watch television. You'll refuse to tell me who you've been talking to on the phone, and I'll make a scene. You'll cry and your nose will get red. Then I'll console you and you'll wipe away your tears. We'll live together forever. We'll give each other little presents. We'll have a garden with flowers. We'll buy each other books, records, pictures, and lots of precious little things that the children will break. Oh no, they won't break them because they'll be afraid I might scold them in my loud voice. Eyes closed, Helène listened. The Doctor suddenly burst out with his horse's whinny, and Helène's head, decapitated, jounced on his knees. You'll get over it all right, and I'll go crazy. Why do you say such things? He stood up and walked back and forth in the disorder of the living room. Because I'd like to know why it's all impossible. There must have been a moment when all of it was possible, normal, certain. But when? At what *exact* moment did I make a mistake? I'm trying to remember the day, the hour, the minute . . . the different paths must have resembled each other like peas in a pod. Why not this one? Why not? I took the other without a thought, and since then I've been advancing farther and farther into an endless landscape. Of course, my friend, you'll say to me: why don't you turn back!

My answer is that I can't. Briars, thistles, trees, and bushes have grown up behind me with infernal speed, and this cursed vegetation has devoured the path and my footsteps. So I'm condemned to move on. Condemned by whom? Who's judged me? When? All this must date back to prehistory, and if I had a fabulous memory maybe I'd know something about it. This said, my friend, melancholy is vile, and rest assured, I'm the happiest man on earth. I'm waiting for the day when someone dares claim he's happier than I am. Get dressed; we're going out to eat. I'll smoke a cigar. No, Helène said, I don't feel like going out. You go by yourself.

One day, Helène made this remark: "When you leave in the morning, I always feel that you'll never come back; that I'll never see you again. It's probably because you take everything with you, you don't leave anything of yourself with me." He answered: "You're very bright." And she: "No . . . Sometimes women don't think. All of a sudden there's just a complete void in their head. Then, other times, they understand everything."

(The Doctor, mouth open, snored behind his folded arm.)

Another day, she said: "You think you're smart and I lie to you all the time, I lie to you constantly. I swear I do." He said: "Why did you say that?" "So that you'll get mixed up, so that you won't know where you are any more. You haven't given me anything. I haven't given you anything. You're a filthy egotist and I'm glad I lied to you all the time. I was keeping my eyes open too." He said: "It doesn't matter to me. Lies or truth, it's all the same to me. So you're caught now, aren't you? You lied to me for nothing. Everyone lies all the time. The way they

breathe. If you think you're going to get off that easy
. . . besides, you haven't lied to me." Afterward, she
confessed: "When I told you: 'I swear I do,' I had my
fingers crossed."

Still another day, she said: "Maybe I'll ask you for
things you should refuse me. Please go on refusing. Even
if I ask for them . . . If you knew . . ." He answered:
"I know which ones."

(The Doctor was snoring, his face relaxed.)

She said to him: "Once, you were God. But afterward,
I knew that you were only a monster. So I want all the
girls to sleep with you. You'd like that, wouldn't you? Tell
me you'd like that, go on, tell me! If you don't, I think
I'll go crazy. I'll kill myself." He answered: "I'd like it a
lot."

(The Doctor was sleeping. Peace was upon him.)

Women, Alex and Eugène said, women are like cats,
you drop them from the fourth floor window and they
land on their feet. Then both of them wondered if "they
suffer." Yes, they suffer a lot, but not for long; otherwise, with their insistence on taking everything on themselves, they'd end up dying of it. Girls, Alex said, girls
recover quickly. Like good boxers. You think they're
worn out, they head for their corner staggering, and in
the next round they start up fresh as a daisy. Then Alex
went into a long explanation in which he proved (for
Eugène reminded him that all the same Khadi did die of
it) that the Ayrab had had his accident first and didn't
die from Alex's punches. Girls, he added—it's the same
thing. Actually, you never kill them, you finish them off.

And when they cry? Oh, Eugène said, I can't stand that. I clear out. Alex said that Guitare had a whole drawer full of photographs of women, big photographs, "portraits." "These are the women in my life," Guitare used to say. Sometimes he arranged the portraits on a stand and passed them in review. Or else he brandished a big revolver and fired at the portraits until the cartridge was empty. The photographs remained intact because the revolver was loaded with blanks. It was a revolver for self-defense. Harmless. It was to keep from getting scared. But the gunpowder smelled good in the room, mingling with the heavier odor of the perfumes. Or else Guitare arranged the photographs on the bed. "I'm telling fortunes . . ." Queen of hearts, queen of spades, queen of clubs, queen of diamonds. That one was called Dany, she was cute. That one married a guy from the Auvergne who owns three cafés; she's gotten enormous, big as that, and she's growing even fatter behind the cash register. When I'm in the neighborhood, I go into her café and say hello. I kid around a little and she turns as red as a girl at her First Communion: "Come on, Guitare, be serious! . . ." That one, I wonder what the hell happened to her . . . Mary Lou . . . She used to drink coffee without sugar and put salt on oranges. That one used to tell everyone she was my wife; I swear! That one read movie magazines all the time. And that one was really cute, really nice, she liked to do the cooking without anything on. That one's name was Fannette . . . When she was mad she used to write me letters, rush out into the street, then come back upstairs and say, "Did you read it?" "Yes . . ." "All right, that's that!" And it was over. Writing letters calmed her down. I think that one's in jail. That one spent her whole life in the tub. That one compared horoscopes in all the newspapers she bought: she was a Ram. She said I was a Fish. So when it was all right for the Rams and the Fish in the papers, she adored me. When there were "dangers of quarrels and disagreements," she would cry. That one's Juju; she used to smoke cigars. That one married a jockey. I used to like that one, but she talked in her sleep. That one wore glasses to the movies. That one, the minute she went anywhere—a dance hall or a bar or a restaurant—she wanted to leave right away. That one was jealous of every woman around and kept accusing me of "you know," getting it up as soon as a skirt passed a mile away. That one thought everybody wanted to rape her. That one, all she talked about was her "periods" and her ovaries, her name was Solfegina. That one, Kiki, her handbag was a drugstore; she kept taking pills for everything and she almost believed me when I told her that in America they made pills for automobile accidents. That one, when she was mad she counted her dresses and paid her debts. That one, Josette, she kept saying all the time that she loved her husband and wanted him to take her side when I got mad at her. That one gave money to beggars whenever she saw them. That one . . . Guitare had an elephant's memory. He scraped up the photographs like a card player, shuffled them, cut. "Now we'll see which one I love. Conchita! Good, I love Conchita! . . ." Eugène told Alex about terrific pickups; Jeanne was jealous as a tigress. And serious, her eyes always lowered—it was easier to be serious that way.

"You cheated on her?"

"Oh, now and then . . . you couldn't really call it

cheating. I loved her. No one else. Match is right. He says women don't understand that the more you cheat on them the more you love them."

"What does he know about it?" Alex asked, "Match never touched a woman."

Match was holding his breath. Eugène described the scenes Jeanne made. Then one day she changed her tune. She looked up and started being flirtatious. Began smiling at one guy and laughing at another. At the foreman? Not especially. It used to get on my nerves, like a mouse gnawing at a string. One day, Sna-a-ap!

"Jeanne, you're cheating on me!"

"Not yet. I have to make up my mind first."

"You're cheating on me!"

"And you?"

"Yes or no, are you cheating on me?"

"Darling, I'm telling you: not yet!"

She was peeling potatoes, using a little paring knife with a very narrow blade from being sharpened so often. She was peeling potatoes carefully, slowly, with a smile that twisted the left corner of her mouth; a smile I couldn't stand, a smile that drove me crazy.

"Stop riding me!"

She was still peeling, slowly, digging out the eyes of potatoes with a quick gouge of the knife point. Eugène could still see the red-and-white checked tablecloth on which she was setting down the soft yellow potatoes; he could hear the rustle of the knife blade sliding around the potato, between the skin and the flesh; he could smell the stale, sweetish odor of the peels.

"But I'm not riding you, my poor darling."

"I'm not your poor darling!"

"Oh!"

She was still smiling.

"Would you rather have an omelet or scrambled eggs with your fried potatoes?"

"Jeanne, shut up!"

"All right, all right, I'm not saying anything."

"Jeanne, swear you won't cheat on me."

"I never swear."

"Swear!"

"No I won't . . ."

"Then you've decided to . . ."

"Maybe yes, maybe no."

She spoke this last phrase with a coquettish movement of her shoulders, wrinkling up her forehead like a vaudeville soubrette. Eugène's hands began to shake where they lay on the table, then jerked away and swept off the cloth with the potatoes, the plates . . . Jeanne stood straight and pale, her knife in her hand. She didn't recognize Eugène. He was . . . repulsive. His lips rolled back from his teeth; red patches stood out on his skin; he had no more neck; one of his eyes was half-closed and he was trembling, trembling, trembling where he stood nailed to the floor by the dread of what he was going to do and what he read in Jeanne's eyes. She didn't move. She stared at him. She tried to get rid of the smile twisting her face, but couldn't.

"Bitch, bitch! Whore!"

She guessed the insults she couldn't hear from the slow movement of his lips. He advanced toward her. She raised her hand that was holding the knife. A flash and he grabbed her wrist, twisted it. Slow motion—as if they were fighting under water. A second flash and the blood splattered from her slit throat. Eugène stabbed, stabbed, stabbed. Jeanne smiled her eternal plaster smile. She slipped, fell.

"It was a crime of passion," Alex said.

During the night, Alex woke up. An idea was running through his mind. He sat down on the edge of his mattress, careful to keep it from rustling. Alex had an idea and that was rare; but it kept running through his head with lizardlike timidity, and each time that he tried to put his hand on it, it vanished, scared off. He played hide and seek with the idea for half an hour, then he set his bare feet flat on the cool floor of the cell. Immediately this coolness invaded his feet, his legs, made its complicated way through his belly and his torso and rose to his head. Alex no longer thought. To think—he thought—you have to have a warm head. I'm cold. He stood up and walked around the cell. Without a sound. Not even a rustle. He stopped under the skylight and stared at a square of sky where a few stars twinkled in the vague night air. One, two, three, four, five, six, seven, eight, nine, ten, eleven stars. He wondered, with a colossal effort of thought, what the stars are for? What are they made of? Why do they shine? It's the first time I've asked questions like that. What are questions for? Alex was completely naked. He breathed deeply. He walked, and his member, which happens to be long, dangled free. His eyes were used to the dark; a tip of the moon had slipped into the left corner of the skylight and soon everything in the cell emerged from the darkness, bathed in an ashen light that is tender to the eyes. It's warm. I'd like to go swimming in the sea. Alex, naked, imitated the movement of a swimmer with his arms. I'm swimming. He was sweating. Is it summer? The sweat flowed from his armpits and the back of his neck. He rubbed his neck, his torso, his belly, and his hands slid over the wet skin as if they were smeared with a sour liniment. Now the smell enveloped his body like a piece of material, floated and swelled with each of his movements. If I were dancing, the folds of the odor would brush against the walls of the cell. He leaned over the mattresses where the Doctor, Match, and Eugène were sleeping. The ashen light carved the faces out of a strange white paste. Eugène was asleep, the fringe of his long lashes carefully curved over his eyes; the bar of his eyebrows very straight; his features carefully organized by sleep. What did the sleep of that handsome face imprison? The Doctor was asleep, his head thrown back; you could see the two black holes of his nostrils where the air spurted out in regular jets; the dome of his forehead . . . What does he remind me of? Oh yes, I remember, I had strained a vertebra and Monsieur Simèon sent me to a kind of clinic where nurses and masseurs were laying the guys out on planks of wood, attaching leather collars—stiff and greasy with old sweat —around their necks and ankles and setting up pulleys and levers to stretch them out. Some were actually hanging by their necks, arms dangling; others were lying on slanting benches; others were crucified on easels. All of them were stretched out motionless, with faces of painless martyrs. That's what the Doctor looks like. He looks like a hanged man only not suffering. Invisible hands are drawing him by his ankles, stretching out his neck, farther and farther. He's growing lengthwise, as if he were lying only on the tip of his skull and his heels, the rest of his body suspended over the void. I've seen that in the music hall. Guys laid out—neck and ankles—on two chair backs. Then the magician takes away one chair, then the other, and the guy was floating, stiff, his belly up. Match was curled up on his right side, a blackish fetus, his cheek abandoned in the shell of his hands; his forehead was only a gleaming knob of light; his pinched nose—a beak—curled into the hollow of his shoulder. Monsieur Match, you're a skinned rabbit after the cook has torn its eyes out; then he rolls the body into a ball, cracking the spinal column a little, and tosses it into the pot. Monsieur Match, you're an old skinned rabbit cooking in your sleep.

One, two, three faces . . . do I have a skull, too, in the moonlight? Why do people never think of being photographed while they're sleeping? They'd get a surprise. All these floury faces, what are they for? Why is it living, this moon flour? Good evening, Doctor Flour! Good evening Eugène Flour! Good night, Match Flour! I pour water on you, I mix it up, and what do I have?

One, two, three faces . . . What use is a face? What's it made out of? Why does it shine in the gray light of the cell? Why does it sleep? Alex leaned against the wall, facing the beds, sometimes stared at the faces, sometimes at the stars. He went over to Eugène, lay one hand on his shoulder, shook him the way you wake the man you've chosen to be your companion in an escape, who will get out of bed on tiptoe without disturbing the other prisoners. The fringe of lashes rose over Eugène's startled eyes.

"What?"

"Shsh! Shsh!" Alex said.

"What?"

"Shshshshshsh!"

Alex didn't dare bend over the mattress, and remained standing, naked, one finger on his lips. Eugène threw back the blanket, intrigued, and got up. Now he was standing, naked, next to Alex.

"What's happening?" he whispered.

"I'm sorry," Alex murmured, "I'm sorry but I wanted to ask if you had killed your wife."

Eugène shrugged his shoulders.

"And the foreman?"

Eugene shook his head.

"Then why are you in prison?"

"Because I'm a criminal."

"Who did you kill?"

"Let me go to sleep. I'm tired, and we'll wake Monsieur Match and the Doctor. Come on, go back to bed or you'll get out of shape."

"Yes . . . Yes . . . In your opinion, did the Doctor kill Helène?"

"No, of course not!"

"What are we guilty of?"

"Getting out of shape and asking silly questions in the middle of the night. All right, get to bed!"

"Yes . . ."

On tiptoe, the two men went back to their mattresses; the straw rustled; they pulled the blankets up to their chins.

"I told you, you started by putting both hands flat on your chest."

"Like this?"

"Yes, perfectly flat. You looked like somebody protesting his innocence in a rather theatrical way."

"Interesting, continue . . ."

For the third time, Match was telling the Doctor about the fit the Doctor had three days ago. At each new telling, he remembered a forgotten detail and the Doctor would exclaim: "Ah! Interesting, you hadn't told me that before!"

"Then . . ."

"Think carefully, take your time. We're not in a hurry. We're lucky about that."

"Then, you seemed . . . absent. You looked at me without blinking. It was pretty hard to take."

"As if I were going to talk to you?"

"No. As if you were astonished to learn of some news that had taken your breath away."

"But before resting my hands on my chest, what did I do?"

"You had stretched out your neck and opened your mouth, spasmodically. I thought you were going to vomit."

"How many times?"

"Five or six times, I guess."

"That's it: precordial paresthesia simulating pectoral angina, a fit of asthma or of spasmodic coryza, gastrologic crises, nausea or vomiting that constitute the prelude to the convulsions or alternate with them. Perfectly correct. Afterward? Or rather, before that? Try . . . Oh, Monsieur Match, how kind you are! And before that?"

"Before?"

"How did you tell the crisis was coming? At what

moment did I stop being normal?"

"You were leaning against the door. Without any warning, you took a step forward, as if the door were burning your back. Then you went over to the basin and you stared at it strangely. I could have sworn you no longer recognized the cell and were wondering why you were here."

"Sudden dissolution of the psychic functions. Collapse of the temporal-spatial framework . . ."

"I beg your pardon?" Match asked.

"Shut up! Mental vertigo reaching the point of complete obnubilation, deterioration of the psychic syntheses, alteration of reality principles, this syndrome plunges the patient into a state close to that of dreaming which is called, in fact, for this very reason 'confuso-oneiric.' The ordinary framework . . . Oh, I don't remember any more."

The Doctor pondered, holding his head in both hands, then continued in a hurried rhythm, like a student reciting a lesson learned by heart: ". . . I've got it: the ordinary framework of perceptions then grows animated and dramatic: this mattress becomes electric, that shoe a case of explosives, this cell a crematory oven, Monsieur Eugène a policeman. The oneiric scene creates an actual scenario which generally unfolds with cinematographic precipitation in an atmosphere of terror and anguish. Hallucinations of all kinds participate in this significant syndrome. Very good, Monsieur Match. And then?"

"You lifted up the basin, turned it over to examine the underside with maniacal attention. You repeated this movement eight times. Then you went over to your mattress, then back to the basin, then back to your mattress.

Then you walked very quickly, head down—"

The Doctor interrupted, reciting: "The most interesting of these cases of epilepsy are those in which the dissolution of the higher functions favors the appearance of impulsive automatic actions. Most frequently, these are uncoordinated actions quite harmless in themselves: strange running movements—precursive epilepsy—sometimes dangerous, however, for the patient insofar as they are possible causes of accidents. Their epileptic character may be recognized by their suddenness, their brevity, the simplicity of the gesture, its generally absurd character, its stereotypic repetition. Serious cases are those in which the psycho-motor automatism is accompanied by impulsions capable of ending in dangerous reactions and in antisocial actions: impulses to drink or dipsomania, attacks against public decency, thefts, arson, suicide, murder. Murder! Murder! Monsieur Match . . . All these acts are remarkable for their suddenness, their absurdity, their absence of motives, and an often revolting brutality. A patient kills a stranger or his own child; he perforates the body with stabs, tears it to pieces, disfigures his victim with pitiless savagery, sometimes even devouring bits of it! . . ."

The Doctor burst out laughing. Hysterical laughter. He was shaken by it . . . It made him cry. Then he repeated between gasps: "Devours it . . . Hee! hee! Sometimes, hee, hee! bits, bits . . . he devours bits!" The tears of laughter hadn't dried on his cheeks before he continued:

". . . the chief characteristic of the psycho-motor automatism, gentlemen, is, if not complete unconsciousness, at least the total amnesia which follows it. We see, gentlemen, that the medico-legal problems thus posited can be very difficult to solve. Before the law an impulsion, even an unconscious one, is suspect; the amnesia may be considered as simulated, and as a means of defense."

The Doctor stood up, thrust his thumbs into the armholes of an imaginary vest, and, clearing his throat, seeking inspiration, continued his discourse, his voice in a higher register than usual.

"The problem is still more delicate in the relatively frequent cases in which amnesia is incomplete, retarded, or even totally absent. This impulsive, conscious, and amnesiac action may retain certain peculiarities which permit us to suspect its epileptic nature: total absence of premeditation, of motives, of relations with the patient's previous feelings."

The Doctor's voice grew still shriller. He adjusted invisible eyeglasses over his nose, grimaced. Eugène and Alex screamed with laughter and applauded.

"There is a record of the case of an epileptic who murdered his father and mother without any apparent motive for the crime: 'It had to be done,' was his only explanation. In other cases, there is an accession of impulsive rage which explodes for only the slightest reason: a word, an observation, a reprimand . . . the subject screams, grows agitated, becomes crude . . . Have I been crude, Monsieur Match?"

"No."

"The subject strikes the persons around him, often those he loves most; he breaks objects, furniture, mutilates himself or attempts to commit suicide. The accession comes to an end quite suddenly and is succeeded by a great lassitude. After his return to the normal state, the patient experiences considerable shame for his conduct and asks forgiveness."

"Later—" Match said.

But the Doctor interrupted him wearily: "No, don't go on. Thank you, Monsieur Match."

Silence. The four men fell silent. The scraping of a shoe, a sniff. Eugène, who was testing his tongue against a hollow tooth, made a brief mouse squeak. This noise exasperated the Doctor. He could easily kill Eugène when the latter plays with his hollow tooth. We are four men between four walls. All the kindness and all the savagery of the world burn between these four walls. We celebrate the highest Mass in the world between these four walls. We are radiant, crowned with roses, and dressed in white between these four walls. If we say nothing until the densest silence falls, something will have to happen. We will find the answer. We don't move, we are careful not to raise our heads and look at each other, we breathe carefully . . . We remember that November eleventh in our childhood when the bugle call for the dead rang out in the morning air dirtied with cold and human spit. We were a few yards away when the soldier put his bugle to his mouth and his cheeks swelled, red and ridiculous. The brass notes come from nowhere; the soldier with red cheeks is only a statue. The call comes from too far away not to be as eternal as this cold, foggy morning, from too far away for a boy in khaki with red cheeks to have blown it into a brass object. Oh, the horrible sob of the living and the dead . . . with one same slow gesture, the men have taken off their hats, berets, or caps. For the first time in my life, I took off the red wool cap decorated with the blue pompoms that some grandmother had knitted for me and with seven-year-old gravity I saluted death. A little later, my hand grasped my father's, during the "moment of silence." A few seconds more and we would have cried out in fear. A few seconds more . . .

"It was terrible," the Doctor said. "My knees began trembling, and a pincers squeezed the back of my neck. A wave lifted me off the ground and I saw all those motionless men with their pale empty faces circling slowly around me. They were motionless like those figures, kings and queens, who at the stroke of twelve begin their procession on top of clock towers or town halls in Germany, borne out of the stone and vanishing back into it. They circled and never moved. Then a scream formed in my throat; I held it back behind the barrier of my clenched teeth, but I was about to die of fear. The scream came out and life started again. My father shook me; a lady put my red cap with its blue pompom back on; a thousand faces turned toward me. My father dragged me away. He was walking quickly and we made our way through the crowd. I was sad but happy. I was crying with happiness for being alive. . . . My father was taking enormous strides, I was trotting along beside him and everything was moving around me again. I was crying and laughing. 'Why are you laughing, you fool?' my father asked me. 'He's not laughing, he's crying,' my mother said, drying my tears. 'Are you laughing or crying?' 'I don't know.' 'Why did you scream?' 'I was afraid.' 'The child is hypersensitive.' Well? Did you ever have anything like that happen to you?"

"In church. At the Elevation," Match said. "The choir boy shakes his little bell and all the heads lean forward in infinite submission when the priest, dazzling with gold, raises the chalice. A hundred times, I lowered my head. If you look, I told myself, you'll commit the most abominable sin of all, and you'll die on the spot, contaminated."

"And you never screamed out in the silence?"

"There's never real silence, in a church. There's always a missal falling, a chair clattering, an old man sighing, a deaf old bigot murmuring, a candle hissing, someone coughing . . ."

"Even so, were you afraid?"

Again the Doctor's eyes gleamed with curiosity and his features, which had gone limp as a sail when the wind drops, were smooth and tense again.

"That is . . . I was waiting for the answer too . . . the event . . . a thunderbolt was going to fall on these bent necks, the vault of heaven would open and a white light would explode in the church and burn us all up. We would leap up in pain, cling to the columns, run through a chaos of chairs and overturned benches. My father would cling to his dignity as long as possible, then the heat would fasten on him, too, and he would leap up like all the rest—once, twice, three times!—and with his mouth full of screams he would dash across the transept and collapse in the chair, stand up again, dash toward the altar, make a sudden ridiculous swerve, run backward, run into a pillar, whirl around like a crazy top. If I raised my eyes, I would release the apocalypse, and everything would be 'fulfilled,' as it says in my Sunday School books."

"Yes . . ." the Doctor whispered.

"That was the most hideous sin I ever committed, that day. I renounced paradise and life eternal, and dragged my father down to hell."

"You looked!"

"With a slow and terrible effort of my stiffened neck, I raised my head. And my eyes fastened on the priest, who was lifting over his head . . . what? I saw nothing. I saw nothing but—and *this* was the crime—I looked."

"And then?"

"Then, no thunderbolt. No heavens opening, no white light, no burning in our loins, no sudden wind filling my lungs. No one moved. My father didn't leap up, didn't explode . . . Nothing, you understand, *nothing* happened! Maybe I wasn't even damned! But one certainty will be my secret: you don't get punished for committing the worst crimes of all. One day, yes, that day, I was ready to do *anything;* one day, yes, that day, I made up my mind and chose hell . . ."

"Out of curiosity," the Doctor said.

"No, out of despair!" Match cried.

"It's the same thing."

"And I wasn't even taken seriously!"

Silence. The four men fell silent. The sound of a clog scraping against the floor, a sniff. The squeak in Eugène's hollow tooth. Waiting. Be quiet. If we create an absolute silence and our thought grows strong to the point of unendurable pain, we might hear the answer.

The Doctor said: "The most terrifying story in the world is the story of Robinson Crusoe. I used to read it and shiver when I was a child. Why? A man alone on a desert island who doesn't go crazy? Who doesn't one day begin examining his hands and noticing how monstrous it is to have hands with nails and to be able to say aloud: I have hands and nails. I have hair, sex, teeth, I'm hungry. I'm an animal. I'm alone and I'm afraid of myself. Of myself! Of myself! And this question that fills my head and explodes, destroying everything: 'Who am I?' In my empty skull, the question echoes like the last cry of a man whose throat is cut in an empty, echoing cathedral: 'Who am I?' Tell me, tell me, oh, tell me! I've run around the island whinnying, transfixed with fear; I've scratched the sand with my nails, feverish. And I've howled. I've crawled to the clear lagoon and surprised my scared, animal face in it. To the motionless coconut palms, to the horizon that flares and trembles under the white sun, to the sand, to the rocks, to the living flowers, I bawl my question. . . . Tell me, tell me, tell me. I'm losing my wits. My mind, I feel it evaporating . . . My God! I'm a bottle of ether that's been unstoppered, and I'm going mad looking for the lost cork . . . my madness has scalped me, I'm evaporating out of the top of my skull. I press both my hands over the orifice, but my reason oozes out between my fingers, and I am becoming *no one*. All it needs is three words—'Who am I'—and the hemorrhage of reason begins. But what vein can I press, what invisible limb can I ligature to keep from becoming a rat, a snake, an ant, a turtle, and to continue swearing to myself that man exists, somewhere? When I lived in cities, I had one recourse when the question broke over me. I would go out into the streets and walk in the city, staring fiercely at the faces . . . when I empty myself . . ."

"When you go crazy?" Match corrected politely.

"No, when I empty myself . . . No, when I lose myself . . . No, no . . . When I see myself, when I think myself, when I'm the other person that I am, all I need to do is to see a face, hear a voice, and soon the panting stops, my terror subsides. One day, in the square, I looked so strangely at the children playing there that the parents came over and without a word took their offspring elsewhere. I remember one mother's look: full of hatred and disgust. Yet my intentions were neither pure nor impure; I was simply watching these creatures so seriously occupied with living; I was feeding myself on their peace, and in their eyes I drank life itself. That's it . . ."

Eugène, Alex, and Match were waiting, but the Doctor had stopped thinking aloud. Like a spring that suddenly disappears underground, the Doctor's thought plunged into silence. There, he thought: that's what innocence is. There's the Paradise Lost of comprehension. On pain of madness, one must be the reflection and the mirror, the mountain and the echo, the gesture and the intention, the act and the will. He examined his patients. He was astonished to hear voices rise out of these envelopes of skin stretched over the armature of bone; to see two eyes shining in a shapeless mass of collapsing flesh. Living souls, he thought, living souls! Useless, but clinging to their skin, to their grease, to their bones, to this mass of sick filth, to this pale obscenity they expose and invite me to palpate, listen to, love. Why do you want to live, to creep down your streets, your stairs, into your offices, your factories? Why do I cure you? In the name of what? Life disgusts me. Your life disgusts me. Your rotten, stinking, hairy, deteriorated, gangrenous, ruined bodies disgust my sight. Well, Doctor? Well, I couldn't care less. You're not going to die today, but tomorrow, and if it's not tomorrow it'll be a little later on. It all comes down to the same thing, and if God doesn't exist, I couldn't care less, my friend, my brother, my neighbor, my image. If God doesn't exist, my friend, my brother, my image, and my neighbor, the hell with you. You're only a poor chattering lump of shit, O man!

O Man! Man! The Doctor collapsed on his desk, his head between his arms. He stood up, twisted his hands. I've had crying jags, gentlemen. I've been terrified of loving no one. I've suddenly opened the door of my office, climbed the stairs four at a time, caught my breath in front of the living-room door. Then I'd open it. I'd walk toward Helène. "Speak to me . . ." I'd tell her. "Say anything, anything, but talk!" She would gaze at me, her eyes full of resignation. "That's it, look at me! I beg you, look at me for a long time . . ." I walked up and down the living room, moored to Helène's mute stare.

"Feel better?" she would ask me.

"Yes . . ."

"What's the matter? Tired?"

"Helène . . . I have to love you. Helène, I love you. Tell me I love you."

"You love me."

"Are you sure?"

"Yes."

"Why do you always send me to other women?"

"I don't know . . ."

I knew. Because she knew I was afraid of loving and because she loved me . . . Listen to me, Helène, listen to me, my love . . . I'm the guiltiest being on earth, the vilest. . . . On certain nights, in certain nightmares, at certain moments between sleeping and waking, when my lucidity became unendurable, I even knew I was the most insignificant man in the world. On certain nights, I understood everything, absolutely everything, and I was the master of total knowledge. I can't describe those moments to you: they're not comprehensible. But on certain nights, if you knew how simple everything is, how obvious: before and beyond this life there exists a simplicity that must —I swear it, *must*—be at the very heart of things. Helène—and I call you Helène so my voice won't be futile if it forms the letters of a name—I know everything's simple, but I dare not love or die to prove it. Besides, no one will believe me, and I'd love for nothing. Helène— if I repeat your name, it's to sustain myself on its litany— the guiltiest man is not the man who *does* evil, but the man who *knows* good and doesn't let himself be engulfed by it. I've seen the worst criminals aureoled with grace, innocent of everything. I want someone to show me a man in peace so I can go to him and say: "Give me that peace!" But if he gives it to me, he'll lose it, so great is my anguish and so many are my questions. Then I'll say to him: "Hear me out, and then, even so, give me peace!"

Then, you see, if he does, if he keeps his peace and gives me peace too, then God exists!

Helène, here is the most absurd prayer human lips have ever dared to form: Love me so I can innocently implant evil in you. Love me without knowing you love. Love nothing. Love no one. I want to be a pebble to you, a shard of bottle, a handful of water. I'll be nothing, and nothing will be my fault.

"You see, Helène (and I'll say your name a thousand times over, to the tree, to the telegraph pole, to the escaping road, to the opening sky, to your absence), it's not that I'm crazy ('I know . . .' you'll answer with your Gioconda smile); on the contrary I claim that no one is more banally rational than I am. One plus one equals two; which means anyone who wants to ride far takes good care of his horse, and I sleep at least eight hours a night. But I live by accident, and if you have the nerve to tell me you love me, I'll scratch the walls and my face, and I'll frighten you.

"She was cunning, she knew how to take care of herself, Monsieur Match. She had simply decided that her fate was to love me. Her fate, hee! hee! You understand? All I had to do was cross my arms and pour it on . . . I was her prisoner, and she fattened on my love . . ."

"Love fills women up," Alex said, delighted with his joke.

"Women are infinitely cunning . . ."

The Doctor's voice faded away. He shook his head and said in a last murmur: "Unimaginably cunning!" He lay one hand on Match's knee and fell silent. Alex had pulled a piece of plaster out of the wall and crumbled it to dust, crushing it with his wooden clog. With a little straw, he made a kind of clumsy sponge and now, with the plaster powder, he was polishing the back of his pan. He spat, worked the plaster into a lather and scrubbed, holding his wad of straw with three fingers. All you could hear was the sound of the rhythmic scrubbing. Sometimes Alex changed his rhythm; instead of rubbing straight across, his wrist made a circular movement. The three of us watched with extraordinary attention. Eugène was a little annoyed at not having had the same idea, but now it was too late, and this pleasure could only belong to Alex. Alex had thought of something and rubbed on, smiling lovingly at his work. Children form a circle around a playmate sharpening his knife on the edge of the sidewalk; they all have a knife in their pocket and yet they form a fascinated circle around their playmate who has discovered a smooth fault in the sidewalk, in the hollow of which he works his knife blade in and out. And all of them admire the artist and are a little jealous of him. That's what's called having an idea. Alex had lots of stupid little ideas at his finger tips. He had a kind of genius. The stupid genius of a fool who knows how to do everything.

"I know how to do everything," he said.

He had ideas in his body like those schoolboys who know how to make coconuts, boats, bombs, arrows, and airplanes out of paper, but whose faces are smeared with panic by the question "What is the subject of the verb *to be* in the sentence 'I am lazy'?"

"I can do anything," he said.

He taught us the calisthenic fly; he made sleeping pills out of bread crumbs and grease; he invented *The Torture of Joan of Arc,* a machine for telling when the guard is coming, etc.

"If there's sun tomorrow, I'll give a performance of *The Torture of Joan of Arc.*"

"For a Christian, a game like that seems rather irreverent to me," the Doctor said to him once.

"Ir . . . ?"

"A blasphemous joke, a sin, if you prefer."

"Oh," Alex said, "it's not nasty, it's just in fun. It's a way of killing time. I'm a murderer: I kill time."

In summer, we would have many performances of *The Torture of Joan of Arc.* Here's how it was done: Alex, always smiling, always ingenious, had constructed a little cage in which he imprisoned all the cockroaches he could capture in the cell. On torture days, he would dig into his reserve and tie a martyr cockroach to a straw with threads pulled out of the mattress cover. Around the straw that was fixed into a tiny socket or pedestal, he would raise a pyre of straw from our mattresses.

"Neat, isn't it?" he said as he went about these miniaturist operations.

Then would come the hardest part. A complicated and ingenious system of shards of glass (scrupulously camouflaged so that they escaped the guard's searches) captured the sun and reduced its beams, by a successive play of lenses, until they transformed the gentle ray into a fiery point. The latter was trained on the lower part of the pyre, at the center of which rose the straw to which the cockroach was attached.

"Confess you're not a saint," Alex said, "or else the fire of heaven will consume your flesh amid hideous sufferings."

The cockroach said nothing.

"Confess!" Alex thundered, "there's still time!"

The cockroach said nothing.

"Confess that the Demon has inspired you! Confess that you are nothing but a prostitute and a whore to the soldiers!"

The cockroach said nothing. Alex's tone would grow more urgent and the words would leap out of his bull neck. He would get impatient. When he took the game too seriously, the worm swelled up in the middle of his forehead.

"Confess! Renounce your master Satan and you'll be saved! You'll return to the . . . Shit, what do you call it, Monsieur Match?"

"To the bosom . . ."

"You'll return, thank you, Monsieur Match, to the

bosom of the Church!"

"And perhaps you'll be forgiven, perhaps you'll see the Lord face to face," Match murmured, staring at the cockroach with unimaginable fixity.

Alex and Match would sometimes form a choir, sometimes alternate their prayers.

"Confess, whore, witch, criminal!" Alex shouted.

"Confess. Break the hard stone of pride within your heart!" Match intoned.

"Ask pardon from God!" Alex said.

"Confess that the Prince of Evil has appeared to you and seduced you, but that you see the light and that repentance floods your heart!" Match said.

The fiery point began almost imperceptibly to gnaw at one of the straws. "It's catching . . ." Alex said. "What did she say? Listen!"

He pressed his enormous ear quite close to the cockroach. He stood up again.

"Did she scream something?" Eugène asked.

Alex turned toward us, his face twisted with impotent hatred.

"She screamed she was innocent!"

"She's prayed to Saint Michael the Archangel!" Match said.

The tiny pyre crackled. The fire attacked the rear of the cockroach, which disgorged a whitish fluid.

"She's damned," Alex said. "God forgive her!"

"*Oremus!*" Match said.

End of *The Torture of Joan of Arc*. Sometimes the mystery play lasted half an hour. It was a matter of making the fiery point approach the stake quite slowly. By autumn the sun wasn't hot enough, and performances were suspended until the following summer. Eugène enjoyed this spectacle enormously. The Doctor was less enthusiastic about it. Once, when Match was interrogating the cockroach and pleading with it to confess its crimes, he said: "You'll be stuck the day she confesses."

Alex was rubbing, still rubbing the back of his pan.

"What are you doing?" Match asked him.

"Haven't you guessed? It's a mirror. There we can look at ourselves as long as we want."

"Now that's an idea!" Eugène said.

For years and years, no mirror has reflected our faces. Twice a week we're taken to the barber whose "shop" has no mirrors in it. And the barber, like us, is a prisoner, but he possesses an oval pocket mirror on the back of which, under celluloid, undulates a naked woman. To his friends—for the barber has his favorites—he furtively shows the mirror and some prisoners have the privilege, for a second or so, of seeing themselves in it. Sometimes the barber even lets them admire the naked woman for two or three seconds. She's been baptized "Cleopatra" and many prisoners have fallen wildly in love with her. Since the barber doesn't like the four of us, none of us knows "Cleopatra" and none of us has ever been able to glance into the mirror. As for women, none of us has more than a memory. What is a woman? How is she made? What does she look like? What does she say?

"What's a woman?" Eugène asked.

"Whatever idea you have of her," the Doctor answered.

"A bitch," Alex said.

"Doesn't exist," Match affirmed.

"She exists since we're in prison because of her," Eugène said.

And the eternal argument began again. The Doctor maintained that we're in prison because it's good to be here. We're warm. We're comfortable. Protected. We're taken care of. "We're happy," he said. "Inexpressibly happy. During earthquakes, have you noticed, prisons always resist; that's how strong they are!" Eugène repeated his last assertion and swore that the foreman killed his wife. "I'm innocent," Alex said. "Me too," Match said.

We're four wretched little innocents. Actually, our faces couldn't have "come back" to someone. To whom?

"Society," Match said.

". . . Society—society's stuck us with the crimes that look like they were ours. Bravo!"

"We'll be able to look at ourselves all we want," Alex said, still rubbing. "Once I thought it up it was easy."

He spent three days polishing the back of his pan, which now shines like a white sun. And for hours at a time he stared at himself. At first he laughed, yawned, made faces, ogled himself, and then, after a week, he stopped playing. Now he just stared at himself, for hours. He fell asleep. "I'm hypnotizing myself," he said. Eugène used the mirror now and then but became sullen after looking at himself and plunged into silence. As for the Doctor and Match, they refused to look at themselves.

"What are you thinking about, Monsieur Alex, when you look at yourself for hours at a time?" the Doctor asked.

"Me?" Alex said.

"Yes, you."

"Me? Me?"

He repeated "Me?" with a startled expression. Anxiety veiled his eyes. "Me?" Stunned, he repeated again: "Me?"

and glanced anxiously at the Doctor, as if the latter were speaking to someone else standing behind him.

It wasn't me, it was someone else. Really. He could never get used to having a name, to being named. When Alex was tried, the reporters wrote that the defendant, during the testimony, looked continually surprised at being there. He kept shooting amazed glances at the policemen, the lawyers, the judges, the public. Each time the judge asked him a question, he said: "Me?"

"Yes, you, and stop repeating 'me' all the time. You're the defendant, don't forget it."

Get him! I'm the defendant . . . all this, these judges, these policemen, those people out there, these lawyers, the whole thing . . . this courtroom, these papers being read, these words being spoken, all on account of me. One afternoon, Alex felt like laughing straight out. He thought it was stupid of them to bother. Don't they have anything better to do than trying me? Still, they seem quite serious. He didn't listen to a word of their crap. Defendant, I must ask you to pay more attention to the proceedings. What? Alex was sick and tired of it. What? He stood up, very calm. What are you doing?

"Me? I'm leaving, Monsieur le Président."

"You . . ."

"Yes, Monsieur le Président, I'm leaving. I'm tired of being here. I'm bored."

The policemen who surrounded Alex made him sit down again. The public burst out laughing and Alex smiled back politely, nodding his head as if he were thanking them. The judge rang his little bell, pounded the desk with the flat of his hand, and threatened to have the courtroom cleared.

"That way we'll all get out of here together," Alex said.

The laughter was twice as loud. Alex was having a good time now. A teacher being jeered is always funny. Amazing how much that judge looks like my old tight-ass teacher. I'm the toughest kid in the class. The others laugh, but then they back down.

"Did you have arguments with Pierre Lechantre?"

"Pierre Lechantre?"

"With Guitare," the lawyer whispered.

"Sometimes."

"Was it after these arguments that you stabbed him?"

"That I stabbed who?"

"Lechantre."

"Guitare," the lawyer whispered.

"I never stabbed Guitare, monsieur."

"All right, now . . . why do you continue to deny it?"

"It wasn't me, monsieur."

"Maybe it was me?" the judge screamed.

"I wouldn't know, monsieur."

"I warn you, denying the evidence will not make things any easier for you."

"I'm not denying anything, monsieur, I'm just saying it wasn't me."

"Then who committed the crime?"

"That . . . you know . . . I wonder," Alex said, staring around the courtroom with an astonished expression.

"So you insist on claiming you're innocent? You haven't killed anyone?"

I almost said . . . I caught myself in time. With a Judge like old tight-ass, you never got done with anything! What crap!

"You almost said what?" Eugène asked.

"I almost said: Khadi! But then, you know, all that crap—he'd never understand it, and besides I'd have gone straight to jail."

"But that's where you are," Match said.

"I am and I'm not."

Alex picked up his pan, wiped off the back with his sleeve, and looked at himself, sticking out his tongue. "I am and I'm not," he said. He added: "That judge was funny. Some days he accused me of killing everyone: Guitare, Maridge, everyone . . . You know, sometimes! . . ." He stuck out his tongue.

Then he declared that, in his opinion, it was all rigged by Maridge. "But wasn't she dead?" Eugène asked. Alex said: dead, dead, not so dead as all that . . . Maybe she was jealous of Guitare, so elegant, so perfumed. I loved him like my brother and still, with his thing about perfumes and all, he made me feel like laughing sometimes. He used to say: "You give her a few smacks at least, don't you?" "Yes . . ." "But you get angry, don't you?" "Yes . . ." Guitare was lying on the bed, his head deep in a pink pillow with a lace border. He looked like a very tough baby Jesus. He shook his finger at Alex. "Tut! Tut! *Chéri!*" (He called you *chéri?* Sure, he called everyone *chéri*.) "Now there's where you made your big mistake. You should give her a few good ones—calmly, and very hard. Like this, look!" He grabbed the pillow, and sitting up on the bed, began smacking it back and forth with the palm of his hand. I can still hear the sound of it. Guitare remained impassive, his lips slightly twisted by a tiny smile. "You're going to kill her," I told him. He stopped. He tenderly embraced the pillow before leaning back against it again. "There, you see, that's a workout for you!" Guitare really liked me and I liked the way he liked me. "I want to teach you," he used to tell Alex. "When you give them a few, first principle: keep calm. You know? Get that through your head, otherwise you'll never understand anything. Second principle, and very important, crucial . . . I don't even know if I should tell you, it's so important . . . it's a secret . . . If I tell you, it's like I was making you my heir. It took a long time to find it out, and I discovered it all by myself. Lying in bed playing the guitar, I don't look like I'm doing anything do I? You're wrong. I'm thinking, I'm figuring things out. I'm *reflecting*. And I've discovered a secret like the atom bomb. I could sell it to the Germans or the Japanese, they buy everything; but I'm a nice guy so I'm giving it to you. Second principle, listen carefully: when you give her one, it has to be *without any reason,* without any motive, without any excuse. Get that through your skull: she should never understand why she's being hit. If she understands she won't like it and she'll turn on you. If she doesn't understand, she's afraid. *Verstanden? Gut! Gut! Verboten! Papieren! Ja und auf weidersehn!* For instance: one day she doesn't come back with much money and she's scared shitless. But you're sweet as honey and you don't notice a thing. She's caught off guard. She was expecting the treatment and all she gets is a Pepsodent smile. Another day she comes in with bunches of money in her bag. You kiss her and then an hour or two later, just when she's expecting it least, you give it to her. For nothing. She doesn't know where she is any more. She doesn't know whether you like her, whether you hate her, what you want, what you don't want, she's completely lost. Now I'm going to teach you a couple of other little tricks . . . you have to have *moods*. One day, just for the hell of it, you decide you've got to have rabbit with fried bananas and gooseberries; another day, you tell her she's got to wear purple satin shoes; another day you forbid her to smoke tobacco because it makes her teeth yellow; the next day, calm as John the Baptist, you swear the opposite. Gradually, her head starts going around. She gets everything mixed up. Things get blurred. And she's always trembling at the thought she might do something that will set off the explosion. She's walking on eggs and you have her in the palm of your hand. Now look, it's not easy! It takes skill. Me, I've been doing it automatically, but I'm talented that way. *Verstanden? Jawohl! Adios bébé und guten tag!* If you listen to me, you'll be all right. And keep away from her snatch. Never compromise yourself. Behave like a kid four years old, and then at the right moment, bang! a good smack out of nowhere I have spoken! *Ja!*

Unfortunately, Alex wasn't talented. For all his good will, he stumbled over the slightest pebble in the path of Guitarean perfection. He lacked his friend's feline grace. He imitated. Guitarean cruelty wasn't easy to learn. It was an intuition. A talent. Guitare was overflowing with it. He had the gestures, the cut, the manner, the chic. He looked at a whore and his eyes were full of total indifference; he looked at her as if she were shit, and then suddenly, his eyes flashed and immediately went out again.

He did this at will—as if he were pressing on a button—once, maybe twice. The whore would fall apart. I swear, it was something to see! Alex sweat blood trying to make lace with a sledgehammer. "Actually," Guitare told him one day, watching him repairing a cigarette lighter, "you're an artisan, not an artist." Alex answered: "I know how to do everything." Guitare sighed: "That's your trouble. In life, the thing is to know how not to do anything." Alex said: "You know how to play the guitar." Guitare shrugged: "Playing the guitar and wrestling, *chéri,* that's what you call art!"

Alex turned toward Guitare with a sullen look, and the worm began to swell. "Feel like giving me one?" Guitare asked, his voice calm and playful. "Yes!" Alex said. "Go ahead, if you want to," Guitare said in the same tone of voice; "I'll let you do it, but don't forget that I could break you in two if I felt like it." Alex went on repairing the cigarette lighter without answering. Guitare threw himself flat on the bed and laughed, burying his head in the pillow which, that day, was blue.

Maridge wasn't fooled. She saw the slaps coming. "I knew you were going to hit me." If Alex asked her to make rabbit with gooseberries she said: "You feel like it?" And even though he'd wrack his brains for incredible things to say, she always answered: "All right . . ." sighing like an old woman whom nothing astonishes but everything exhausts. Poor Alex was going crazy. She would get up, make the coffee, rub her high breasts with cold water ("so they'll hold"), sigh, feel the stockings she had washed the night before to see if they were dry, serve Alex his coffee, sigh, pick up *l'Equipe* that the concierge had slipped under the door, hand it to

Alex, sigh, get dressed, powder her pointed nose, make up her eyes with tiny jabs of the black pencil, sigh, pull on her clothes, stagger around on her high heels, tug the strap of her bag over her shoulder, sigh again and say: "All right I'm going! *Ciao!*" Alex wouldn't answer. To-night I'll get her. He got her. She warded off the blows with her thin arms. "I brought you some stuff to eat." He yelled: "I don't want it. I want orange juice with three egg yolks beat up in it, go and get it!" She answered: "All right, I'm going." If she keeps on like this I'll go nuts. How would Guitare manage with a girl like this? He told her: "I'll kill you . . ." She didn't answer. He said: "An-swer me!" The pointed nose described a quarter of a circle, the eyes on each side of this nose stared at Alex without submission and without defiance, the red mouth underneath this nose twitched, and out of it came this noise: "I don't care . . ." Alex stood over her: "Look down!" She looked down. He squeezed the back of her neck hard. "I'll strangle you." She didn't move. He saw the roots of her cropped hair, the two vertebrae that stuck out at the top of her spinal column. I'll strangle her. He let go, lifted up the limp head. Two slaps. The head snapped from side to side. "You scared now?" She shakes her head no. He lay down on the bed, stuck a pillow be-hind his head. Like Guitare. She stared at him as if he were shit and Alex was the one who was afraid. "Screwed up," he thought, "completely screwed up."

"I can see how a guy could have strangled her," Alex said. "A cunt like that gets on your nerves. They're like cigarette lighters that don't work. Everything's in-side: fuel, flint, wick, even the spark. And no light! So you wind up and heave the thing into a corner. That's what the guy should have done. Besides, they found her all hunched up in a corner of the room. The guy strangled her and threw her there. Until the last minute she said she didn't care, she wasn't even scared. In a way, you could say she died of stupidity."

"Because she was stubborn as a mule," Eugène said.

"I call that stupidity," Alex said.

"Childishness," the Doctor said.

"Exactly!" Alex said.

It was raining. It hadn't rained for several weeks and the drought, according to the news bulletins, was worrying the government. Yesterday, on the ten o'clock news bulletin, Match told us that cows, oxen, sheep, were dying by millions. Whole herds were in their death throes on fields as bare as the Place de la Concorde. In Normandy, now a Sahara, the corpses of animals that were nothing but skin and bones spread a terrible stench nonetheless. Typhus was reported in Lisieux. Because of this unprecedented national catastrophe, the news of the invasion of West Germany by the East German armies took second place. As did the reports of the increasing number of arrests made throughout the country.

"They'll end up arresting everybody," Eugène said; he wasn't interested in agricultural crises.

"They're nuts," Alex said.

"It sounds like Russia under Stalin," the Doctor said. "Stalin ended up arresting everyone."

"So did Napoleon," Alex said.

"Napoleon?" Match asked, stupefied. "No, he didn't!"

"Oh! Excuse me," Alex said, "I thought . . . I heard

something like that. Are you Corsican?"

"No," Match said. "I'm not Corsican, but I respect historical truth. Napoleon was an exceptional man. Thanks to him we have our Civil Code and . . ."

And nothing. Match nibbled his upper lip, swept a long limp hand over his forehead and nervously stood up, then sat down again. The Civil Code and nothing. In his eyes gleamed a futile and suffering sagacity.

It was raining. Gold was falling. The farmers of Normandy and the Vendée were crying with happiness. The water from heaven and their tears sprinkled the earth, in which cracks were opening, swallowing up the fleshless corpses. For no reason, Alex began walking around the cell limping on both legs. The Doctor, Match, and Eugène stared at the gray rectangle of the window hatched by the thousand arrows of the rain's dim crystal.

"Yesterday, the sky was blue," Eugène said.

"Today, it's gray," the Doctor said.

We're very sensitive to the colors of our rectangular piece of sky. The blues, grays, pinks, and mauves are never the same. The most complex and the subtlest are the grays. Because of his insomnia, Match knew most about the night's velvet and the stars wandering across our patch of sky. Crouched like an Arab storyteller in the middle of the cell, he observed the movement of our stars. In June, there was a very brilliant one that followed the top of the skylight. We called it "Brünnhilde" and it belonged to Match. In September there was one that appeared toward midnight, rose to the middle of the square, and disappeared deep in the sky, swallowed up by the night. We called it "Gethsemane" and it belonged to the Doctor. The one twinkling in the left corner of the square was called "Bull" and belonged to Eugène. Alex's, baptized "Uppercut" by him, was a big April and May star. Subject to insomnia, Match kept an eye on them. "Doctor, here's Brünnhilde!" He wakened him carefully. "Oh, yes?" The Doctor crouched in the privileged spot in the cell. "Soon Uppercut will be here, it must be the end of March," Alex said. "Wake me, Monsieur Match, don't forget!" "I won't, Monsieur Alex." Match did his job conscientiously and we all believed he was the world's best star-watcher. "If I'd known, I would have been a lighthouse keeper," he said one day. "Or an astrologer." He claimed the stars played a role in our life and offered as proof Gethsemane's calming influence on the Doctor's nerves. We've watched the rain falling all day. Our contemplation was so intense that we didn't hear the guard open the door to hand out the soup. "Hey! Sulking? Hunger strike, kids?" Alex, less absorbed than his companions, held out the pans.

"Raining buckets," the guard said.

"Will it last long?" Alex asked.

"With weather, you never know."

"That's right!"

"For weeks, not a drop, and then all of a sudden, the deluge. Always not enough or too much," the guard said. "This rain isn't the right kind, anyway. Too strong. A slow penetrating rain would have been better. But still, it does the farmers some good."

"That's right!"

"Limping?" the guard asked Alex as he walked toward the mattresses with the pans.

"On purpose," Alex said. "It relaxes your hips. I'm training for the championship."

"Is it soon?"

"You'll have to ask my manager."

So Alex wasn't limping "for no reason." He was in training. Was Eugène in on the secret? Probably. In matters of training, Alex would never have dared take such initiative on his own.

Tonight, Alex got up and limped around the cell until dawn. When the day whitened our sky, he fell down in exhaustion. Eugène reprimanded him severely. The blade of straw—in other words a "cigar"—in his mouth, he scolded Alex in a kindly but severe manner, trying to resemble Monsieur Siméon as much as possible. With Alex giving him clues (for Eugène had never seen Monsieur Siméon), he repeated the series of scoldings until Alex exclaimed "That's it!" The hardest thing was to catch the exact inflections. "I've already told you not to train after sunset, kid, haven't I, yes or no?"

"Yes, Monsieur Eugène."

"Well then?"

"I felt like it, Monsieur Eugène. I wasn't sleeping and I told myself, 'You might as well train!' "

"It's not what you tell yourself that counts, it's what *I* tell you, get it, kid?"

"Yes, Monsieur Eugéne."

"Now you're not going to try that any more, are you?"

"I promise, Monsieur Eugène." Eugène slapped Alex affectionately on the shoulder and Alex smiled a stupid, crooked smile that showed the tip of one tooth.

"It's good to work . . . I don't like talented types, I like guys who can't stay away from the gym. But you've got to do what I tell you. By the way, kid, if the press asks you how you train, not a word, get it, not a word about the limping sessions."

" 'Claudication sessions' would sound better," the Doctor said.

"Thanks, Doctor."

"You're welcome."

"Not a word about the 'claudication sessions.' You'll get so that Sugar Ray's hooks will go right by you without touching a hair on your head. All right, that's enough for today. Go back home and read magazines. Or have a game of solitaire. That'll relax you."

"Okay, boss!"

Eugène spit out his straw. That was all for today. It was still raining. Only Match continued staring at the gray sky. The Doctor sat down beside Eugène. "Shall we talk?" he asked him. "Sure," Eugène said. "What shall we talk about?" "I don't know." They remained silent, sitting side by side. Motionless. Hands resting on their knees, a little stiff. "I've seen photos," the Doctor said, "where men were sitting the way we are. On electric chairs." They fell silent. "Shall we talk?" the Doctor asked. "Sure," Eugène said, "let's talk." They remained silent.

"Do you think they'll kill us, Doctor?"

"In my opinion . . . no."

"Which would you prefer, Doctor, the electric chair, the guillotine, the rope, or a firing squad?"

The Doctor laughed and said: "Tuberculosis. You sweat, you spit. Life seeps away in sweat and blood, your eyes gleam. I love tuberculosis and I strongly regret the fact that it's on the way out."

"I'd rather be shot. As a favor I'd ask them not to tie my hands or blindfold my eyes. Standing in front of the stake, I'd rush toward the rifles and then I'd fall as I ran, like in the movies, with a dance step."

With his raised index finger, he sketched a spiral. A last dance step and it would all be over.

"They won't kill us?"

"In my opinion, no."

"Oh!" Eugène said. "In that case . . ."

"In that case?"

"I have the impression that changes everything."

"But what?"

Eugène said that up till now he had believed they were going to kill him, then he got his words confused and despite the tortures he inflicted on his brain, he couldn't manage to make his thoughts clear, and he begged the Doctor to help him. "You understand . . ." and he made deaf-mute gestures.

"I don't understand anything," the Doctor said. "Do you want to say that the thought of not being guillotined or hanged comforts you, relieves you?"

"No."

"Well?"

"If you help me, I'll figure it out. Try something else . . ."

"Do you want to say, for instance, that you're less interested in the movements of your star in our sky?"

Eugène reflects. "Something like that, but that's not it, either, because it might be just the opposite."

"Now, let's see . . . Do you mean you might admit you killed your wife?"

"Doctor, that's not playing fair," Eugène said.

Today, the foreman's nerve was beyond belief. He came under *my* roof after *my* wife. He told her I wasn't worthy of her, that goon with his yellow boots. Alarmed by her lover's boldness, Jeanne begged him not to come. The foreman killed her in a fit of passion. He was jealous of me! That was it! Actually, deep down, Jeanne still had a certain amount of bourgeois morality, and those words "I'm cheating on my husband" scared her. Did she love that guy? He talked nice, he was clean . . . His white hands with their carefully clipped nails made Jeanne dream about him. A boss's hands. In the dance halls, she had never seen anything but solid, clumsy hands, not washed but scrubbed after the day's hard work. For her, that guy's hands were the hands of the bosses to whom she had always said yes, monsieur, certainly, monsieur. And those boss's hands, bishop's hands, doctor's hands, were now squeezing hers. Gently. Don't touch me. He looked at her. Don't look at me like *that*. He smelled good and wore silk ties. I told you not to look at me like that or I won't see you any more. I think you're beautiful. You're making fun of me. Sometimes, with Eugène, she felt safe because there was no humiliation when he looked at her; sometimes she was horrified by his simple male beauty. His beauty was stupid.

"Don't cut the bread with your knife."

"Why not?"

"Because you're supposed to break bread with your hands."

"Works better this way," Eugène said, continuing to cut his bread. "We having dinner with the President?"

He laughed, and Jeanne hated that laughter of his. She stood up and walked out into the kitchen, her back straight and her nose white, which proved she was angry.

That guy spoiled her for me completely. Eugène had married the world's most beautiful servant and found himself facing a judge. I couldn't move any more. She was spying on me. One day I watched while she was emptying out my trouser pockets before ironing them. She took out the cigarette lighter, the American army kind with the top that comes up automatically, and tossed it onto the oilcloth, where it slipped and fell onto the floor. Eugène said nothing. She picked up the cigarette lighter and tossed it on the table. Clack! She took out a crumpled blue-and-white checked cotton handkerchief. She held it in two fingers, with repugnance, the way you hold a dead rat by the tail before you toss it into the sewer. She took out my knife with the black handle, and tossed it on the table where it slid off and fell onto the floor. She picked it up and set it on the table. Clack! She thought it was silly to carry knives, like a criminal! Three coins, one hundred-franc piece, two five-hundred-franc pieces. A brass ring I found. Clack! A button. She turned out the gray canvas pockets and shook the tobacco dust onto the oilcloth. I realized she no longer loved me. I remembered other times when the cigarette lighter was a diamond, the handkerchief precious silk, the knife a magic weapon and the button a pearl. One day she even kissed the cigarette lighter before lighting it and holding the flame for me. She didn't love me any more. All these objects accused Eugène of some secret crime; they denounced his poverty, his misery . . . the word "vulgarity" rang in his head. Not long ago, cigarette lighter, knife, handkerchief, tobacco dust told her about a man and his love. Tonight, they said that Eugène was a work-

man who put on a white shirt Sundays and slicked down
his hair with ridiculous care. A clear, crystalline hatred
hardened her heart and whitened her face as she pursed
her lips. "Little bitch!" Eugène thought. Jeanne was
thinking she'd been a fool to marry this crane-operator
with his pockets full of tobacco dust. Eugène's eyes, the
hell with them, she couldn't care less! His handsome
face! She was tired of it. The way he walked? Like a
sailor out of work. She pressed the trousers with long,
furious strokes of her iron. Eugène was reading the paper
and smoking a cigarette.

"Iron them good," he said.

She didn't answer.

"I told you to iron those pants good."

"If you think I'm not doing it good, do it yourself!"
She held out the iron.

"It's not my job, it's yours. Iron them good!" He said
all this without looking up and without raising his voice.
But she no longer loves me, she'll never forgive me for the
way I took her. She was hot for me. And now she's
ashamed of it and I disgust her. In a little while, when he
takes her, she won't move but somehow she'll escape that
embrace, that bed, that house, that past. Eugène felt a
sticky sadness explode in his mouth. For the first time in
his life, he no longer had confidence in his body, his
face, himself. Eugène was lying flat on his bed letting this
infection invade him.

So he wasn't invulnerable? Once he walked and
breathed with all the strength of egoism, and his footsteps
rang firm on the earth. He was the ruler of a kingdom
whose borders no one dared cross. From the height of
his throne, from the height of his crane, he decreed simple

truths against which nothing prevailed. Girls: you have to know how to handle them. This year, a Dutchman will win the Tour de France. Rabbit's better for you than chicken. If you buckle your belt over your navel your movements are freer because your belly can breathe. Happy, closed, solid. Every object around him resembled him. He suspected the enemy's presence, but on his own territory Eugène knew he was invulnerable. Jeanne had carried the gangrene. I'm sick with something but I don't know what. I still have the same body, the same strength, the same way of walking, and I'm not the same any more. Eugène thought of the days when he used to walk with Jeanne on his arm and they played the game of watching people on the streets. They played.

"Look at that guy," Eugène used to say, "what do you think of him?"

"Pretty good-looking."

"Would you sleep with him?"

"I'd rather die." Eugène concluded from this that you could be good-looking and disgusting at the same time. His own secret was to be good-looking and please Jeanne at the same time.

"You understand, Doctor, I didn't dare touch her any more. I felt like I was a grease-monkey trying to arrange the pleats in a bride's dress. I didn't want to touch her and yet I had to. It drove me crazy. Then, of course, when I did touch her I was furious. I got everything dirty and messed up, but I didn't care. Except, afterward, a bad feeling made me go out and walk in the streets and drink."

"You drank?" the Doctor asked in his clinical voice. "This is the first time you've ever mentioned it."

"I forgot. Didn't I ever talk about it?"

"I don't remember."

"Well, I drank. Since she said I was disgusting I might as well *be* disgusting, right?"

"Of course!"

"Oh, yes, I remember once! Once when I came home to the house I took her crocodile handbag, she said it was only imitation because the foreman had given it to her, but I'm sure it was real, and guess what! I threw up in it and then I put it back in the drawer. In a way, I sort of behaved like a kid. She didn't stop me from drinking. She wanted the neighbors to know I went to work drunk. It seemed to please her. Almost as if she led me around on a leash and said: 'Look how drunk he is!' After that, the foreman picked her up all set to go."

He came home one night at three in the morning and swore the foreman was hiding in the house somewhere. He looked under the bed, in the closets, emptying them with great clumsy gestures; even the dresser drawers, the garbage pail under the sink. "He's hiding!" he shouted. "Show yourself, coward so I can beat the shit out of you!" He searched the bed. He even looked under the oil-cloth in the kitchen. "You're a little pimp, a tiny pimp, but I'll find you. There he is!" he shouted, seeing his own reflection in the bathroom mirror. "Please," Jeanne said, "don't be crazy! Don't drink. Don't be jealous. I love you, don't you understand that I love you? I swear I'm not cheating on you. I swear it on the head of the baby I'm going to have, here . . ." she touched her belly with the palm of her hand. "A baby? From that mosquito? Ho, ho, ho, ho! Madame's pregnant by a mosquito!" "Eugène! Eugène! Don't say that! Don't do that!" He kicked

Jeanne's belly . . . He grabbed her by the hair and threw her onto the cold floor of the bathroom. With all his strength he kicked her in the belly once, twice, three times . . . He counted them . . . Four, five, six . . . Thirty-eight! He stopped because he was tired and she had stopped moving. He staggered toward the bed and fell asleep, fully dressed. Jeanne's agony, according to the doctors, lasted at least five hours.

"Then," Eugène said, "when she realized she was pregnant by her lover, she decided I'd kill her if she told me about it. So she decided to commit suicide."

"That doesn't make sense," the Doctor said.

Eugène gnawed one nail. "You think? Well, what did happen, in your opinion?"

"Were you jealous?"

"Of a mosquito? Of course not! And I love kids . . . I wanted a son. I'd have sat him on my motorcycle, between my legs, and zoom! On your way, boy! And I'd have gone down on all fours so he could ride around on my back. Gidyap, gidyap, Papa! When he was fifteen, I'd have taught him how to handle girls."

Lying on the mattress, hands behind his neck, Eugène took a two-hour nap. He woke up, stretched, yawned, and went back to his place beside the Doctor, who hadn't moved. "You haven't slept, Doctor?" "No. I was thinking." Eugène looked at the Doctor very respectfully. Thinking for two hours . . . Talking, yes, but thinking! Alex said thinking gave him a headache. He couldn't manage, he said, tapping his forehead, to get it up in there!

"We could go on talking," Eugène said.

"Glad to . . ."

"I was changing, and the guys at work noticed it. Since I got married . . ."

He had no more exploits to tell about on Mondays. Picnicking in the country, walking around on the boulevards, or sucking an Eskimo pie between Westerns— hardly exploits worthy of a Eugène. He had to walk slowly so Jeanne could keep up with him: two of Jeanne's steps were equivalent to one of his own. That's what gives guys glued to their wives on Sunday that slow, funereal walk. For a lifetime, for a thousand, maybe two thousand Sundays, he'd be forced to walk that way, as though a chain bound him and measured his steps. To top it off, in five or ten years a whole trail of kids would be stretched out behind them. *Her* kids. *Hers.* Eugène didn't like kids. They cry, they piss, they're sick all the time, and they cost a fortune. He could still hear his mother blaming him for being born, still feel his drunk father buffeting his head. He hated his child, didn't want him. Why? Because that's the way it is, because I don't want one. At fifteen he felt free once he entered the world of men, the gangs . . . If his mother made a fuss it didn't matter any more, and his father didn't dare touch him now. A blue-and-white striped shirt molded his young athlete's body; he had broad shoulders and wore a copper ring—a seal ring—that turned the middle finger of his right hand green but made deep cuts in the faces of his opponents. From this period until his marriage to Jeanne, Eugène liked himself. Now, I'm dying, wasting myself. "You're turning sour, Eugène!" someone at work said to him. He was right. They went out walking Sundays without a thing to say to each other. And before the walk there was the torture of getting ready. In the old days, there was the white shirt, the blue suit, the black shoes with pointed toes the way he liked them, the tie quickly knotted, the palms of his hands greased with brilliantine rubbed over his hair three or four times, a skillful touch of the comb the way he knew how to do it (even at the barber shop, once the barber was through cutting, he would take the comb out of the man's hand and fix his hair himself), and then out with the boys! All right, what's for today? Pick up something? Slumped in a chair, eyes down. "What are you thinking about, darling?" About nothing. Ready for over half an hour, he watched Jeanne dressing. "I'll be ready in a minute." She walked by for the third time, in her panties and bra, flustered and talkative. She described what she was doing and Eugène nervously tapped his heel. "I'm wearing light stockings today. Damn my garter belt, where did I put it?" She stuck a wad of cotton between her toes, otherwise her pointed shoes hurt her. "No, my green dress is too wrinkled . . ." She passed back and forth, spreading a cool odor of soap. "I'm ready." She was still looking for her garter belt. God damn, God damn, God damn, I'm fed up with this! Eugène thought. It's crazy how a girl can cover herself with all that elastic and those onion skins everywhere, all over her legs, on her breasts, on her ass! With all those buttons, that rubber, those lace things, and cotton between her toes to boot! And the makeup, finished at last? Yes. Good. "I'll wear my green dress after all, so what! I'm ready. Look, I think I'm getting fat." And the necklace, the earrings, pounds and pounds of scrap metal and pebbles she stuck on herself. Why all this fuss? To go wear out her shoes on the boulevard as if she were walking to a funeral. Each Sunday, he buried his youth, he buried Eugène. On the other hand, Jeanne got younger week by week, gleaming with joy and health. Overcompressed, backfiring, she dragged him from one shopwindow to the next, compared prices as fast as a cash register, took in the surrounding female society with a series of stares that would disintegrate uranium, and chattered constantly. She saw everything, heard everything, noticed everything; she had a hell of a time.

"Conclusion, Doctor; a man isn't made to live with a woman. People who say anything else are sick. What was I good for when we were wandering around? Nothing. I was her cane. She leaned a little more heavily on my arm when she was tired. Aside from that, I could have been made out of wood: it all came down to the same thing. She talked to herself; she asked me questions and gave the answers herself. I was a dog. 'What do you think of that plum-colored knitted wool suit over there, that one?' What would you have thought of it, Doctor, the plum-colored knitted suit over there?"

Alex puffed out his cheeks and started laughing. Match's face, on the contrary, relaxed with tender delight. The Doctor pinched his nose and reflected.

"Crêpe de chine, mimosa, taffeta, organza, tangerine, velvet, satin, marmosette, astrakhan, and zebra skin," Alex recited, choking with laughter.

"Frankly, Doctor . . ."

"This way, ladies," Alex said, between gasps, "the Maison Alex offers reasonable prices, good buys everywhere you look!"

Alex was shaken by so noisy a fit of laughing that the Doctor no longer heard Eugène telling about his troubles and his deaths. When she left with the foreman,

Eugène said he was relieved. That's what he tried to explain to the judges. He told them: "Why should I have killed that foreman?" But Jeanne's testimony spoiled everything. After taking the oath, she said he was "morbidly jealous." "She spoke with her head down. The bitch didn't look at me, not even once."

"Crêpe de chine, crêpe de Congo, de Venezuela, de Canada! Crêpe de Cameroons!" Alex said, holding his belly with both hands.

Match, still plunged in a kind of tender reverie, repeated "crêpe de chine" and saw thousands of Chinese women draped in mourning. When he was fifteen the gates of hell opened for him. One day he admitted his ugliness to himself. He whispered to himself about it in a shed filled with old tools where he went and locked himself in. The neighborhood cats came there to have their kittens on a heap of sacks in the corner. "Once I knelt down before a big plowshare that the blue dust had made into a stiffened angel's wing, and I prayed. What did I ask my God that day? Not to live, I think, and yet I didn't want to die. To stop living, I think, and yet I didn't want to die. I asked him to *be* no longer . . . To stop *being* . . . To be oblivion. Imagine a fifteen-year-old Hamlet on his knees in front of a plowshare, asking God to be and not to be, while a litter of kittens yowled in the corner."

"And you never killed them?" the Doctor asked.

No, he made them speeches, and the mother cats got used to his presence. "At fifteen, I was . . . it's on account of your crêpe de chine, Monsieur Eugène, that I'm thinking about all of this."

"Oh!" Eugène said.

"Funny!" Alex said.

Because all his memories of that time were wrapped in that material with its funereal name. It lay over the shed, over his eyes and over his hands. Soft as the nest where the kittens were lying. He stuck his hand into that warm, living, hairy hole. At fifteen, he was a funny boy. Stupid, that's it, and "slow," the way they say, and yet very intelligent, that's it, and "advanced," the way they say. Actually, he was "monstrous"; slow and advanced.

"Never on time!" Alex said.

"That's it! Monsieur Eugène was *on time,* if I understood correctly, between fifteen and his marriage. You, Monsieur Alex, you were *on time* during the period of your glory, before your sight was impaired. Me, never."

Match was never comfortable in his age and in his skin, his ideas were never clear in his head, tools were never accurate in his hands. One day my father told me I was going to end up digging ditches. A failure. A ditch-digger, a nobody . . . A rough draft. For what? At fifteen you couldn't figure it out, and you knelt in front of a dusty plowshare. Today he knew. He was a rough draft for a man, a body, a son, a saint, and a toad. As in rough drafts, only one phrase came out readable and beautiful: his hands. Later, the world might have been a consolation to him, but everything there was a failure too, and no one was comfortable there, either; the trouble was, other people invented tricks; they blocked up a hole, drew a false window, they had ears that filtered out sounds, eyes accustomed to one horizon or another. When you were *on time* once, just once, you never forgot it, and afterward that's what helped you to live, even approximately. To live, you had to remember having been perfect once. Afterward, you cheated, you lied, but it didn't matter. It was there, the great secret left in those churches he never went into any more. All he needed was to slip into that coolness, prostrate himself in a dark booth and murmur the words in front of a grill where a faceless human voice would answer: "Go in peace, my son, and be forgiven!" But how was he to cross that threshold? Besides, he had nothing to confess. "After killing my dear mother . . ."

"Your father or your mother?"

"I killed my so-called father, but my mother died on account of me."

"There's a difference!" Alex said.

"The first thing I did was throw myself on my knees in front of the priest and kiss the bottom of his gown. On this earth, there exist men dressed in black who in the name of God forgive you for everything! Why don't we take advantage of it? Why do we want to be guilty, ruined, lost? Why not believe in them?"

"I believe in them!" Alex said. "Those little priests are good guys; I always defended them. When a guy was kidding around about them over at Monsieur Siméon's, I used to say: 'Don't talk about stuff like that! There are things that you don't understand, but that's no reason not to respect them.' Besides, boxers have medals that they kiss in the dressing room before going into the ring. Us boxers, we don't go to church, but we believe. We're not animals."

Why not believe? He wanted to and didn't want to. He missed the appointment again. She asked him—he was sixteen—and she was patching up some old trousers his father wore to water the garden, she asked him as her

needle grated against the silver thimble, she asked him:
Match . . . She didn't call him "Match," of course, she
used a diminutive of his name. He didn't want to remember that name. Not for anything in the world! He
was Match. Only Match. With a resigned inflection in
her voice, she said: "Why don't you talk to your father?"
He was sitting in front of her, putting new laces in his
shoes. "You should talk to him, it's your duty to make an
effort, you're younger than he is, he's always been so
good to you, in spite of everything . . ." She told him
that, but he'd always known he'd kill him some day, that
skinny man who was too tall, whose breathing, when he
read his newspaper, blamed him for living. She told him
it was his duty to understand, he was a big boy now . . .
Standing in front of the window, a pain ran down his
ribs and he leaned with both hands on the window sill to
keep from sliding down to the floor and sitting there. She
said: "You're a big boy, you understand, it's not up to
him to take the first step, he thinks of you as a man, and
after all, deep down . . . He loves you." With a voice
husky with tenderness and shame, he said: "It's not true,
Mother. He can't bear me."

"Of course he can, don't be silly."

"Mother?"

"Yes . . ."

"It's not true and you know it: he told you so himself!"

Mother, be patient a little longer and I'll leave soon.
When I'm eighteen I'll leave this house where I'm washed
by the warm flood of your love and the icy waves of his
hate. I'd like to kill myself, but I'm afraid. A year ago, I
got everything ready in the abandoned shed: around a
winch I attached a new rope smeared with soap, but the

knot slipped. Now and then a cat stopped washing her
kittens with broad swipes of her pink tongue and questioned me with her green eyes. Everything was ready,
but I was afraid. Then I said: "If Mother comes back
from Mass on his arm next Sunday, I'll do it."

"And she didn't take his arm, since you're here," Eugène said.

"Yes!" Match said.

"Well?"

"Well, I'm here!" Match exclaimed.

"Hey!" the Doctor said, "don't shout, you're among
friends here."

"I'm sorry."

I'll go away, Mother. Don't worry. I'd like the cat to
lick my face. I've smeared my forehead and cheeks with
sugared milk to feel the rough tongue that gives me little
kisses. I'll go away. I saw the road where I would walk
alone, a road that vanishes into the distance like railroad
ties; cities, ports, ships, Africa, the Sahara . . . I was
only fifteen and I couldn't imagine traveling without long
roads, without ships and palm trees.

"It's not true," his mother said. "He didn't say anything of the kind. He's very kind, and eager to love you,
but you—it's as if you don't want his affection."

Leaning on the window sill, Match no longer saw the
laundry drying on the terrace of the next house. He closed
his eyes, but the tears welled up under the eyelids and
slid down to his upper lip. She said: "You're my son,
and sometimes it seems as if you forget it."

We ate our food with a good appetite tonight. We were
all feeling good. Eugène sang an obscene song to the tune

of the "Blue Danube," and Match beat time. Alex imitated the cries of several animals; he ended with a fart that he calls "the cry of man at the summit of glory." Only the Doctor betrayed some nervousness, for he was preparing to contemplate Gethsemane, his star. Pewter mugs raised, we toasted his luck, congratulated him and swallowed a mouthful of water together. The next day Match sang obscene songs for over an hour. Then he declared that he was a dreadful child, that his stepfather was the best of stepfathers and his bitch of a mother always managed to poison the relationship between her husband and her son. Out of jealousy. She wanted us all to herself and couldn't bear our male complicity that she felt was directed against her. By blood, I was my mother's son, but it was my stepfather I loved at the bottom of my heart. I had disrupted the natural order of my affections. Eugène said such things happened, he had heard of things like that. He knew a widow who remarried, and the new husband loved the daughter from the first marriage more than the mother did, because the little girl reminded the mother of the first husband she wanted to be rid of. "It's true," Eugène said. Alex and the Doctor agreed that it was true, and that a woman, even a mother, always ended up jealous of two men. All of a sudden, Match's good humor soared hysterically and he felt unlimited gratitude toward his friends. If the sky hadn't been so cloudy that night, if the Doctor had been able to contemplate Gethsemane, our happiness would have been complete.

It took me a long time, years and years, before I realized that my mother was a bitch. In her own way, of course. What I took for kindness was only indifference. A single thought preoccupied her: my stepfather. Like many women, she had made love into a task, and she loved with the clear conscience of a hard worker. My father—her first job, in a way—had collapsed between her fingers; all she could do now was to work unceasingly to construct a second monument, her second love. I got in her way a little; I cluttered up the place. Actually, for everything to be in order, I should have died at the same time as my father, in an accident, for instance.

"But didn't she tell you: 'you're my son'?"

Yes, because she tended to forget it. From time to time she'd exclaim: "You're my son" with a sudden impulse of tenderness, and then she'd consider herself quits as far as I was concerned. With antlike stubbornness, she'd go back to her serious work: loving my stepfather. How could Match have wanted her to love him? Love, love's a gesture, a glance, a caress, a word that's both like and unlike other words. Love's not an obligation, Doctor.

"I'm not so sure about that," the Doctor said. "Do you know what love is?"

Loving Match would have meant making him hand-some. Wrong! Three or four times a year I went to the cemetery with her and we visited my father's grave. She bought flowers at the gate and I arranged them at the foot of the granite cross. One hot summer day, rummaging through the drawers, I discovered some photographs of my father; a bundle of photographs held together by a rubber band. I wasn't startled to resemble a dead man. This man sitting on a high-backed chair between two pots of ferns, his hands spread on his knees and a mustache shadowing his upper lip—I'd already seen him somewhere. I take a stick of charcoal and decorate my upper lip with a mustache. Glance into a mirror, glance at the photo . . . That man is me. I'm the living portrait of a dead man. If only she'd let me love my step-father! The viper always managed to be a third person between us, so finally I detested both of them. If I had a conversation with him at the dinner table, she'd always get involved. If he gave me a bicycle then she'd decide on the color and the shape of the handlebars, which, as Monsieur Eugène knows, are the two essential things about a bicycle. She slyly stole away the affection he gave me and left me only the crumbs. When I understood her strategy, I was about fifteen, and I began to take my revenge. Patiently. She died of it. Parents should never forget that children grow up, and that they remember.

"And your stepfather—why did you kill him?"

"Did I kill him?"

"Apparently . . ." Eugène said.

"You're getting everything mixed up," Match said, "My stepfather's death has nothing to do with what I'm telling you. It happened six or seven years after my dear mother's death. Don't confuse the sheep with the goats."

Today, Match killed no one. His mother, he said, died of grief and despair. It was her own fault. For noticing, with the years, that the hatred—which was her own work—of her son for her husband had become a fire that was devouring everything. When she understood her mistake and realized that she had lit the match herself, she chose to die. So Match killed no one, today. His lawyer said that the gentlemen of the jury wouldn't condemn him on the evidence of malicious neighbors. To have heated discussions with someone, to get angry with that person, doesn't mean that you plan to kill that person.

Besides, my client is a frail boy, who all his life has shown
a horror of violence. Can you see him turning against an
old man and smashing his skull with a candlestick? Of
course my client gambled—and lost—like all gamblers,
and was in great need of money. Would he have killed
merely to inherit the modest fortune of his victim? No;
many times over this same victim had declared to his
stepson: "When I die you won't get a penny: I've seen to
that!" And then the lawyer worked out a complicated
theory relating to the psychology of the gambler.

"You used to bet?" Alex asked.

"A little . . ." Match said.

According to the lawyer, the gambler is a weak man.
Superstitious, he lives in a universe full of omens. He's
not an active but a passive personality. Here the lawyer
read texts by psychologists and psychiatrists in support of
his thesis, and opened a huge book, showing the title to
the jury: *Psychopathology of the Gambler*. Passive, the
gambler waits for luck, and provokes; "forces" it only by
magical operations. At most he steals, and there's an endless list of honest men who dig into the cash drawer in
hopes of repaying the next day. He steals, but the gambler's theft is a theft of a particular type. It's a secret loan,
and thanks to luck—the gambler thinks—the secret will
never see the light of day. In short, the action is retrievable. Let us not forget that the gambler lives under this
sign: the retrievable. He loses, wins, loses again, wins
once more, everything dissolves, grows confused, is lost
and found again, and nothing is ever won, just as nothing
is ever lost . . . In his everyday life, the gambler acts on
impulse: he's not a man of decisive actions, of brutal and
definite decisions. As a matter of fact, for him, the will

doesn't exist, for he knows that to *want* to win is an absurdity. The will, after all, is a virtue for which he feels no need and of which he makes no use. Actions have a double face, for he interprets them. Gamblers who find out while they're betting that their wives have been unfaithful appear to be delighted by the fact, for as you all know, gentlemen of the jury, there is a legend that luck falls heaviest on deceived husbands. Hence, I deduce from this that my client cannot be a murderer. To kill, indeed, is to perform an irretrievable action, an action it is impossible to remedy, an act closed and over. A gambler, gentlemen of the jury, would put his wife and children, father and mother out in the street, but he wouldn't kill them.

"Your lawyer talked good," Eugène said.

"Did your stepfather die right away?" the Doctor asked.

"Death was instantaneous. His whole skull was bashed in."

"Who killed him?"

"A prowler, in my opinion. The kind specializing in rich old men."

Alex's training session. In a month, he would face Sugar Ray Robinson in Madison Square Garden in New York. When you train, you don't think about anything. What could you think about? About broads. How do you think about them?

"Well," Alex said, "you'll laugh, sometimes I think about them . . ."

"Any one in particular?"

"No, all of them. Us boxers, we say 'broads.' One

broad doesn't exist."

"Weren't you ever in love?"

"No. What's that? I don't even know what it is. With Guitare, when we went to the movies and the guy was kissing some broad, that was when we laughed. We nudged each other and groaned and kissed the backs of our hands until the sound filled the theater. Since we were big guys, everyone was afraid to do anything. When the girl cried because the guy left her, we cried too and made a lot of noise. It was great."

"Well," the Doctor said, as if he were explaining multiplication by twos to a dunce, "love . . ."

Alex came to his assistance: ". . . is like in the movies. A rich girl sees some tough guys beating some guy up. When the guys have gone she takes care of the guy. She wipes off his face with a wet towel and she gives him a drink. The guy opens his eyes, that aren't black-and-blue or cut or anything, and he looks at the girl. She looks at him. But the guy stands up, pulls up his belt that has a gun hanging from it, and walks out without saying a word. The bartender comes out from behind the bar where he's been lying flat, takes a deep breath, and says: 'Johnny's gang just took care of Big Bill. They're all gangsters!' The girl understands that her guy's a gangster too and begins sweeping up the broken glass without a word. But Johnny's gang sets fire to the ranch where Big Bill grew up and the ranchers who brought him up are fried. Then Big Bill starts killing all the guys in Johnny's gang, one after the other. The girl in the bar is scared for him. Especially since the police are looking for him all the time. One night he knocks on the shutters; she opens up. It's him. She's scared but she lets him come into her room. . . . He's dirty, sweating, and panting. He says: 'Can you hide me until morning?' She says: 'Yes!' He sits down in a chair and she gets into bed with the covers pulled up to her chin. He falls asleep and she watches him. In the morning they kiss. He jumps out the window and disappears. But Johnny's been tipped off by the sheriff and he catches Big Bill just when he's trying to unhitch his horse. Big Bill fires and kills the sheriff. Then there's a revolver duel between him and Johnny in a cemetery. The revolver shots break the wooden crosses; they crawl around behind the tombs. In the end, Big Bill finally hits Johnny, who falls back into a grave dug just the day before. But Big Bill's been hit, too, right in the belly. He gets on his white horse and makes a lot of faces and gallops to town. The blood gushing out of his belly runs all over the white horse. That's terrific, that part. He gets to the bar, pushes open the door, grabs his belly, staggers in, and falls down flat. Unconscious. The girl rushes over, washes his face and gives him a drink. Like at the beginning. Then he opens his eyes, and this time he says: 'Thanks.' She tells him she loves him, and again he says: 'Thanks.' Then he dies. The end. That's what love is. Guitare and I thought it was funny as hell when he went into her room and fell asleep in the chair with all his clothes on."

"And you've never been in love?"

"Never. I just told you, it's a gag! But Guitare was the sentimental type. He knew all those stories about princesses getting married and all that, and every week he read all the papers. When it didn't look so good for princesses, he felt sad. He went to the movies four times to see Margaret get married. I only went twice. There were two things at the movies he liked better than anything; one was princesses and the other was atom bombs. Each time he went to the movies, when an atom bomb went off, he opened his mouth and said: 'Now that's something. Compared to that,' he used to say, 'you're nothing. You can be big as you want, but you're nothing compared to that.' "

"But you said you used to think about girls sometimes . . ."

"Oh sure! I think about them, and then all of a sudden I change the subject. For instance, I think about girls naked with feathers and all that, and then right away I'm working in a garden and planting vegetables, watering the cabbage, cutting down trees, or else I'm playing dominoes in a café—Why dominoes? I've played twice in my life. Or else I'm throwing money to some guy who's lifting dumbbells in the street and eating fire. Sometimes at night before going to sleep, or in the morning when I'm half awake, I decide to think about them, but I always end up cutting down trees, playing dominoes, or applauding the fire-eater. And there's nothing I can do about it! I can't help it."

These last six days we haven't talked. Morning and evening Match would recite the news but, in the interval, the most complete silence reigned in the cell. "Behaving pretty nice," the guard said. No one answered. These periods of silence would arrive unexpectedly and for no particular reason. One morning, Eugène got up and said: "Good morning!" We answered: "Good morning!" Then not a word more. The Doctor stood up, sniffed.

Not a word. Match stood up and cracked his knuckles. Not a word. Alex stood up, cleared his throat, inhaled, raised his head, aimed carefully, and spat out of the skylight. He never missed. Not a word. Fifteen minutes went by. No one spoke. The guard brought the coffee. We drank. An hour passed. No one spoke. After two hours it was too late. We started off on hours and days of silence. It became completely impossible for us to open our mouths. In the cell, we walked without a sound, and all our gestures were wrapped in cotton; we were like those big fish that pass each other in an aquarium, and the cell was full of thick green water. We set our pans down carefully so they wouldn't clink; we sat on our beds, one buttock after the other, so the mattresses wouldn't creak; we held our noses when we sneezed so the noise wouldn't leave our throats. In summer, around four, when the air turned heavy between the walls of the cell and the city was dying around the jail, the distant sounds came to us, carried and muffled at the same time by the vibrations of the heat. Two years ago, we heard a dog bark; last year, the echoes of a song got into our cell. Soldiers leaving on maneuvers in the middle of August? Boy scouts marching to the beach? Were we near or far away from the sea? Alex said the sea was close by because our iron beds are covered with rust. We often discussed this problem. Eugène suggested that we ask the guard. Which we objected to: *primo* because he might not answer us, *secundo* because if he did answer us we'd know and then we'd stop asking each other. Such reasoning did not convince Eugène, and Match proposed a compromise solution. As follows:

"We'll ask the guard but first we'll ask him not to answer. Then we'll interpret his physiognomy."

Solution adopted. We fixed a precise date for the interrogation of the guard. In the cell, still the same death. Sometimes we kept still like this for over two months. Each day added another layer to the silence and we were all just about certain we'd never speak again. Why should we ever articulate words again? What event would force us to utter sounds? Why not keep still forever, until death? We all admitted we had had the same thought: if one of us dies, will we talk? And we all decided to say nothing. After that, there was nothing else to do except to imagine one of us lying in agony in front of his three friends, mute as fish, and watching two guards carrying away the body. It was Match who began talking in his sleep one night. He woke us up and went right on: "What, what? Who are you?" he screamed when he came out of his nightmare and saw us standing around him. "What was I saying?" We told him. He wasn't saying anything. He was pronouncing words: pilot comb ceramic curtain hacienda maximum clog. After he woke up and all the following day, Match tried to reconstitute his dream. We decided to help him, and each of us made up a story using those seven words.

The Doctor's: Monsieur Match lost a maximum amount at the gambling table because the clog—in other words, the roulette wheel—was bad for him. He wants to go to a hacienda in South America, and takes the plane, sitting behind the pilot. He disguises himself with a wig that he combs carefully, but a policeman hidden behind a curtain surprises him in the airport washroom decorated with ceramic tiles.

Eugène's: Using a curtain, Monsieur Match strangles someone reading a newspaper with clogs on his feet. Afterward, he steals the maximum, etc.

Alex's: Monsieur Match makes a pair of clogs out of curtains because his feet are cold when he walks on ceramics. Afterward . . . What's a "hacienda"?

"A farm, in Spanish."

". . . Afterward," Alex continued, "he pilots a plane," etc.

So, that time, we found words again. This time, on the morning of the seventh day, the Doctor, after drinking his coffee, picked up his spoon and whacked the bottom of his pan, shouting: "Boom! boom! boom!" Alex imitated him: "Plan! Rataplan! Plan!" Eugène and Match joined in and brayed a kind of military march: "La la tra la la tra la la! . . ." The guard came, his face all red. "Atten–shun!" Alex shouted. Our spoons on our shoulders, we saluted the guard, who snatched the pans and spoons out of our hands, and we had to go without lunch. Afterward, we talked. Each of us has his own way of talking. Match happens to have a sour but rather distinguished voice. He emphasizes certain words by articulating them the way some people do once they're cured of a stutter. Alex has a rough but kindly voice. Eugène gives the impression, often, of not talking to anyone, just giving a monologue. He's reciting obvious facts, apparently not expecting any answer. The Doctor talks in a low voice and his words describe an uninterrupted thought. Before he talks, you can tell he's thinking. After he's through, you know he's still thinking. There's a reason for that: he's afraid of his "absences."

If he thought all the time, he wouldn't fall into the hole of his absences, his madness. He asked Eugène: "Did we have lunch?"

"Yes, Doctor."

"You're sure?"

"Yes, Doctor."

"Ah! . . . and what did we eat?"

"Chick peas with salt pork and spinach. And for dessert we had applesauce, which was pretty bad. It was too loose, and there wasn't enough sugar in it."

The Doctor nodded.

"And before dinner, what happened? Did Monsieur Alex train?"

"Not today, Doctor."

"What did I do? What did I say?"

"You drank some water out of the faucet. You brushed your teeth with two fingers. Then you put your left shoe on your right foot and you—"

"Right shoe on my left foot."

"Exactly! And you walked around like Chaplin because of that."

"Did I notice it?"

"Yes."

"What did I say?"

"You said: Damn! Damn! looking hard at your feet."

"Maybe I'm going to have a fit. What do you think, Monsieur Eugène?"

"You shouldn't think about it, Doctor, you shouldn't think about your fits."

"They think about me. I feel I'm being followed. There's someone behind me who never stops looking at me; who's watching my gestures, playing tricks on me.

She's the one who played that trick with the shoes on me."

"She?"

"Yes, *she,* it's not something masculine."

"Do you know her?" Eugène asked, impressed and beginning to turn pale.

"I have my suspicions."

The Doctor grew animated. His shoulders moved up and down. His eyes grew wide and pale. "Some day," he said, "I'll turn around fast, and I'll catch her. I'll look her straight in the face; I'll look her straight in the eyes and mine'll be like two daggers, and she won't get away from me! I'll kill her! I'll grind her down to dust! I'll burn her up and she'll vanish! She doesn't have the right to spy on me, to follow me, to beg me, and whisper things to me. No, she doesn't, oh, no! I'm free, Monsieur Eugène, and I don't bother about anybody. Don't forget what I'm telling you, will you? And above all, don't forget that I'm asking you to keep track . . ."

The Doctor stood up very straight now and walked back and forth in the cell. Match, Alex, and Eugène, sitting on a mattress, are attentive spectators of this routine. "Let's remember his words carefully," Match murmured into Eugène's ear. "Later on he'll ask us to repeat them to him exactly."

". . . Don't forget, you three, because you'll be my witnesses and you'll have to speak the truth, and swear to it. You'll be believed if you say the same words, exactly the same ones. Other people's business doesn't interest me; I'm alone. I didn't ask anybody to bother about me or talk to me. Leave me alone! Ho ho ho!" and he whinnied like a horse. "You'll notice that I'm laughing, and that I'm giving no indications of anxiety whatsoever. So I'm not the guilty one. If she follows me, that's her business. My only desire is to smoke my pipe, sit on a bench and smile at the children singing mysterious songs while they're skipping rope. My only desire is to practice my profession and inform my patients that they're all done for, doomed to die. I'm not dying! If I turn around suddenly I'll catch her in the act, shadowing me. Does she suspect I might turn around suddenly? I know her. She's a coward, she'll run away as fast as she can go. Or else she'll have the cheek to claim she just happens to be there by accident. Or else she'll make trouble for me by saying: 'I don't know this man! . . .' Did I ask anyone to follow me? I'm alone, I am! All this is harder to stick together than the pieces of a broken pot that's gone through a pulverizer. There's no simplicity left, it's all ground to dust. No one in the world can put a pot together again from dust. Don't forget, Monsieur Eugène, and you, Monsieur Alex, and you, Monsieur Match: you'll be called on to bear witness to my extraordinary patience. If they try to catch you up, you answer: 'He was patient!' They've examined me. I was searched, undressed, auscultated by seven doctors. Questions, analyses, examinations . . . I knew more about it than they did. At the end, when I saw how perplexed they were, I joined the discussion. There were eight doctors—including myself —considering my case. A real anatomy lesson, the same faces as in Rembrandt's painting, except that here the corpse was talking and giving his opinion. I watched them so ironically at first, like an inspired magician before whom seven colleagues were doing their acts—

that they lowered their eyes. I decided to help them out."

"That's like the story about the guy who's good at fixing things," Alex said.

"What story?"

"Don't you know it? It's a good one. They were going to guillotine this guy. And the head of the prison, the chaplain, the lawyer, and all those guys were there, you know? The guy puts his head in. Click! It doesn't work. They try again. Click! It's busted. The executioners try to fix it up. No use. So the condemned man says: 'Let me try, I'm good at fixing things.' And in fifteen minutes he gets it fixed. He stands up and says: 'Now it ought to work.' He sticks his head into the hole and clack! It falls right off into the basket."

There were eight of them passionately discussing the Doctor, and in the heat of the argument they had completely forgotten that they were talking about one of their number. The patient had evaporated.

Before setting forth their conclusions, they handed me over to the police all the same. Fools! According to them, I had committed the murder during one of my fits; either in the fit itself or in a "latent" state. Now, I'm not lying: I say she's not dead and that I'm the victim of a tremendous and loathsome machination. Gentlemen! . . . You're hiding the truth from me, she's not dead, and I didn't kill her. Where's the body? Who's seen it? They've hidden it from me. Why should I have killed her? She died on her own. Why should I have killed her *since I was killing her?* Standing before us, the Doctor showed us his hands; they were white, open, and empty.

The day of the event, we took a walk in the woods near

the city. She submitted to all my whims, and on that day I felt like walking in that woods. Our feet—it was October—sank into a spongy carpet of dead leaves. We walked without saying a word. At noon, the woods suddenly ended and we came to a farm. I threw stones at a yellow and white dog that followed us, yapping. He ran away, sat down, and kept watching us until we were out of sight. It had rained the night before, and an odor of moss, wet wood, mushrooms, and vegetable rot rose from the earth. Nostrils dilated, I breathed deeply and gorged myself on this odor that was so sweet it hurt. I pushed aside the branches that whipped my face to open a path for her. "I'm tired," she told me. We sat down on a sticky wooden bench in a clearing in front of a hut. She asked if we were going to walk much farther. I answered that I felt nervous and wanted to exhaust my body. It was late already. Night was slipping between the branches. Let's go back to the road. Suddenly I said to her: "Something's wrong . . ."

"You're sick?"

"Shh! Don't touch me! I'm not sick. Something's wrong."

"What's wrong?"

"Something."

"What?"

He didn't answer. His eyes, gazing at her looked so blue they were white, and in them she read something beyond despair, beyond distress, something beyond everything you could read in *human* eyes. He went over to a tree, pulled off a fragment of bark and crumbled it between his fingers.

* * *

Guitare used to say that the way women liked little things made him nervous. Lipsticks, compacts, nail files, handkerchiefs, brushes, pins, pencils, perfume bottles, all that. Their bags were always a tool box, like the kind plumbers carry around. And all day long, as soon as they had a minute, they started repairing something.

He picked up a handful of dead oak leaves and crumbled them.

"I'm the one and only spectator," he said. "What shall I do with what I see? Suppose you were walking in the most beautiful city in the world, intact but deserted? All the inhabitants are dead and you're alone. No one. Not one human being, not a cat, not a bird, not a fly, not a mosquito, what would you *do* with what you saw? In the middle of a huge empty square, I screamed at the top of my lungs. What's there to do? I want to walk just like a hundred thousand other men; I want to participate in a fishing contest, or I want to be a Chinaman along with a million other Chinamen carrying dirt in a little basket all day long. . . . I've seen that in the movies, and with all my heart I longed for the destiny of one of those random ants. . . . I'd like to spend my life in a subway car."

Kneeling at Helène's feet, he rested his old child's head in the hollow of her thighs. Gently, she caressed that poor head full of emptiness and madness and cried. I don't like men, Helène. I couldn't care *less* about what people call men. Women are something grafted to a man's body when he leaves adolescence, aren't they? Hee, hee, hee! As a child, when I saw crowds, I wanted to kill everyone; I dreamed of grenades exploding, tearing apart the stupid bodies and plastering terror all over those faces. One day I went into a dance hall and I saw a whole crowd of men and women dancing; there was a pain burning in my belly and I came outside to throw up. I would have killed the first man or woman who touched me. I don't want to be touched. If anyone even brushes against me, if anyone touches me, I scream; I fight; I kill. At night I woke with a start. Someone was wandering around in my bedroom; his enormous hands, the palms covered with warm velvety hair, caressing the darkness, searching for my body. Those hands, those hands had no body and floated in the silky night like bats. What could I do against those hands resting on my body, covering it completely? At the end, huddled in my terror, I fell asleep. As long as they don't touch me, I can love men. What happens when I'm not here? What do they do to me? What do they say around me? If I drool and roll on the floor, my eyes popping out of their sockets, a hundred thousand people will watch me with their eyes where they belong. Me, me, where will *I* be, me? Where am I being watched? In what street am I spied on? At the foot of what tree will I die?

This happened in a resort where my parents were taking a cure. I was nineteen and I was still walking behind them, on the invisible leash of childhood. They said I hadn't had a fit in a long time. Some idiots told my father that once my adolescence was over, I might enter a period of relative calm. That old bellboy who came in every morning pushing a wheeled cart with my breakfast on it and then opened the curtains, that bellboy had a sad sheep's face. The bottom of his face was pointed, the lower lip wet and pendulous, his eyes protruding. When he pushed the cart, leaning over, the illusion was powerful and I heard him bleating his "Good morning, monieur!"

He reported how when he had poured out the coffee, the young man in 535 had suddenly thrown back the covers and leaped out of bed. He was startled and dropped the coffee pot. "Then the young man in 535, without a word, without a sound, threw himself on me and began scratching my face. I had just time enough to protect myself. I stepped back, overturning the tray; he chased me, kicking me, but since he was barefoot, he didn't hurt me." The old sheep ran away, terrified.

The manager called his father, who turned gray and said: "I'm terribly sorry, monsieur, my son is a very nervous boy!" The manager said that he would speak a word or two to the boy. . . . His father asked him to do nothing of the kind . . . "In that case, I'm terribly sorry, sir . . ." "Of course, I understand, we'll leave at once." When he came to himself, they had put the room back in order but the mirror on the dressing table was broken. This time, his memory was intact until the moment the old man ran away. Knocked out by sedatives, he talked in a limp voice, but with his memory intact. It wasn't his fault; that bellboy always came into my room at the same time, and every day his resemblance to an old sheep grew more and more hallucinatory. Every day he made exactly the same gestures: drew the left curtain, then the right. Noise of the curtain rings clattering on the brass curtain rod. Turned to the left. Eight steps to the cart. Leaned over. Pushed. Took hold of the coffee pot, poured. With three fingers, picked up the handle of the milk pot, poured. Smiled. Turned left. Six steps. Left. The door slammed. This trained *animal* drove him crazy. He didn't feel responsible, and maybe it was only the effect of the sedatives, but he smiled at his father.

"You know, they said I was faking," the Doctor said. "Well . . . then there was some doubt and they condemned me."

A little while ago the Doctor received an electric shock, and we thought his fit had started. But, no. On the contrary, he seemed relaxed by it, and talked calmly. In fact, he discoursed.

"Are you a faker, Doctor?" Match asked.

"Fakers—I knew two in the army," Alex said.

"So you think I faked a fit," the Doctor said, "in order to kill Helène. Is that it? Well, that doesn't quite hang together, you know, because after all, why should I have killed her?"

"To find out," Match said.

"To find out what?"

"Ah," Match said, "you're the one who has to answer that. There are always reasons for killing someone. For instance, there are people who can't live if someone else exists. There's not room enough for two. Besides, I think you once said, and it made pretty good sense to me, that murderers are always in a state of self-defense. It doesn't take much . . . You kill someone because he has an obsessive wrinkle, a voice that bothers you a little more every day, because he has a funny smell, because he laughs . . ."

Because one day, suddenly, he's flesh, meat, a meaningless body. Bodies don't count: battlefields are covered with them; they rot by the thousands under the ruins of bombed cities. You decide that someone's a body, a corpse, and from then on you're a butcher. The judges will never understand that. They see souls everywhere. For them, carrion immediately suggests spirit.

"All right, all right," the Doctor said. "Let's concede I'm a faker."

He smiled, sanctimoniously. A fake madman. He never had fits and his whole life was a farce. Since he began faking in short pants, it was impossible to stop. He fooled his parents, his friends, everybody . . .

"Like in the army," Alex said. "Once you begin faking, you have to go on, otherwise it gets tough!"

When life became too dark for him and spattered him with questions, he clapped his hands, like in fairy tales, and he was crazy. "It seems to me, my friends, that either no one's crazy, or else this earth, our dwelling place, is an asylum. My fits began after my brother's death. My parents had transformed the house into a museum and appointed themselves curators of their 'immense grief.' Hee, hee! Forgive me, I can still see their long faces, their black clothes; I can still hear their silence. Ridiculous! They didn't give a damn about me. I ate, drank, slept, and went to school. My feet were all right, my eyes, and my head. I was a well-adjusted toy that walked all by itself. In my little snake's head, I decided: Wait and see, just you wait and see . . . That's how I fell sick—quite deliberately. Crazy people, I thought, are individuals who are terrifically brave, and madness is only a superior form of nerve. My dear friends, I'm quite shy, you know. When I saw a boy walk up to a girl, I used to say: 'He's crazy!' When I saw a friend go to the blackboard and recite his lesson without stammering, I'd think: 'He's crazy!'

When I saw a kid who wasn't even shaving yet buy a ticket for a film you couldn't see unless you were over sixteen, I'd say: 'He's crazy!' My timidity became pathological. Knowing my lessons by heart, in class I pretended not to know them so I wouldn't have to recite. I'd rather have died."

"How did you get through your orals?"

"Drunk."

To talk to a human being, to ask someone on the street for a light, to look at a woman, smile at her—such things constituted, in my opinion, acts of pure madness.

Then the Doctor said he had made up the story of his dead brother. He said he was an only child. He attributed his misfortunes to his timidity. He said he invented the story of the brother because the brother would have been another self, and *he* might have learned how to love his parents. I didn't dare love them. I thought it was obscene. When my mother kissed me, I blushed to my ears. When I was bigger, I pushed her away.

"You a faker . . ." Match said in a thoughtful tone, as if this idea opened new horizons to him.

"Suppose I admit that. But then why would I have killed Helène?

"My Helène! My darling. My sweet sugar!" he stammered in a tearful voice. "How I loved you! O my bird, my sea! O my star and rocket, my zodiac, my sailboat!" Nothing was more upsetting than when the Doctor played the clown. It spread discomfort in the cell. "Oh, my Helène, how I loved you!" End of the clowning. Normal voice: "Why did I have to see you one day? From that moment—which lasted three seconds—I knew it wouldn't be difficult for me to . . . *suppress* you. Something exploded in my head: you didn't have any meaning. Your presence beside me couldn't be explained. I didn't have to talk to you; you didn't have to love me. Your presence, here, was absurd. In the past, when I walked toward you, an invisible shield protected you; I touched you and you were solid; your hair was alive between my fingers that twisted it, and your body was inhabited by a hundred living springs. But now I had *seen* you, and I knew that from now on I would pass through you the way you walk through a fog, the way I could walk through the mirror and continue on my way, hee, hee, hee! Toward what? That's my little secret! I intend to die with it. I won't write any will. I'll take this formula with me. It will be the obol the Ancients slipped into the dead man's mouth so he could pay Charon for ferrying him over the Styx. On the other bank, I'll confess everything. Not before. My Helène! I knew her all right! When she saw I had seen her, she was *really* scared. She told me: 'What's the matter? What's happening? What are you thinking about? Why did you look at me that way?' Sly as a fox, I assumed an innocent, harmless expression—I have my ways when I'm at my best . . . and I said: 'What? What? I wasn't thinking of anything, I was admiring the way your hair looks. Right off the tip of my tongue! I finished off her gestures, her moods, her thoughts. Sometimes this game amused me, sometimes it bored me. It taught me that she loved my madness. You know, women are funny. When they've decided to love—'love,' the way they mean the word—nothing can stop them. You give them a madman? Fine, then a madman it is. Shall we wrap him up for you, madame? Shall we send him home for you? No no, I'll take him with me! You give them a drunk like Monsieur Eugène? Fine, a drunk! A brute like Monsieur Alex? Fine, a brute! A gambler, like Monsieur Match? Fine, a gambler! Disease, madness, vice, it's all included in the price. It's the tip!

"Me, the adored doctor, I was crazy, it seems. She had bought the madness with the rest. With my childishness with, hee, hee! my charm, with my cowardice, since I can boast of never having met anyone as cowardly as I am. Are you a coward, Monsieur Eugène? And you? And you?" Match, Eugène, and Alex searched their memories as fast as they could. They rummaged hastily through their actions, the way you look for an umbrella in the miscellanea of a dusty closet full of moth-balls and spiderwebs. "Silence!" the Doctor shouted, "I know what you're thinking! You're trying to remember if you helped a drowning man, trembled before the enemy, and bowed to the stronger. You're making a mistake, my friends. Some day, I'll tell you about real cowardice. All you need to know today is that it consists of not vomiting yourself up, every last piece of gut. She loved me, but did she know I'd kill her? *That is the question* I can't answer. Did she know, or didn't she? She didn't know? Then I've won! She did know? Then I've lost, and she had me! Did she figure me out, that day when I looked at her— for three seconds—without the shadow of any tenderness, without anything. Look at that wall, Monsieur Alex! Don't move! Open your mouth a little bit! Don't think of anything! No, that's not it!"

We set up a contest of "absent" looks, and all stared at the wall in turn, our minds blank. The Doctor has tried to "reconstruct" his expression of that day, but he hasn't managed it yet. All the same, he's won the prize so far. Match, whose eyes are too deep and too dark, always has something "expressive" about him; Eugène isn't bad, but his long eyelashes conceal his expression; Alex can't help looking angry. This contest took us a good hour or so.

"Or did she think she'd get away with it, the little fox? In that case, I had her, and the glory's all mine. In any case, she played the game pretty well."

"Please . . ."

"If it's *me* you love, who are you saying please to?"

You understand, if it's *me* you love, I'll realize it; a door will open. If it's *me* you love, I have to behave myself in such a way that it's impossible for you to love me. And I say: Impossible! Impossible! And I run my head against the wall; and I cut open my forehead against the wood of the Louis XVI bed! It's impossible for a circle to be a square! I drool and I bite my tongue, the blood spurts out on my cut lips, I say nothing, absorbed in ridiculous reading, I go down into the street, I come back, I draw the curtains, lock the doors, and with my dislike of electric light, I light a candle and stretch out on my bed, eyes wide. If you love me, the face of the world will be changed forever; history will reverse its course; nothing will ever have happened; everything can be invented and constructed . . . all we have to do is break this seed of malediction and we'll be the husband and wife who, mingling their breath, begin the world. But I laugh, my dear, because all is lost. Somewhere, someplace, everything's been wagered and lost. We're pieces of shit, my shadow.

"As far as I'm concerned," the Doctor said, "I swear

that I've always believed in original sin.

Beg your pardon? What? The Doctor was speaking to an imaginary interlocutor. "You asked me, sir, why she stayed with me? I tell you, I asked myself that, too. Hadn't she been sent to me? Wasn't she obeying someone's orders? Whose? For example, God's? The world's full of gods, you know, there are some everywhere. This cell, don't make any mistake about it, is full of them."

He sat down, dropped his arms alongside his body and said, overwhelmed: "How innocent I am!" But who will imagine my innocence? Who'll believe me if I don't tell everything. But how can I tell *everything* if words fail me? Look, I'm alive, I open my mouth, I grind my teeth, I open my hands, I clench my fists, I pinch my nose, I sleep: therefore I'm innocent. If I were guilty, I'd be dead! One day, we were visiting a museum and walking past portraits of sad kings—painted by famous painters —and their eyes waited for us and accompanied us. I told Helène with a sweet smile and slowly raising my eyebrows . . . I remember having slowly raised my eyebrows but I'm not sure about sniffing . . . I told her: "I'm dead too. I look alive but I'm fooling everyone: I'm really dead and buried. I'm not moving either. You're moving, you enjoy living. Go away, come back, and you'll see: I won't have moved. Weep for me, Helène. No luck, no luck being the widow of a living man or in love with a dead man." She didn't answer. I took her arm: "All right, come on, let's be happy and admire these beautiful canvases!" During the day that preceded the murder, I cried a lot. I was afraid because I'd already killed her and she didn't know it. Of course, I don't know anything sweeter than living with someone whose death you've already decided. It's an emotion of an absolutely disgusting sweetness. There's also something absolutely irresistible about the comedy of it, and therefore about the tragedy of it. God alone, Who counts and measures our days, can know it in its plentitude, but in my humble circumstances I savored its profound delights. I trembled at making a mistake, because I wanted her to be *natural.* How many plans I told her about! How many futures I described to her in brilliant colors! At the end, my love, the scaffold! I press a button, the scaffold opens and swallows you up. My power was the enormous kind you have over a blind man when you take his arm to help him cross the street. She had the bathroom repainted, oh, I have a memory! . . . Someone gave her a Persian cat and she began training it, housebreaking it, and promising everyone kittens. She stored her furs until next winter. She was learning Italian because we were planning a trip to Rome. I laughed hysterically—in bad taste, because it wasn't very funny, I admit—the day when I saw her come in carrying two suitcases and said: "It's for the trip . . ." I had produced a real prodigy: her gestures meant nothing; her words were only noise and wind; she walked on a carpet of expressions which, out of pure clownishness, I could set fire to at any moment. Her life sounded hollow and I weighed it in my hand, lighter than the shell of an egg that's been blown. Poor love, what a furious laugh I had on you!

"I'll say!" Match said.

Did she have any suspicions? Never! That's the human race for you. Eggshell, I'll smash you. I'm not afraid, I'm used to the game. I die all the time. A hundred times death has bumped into me; a hundred times I've felt its cudgel on my neck and I've crawled toward the hole on all fours. But I know. I know. I'm a thinking eggshell.

This morning, Match suggested that each of us talk about his faults. "Monsieur Alex?" Alex wrinkled up his forehead, reflected . . . "All right, think it over, we'll come back to you later." "Monsieur Eugène?" "I hold grudges." "That's all?" "Yes, that's all . . ." "Monsieur Match?" "I tend to tell lies." "Doctor?" "I'm dead." "That's not a fault." "It's not a fault? Well, in that case, I'm a glutton." "Monsieur Alex, have you found anything?" "No." We all declared unanimously that Monsieur Alex was perfect. We congratulated him and shook his hand.

Today we decided to clean house. We shook out our mattresses; the straw had been matted by the weight of our bodies. Where did all this dust come from? We cleaned the pans, polished our shoes. In five minutes we were through. Yet we had counted on having work for the whole day. We began again, more intensely. Shaken too hard, one mattress split and a cloud of straw filled the cell, now we had work for the whole day: picking up the straw down to the last stem, stuffing it back into the mattress and arranging it there. The guard lent us a needle and thread but watched the mending of the rip (performed by Alex, who knows how to do everything) and then we had to give him back the needle. Match's latest news bulletin informed us of the birth of the Queen of England's fifth child. The royal baby weighs eight pounds and is in fine condition. As is the Queen. Let us hope this birth will bring balm to the heart of the sovereign and help her support the cruel bereavement she has recently suffered.

"What bereavement?"

"Her husband got himself killed in an automobile accident last November," Match said.

"Poor guy!" Alex said.

Match announced that the murderers of nurses continue to commit their detestable crimes with impunity. The day before yesterday, seventeen new victims were disclosed. A slight improvement had been noted in the Pope's state of health, but a relapse was feared, which might prove to be fatal. In Yugoslavia, all civil powers had been assumed by the army until new elections could be held. The dispute between India and Pakistan, according to neutral observers, was about to degenerate into open conflict, and the unexpected eruption of volcanoes in the Auvergne was sowing panic among the inhatitants of the Massif Central. Despite the desperate efforts of the Paris firemen, the blaze ravaging the Comédie Française had not been brought under control. The conflagration had spread to adjoining buildings, and it was feared that the Bibliothèque Nationale would fall prey to the flames in the next few hours. General Eisenhower, ex-President of the United States and former European commander-in-chief during the Second World War, was buried today at West Point. In Manchuria, where the adversaries, by common agreement, had abandoned the use of atomic weapons, the Japanese army continued its advance.

"Against who?"

"I don't know."

Yesterday in Philadelphia the American track star Jeff Moore jumped two meters eighty-four centimeters from a standing position, beating his preceding record, which was two meters eighty-two centimeters. The Brazil soccer team beat France by a score of two to zero. Finally, according to the week's last count, seven hundred thousand individuals of both sexes have been arrested in France. This ends our news broadcast.

Before going to bed, we commented with some animation on the birth of the royal baby and General Eisenhower's death. We then wished each other good night.

"I don't understand," Alex said, "why the radio never mentions my bout with Sugar Ray Robinson!"

"Never mind . . ." Eugène said.

"It isn't fair."

So great was his agitation that he didn't have time to dress and wandered around the cell naked as a worm. The press, the reporters, the radio, they're all corrupt. When I think of the money I greased those bastards with! Alex his member dangling from his hairy body, screamed louder and louder. It was the first time Match, Eugène, and the Doctor had observed this regal spectacle: a *naked* man in a rage. Here was anger in its pure state, without the help of robes (indignant lawyers), without a switch to lash its boots (cavalry officers), without a cigar stubbed into the ash tray with a flick of the wrist (businessmen). Alex was suffering the wrath of Adam, whose Michelangelesque musculature he possessed, and Match imagined household scenes in Eden. The joy of seeing our mother Eve, naked under the apple tree, a half-devoured apple in her hand, receiving from Alex the most splendid scolding in the history of humanity. Since that day, we have dressed up our angers, and the richer the clothes the more men tremble. Alex's rage grew from moment to moment, and he became terrible. On his forehead, the mauve worm had dilated its coils, and he struck the air with his fists. Why do men get angry?

"The attribute of Jupiter," the Doctor said, "was the thunderbolt."

Then Alex realized he was naked, and his frenzy evaporated as though by magic. The worm deflated, and he pulled on his pants.

"And suppose it was fixed by fat Lucienne? After what happened to Khadi, he started slipping. Because, you know: that big piece of shit always picks up Bics for his fighters."

"Bics?"

"You know, Arabs—that's what they call them. Ever since he worked Coco Saïd up to the European championship . . . you remember, don't you? Against Di Lorenzo . . . Ever since then, these Bics were all over the place. You stepped on Bics in the gym, there were Bics everywhere. They all thought Lucienne would get them up to the title, but for one Coco Saïd, how many Yousoufs were there?"

"Yousouf?"

"The one who went crazy and killed his two wardmates in the hospital. There was a lot of talk about it at the time. So anyway, Lucienne didn't have anybody except Bics. Why? It's easy: because Bics aren't very sharp and you can cheat them on the take; because for Bics, boxing's a matter of getting out alive or croaking: those guys don't think the way we do. Life doesn't mean a thing to them, they're savages! You know, they're all fatalists. And when you come down to it, they're pretty good. As long as he can stand on his legs, a Bic will let himself be pushed around the ring. He brings in cash right up to the end. Lucienne did pretty well, you know. Whenever anyone was arranging fights—in Paris, in the country, anywhere—he sent his Bics out. All right, fine. But after Khadi, the Bics got the score. Especially, I guess, because Lucienne didn't even send the body to Algeria so the family could bury it the way they do out there. They cry and they sing and they eat cous-cous, it's a real party. They call it a *nouba*. They enjoy themselves in their own way. The ones around the gym must have chipped in to pay for sending the body, and that made a bad impression on all the others, and they got mad at Lucienne because, you know, those Bics hold grudges. Then they boycotted the gym and the old queen's business started to slip. Of course Lucienne never forgave me for that, and he took his revenge every way he could. One thing's sure, if you think about it, the guy who came out ahead was Monsieur Siméon. First because I knocked Khadi out of circulation, and that Bic could have been champion of France in two or three years; second because Lucienne's gym, once the Bics left, couldn't compete with Monsieur Siméon's. So I say to myself: Alex, boy, suppose all this is just a trick of Monsieur Siméon's?"

Alex will talk for two hours. He'll talk to himself. He'll ask himself questions, give the answers. During his endless monologue, his conviction will grow stronger: Monsieur Siméon knew Khadi had been in a motorcycle accident or something—had been hurt, anyway. By whom? No one's ever known. The other guy was never identified. And suppose the other guy happened to be Monsieur Siméon in person, or some Corsican he paid to do it for him? Veils fall in Alex's head, a great light dawns in all the corners of his brain and his ideas rise up in a storm. Never has Alex felt so intelligent. He *is* intelligent—he knows it—he feels it—and like a boarding-school girl intoxicated by the first glass of wine she's ever drunk, he abandons himself to the unheard-of delight of expressing his intelligence. If he stops, it's all over, he'll lose the thread of his ideas. He "follows through," as they say in boxing, he walks all over his adversary who has emerged from the shadows, and the more he talks, the more the ideas cluster around him. There's no doubt about it: Monsieur Siméon knew he'd kill Khadi and that then the Bics would desert Lucienne's. It was a deliberate, premeditated murder arranged by Monsieur Siméon, for whom Alex was only a crude instrument. So I'm innocent. I suspected as much all along, but now I'm sure of it. With a joyous movement, Alex tore Khadi's death out of his heart and loaded it on Monsieur Siméon's back. He washed his hands of it. He whistled. He hummed. He'd like to circle around Monsieur Siméon, hopping from one foot to the other, thumbing his nose at him and repeating in a monotonous sing-song: "It wasn't me, it wasn't me, it wasn't me . . ." Crazy with happiness, Alex disgorged the lustral waters of the innocence that flooded him, and his eyes gleamed as they never gleamed before, with the candor of a new-born baby. It wasn't me! "I'm hungry!" Alex said. His happiness suddenly made him hungry. He took a crust of hard bread out of his pocket and chewed it up in three bites. He was sweating.

"Bravo!" Eugène said.

"Yes," Match said. "Still . . ."

Alex glanced at him sourly. Was Match going to steal his victory away from him?

"Still," Match said . . . "Lucienne *also* knew Khadi had had an accident. Why should he have deliberately sent Khadi to his death?"

Alex had a sudden desire to throw himself on Match and knock him out, but he controlled himself, for no such thing could be allowed to happen in the cell. On the contrary, he must answer. Here he had just managed to construct his castle of arguments and reasons, the whole thing was standing there in front of him, and now Match was blowing on it to test its solidity.

"Why should he have deliberately sent Khadi to his death?" Alex repeated, to gain time.

"Should he have deliberately sent him" irritated Alex. No one talked like that. Match expressed himself like a judge. Should he! Deliberately! . . . Judges always talk like that when they're trying to corner someone.

"Yes," Match said, speaking more and more elaborately. "Why should fat Lucienne, aware that Monsieur Khadi risked dying at the end of his fight, not have conceded the bout in order to save his fighter?"

"Out of pride!" Alex said.

"I don't understand," Match said.

"So as not to back down. Lucienne thought: 'Let the Bic croak, I couldn't care less!' "

"You mean fat Lucienne deliberately sacrificed a boxer who you yourself, Monsieur Alex, believed likely to become champion of France? You must admit . . ."

"I don't admit anything," Alex said. "I say that queens sometimes have pretty crazy ideas. Queens are like that: they know when they're going to get drowned and they throw themselves into the water. Listen to me, Monsieur Match: the old pigs who prowled around Guitare, they knew that if Guitare bothered with them all it would be just to give them a couple of good ones, but even so they went right on. 'Pay in advance!' Guitare used to say. And they paid. 'And you'll be nice?' the old pigs used to ask. 'Maybe, maybe not!' Guitare would answer. Can you explain that, Monsieur Match, can you explain that?"

"They were masochists," Match said.

"Well that's it, then!" Alex said triumphantly. "Lucienne was a masochist!"

"All right, let's say she was," Match said. "But you, Monsieur Alex, didn't you know Khadi wasn't in a fit state to fight?"

To this question, Alex had twenty answers. Which one to choose? All. No, he didn't know. He was busy training. His job was to fight, not to "know" things. Yes, he knew. And so? Was he to raise a finger and say: "Excuse me, referee, this fighter isn't in condition to fight me!" He knew because he'd overheard a conversation between Monsieur Siméon and a ticket-seller who also took bets.

"I was on the table in the massage room, relaxing, and I heard the bookie saying: 'Is it true, Monsieur Siméon, that business about the Bic's accident? He gets headaches? And throws up all the time when he trains? Pretty risky, isn't it?' And Monsieur Siméon answered: 'Yes, but shut up about it! Let him go on as the favorite! . . . and put as much on Alex for me as you can!' "

"Ah! Then you knew!" Match said.

"Just a minute; just a minute! I *heard* but I didn't *know*. I have ears and I hear, but between hearing and knowing, just a minute! There's a difference!"

The bookie and Monsieur Siméon left. On the massage table, Alex closed his eyes. No one even suspected his presence. Did he know or didn't he? What should he do? Nothing. He got dressed and left. He called a taxi. The driver told him he'd been riding around with a drunk American in the back of his car for two hours.

"You knew he was drunk!" Alex said to him.

"Listen, I'm a taxi driver. When the customer doesn't tell me to stop, I drive. Drunk or not drunk, it's not my business."

Noisily, Alex approved. He was a boxer. Accident or no accident, I'm a boxer and I box. Throwing himself back against the seat, Alex decided he didn't know what he knew.

"Guitare, suppose you were a boxer."

"*Yawohl.*"

"Why do you talk German?"

"Because of the police!"

"And suppose you knew that the guy fighting you could hardly stand up . . ."

"*Ya!*"

"And if you hit him on the head, he might get a cerebral hemorrhage. What would you do?"

"I'd buy an iron, I'd hide it in my glove, and I'd smash his skull open like a lemon."

When Guitare heard about Khadi's death, he said to Alex: "*Chéri*, I'm getting to like you more and more. You're a dope, but you can go far." "How far?" Alex asked. Guitare raised one finger and said, "All the way, baby, all the way!"

At noon, the Doctor informed us that his next fit wasn't far off. Really? Yes, something told him. Sitting on the mattress, barefoot, he spread his toes, one by one. "Which of you can do that?" "Me," Alex said, taking off his shoes. Eugène too, Match too. We all spread our toes one by one and measured the intervals. The Doctor was proclaimed champion. "And who can do this?" Match said, turning his thumb down till his nail touched his wrist. No one. Alex was filled with admiration. "I could never do that, that's really something, Monsieur Match, that's great." He shook Match's hand; Match was very proud and kept turning his thumbs down for about a quarter of an hour before our dazzled eyes. "Who can do this?" Eugène said, wiggling his ears with little jerky movements. The Doctor tried but only his right ear moved. Alex grimaced comically. "No, Monsieur Alex, without making faces. Like this." Alex grimaced. He took his pan with the highly polished bottom and checked his exercises in the mirror. He grimaced and thought of Khadi. I look like Khadi when he took my right in the first round. The more I hit him, the more he looked like he was laughing. It was as if he liked getting his already broken skull smashed to a pulp. Before the third round, when Lucienne was sponging off his neck and talking in his ear . . . In the polished mirror of the pan, Khadi was sitting on the ringside stool, his arms stretched out; he rested his two gloved fists on the ropes; his legs were wide apart; the skinny legs of an Arab, with hard knees that stuck out like stones. Not a hair. Did he shave himself? No. The idiot wasn't even winded and if it wasn't for his broken head he'd give me a lot of trouble. What wind! Those Bics, they almost never smoke and they never drink. How old was he? A kid. He was sweating and his kinky hair shone. The public applauded Alex, but a contingent of Bics shouted whenever Khadi even made a feint. He spat out his toothguard, like a big wad of pink blood, into the basin Lucienne held for him. He was protecting his teeth! What good will his teeth do him! All right, boy, no more cous-cous for you! But he was still smiling. Laughing? The guy's nuts! But he stared at Alex with a kind, sweet smile. They're okay, those Bics, and Alex almost went over and gave him one of those clumsy embraces boxers always give each other after the fight. "You know where to hit him, kid?" Monsieur Siméon murmured. "Yes," Alex nodded, still staring at Khadi, who didn't lower his still smiling eyes. Christ, I like the Bic! "A boxer," Monsieur Siméon said, "doesn't have to be 'mean,' you understand? When a boxer loses his control, he gets mixed up and comes in like a lion and you take him out like a lamb. A boxer," Monsieur Siméon said, "has to be careful, stubborn, and disciplined. Not mean. You know where to hit him, kid, don't you? Yes . . . All right, go in there and give him short hooks! Don't get excited. Take your time, but hit him sharp and short." At the bell, Alex jumped out of his corner while Monsieur Siméon quickly pulled the stool out of the ring. You understand, boxing was my whole life. I liked it more than anything. I didn't care much about the money, the prizes, the guys I was fighting. In the dressing room, when Monsieur Siméon was bandaging my hands, when he slapped me on the back, when those guys with cigars in their mouths walked around me like they were looking over a thoroughbred . . . O.K., Alex? O.K., Monsieur Pierini! O.K., kid? O.K., Monsieur Stoffer! When Monsieur Siméon helped me put on my silk robe . . . I was clean-shaven, combed, lotioned. . . . I smelled of cologne and my muscles sang a waltz. . . . When I walked to the ring with Monsieur Siméon, when I saw the ring, the only thing lit up in the whole place, and I walked toward it like it was a throne, when I stepped over the ropes and did two or three knee-bends to loosen up the leg muscles, when . . . I swear it was like I was with a woman. Did you . . . ? Sure! Then the bell rang and I was in Paradise! Happiness, Happiness! Alex knows what happiness is. It's when you understand everything, when you're doing what you were born for. I was born for that minute; for twenty-six years I was walking toward that cone of white light and thousands or millions of men held their breath in the dark around me and stared at me. More than happiness! I was like a madman in front of the most beautiful woman in the world who really wants it. When I stood up at the bell, for the third round, I understood: Khadi wasn't looking at me and it wasn't me he was smiling at, it was at nothing. At himself, at the Angels. He didn't move, he was that happy, and fat Lucienne had to wake him up and push him out into the ring. I couldn't have cared less if I croaked in the ring. Maybe Khadi was happy and thanking Alex for killing him. Sometimes I envied that Bic. I swear I cried when I heard about his death. I was playing the pinball machine and I didn't even see the balls through my tears. I remembered his smile, his knees, and his Angels and that fat queen whispering in his ear that he should go out and get himself killed. While I was going up the stairs I cried, but when I got to Guitare's door I blew my nose and waited a while before I knocked. Khadi's dead. Guitare was knitting, lying on a pile of pillows, knitting a black sweater with huge red needles. He said it was relaxing, and the proof was that every pregnant girl was always knitting, wasn't she? "You don't look so good today," Guitare said. "Khadi's dead." "One less." "One less what?" Alex asked. "One less dope in the world!" "How do you know that Bic was a dope?" "That's all there is, dopes!" "What about your princesses?" "Don't you worry about my princesses!" I watched the red needles sliding between his fingers and pricking the black wool. "I think I'll chain-stitch the whole thing and finish off with a turtle-neck," he said, laying the part already knitted on his chest.

"No faces, Monsieur Alex; the ears move but the rest of the face remains motionless. Like this!" Match could move the corner of his left ear, but that was all. "A little practice," Eugène said, "it takes time but you'll get there." "Who can do this?" the Doctor asked, crossing his eyes. One for Eugène, whose eyes go almost completely white. Zero for Match. Zero for Alex. The Doctor and Eugène, still crossing their eyes at each other, shook hands and put their faces together until the tips of their noses touched. "Who can do this?" Alex asked, making his irises disappear under the lids. No one. One for Alex. With his eyes turned up, he looked like Helène when I carried her body to the bed. "Who can do this?" Match asked, puffing out his cheeks, pursing his lips and making a tiny sizzling noise. One for the Doctor and Alex. Zero for Eugène. "And who can do this?" Alex asked, rolling up his shirt and undulating his navel without moving his hips. No one. One for Alex.

"Tonight," Match said to Eugène, "your star 'Bull' appears."

"Let's hope I won't have any clouds. Three years ago I didn't see it once. You remember those clouds, that rain?"

"No," Match said.

"You've forgotten?"

"It wasn't my star, it was yours," Match said dryly.

The Doctor, once again, promised us a fit for this week. If I'm not mistaken, in two or three days . . . something tells me. What?

"I'm waiting. It's prowling around. It's watching for me. I won't get away. It's everywhere. It's this humidity that seeps out of the walls; it's the night that envelops the jail. I know it's here, like something hidden, but I can't find it. Who's hidden my fit from me? It hasn't been stolen, it's been hidden. Who? You? If you weren't here, maybe it would come. But you frighten it off . . . It's so timid. Come on, dear, come here, little girl, come on, darling! Don't be afraid of the gentlemen, they'll be nice to you, they'll like you, they won't hurt you, they'll just watch you play with me . . ."

The Doctor winked and put a finger to his lips. Shsh! Don't move. Two pink spots on his cheekbones emphasized the pallor of his face. If you scratched that chalky face with your fingernail, it would crumble, it would become more terrifying than a gargoyle's head corroded by time. "You understand, I'm trying to tame it," he said in a murmur, and, still winking his eye theatrically, "I flatter it and tell it stories. Actually, maybe I'm just wasting my time, maybe it's not there, but ten thousand miles away. Ho, ho! It comes pretty fast if it wants to; faster than the speed of sound. Or else—and this is its usual manner—it trots along, taking tiny steps on its thin legs, like an ant. Or else it turns itself into a slug and crawls! Heeee! One night, I tried sleeping on the floor where I had spread a huge white sheet, and all around the sheet I put ink. You know what I found next morning? My nice white sheet with footprints all over it, a thousand tiny black spots all around it, outlining the white shape of my body in the center. Another night it was disguised as a slug when it visited me, and that night my nice white sheet was covered with black lines forming arabesques and complicated hieroglyphics around me. Or else it grows big and crawls through the underbrush in order to spring at my throat. Is it male or female? I don't know. In any case it has a remarkable strength, the kind of strength all demons have. It creeps up and I'm the sentinel frozen with fear in the night, when the running of a field mouse makes him clench his hand on the cold steel of his gun. I fire at fear and I fire at the night. If I turn in this direction it leaps at my throat; if I turn in that direction it stabs me in the back. I love it, it's my friend. What would I do without it? *What would I be?* It creates this miracle of coming, of being here and of leaving at the same time! Sometimes we argue and I threaten I'm going to leave it; then it begs, promises me to be good and behave over in its corner. By the way, it can't always help it, because sometimes I'm nasty to it. Sometimes, you know, even though we've already known each other more than ten years, I leave for a trip without warning it. At that very moment, I see everything again. You know, I'm endowed with a monstrous memory. But if you don't believe me, what would my memories become? Listen . . .

"Sometimes the cell enlarges, its walls move back to infinity and I lose sight of you, my friends, my dear friends; sometimes it shrinks and crushes me. Sometimes, finally, the two movements succeed each other in a rhythm and I am lodged within a lung. If the movements accelerate, I smother."

The Doctor has spoken so well and so long that the fit hasn't come. We were almost disappointed. Alex's disappointment was close to bad humor. To be frank, Doctor, I was actually counting on it. . . . We were disappointed.

"When will he come back, Doctor?"

"Who?"

"Your angel, like you said."

"That, my dear friends, God alone knows! I wonder myself where he's gone. Yet I swear I felt the wind of his wing brush my temples."

"Where the hell has he gone?" Alex asked.

"God alone knows."

There was a sound of fingers snapping, and Match, who had been dozing, said that if God exists then not everything is permissible. "Monsieur Alex, is everything permissible?"

"Not in boxing."

"And outside of boxing?"

"Outside of boxing? Where?"

"In life."

"My life is boxing."

"Thank you, Monsieur Alex. You're excused. Next! Monsieur Eugène, is everything permitted?"

"No."

"Why?"

"Because of the police."

"And if the police didn't exist?"

"They do exist."

"And if you didn't have to worry about the police?"

"The police worry about me, and put me in prison."

"Suppose you escaped?"

"Sure, if I was invisible I could do anything. Everything would be permissible."

"Would you do harm?"

"Harm and good; I'd mix them up. I'd know everything. Every secret. I'd have known if my wife was cheating on me with that bastard. I'd have followed them, I'd have gone into the room with them and sat down on a chair to be the invisible witness of their calisthenics. At just the right moment, I'd have strangled them."

"Excuse me! You say on the one hand that if you'd been invisible you'd have known if your wife was cheating on you, and on the other hand you say you'd have strangled her because she was cheating on you."

"I'm telling the truth."

"Thank you, Monsieur Eugène. Next! Doctor, is everything permissible?"

"It pleases me," the Doctor said, using his consultations-between-two-and-five-except-for-Mondays voice, "it pleases me that everything should be forbidden. I want to be forbidden to raise my little finger, I want it to be set down in a big book that my whistling cane cuts down the wild flowers along the roadside, I want exact count to be kept of my coughs, my glances, my sighs, I want no one to forget the slammed door, the lost handkerchief, the hidden cigarette, the broken shoelace, the bad breath, the broken bottle, the half-open eye; I want to be bound so tight that at the slightest movement the chains will bruise my flesh. I want every grain of sand I walk on to be counted, I want to be pierced by light, I want to be absolutely pure. My intention is to be guilty (the Doctor snapped his fingers) of that! I hope with all my heart that God is a maniac. *Amen!*"

"So, Doctor, not only is not everything permissible, but worse still, everything is forbidden?"

"Absolutely everything! Your presence is a crime. Your body stinks, your eyes make everything filthy. We deserve to be burned up and our ashes mixed with the mud. Tell me, Monsieur Match, do you like animals?"

"Yes . . . some."

"I don't. I don't like their tails and their legs. When Helène told me she'd like to have a cat, I answered: 'All right, but I'll cut off her tail.' We had a long argument over animals' tails, and I patiently explained to her the disgust they made me feel. *Amen!*"

The cat that belonged to Madame Saint-Roman and sat on the window sill watched me intensely, and its Godlike gaze gave me the shivers. I saw it from the end of the street, and I could have made a detour to escape its oracles, but it called to me. Then I gave up and asked my mother what cats think about. Then I abandoned all honor and I denounced the cat for staring at me. It spied on me. The sight of the animal threw me into such anguish that my father had to go and "explain" to Monsieur Saint-Roman. Soon the whole neighborhood heard about it and you can imagine the jokes people made when I went by.

"Thank you, Doctor. Next!"

Then Match, talking to himself:

"Now, let's see, Monsieur Match, is everything permissible? I warn you, Doctor, that if everything is permissible, I'll scratch your eyes out of their sockets tonight with my own nails."

"Do it then!" the Doctor said.

"But if everything isn't permissible, I won't do it. Which will I decide?"

"I don't know."

"Decide for me, Doctor."

"That takes some reflection. Let me think about it for a week or so."

"Gladly."

We lived through a great period of suspense. Would Match scratch the Doctor's eyes out? What would the Doctor decide?

"I've decided, Monsieur Match, that you'll scratch my eyes out. But only the day I ask you to."

"Fine."

Such were our games.

When he saw her coming, dancing along the dirt path, so light among the bulldozers that roared beside her, so desirable in her yellow dress that matched the sun . . . The guys at work whistled with admiration or fell silent as she passed. Up in his crane, he knew that the nymph was dancing along to meet him and that all her beauty had been created for him, to be offered to him, to him, Eugène. I love her, the bitch. He wouldn't have been surprised if she rose from the ground and came all the way up to where he was. The bitch! The impulse that hurls you toward someone appearing at the end of the path, that's what love is, the filthy bitch!

"What did you make for me today?"

"Tuna, to begin with, and then a nice little veal stew with shallots. And there's some cheese, too."

"Sounds great! Are you leaving?"

"You want me to stand around and watch you eat?"

"Stay awhile . . ."

"I bring monsieur his hot lunch and monsieur wants me to watch and applaud each time he swallows a mouthful? That's the end!"

She slapped her thighs. Two nice loud slaps on two firm thighs. I thought of her thighs, not the slaps. Her gesture was vulgar but it excited me.

"One thing that always amazes me," Match said, "is people's familiarity with their bodies. They're always touching their breasts, their thighs, rubbing themselves . . . and when they make love they do it together!"

Match caressed his domed forehead with his long hands as if he were caressing the idea which lodged there now. Since Jesus was born of a virgin, why not me? How much I wanted to be brought into the world by a virgin! As you grow up, you learn monstrosities . . . that there had to be a man . . . and that this act has a name. I have the shame of my body and the pride of my soul. I'd never do *that*. No woman will touch me. Are you a virgin, Monsieur Match? Yes.

The steel beam, what luck! mashed him to a jelly. The legs cut off right at the top of his boots! Two boots standing there like in a shop window, but with two bloody stumps sticking out! Poor foreman, so elegant when he walked around arching his back! The likelihood of an accident was so faint. Besides, he had changed a lot lately. Often he argued with his wife when she brought him his lunch. He drank. The accident happened at three in the afternoon. They didn't question him that day. What was his behavior after the accident? He came down out of his crane . . . Quickly? Yes or no. He looked at the corpse, if you could call it a corpse. Was it true that he smiled when he saw the boots? Yes or no. He got home before seven. Jeanne was surprised. Why are you here so early? Your boyfriend's dead. Who? The foreman. Freak accident, you know? Sliced in half by the steel beams I was picking up with the crane. You killed him? Eugène, you're a murderer! Murderer, that's a word, just a word. I'm not a murderer. You swear it? I swear anything you want. Afterward, he sat down at the table and rubbed the oilcloth with the flat of his hand. This oilcloth's greasy. You should wash it with cleanser. With Bon Ami, it's great stuff. They use it at the canteen, and the dishes get done in no time. I didn't know what to say. In my case, the Doctor said, it was very different. I put both elbows on the table and I said to Jeanne: That's quite a little piece of news, isn't it? Since we have a cellar, we should use it and buy our winter coal now; it costs less in the summer. Did you ever think your boyfriend there was doomed to die in the prime of life? What did you fix for dinner? I feel like lamb chops and spinach, fresh spinach. Tomorrow the police are coming to question me. If you tell them that bastard was your lover, they'll poke their long noses into everything and try to prove it wasn't an accident. On Sunday, we'll go to the music hall and listen to that singer you like. Of course it was an accident, I'll prove it: a workman, an engineer, *anyone* knows it's dangerous to stand around under a crane picking up stuff. If I wanted to kill the foreman, if I had an idea like that, I could have waited a thousand years before he stood under my crane and another thousand before the crane was picking up beams and another thousand before the beams would fall right on him like that from such a height. A man who intends to kill doesn't wait for miracles. He buys a revolver and shoots. So there was one chance in a million that the foreman, who knew his way around construction sites, would stand under the crane; another chance in a million that no one would say watch out, it's dangerous to stand there; another chance in a million that the same day, at the very minute when he stood there that way, I'd be picking up beams; and another chance in a million that they'd fall exactly on the target. If I wanted to kill him, I wouldn't have waited for one chance out of millions and millions. I'd have made my own chance. They said a clumsy maneuver was unlikely. I said how did I know that the guy was underneath? *Did I know, yes or no?* No one's ever managed to clear that up.

Today, Eugène hasn't killed the foreman, but when he saw him dead, he thought of something. He'd let

Jeanne suspect—just to scare her—that it had been a crime. Since the guy was dead anyway, he might as well take advantage of it and brag a little about a crime, which was actually a stupid accident. Jeanne will see what I'm made of then, and she'll know that if she ever looks at another man she's condemning him to death. Eugène's idea was to dose out the confession of his "crime" so Jeanne would never be sure. . . . Did you kill him? Yes. Did you kill him? No, I'm just kidding. It was a mistake to brag, to give too many details. Because he played the murderer so much, Jeanne began believing he really was one. He was condemned for kidding her.

"Your jokes were your downfall," Match said.

"Your sense of humor," the Doctor said.

"They didn't get a murderer; they got a fibber," Alex said.

Our prison must have been located in a region with a very hot climate. As a matter of fact, we never suffered much from the cold, but the heat bothered us for months at a time. Match, who handled the news, was also assigned to keeping our calendar up to date. What day is it, Monsieur Match? What month? What season? Unfortunately, he often mixed up the years and, more frequently, the seasons or the months. For instance, the Doctor expected his star, Gethsemane, in February, though it appeared only in September. Similarly, when we were roasting in the August heat last year, Match swore it was January. All this mattered very little, except for Alex, who wasn't sure when he was supposed to fight Sugar Ray

Robinson. Match actually went so far as to maintain, one day, that the fight had already taken place.

"According to my calculations, Monsieur Alex, you've fought Robinson."

"And who won?"

"I don't know. But it's December now; and the fight was arranged for September. So it must have taken place. Try to remember."

"Monsieur Eugène, do you think the fight came off?"

"Impossible," Eugène said. "First of all, I'd remember; and second, Monsieur Match would have announced the results in the sports bulletin. Don't forget, when the world title is fought, it doesn't pass unnoticed." Match yielded to this reasoning and confessed his error. When it was hot, we all sweat a lot—except Match, who was insensitive to variations of temperature—for the sun strikes the outer wall of the cell. Eugène disappeared in endless naps and slept with his mouth open; the Doctor, his shoulders hunched, his steps dragging, walked around the cell uttering strange groans—of pleasure, it sounded like. Alex, naked to the waist, lay down on the cement floor of the cell in order to receive the sun, through the skylight, on his face and body. In the course of his peregrinations, the Doctor was obliged to step over his body. "Am I getting tan?" Alex asked. He moved a few inches at regular intervals. "Otherwise," he said, "because of the bars I'd look like a zebra." The sweat streamed from his body and formed beads at the roots of the hair on his chest. He rubbed his sides, his eyes closed, with broad caresses. "Sweat," he said, "is the best liniment." He also said: "I couldn't live without pectorals. If someone gave me a choice: a brain or an athlete, a boxer—I wouldn't take long: I'd choose to be what I am. Who sees your brain in the street? But if you're a big guy, everyone turns around when you walk by!" The Doctor kept stepping over Alex's body.

"Am I in your way, Doctor?"

"Not at all. On the contrary."

"Doctor, could you tell me, if you don't mind, when the sun moves? Otherwise I fall asleep and I'm back in the shade again."

"Of course, Monsieur Alex."

"I'm getting tan, aren't I, Doctor?"

"It's coming."

It's great. All I have to do is close my eyes and I'm back at the swimming pool with Guitare. Guitare used a depilatory. Along with knitting and wrestling, it was one of his chief occupations. He had this mad queen for a friend, a hairdresser he called Lady Mimosa; he always said Lady Mimosa was great. Just because she came to Guitare's house to pull out his hair with hot wax. "She's a real genius," Guitare used to say.

"Tomorrow, Lady Mimosa's coming. If you want to watch . . ."

The queen would arrive, fluttering as if someone had slipped itching powder down her back. "Good morning, Monsieur Guitare," she'd say, pursing up her lips and lisping. "Good morning, Monsieur Alex." "Good morning, Lady . . ." She took a striped silk blouse out of her little bag, put it on and wound a yellow turban around her head.

"Why do you get all dressed up like a Hindu, Lady Mimosa?"

"Because it's mysterious and chic, Monsieur Guitare."

"Right!"

"Did you do your military service, Lady?"

She would burst out laughing, and cross her legs like a virgin surprised in her bath.

"Yes, Monsieur Alex."

"In what?"

"You'll never guess . . . in the Chasseurs Alpins! Naturally they used to call me the Chasseur Alpine . . ."

"Alpine!" Alex roared, bursting out in a laugh that shook the building.

"Now let's see, let's see, where's our little stove, here we are, our little casserole, our little spatula . . ." Lady Mimosa said, arranging her instruments. "There we are, all ready. You know, Monsieur Guitare, I swiped some American wax for you from the salon, nothing but the best for you. Madness! Shall we do the legs first or the chest today? The legs? Fine, fine, fine! Now you just stretch out while the wax is heating up."

Next she would lay out the hot wax on Guitare's thighs, spread it with a spatula, and then pull it away quickly, the way you tear off a bandage that's stuck to a wound.

"Ouch!" Guitare shrieked. "That hurts."

"Oh, you must suffer to be beautiful."

"Handsome!" Guitare said, his voice hard.

The queen lowered her eyes.

"You'll have thighs smoother than a marble statue. A few sunbaths on top . . ."

"Ouch!" Guitare shrieked. "If you pulled it away slower . . ."

"No, then it would hurt even more and the hair wouldn't come out. There. Two more times and we'll be

222

through. How cute your apartment is, Monsieur Guitare!"

"Handsome!" Guitare said.

"Yes, handsome."

"Do you want some coffee, Lady, or tea?"

"I'd love some tea."

"Listen, Lady Mimosa, did you know that my friend Alex here once killed a man with his fists?" The hairdresser clasped his hands and emitted a little shriek:

"No!"

"Yes, he did, Lady! Isn't that the truth, Alex?"

"He's dead."

"But that's dreadful," Lady Mimosa squealed. "Was it an argument?"

"Not at all. The guy had done absolutely nothing to him!"

"Well what was it?"

"It's a riddle, Lady. When can you kill a man who has done absolutely nothing to you?"

"Never, you know that!"

"Yes you can, think! You have the right to kill him and they even pay you for it!"

"In wartime? That's it! I guessed it!" the queen said, clapping her hands.

"That's right! But that's not it. You're getting warm . . ."

"It's a game! When you're out hunting? By mistake?"

"No . . . he killed him with his fists, and he did it on purpose."

Alex was about to protest. Guitare, a finger on his lips, insisted on silence.

"I can't think any more . . ."

"Come on, Lady, make an effort . . . Look at Alex carefully. What does he look like?"

Lady Mimosa stared at Alex, then lowered her eyes.

"It begins with a *b*," Guitare said.

"A boxer! A boxer! I guessed it! My Lord, you're a boxer, Monsieur Alex?"

"I'm Alex the boxer."

"And you killed your opponent?"

"He's dead."

"Ooh! Poor boy! Goodness, what a profession! Heavens! You're going to have a skin softer than a baby's, Monsieur Guitare," Lady Mimosa said, massaging Alex's thighs with eau de Cologne before rubbing them with softening cream.

From the month of May on, we both were crazy to get suntanned, Guitare and me. Arm against arm, in the evening, we'd compare the color of our skins. You're more coppery but I'm darker.

"How do you manage not to sweat, Monsieur Match?"

"Aren't you hot?" Eugène asked.

"No."

"Strange!"

"And not cold either?"

"No."

"Strange!"

"You're like a snake," Alex said.

"Snakes get cold. I can prove it. In fairs, the boas and the pythons and all that . . . they're in heated glass cages."

"Then what's the animal that doesn't get too cold or too hot?"

"There *is* none," Match said. Me.

"Have you ever seen two snakes fight?" Match asked.

"No."

"I have. The biggest one always wins. He winds himself around the other and then their two bodies beat the ground. The big one grabs the throat of the smaller one between his jaws and strangles him. Then he swallows him, beginning with the head. It takes forever, but it's funny to see the big snake expand by exactly the diameter of the smaller one sliding down his throat. When the operation's over, he falls asleep and starts digesting."

"And where did you see that?"

"In Africa."

"You know Africa?"

"A little." Match often had surprises in store for us. Apropos of snakes he told us without a word of warning that he'd traveled in Africa.

"What's Africa like?" Alex asked.

"Hot, humid, full of mosquitoes, spiders, cockroaches, ticks, worms, caterpillars scorpions, termites."

"What about the Negroes?"

"Nice," Match said.

"It's crazy how black they are!" Alex said. Once I fought Kid Omar . . . the bout was a draw. We met in a night club after the fight. I walked in and asked if Kid Omar was there. Yes . . . I looked around . . . No one. Finally I saw a white collar in the dark and the Kid's head right above it. He was so black I couldn't see him."

The Doctor interrupted his walk; Alex turned over and lay on his stomach "to tan his back." "This heat," the Doctor said, "is hard to bear. You'd think they were roasting the prison until there's not an ounce of flesh left on our bones."

The feeling of suffocation didn't diminish after sunset; the thick walls gave off the heat accumulated during the day. In the middle of the night, Eugène wriggled feverishly on his mattress. You asleep? No. No one's asleep.

"I'm cold!" Eugène said. We covered him with our shirts and canvas trousers. Eugène was always cold. We threw a mattress over his body. He shivered.

"What's the matter with me, Doctor?"

"A high fever."

"And what is it?"

"A kind of grippe."

At dawn he was still feeling bad, but refused to go to the infirmary. He preferred to be cared for clandestinely, by us. Following the Doctor's orders, we applied leeches to him (that is: we pinched the skin on his back hard in about a dozen places); every two hours, we gave him two quinine and vitamin C tablets (bread crumbs rolled into pellets), and in the evening we applied a mustard plaster (a wad of straw wrapped in a shirt). Eugène had a good night and the next day he was back on his feet, entirely recovered thanks to the energetic care we lavished upon him. Thank you, my friends. Don't be silly, Monsieur Eugène.

The heat suddenly stopped; which reinforced the Doctor's conviction; they were roasting the prison. They intended to melt us like pieces of lard. No, Doctor, that's a ridiculous notion! Why not? Wouldn't that be the best way to get rid of us? What's happened to your prisoners, Warden? Melted! Melted, Inspector. Melted? Exactly, Inspector! If you'll come this way, I'll show you what's left of them: some teeth, bones, hair . . . Here, let's have a look, Warden. Of course! Your prisoners were very *fat* then, Warden? Very fat, Inspector. Which explains why they melted under the summer heat, Inspector, like snow in the sun.

"We should send a protest to the government," the Doctor said.

"I can't sign it," Match said. "I'm cold."

"Sign all the same!"

"Impossible, Doctor."

Today, the Doctor told about his brother's death. We were on a trip in the mountains and I pushed him. Afterward, I said he slipped. He fell into a crevasse about a hundred yards deep. Oh, my mother's tears! My mother was so beautiful, behind her veil of tears! But a lot of good it did me! She loved him even more dead than alive, that son of hers with his girl's hair and pink skin. The summer after, she had a marble cross put up at the place where the poor dear had fallen off.

"Here?"

"No, Mother, over there."

"Here?"

"Here. Here . . ."

"Did he scream as he fell?"

"Yes, Mother."

"Did he call to me?"

"No, he screamed."

She had bought a bouquet of roses and white daisies. She handed them to me.

"Here, throw it!"

"Where?"

"Into the crevasse. Where he fell."

"No."

"Come on now . . ."

"I don't want to, I don't want to."

"Why?"

"Because . . ."

I was red. I was furious. My legs were shaking and I burst into sobs. Dry sobs: without tears.

"Why don't you want to throw those flowers?"

"Because they'll scream, too!"

Stupefied, my mother stared at me as if I had been an evil magician; she snatched the bouquet out of my hands, leaned over the edge of the precipice, hesitated, then set the magical flowers at the foot of the cross with loving gentleness. A lot of good it did! The dear child's ghost obsessed my mother to the point of frenzy, and her house was transformed into a museum of sublime grief. Ever notice the obscene taste women have for death? Above all, they adore "losing" their husbands.

Three or four years ago, the Doctor told us that after his brother had been picked up by the rescue party (he died before reaching the hospital) he murmured: "He pushed me. . . ." "Don't say anything," my father told my mother, "I'll talk to him, you keep quiet." "How did the accident happen?" "I was walking behind him" "And were you far away?" my father asked me gently. "About from here to the street corner." "And he was walking along the edge of the crevasse?" "I don't know. I had my head down, I was watching my feet." "Are you sure you're not the one who slipped, and then you caught onto him, or without doing it on purpose, you pushed him when you stumbled?" I resisted the interrogation brilliantly for an hour and answered about fifty honeyed questions without contradicting myself once. I'm lucky that my eyes are so pale you can't read the truth in them. Dark, deep-set eyes like Monsieur Match has would have ruined me. At the end I cried, so as to make my father ashamed of his suspicions.

"No, he didn't push him, I'm sure of it," my father told my mother.

"Then why the accusation?"

"Don't use words like that. His terror when he realized that he was slipping must have been so immense that it distorted his senses. Sometimes when you fall you feel you've been pushed. Besides, children are like that: if they fall out of a tree, they accuse the tree; if they cut themselves, they accuse the knife. Our little boy may actually have thought his brother pushed him. But you have to put that idea out of your mind."

Whatever the case, my mother "changed" toward me. A repugnance checked her rare impulses of affection, and I caught her glancing at me when she thought I wasn't looking. One day I slipped on the waxed floor in the hall, and to keep from falling, I caught hold of a console table, dragged it down with me and broke the porcelain vase standing on it.

"I slipped, I was trying to keep from falling . . ."

I acted out the scene. My mother didn't say a word as

she swept up the fragments of the precious vase. The following autumn I had my first fit.

"And had you really pushed him, Doctor?"

"That's the strangest thing of all, Monsieur Eugène. I don't remember any more. I went back to the scene with my mother, and I hadn't pushed him: I was walking with my head down about ten yards behind him; I heard a terrible scream; I saw his body at the bottom of the crevasse. Everything was in order in my memory. But if I went back and saw the place alone? Maybe I was walking beside him, maybe a kind of empty rage burst inside my head, maybe I would slip or pretend to slip, and maybe with a nudge of my shoulder I would push my brother into the abyss. . . . Would I do it on purpose? Would the movement be involuntary? . . . I don't know. On my honor, I don't know. What do you think, Monsieur Match?"

The story reminded Match of a story that greatly impressed him once. A village poacher, married and the father of a whole tribe of children—but the children have nothing to do with the story—was involved with a young girl of the village. Or rather, he made advances to this young girl and she rejected him. One night, he and his wife (she helped him when he was poaching) went to set their traps and nets (actually they were baskets) in a deep hole where there was a lot of fish. It was a dark night. The water was cold. He pushed his wife in, and the unfortunate woman drowned. He came back to the village before midnight, was *sincerely* surprised by his wife's absence, soon grew alarmed by it, and knocked at his neighbor's door. At dawn, the whole village was aware of the fact, and soon the unhappy woman's body was found in the pond. The husband sobbed and remained prostrate for weeks. The day of the funeral, he had to be supported at the cemetery and then dragged away, so great was his grief. As a widower, he no longer made advances to the young girl and even showed a certain coldness toward her. A few months later, a boy of fifteen, one of those village half-idiots that squint a little and masturbate a lot told his father: "Papa, Joseph drowned his wife. I saw him go with her for the nets and then they went to the pond together. After, he came back alone. He said he went to walk over by Les Granges and that when he came back his wife wasn't at the house and that she had been jealous on account of Josette so she'd gone to the pond. But it's not true, Papa, he went to the pond with her and he came back alone. He didn't go to Les Granges." The father informed the police. Joseph was questioned. He denied everything. He was confronted with the boy. The latter, one finger in his nose, repeated: "You were at the pond with your wife. I saw you." "No!" "You were at the pond with the nets." Joseph grew furious, tried to strike the boy. The police held him back. Joseph got *too* angry. He confessed quite soon.

"Then you pushed her . . ."

"Yes . . . A little . . ."

"You wanted to get rid of her? To kill her?"

"No."

"You wanted to go with Josette?"

"No, she's a little bitch."

"Then why did you push her? Had you thought of it before?"

"Never."

"Well, then?"

"The idea just came to me, all of a sudden."

"The idea of killing her?"

"No, pushing her."

"But you knew she would drown."

"I just pushed her and then it happened."

"And you knew she would drown."

"No."

"But how did this idea come to you in the first place?"

"Suddenly. She was crouching at the bottom of the bank and letting down the basket. I was just above her so then I pushed her with the flat of my foot . . ."

"How?"

"Like this. Just a little."

"Had you been drinking?"

"I never drink."

"Were you angry?"

"No."

"Had you been quarreling?"

"No, we never quarreled. We got along."

"Then why did you push her?"

"She slipped. I only pushed her a little."

"But if you hadn't pushed her, would she have fallen into the pond?"

"No."

"And what did you do then? Did she scream?"

"No, she swallowed a lot of water and choked."

"And you watched?"

"Not long. I climbed up the bank after I pulled out the baskets and I left."

"Because if they'd found the baskets they would have known you had come to the pond?"

"That's right."

"You thought of that, did you?"

"I didn't think of it. I pulled up the strings and took away the baskets, that's all."

"And why were you surprised not to find her back at home? And why did you cry at the cemetery?"

"Because we got along."

"A wonderful story, isn't it, Doctor? It's a little like yours."

"With this difference, that I didn't have any half-idiot for a witness."

"You never know," Match said. "Maybe there was a motionless witness sitting on a rock, someone who saw everything. And who decided to keep quiet, who will keep quiet forever. All 'accidents' have witnesses: sometimes it's a fly, a cat, an eagle, a crow, a chamois. Me, if I killed my friend on a raft, right out in the middle of the ocean, I couldn't keep from looking behind me afterward."

"And would you be surprised to see a head disappear under the water, after shouting at you: 'Hey! Hey!' . . .?"

"Not surprised at all."

The heat was beginning again. The Doctor told us that cranial sweat burns the roots of the hair—sweat contains acid—and that we'd all grow bald if this continued. Eugène was very disturbed and suddenly started fanning himself with the square of cardboard we used for picking up crumbs. Again the Doctor asked us to sign a protest.

"I'm not sweating," Match said, "so I'm not entitled to sign." "I'm getting tan, so, honestly, I can't sign either," Alex said. Only Eugène, who was afraid of growing bald, agreed to sign the protest with the Doctor. The Doctor accepted Match's and Alex's reasons, and even believed that the signers would derive some advantage from the fact that the other two abstained. "If we all four signed, it would look like a kind of conspiracy, an organized and premeditated rebellion, almost a revolt. As a matter of fact, it's natural that out of four individuals, two should complain of their lot whereas the other two should not only accept it, but even find it a source of satisfaction. The attitude of Monsieur Match and of Monsieur Alex reinforces our protest, Monsieur Eugène. We won't look like troublemakers, just respectful complainants."

"I agree with you, Doctor," Eugène said.

"Thank you. Now we must write out the text. Let's see . . . 'We the undersigned, considering that the temperature prevailing in our cell is excessively high, are led to believe that the prison is being submitted to intensive heat. We desire to know the reasons that impel the administration to roast us. In case the heat has purely geographical reasons (prison constructed in the heart of a desert, on a volcano, etc.), we the undersigned will submit to climatic fatality. If, on the contrary, the heat is due to human action, we the undersigned respectfully request the administration to consider means of remedying it.' What do you think of that, Monsieur Eugène?"

The Doctor and Eugène had thought of everything except for the problem of paper, pen or pencil, envelope, etc. Should they ask the guard? He would never agree to becoming a messenger of subversion, an accomplice of agitators. The Doctor's fine project went up in smoke, but still he and Eugène discovered one consolation for all their pains: when the heat is too unbearable for them, they would *recite* the protest, which they learned by heart. Either they would recite it in a tragic tone—the Doctor twisting his hands, rolling his eyes, and intoning: "We the undersigned, considering that the temperature . . ." Or else they would adopt a honeyed, gentle tone—Eugène hunching his back, tears filling his eyes, he groaning and bleating: "The undersi-i-igned, considering that the tem-m-mperature . . ." Sometimes they would assume an attitude of rebellion— head high, eyes proud, they would hiss: "The undersigned! Considering that the temperature! . . ." Or even the tone of a litany, the Doctor droning out: "Theundersignedconsidering-thatthetemperatureprevailinginthecell . . ." Or in chorus. Or in alternating phrases. They would keep inventing new variations, and they forgot to sweat. Match and Alex would have liked to join in these performances, but they had to content themselves with being spectators, since they hadn't signed the protest. The Doctor and Eugène, on the other hand, abandoned themselves to it wholeheartedly, perhaps with a faint affectation of happiness which betrayed a desire to take a mild revenge on Match and Alex. Alex, moreover, was quite uninterested in these dramas performed by the Doctor and Eugène, but Match was sorry not to participate in them, and decided to renounce his spectator's role at any cost. He lay down on his mattress and remained motionless in a strange posture. That is: his hands were half-closed, as if gripping a steering wheel about a foot away from his face.

Sometimes his right hand would describe a semicircle, rejoin the left, and then resume its earlier position. After about a quarter of an hour, Eugène and the Doctor stopped protesting.

"What are you doing there, Monsieur Match?"

"I'm reading."

"You're reading?"

"Yes."

"What are you reading?"

"Poems."

"Without a book?"

"I know them by heart. When I had the book, I opened it all the same, even though I knew all the poems."

"Who are they by?"

"It's an anthology."

"Who's your favorite poet?"

"Dante. And yours, Doctor?"

"I don't much care for poetry."

"What do you read?"

"Medical works, sometimes biographies. In my work, there's not much time for reading. Besides, how can you choose, with all the things publishers flood us with? Can you rely on the critics? They have their tastes, which are not necessarily mine. Best-sellers? I mistrust mass literature."

"Well, four lines of Dante and I feel like something!"

"Ah, Monsieur Match!"

"Ah, Doctor."

"And you, Monsieur Eugène, what do you read?"

"I read ghost stories and detective stories. I think about them afterward, before I go to sleep. Or else I imagine I'm a bicycle racer and I'm winning the Milan–San Remo or the Paris–Roubaix. Since my specialty is mountains, the papers call me "the eagle of the peaks."

"Very interesting!"

"I fall asleep fighting for a lap every night. It's exciting because I wonder if I'm going to win the Tour de France. Three months ago, in spite of all my work, I only came in second. And six months ago I had to give up because of an attack of dysentery."

"You're in the Tour de France . . ."

"About every three months. But I also do a lot of track racing. I've won the Tour d'Italie, the Tour de France six times, and just about all the others except for the Tour de Lombardie. I'm also the world record-holder for speed per hour, and I've been world champion twice on cross-country. Plus a number of six-day races I enter only to make money."

"I think I'm going to get interested in bicycling myself . . ."

"It's great, Doctor. It's hard work but it offers a lot of satisfaction."

"And the ghost stories?"

"I scare myself. I walk in cemeteries dressed in a sailor-suit . . ."

"You're a kid?" Alex asked.

"I don't know. I'm not sure . . . In any case, I'm dressed in a sailor suit. It's winter; night's falling. All of a sudden I hear the gate creaking closed. Impossible to leave: the walls are too high and there's barbed wire on top of them. Poor Eugène, shut up for the night in this God damn cemetery! I light a cigarette and sit down on a grave. Some stinking ravens are perched on the crosses and stare at me with their little red eyes. It's dark, but the moon lights up the gravestones that look like blocks of snow. Midnight chimes. Now I begin to hear sobs, groans, shrieks, voices . . . I see the gravestones gently rising; boy am I scared! I huddle up in bed, I hold my breath, but at the end of the path, I see a long white form floating toward me. It vanishes, hides behind a grave, then it appears much closer, it disappears again and rises up again farther away. All of a sudden I feel it behind me, right behind me. I'd like to get up and run away, but I'm petrified. I don't even dare turn around any more. It goes on . . . and on . . ."

"And then?" Alex asked, completely white.

"I stand it as long as I can. When I can't bear it any more, I open my eyes and I look at the cell, or else I lean over and watch you sleep."

"And you've never tried to stick it right to the end, to see what it would do?"

"It would put its cold hands on me."

"And?"

"I'd rather not know."

"And the detective stories?"

"Oh, they're great. I kill everyone."

"And you, Monsieur Alex, what do you read?"

"Oh, I read *Ring, l'Équipe,* and *Le Miroir des Sports.*"

"No poetry?"

"No."

"No novels?"

"No," Alex said peevishly. "Novels are just stories!"

Today, Alex talked about Guitare without any affection at all. That guy made fun of me a lot, you know. He thought he was king. He asked Alex to make him some coffee. "What, you don't even know how to make coffee? You just take dishwater, a little sock broth, and some tobacco juice, and you mix it with tap water and let it stew. Coffee has to take its time, you know."

"Listen, you can make your own coffee, I'm not your maid."

"*Chéri,* if you don't like it you can get the hell out, you know. There's the door!" Guitare said, with a movie smile. Alex didn't move. There was something about Guitare. You got used to him, to his smile, his smell, his gestures. You felt like killing him, and you fell at his feet. Everyone around him was caught in an invisible net; indifferent, Guitare watched them struggle. Last Thursday, Monsieur Siméon whistled with admiration when he saw the black-striped green handkerchief hanging, carefully crumpled, out of Alex's breast pocket: "Hey, you imitating Guitare now?" Alex blushed. Did Monsieur Siméon notice? "Soon you'll be taking up knitting." After that, Alex watched himself. He was careful not to walk like Guitare, talk like Guitare, dress like Guitare, but it was too much for him: he was haunted. To whom could he explain why he would kill Guitare some day? Who would believe him if he told how he walked under the wrestler's windows at night to see if the lights were on? How he waited for him in the bar across the street, playing dice with the Syrian bartender. When Guitare's windows lit up, he forced himself to play three more games with the Syrian, then crossed the street and climbed the wooden stairs. "Hey, Alex!"

"Hi, I was going by and saw the light . . . Am I

bothering you?" "Not at all. Have a chair, Cinna, and sit down on the ground—the doorman at the Tropicana's always saying that. You know him? He talks to himself and calls all the guests 'Milord.' He sweeps the ground with his little cap: 'Milord Guitare will do us the honor to take a seat, Cinna, and sit down on the ground?' "

At the end, Alex stopped existing. If he went four or five days at what cost! without knocking at the wrestler's door, Guitare greeted him the same way. The immutable "Hey, Alex! . . ." He was about as important as a bowl of water. When Alex told him he felt like leaving France and having a look at South America, Guitare answered: "Good idea, you'll see some country. . . ." With Guitare, you were always caught off guard . . . If you told him about Tahiti, Italy, or Japan, he listened, then answered: "Me, I hate traveling. Only jerks travel. Buying tickets, clothes, suitcases, going to the station, getting into a flea-bitten train, sitting down next to some guy who's snoring, getting out God knows where . . . Oh no! Me, with three hundred francs I go to Japan in the movies. The other day I saw some jerk on television who climbed a mountain about as steep as that wall. I told myself: If you break your neck, I'll buy us all a drink. The jerk reached the top by driving in nails on the way up and then he saluted and waved a flag. I never saw such a dumbhead in my life! Just think, Alex: there are jerks even crazier than that, jerks who do it even without television. And not for money either! For nothing! I tell you, if they killed all the jerks there'd be just enough guys left on earth for a poker game. They ought to shoot all those guys who climb mountains, all the ones who travel or get married

. . ." "Not everyone can be a wrestler." "Alex, I'm going to explain how I look at it: I don't understand how come everyone isn't *me!*"

Alex suffered from Guitare's indifference; he flattered him by telling him about princesses, about the quality of his perfumes, and his virtuosity as a knitter. The wrestler nodded his head, for everything that Alex was saying followed as naturally as night follows day. He reigned as an absolute tyrant over a mysterious kingdom of which he was the sole emperor and the sole subject. They said about me: "He's Guitare's friend," and when I heard it I suffered, because I knew Guitare had no friend. As if, because I sit every day in the park next to the same statue to read my paper, they said that I was the statue's friend. Once, just once, he looked at me as if I was *him*. "So just like that, you pounded the Bic until he croaked? Tell about it! . . ." He listened to me very hard. It was one of the most beautiful moments in Alex's life. He would have killed a Bic every day just to see that same soft light in Guitare's eyes.

"You should have suggested the idea to him."

"It would have interested him for about a week. I know him. One day, he would have interrupted and started talking about his princesses, or the atom bomb, or his latest perfume."

"And that light in his eyes, had you ever seen it before?"

"Never."

"Then you can be happy, Monsieur Alex!"

Today, Alex killed Guitare. With Guitare's pearl-handled revolver. And with a bullet right through the heart. A real colossus, Guitare had the strength to sit down on the bed, his back against the pillows. He took

Alex's hand (Alex had fallen on his knees beside him) and squeezed it. Alex was crying. Guitare looked at him and nodded. Then he died. Why did he nod? At what?

"He understood that you'd killed him," the Doctor said.

"But I don't understand it."

"The victim always knows most. Just before dying, you're so smart it's monstrous."

"Still, I've seen dead people looking surprised."

"Jerks, as your friend Monsieur Guitare would say."

"And what was it that he understood, Doctor?"

"Monsieur Alex, you're a mysterious fellow. Why do you ask me to tell your secrets? What did you do after you closed the dead man's eyes?"

"I forget."

"No, you remember."

"Then you tell me what I did, Doctor."

"Dare me?"

"Dare you!"

"You closed his eyes and kissed them. Then you opened the bathrobe and you asked yourself how the life of this god could have escaped out of such a tiny red hole, a tiny rose tattooed on the hairless chest . . . Shall I go on?"

"Go on, Doctor."

"And you leaned over him as if you were going to smell that rose, but rested your lips on it instead. And then you slowly stood up and you looked in the mirror at your face bathed in tears and your lips red from having so tenderly embraced Monsieur Guitare, otherwise known as Death, for the first and last time. Shall I go on?"

"Yes."

"Then you camouflaged the crime as a suicide, with a

good deal of skill. No one, you were persuaded by certain voices, no one would be surprised to hear about Monsieur Guitare's suicide. He belonged—how had you understood it?—to the race of the divine who don't love life. When he shook his head, he told you: 'Yes, you understood what I wanted . . .' Since Khadi's murder, he had divined certain tendencies in you and had gradually induced you to kill him. Just think for a couple of seconds, Monsieur Alex: do you suppose that if Monsieur Guitare hadn't secretly *ordered* you to, you'd have killed him? Do you dare suggest that you didn't obey him? Be modest . . ."

"And then, Doctor?"

"Oh then, anything . . . You went back to your place, and you inflicted the proper punishment on Mademoiselle Maridge. Although she was quite used to it, your rage astonished her a little. The next day, when she learned about Monsieur Guitare's 'suicide,' she understood. You tore the paper out of her hands and for the first time she was afraid of you. She swore to herself that she'd turn you in if, some day, in order to terrify her still more, you ever confessed what you had done. Your voices warned you, and at the same moment you promised yourself to kill her. That's all. Like my story, Monsieur Alex?"

"Very much."

"Of course, nothing happened that way, did it?"

"Not one true word in it, Doctor, but it's a good story all the same."

"Now you tell the story of the two murders."

"Here's the truth: Guitare advised me to get rid of Maridge, who advised me to get rid of Guitare."

"And whom did you finally 'get rid of?' "

"No one, finally. Believe me, no one! But with things as they are today, just try and find someone who believes you if you say you haven't killed anyone. . . ."

Eugène suffered badly from the heat in the Nice–Marseilles lap. Now he was third. The next lap in the Alps would be the decisive one. We hoped he'd win the Tour. This morning, he told us things that mark professional sports in general and bicycling competitions in particular with hideous scars. The head of the Italian team offered him six million lire if he'd take third and agree to let the Italian Bolzano, present wearer of the yellow sweater, win.

"And what did you answer?"

"I refused."

"And what did he say?"

"*Bene*, that in that case it would be a struggle to the death." And that the Italians and even the Dutch would gang up against me.

"In other words, they put a price on your head," Match said.

"And why did you refuse the deal?" the Doctor asked.

"For honor's sake—because I'm French."

"I have an idea," Alex said. "Why don't we buy Robinson off, Monsieur Eugène?"

"First, because we don't have enough money; second, because you're the challenger and it's up to the champion to buy you off."

"I wouldn't let him."

"Of course not. If you win, the title's worth ten times what Robinson would offer you."

It was chiming three last night when the Doctor shook us, one after the other. Forgive me, my dear friends, but something's about to happen. You're forgiven, Doctor. Alex, naked as a worm, yawned until his jaw looked as if it was going to snap off. Match, on the other hand wrapped himself up in his blanket, blinking his eyes while curiosity swept Eugène clean of sleep. My dear friends, something very serious is about to happen. Listen . . . The Doctor pricked up an ear, one finger laid on his lips. We listened. Don't you hear anything? Nothing at all, Doctor, do you? No, I don't either. Well . . . But just now, while you were sleeping, I heard something. What? Noises. What kind of noises? Nonidentifiable. The Doctor was suffering from a singular agitation, and his upper lip was twisted in a panicked grin. Listen, listen carefully, I beg you, on my knees! He fell to his knees. Absolute silence. We all listened hard. There, did you hear? No . . . I swear that serious, crucial events are about to happen, against which we will be impotent. We'll be petals and cobwebs confronting these events. We'll be swept by a tidal wave, engulfed by an earthquake, roasted by a huge conflagration. But I don't want to die that way. Not yet. I'm not ready. I'm willing to die if I can choose the day, the hour, and the color of the sky. The Doctor stood up and, assuming a woman's voice, caressed the head of an imaginary child. Go on now, go on, jump in the water, child! No, not yet! No, later! No, not right now! In five minutes. All right. Come on now, the five minutes are over, jump in the water! . . . Another five minutes! All right, but this is the last time! There, now those five minutes are over too, this time jump in that water, right this minute. Oh no, oh no, oh no, please, it's cold, and it's so deep . . . If you don't jump in that water, you'll never learn how to swim! Oh no, please, please, please! I don't know how to swim, I don't know, I don't know, I don't, I . . . Ploof! Monsieur Alex, I don't want to die, do you understand? Yes . . . And you Monsieur Eugène? Yes . . . And you, Monsieur Match? Yes, Doctor. I don't want to die *now,* I'm not ready.

The Doctor fell on his knees a second time. I don't want to die. I want to see the white boats again, the plane trees, the circles of dancers in the market place, the little boys dashing down the street on their scooters, and the cat that jumps into the fork of the tree when the yellow dog chases him. Let me see it all again. I'll take my time, I'll sit there for hours at a time, but afterwards, I promise that I'll give myself up to you and do anything you want. Don't take me, don't take me away, first I have to put things in order here, I have to brush, clean, polish. The Doctor stood up, raised one eyebrow, and assumed a tone of command. I want someone to find me a confessor! I want someone to know that I intend to confess my sins once and for all! All! All! And in a high-pitched voice: And you'll tell the truth? He screamed. I don't want to die now, not tomorrow, not ever. Do you understand, never! I won't die! I! Won't! Die! I'll be immortal! Let them call me Himalaya, Egyptian sphinx, Pacific Ocean! If I close my eyes, I can't stand the day! If I open my eyes, I can't stand the night. Let the world be astonished to discover that my life is my power and that I intend to exert it with savagery! Excused! Vanish!

Match, Eugène, and Alex were lying stretched out on their mattresses with their hands under their heads, admiring the Doctor's performance. It is my firm intention not to die. Yes indeed, let someone else die in my place! Who? Anyone! Any innocent will do. Innocents adore dying! They throw themselves under trains, off the parapets of every bridge in the world; they leap into flames, run through deserts of snow and ice, consecrate themselves, sacrifice themselves, open their bellies, shed their blood, their guts, their brains! Let them hang some innocent, let them draw and quarter him, break him on the wheel, lynch him, burn him, drown him, strangle him, eviscerate him, eat him! Me, I know one recipe for being innocent. Would you like me to tell it, Helène? She says she'd like me to tell it, the cunning little bitch! My poor Helène, it's so simple, any ten-year-old child can manage it. Listen carefully, all you need is to be crazy. Get this, light of my life (here the Doctor inexplicably assumed a harsh lower-class voice), I tell you anyone who comes along can do it. You just need a little skill, a little know-how, a little wrap-that-up-for-me, mademoiselle, I'll stop by again one of these days a little please-keep-the-change, my friend. (Normal voice): Light of my life, madness is a gift from heaven and a little star on one's forehead. Cut out the act, you say. Stop clowning, I'm tired and I want to go to sleep. The Doctor walked toward Alex's mattress and leaned over it.

"What did you say? Do you want to sleep, Helène?"

"Yes," Alex said, assuming a whining voice, "I'm tired, my love, let me sleep, I'm tired! . . ."

"So you accuse me of putting on an act?"

Match slid over beside Alex and helped him find the right answers, which he whispered into his ear:

"Yes, my love, you're only a poor comedian without talent who trots out a whole lot of old jokes."

"Take me seriously, darling . . ."

"No. Not for a minute!"

"I'm crazy!"

"It's not true, it's not true!" Alex intoned in a monstrous little girl's voice.

"Have pity on me, my poor fool!"

"You're only a baby with a beard, a baby with a beard! . . ."

"I'll kill myself!"

"I couldn't care less."

"I'll kill you!"

"You wouldn't dare!"

"I'll kill you during one of my fits, my treasure!"

"Then you won't have killed me, it'll be as if you hadn't killed me."

"The fit will be a fake!"

"They won't believe you, they won't believe you!"

"I'll confess."

"They'll believe you still less then."

"Tell me you love me or I'll kill you, girl."

"I don't love you, I don't love you."

"Then why do you stay with me?"

"Because you're rich and I'm a whore!"

"Get ready to die, bitch!"

The Doctor ground his teeth and raised a hand clutching an invisible dagger over Alex, into whose ear Match hurriedly whispered: "Tell him that you love him, quick!"

"My love, I love you!" Alex crooned.

The Doctor caught his breath, lowered his arm.

"Oh! Now you love me, bitch?"

"Madly, my love."

"Say it again!"

"I love you madly!"

"Is it true?"

"Say *no!*" Match whispered.

"No!"

"If you love me, you're nothing but filth."

"Say that you're filth," Match whispered.

"I'm filth."

"If you love me, something will rot inside you; you'll smell bad, I'll spit on you, I'll turn away from you. Leprosy will disfigure you, the plague will swell your belly. . . . You'll be like an old paralytic whose wounds are covered with green flies."

"Tell him he talks beautifully, tell him that's what you want! . . ." Match whispered.

"That's what I want, darling. How beautifully you talk!"

The Doctor fell on his knees again.

"Don't love me, Helène. Go away . . . leave me . . ."

"I can't. I'll follow you to the end of the earth. You've left your mark on me for life."

"You talk vulgarly, my darling . . . Sleep now, close your eyes and go to sleep . . ."

"Someone find me a confessor! I don't want to die without having confessed everything! Right away! And I mean *everything!* Monsieur Match?"

"Yes, Doctor . . ."

"Be my confessor, I'm confessing!"

"I'm listening to you, my son! Will you tell me the truth?"

"What truth, my father? Now you ask for the truth?"

"Of course, my son!"

"That's asking for quite a lot! I'd even say that's going too far, Father. The truth! Won't you be satisfied with my confession?"

"No, my son, I insist on the truth!"

"And if my confessions were lies, Father? How would you know that I'm not telling you the truth?"

"The truth has an odor, my son, and my long nose makes no mistake about it!"

"But, Father, there's no need for a confession to be true, if it's *enormous.*"

"I prefer true little confessions, microscopic confessions, to big lies."

"Father, you're a very bad businessman."

"I'm in the business of souls, my son. I buy them heavy and I sell them light."

"At what price?"

"You won't know until after your confession."

"Give me an idea."

(Alex has fallen asleep and is snoring. Eugène has been dozing as he scales the Aubisque where he takes the lead again. The sports writers predict he virtually has the yellow sweater.)

"Don't insist, my son."

"Tell me at least, Father, what confessions you would like? Big ones or little ones?"

"True ones!"

"Oh! How stubborn you are, Father! Why do you love the truth so much?"

"I neither love nor hate it, my son, I wait for it."

"And what will you do with it?"

"In your name, I will offer it to God."

"And what will he do with it?"

"His intentions are impenetrable."

"And if he doesn't exist, Father?"

"If you confess, my dear son, he'll exist. Sins invent the devil, remorse and contrite confession bring God into the world. Try, make an effort!"

"All right! Father, I loathe myself, I have hair on the insides of my hands, I like the odor of the gas I emit in my bed, and I believe that I've committed a crime."

"I am listening to you, my son."

"Father, what is the truth. Is it when you say anything that comes into your head?"

"Open your heart to me and speak."

"And if I have no memory, Father? If I didn't know what I was doing?"

"You wouldn't have come to me, my son."

"I'll tell you nothing, Father. It's impossible for me to 'isolate' my sins, as they say, I think, in chemistry. Good-by, Father, bless me!"

"It is not in my power to bless your forgetting, your stubbornness, or your silence. But may God the all-powerful have mercy on you."

"Thank you, Father."

Match went back to his mattress. The Doctor's monologue:

"Father, I haven't come to you in order to open my heart to you. What I wanted, Father, was to go into a cool church while the sun was harsh outside; to walk through the silence of its vaults, for the noises of the street displease me. I wanted to sit on a cane chair and contemplate the gildings of the high altar. Sheltered from the sun and the noise, I'd have watched the candles melt, their stalagmites running down the silver chandelier; and I would have breathed the odor of incense and mold that floats in fragile layers in the depth of the chapel; I'd have stopped in front of the wooden Christ in chains that weeps tears of blood lovingly painted red by the artist; I'd have sincerely admired the choir and its Gothic stalls. Over there, a passing priest genuflects in front of the altar. The red gown of a choirboy suddenly vanishes, swallowed up by the shadow of the sacristy.

"How does it happen that even in very hot countries there are no flies in the churches? I've visited the tropics and the flies there were a plague. In the market place, when a housewife went to the butcher stall, the butcher had to take a palm leaf and drive away the flies clustered on the pieces of meat they had transformed into blocks of coal. How could you tell which were lamb, beef, or veal under the armor of flies? The butcher waved his palm leaf; the flies flew away. He quickly picked up the beef and cut off a slice before the carpet of insects fell back on it; yet even in these countries, there's not one fly in the churches! You'll say it's because there's nothing to eat there. . . .

"Father, what I wanted was to smell your bittersweet old man's breath, to sense, in the darkness, the kind gaze of your bleary eyes and to hear your quavering voice. Nothing more. Afterward, I'd gladly have told you about my sins to astonish you, but no sooner did I indicate my intention than you told me that I was talking to God himself. In that case, good night! Since my sins are only child's play and foolishness, God won't take me seriously or be at all surprised. *Amen!"*

This morning, when we woke up, the Doctor's face was lined and he had pouches striped with violet veins under his eyes. He begged our pardon for having awakened us . . . Not at all! It's nothing! Don't be silly! On the contrary! Thank you, thank you. He thought he had heard noises: the grating of a pulley, the hissing of a lighted wick, the clicking of a pair of scissors . . . and he was afraid.

"Those aren't such terrifying noises," Eugène said.

The Doctor answered: "I'm like a woman; when I begin to be afraid, I'm afraid of everything. Didn't you confess me last night, Father Match?"

"You avoided confession."

"It was your duty to insist."

"The heart of a sinner can't be forced like a strongbox. Either it opens or it doesn't."

"Monsieur Match," Alex said, "should have been a curé."

"I was," Match said.

"No!"

"No, it's a joke."

"Oh."

"Does that reassure you?"

"Listen, it's funny," Alex said, "but if you *had* been a curé I'd be scared of you. It's funny and all, but that's how it is: you'd really have put the fear of God into me."

"That's not funny at all," Match said.

* * *

As it turned out, Eugène lost the Tour de France. Against the Italo-Dutch coalition—and despite his lead—his efforts were futile. Besides, the French team, lacking discipline, expended most of its efforts seeking prizes rather than helping its leader. Resigned, Eugène had no recriminations. He told us that the public reception along the route consoled him and salved his wounded pride. At Rheims, more than a thousand young people accompanied him to his hotel and he signed autographs for an hour while still in his racing uniform. "The papers said that from the point of view of my popularity, my defeat was a great victory."

Today Alex stretched his endless arms, heaved a sigh strong enough to blow a sailboat off the ocean, and said:

"All right! It's decided! In two weeks I'm getting out of here!"

Like a spring, Match leaped up from his mattress. His eyes glowing, stammering, stretching out his skinny neck, he said:

"What? What did you say? Mo-Mo-Monsieur A-Alex? You . . ."

"I'm getting out of here! Escaping!"

"Are you crazy?"

"No, why?"

Match hopped from one foot to the other as if the cell floor were white-hot, swallowed three or four times.

"Mo-Monsieur A-Alex . . ."

"Monsieur Alex is escaping," Alex said.

"And your fi-fight with Ro-Robinson?"

"Canceled!" Alex said.

Match staggered, leaned against the wall. He let himself fall onto his mattress. Just as his legs collapsed under him, Alex's colossal laugh made him jump.

"It's a joke, Monsieur Match!" Alex said, patting him on the shoulder.

"Are you sure?"

"How could you believe anything like that?"

"What's happening?" the Doctor asked.

"Oh, is that you, Doctor? Where did you come from?"

"Oh, I was called into town," the Doctor said, turning over on his mattress where he had been lying flat on his stomach, a bolster over his head.

"A serious case? An emergency?" Match asked.

"No," the Doctor said standing up, "an autopsy. A nurse murdered by some maniac—strangled."

"Rape?"

"Not even that."

"You see some funny things in your business, don't you, Doctor?" Alex asked. "Autopsies, abortions, accidents, livers, lungs, abscesses, prostates, blood, ovaries . . ."

"Oh, you get used to it . . ." the Doctor said.

"Actually, it's like the mechanic who fixes cars, isn't it?" Alex asked.

"Yes, almost. You either fix it or you send it to the scrap heap."

"Okay, Grandpa, back to the ironworks for you," Alex said. "Go on, my darling wife, my life's companion, get scrapped. If I was a doctor like you, I'd tell every patient who came in that he was going to croak."

"In a few years, your diagnosis would be the best in the world."

"Everyone's sick, Monsieur Alex, since everyone dies."

Alex lay down on the floor, took off his shirt, and offered his torso to a ray of sunlight. "Listen, if I'm going to die I want to die tan," he said. He fell asleep and woke up two hours later. "If I die, I'll die tan," he repeated, as if he had abolished time during his nap. That was another characteristic of Alex's personality: he was completely lacking in the idea or, rather, the sense of time. For instance, he fell asleep in the middle of a conversation: "So then in the ninth round, dazed by a right hook, I catch my breath . . ." Alex died until the next morning. Rebirth and: ". . . and in the tenth round, I'm back on my feet and attacking." He said:

"A dead *white man,* if I remember, isn't so good to look at, but a dead Negro isn't so bad. How's business at the moment, Doctor?"

"Fine. People seem to be more and more fragile, more and more nervous, sicker and sicker. In the profession, we're rolling in money. How about construction, Monsieur Eugène?"

"Can't complain," Eugène said, "we're building prisons, mostly."

"Modern ones?"

"All the same model; five stories with an interior courtyard. Stone. Solid."

"And no social agitation, no strikes?"

"A few, quickly beaten down in floods of blood."

"And what about you, Monsieur Match?"

"Well . . . excuse me, but I've forgotten which profession it is that I . . ."

"Oh, it doesn't matter which," the Doctor said. "How about a book and stationery shop, would that suit you right now?"

"Yes."

"And is it going well?"

"Well . . . no. Actually, to tell the truth, no."

"The hell you say! Why?"

"First of all, because of television: people read less and less. Reading's become a very old-fashioned pleasure, and our contemporaries treat it as if it were an obscene and painful activity."

"As a matter of fact I treat a few people who still persist in reading . . ." the Doctor said.

"This year, in France," Match continued, "scarcely more than perhaps a dozen books have been published, seven of which, moreover, deal with the new prison regime. People write less and less and instead they use the telephone, the tape recorder, and so forth. With the exception of a few old monks, no one even knows how to write any more."

"And the newspapers?"

"Since they're spoken, telephoned, or recorded, that market is closed to us. Since Gutenberg, we've been living in the age of paper, but that's all over now. Logically, we should be entering the age of speech, but since men express themselves with more difficulty every day, I refuse to envisage the future."

So, for a month, we lived a *worldly* life. Eugène fell in love ten times. He grew thinner before our eyes, refused his food because he was living on "love and fresh air" and came home exhausted. He even slept out three or four times (sleeping out consists of burying oneself under the mattress, not saying good night, and appearing only the next morning, around eleven, dragging one's feet and yawning). Eugène has added to his trophies: 1) A hysterical young model who doesn't wear anything under her skirt. "I figured that out right away because she didn't want to walk over the blowhole when I took her to the amusement park." With a suggestive leer, Eugène added: "Afterward, I checked: I was right." 2) A disconsolate widow of about forty.

"And?" Alex asked.

"And, hairy legs."

"Rich?"

"What do you think I am, Monsieur Alex?"

"Excuse me, Monsieur Eugène."

Hairy legs, rather fat, and a trifle broken-winded. 3) A Swiss governess, twenty, also plump, and squeezed into a lace corset, the kind people wore "in the good old days." Soon she began crying, saying she loved Eugène and wanted to marry him. Nice. Spoke German. Drank beer at meals and stuffed herself on cheese. 4) A servant-girl raped by three soldiers when she was fourteen. Bad breath. Refused to go dancing because she was wearing a sweater and skirt. 5) A cashier in a restaurant. Between thirty and thirty-five. Dark, with the shadow of a mustache. Thick ankles. Also eager to marry. Called Eugène "my big tomcat," and asked him to purr, pressing his head against an ample bosom. 6) The wife of a druggist. Tall, nearly fifty, but dripping with furs. Offered Eugène a job as salesman in the pharmacy her husband owns. Didn't want to be separated from her dog, a black dachshund that kept jumping on the bed all the time. In the middle of the night, Eugène gave the creature a terrible whack on the hind end, sending it off whining with pain. The woman got dressed, furious, and left. Eugène didn't budge and said: "Good-by, old lady!" before the door slammed. She answered: "You brute, you cad!" Eugène, who had slept out that night, came back to us in a good mood. If she'd been younger, he'd have kept her, but secretly poisoned the dog. 7) A schoolteacher. Twenty-three. Asked Eugène if he had ever performed the sexual act on a beach in Brittany ("with pebbles," she specified) at night, in August, and in a strong wind. "No . . ." Eugène answered. Then plunged into a long daydream put to good use by Eugène. Refused to tell her name. Why do you want to know? What's the use? Stared at Eugène, holding his hands and nodding her head. Said: "You're a strong man!" 8) A "pants-finisher." Skinny. Cried. Suggested to Eugène that they "go away." "Where?" he asked. "Anywhere," she answered. Nervous. Bit Eugène's right shoulder. 9) A student. Introduced Eugène to her friends who giggled. Nearsighted and not very clean. Refused to come out of the bathroom. Swore she wanted to go home. When slapped, threatened to throw herself out the window and wake up the whole building. Promised Eugène she'd do it next time. Threatened him, armed with a fingernail file. Cried on Eugène's shoulder, who consoled her while undressing her. 10) Another servant-girl. Brought Eugène three cigars stolen from her employer. Told him: "You don't love me, I know it. What you want is to have a good time." "No . . ." Eugène answered. "I thought you weren't like all the rest," she said.

Eugène confessed that this life was exhausting him and cursed the demon of lust that impelled him toward new adventures.

As for Alex, he took a rest cure to relax his nerves before his fight with Robinson. Twelve hours of sleep. Foot-work. Rope-jumping. A few rounds with sparring part-ners. Lunch. Walk. Nap. Volleyball. Dinner. A game of cards or dominoes. Then bed.

"Well, Monsieur Alex?"

"There's nothing to tell. A boxer's life is like a monk's!"

"But where *is* this farm you've gone to? What's it like?"

"It's a country house a rich businessman lent me. In front is a garden, behind is a lawn with a tennis court and a volleyball court, too, swimming pool and stables. The ring is set up near the lawn, on the tennis-court side. Ab-solutely quiet," Alex said, jerking his head from left to right and from right to left (apparently he was watching his host and his host's daughter play tennis).

Sullen, frowning, Match was gambling away his tiny salary as the head of a tourist office (he gave up the book and stationery shop) in illegal casinos. Sometimes he came back with his pockets full of bills, sometimes they were completely empty. He borrowed money from his father, sold his dead mother's jewelry. He talked of com-mitting suicide, but two hours later he was dealt "a hand with ten trumps," recouped his losses and won a fortune. He suggested that the Doctor accompany him once, just once, to one of the sessions. The Doctor refused and ob-served that gamblers, like drug addicts, like to make disciples. When you live in hell, you want it to be in-habited. The more damned souls there are, the less you're guilty, etc. Nonetheless the Doctor yielded and spent a whole afternoon beside Match in a corner of the cell watching the agitation that prevailed around the bac-carat table. Match commented on the hand, watched the banker, and asked the croupier to place his bets. This afternoon, he lost everything, and the Doctor felt it was necessary to chide him when they left the table. He took his arm as they walked up and down the cell. They came back from the table. Listening to the Doctor's sermon, Match assumed the expression of a schoolboy caught cheating. "I know . . . you're right, Doctor; but it's as if someone took me by the shoulders and pushed me inside, where the gambling is. I'm sucked in." "Now, now, a little will power, be reasonable, be strong . . . Gambling spoils your sleep and your appetite, it's ruining your complexion, your eyes are sinking into your head, your hands are trembling. You're no longer a man, you're a limp rag. Haven't you noticed how the deference the croupiers and waiters show you is tinged with scorn? How close this cottony politeness is to insolence?" "I don't much care about scorn, Doctor, I'm used to it. Some day, I'll break the bank and ruin them all, I'll be covered with gold and measureless pride. They'll crawl behind me as I drop my tips; I'll even forget my bets on the table. I'll lose with a smile and my colossal gains will leave me unmoved. I'll have my chair, my whims, my superstitions of a *ground seigneur*. Everything will bow before me; people will stand aside when I walk by; the lackeys will prostrate themselves. Doctor, *I will rule!* I'll be mad, but they'll be the servants of my madness . . . Besides, what else is there to do in life except to gamble?" "Now calm yourself, Monsieur Match . . . What is there to do in life? Why, there are all too many choices. Why don't you get married? Because women only like men who amuse them, who are handsome or who make a fuss over them. It's true . . . Amuse women! How? Well, be witty, entertaining, tell stories . . . Talk about clothes

. . . Homosexualize your gestures, your apparel, your remarks. . . Stop looking so starved when you're with pretty women—they hate giving charity to the poor, they're frightened if you throw yourself on their mercy. Dampen the fire in your eyes, be casual, give little presents. Beyond your strength? Then be a professional man, work. Take a job in the post office, open a shop, sell hats, shaving cream, brooms, embrace the career of arms, hire yourself out as a museum guard, a juggler, a steward on a boat, a ski teacher. What a funny look you just gave me, Monsieur Match! Do you doubt my friendship? I can't encourage you enough in your love of gambling. Gamble! Day and night! Give yourself up to this passion body and soul. Ignore the prudent and the wise, who will never know what joys you experience when the cards are turned over, what effluvia rises from the green table to your trembling hands. Gamble! Live! Why not? In the name of whom and what? Man lays the bets, but God deals out the cards. Have you noticed how much the gesture of the croupier gathering in bets with big sweeps of his rake . . ."

"Oh, Doctor! It's the fiercest gesture in the world, isn't it?"

". . . how that gesture, I was saying, is stamped with a nobility and a solemnity that are actually divine? As beautiful as a cataclysm, as calm as a deadly weapon? Didn't you know that in the Middle Ages the croupiers were sometimes disguised as angels, in white masks and fitted out with big wings on their backs, or else wearing a red hood with two holes for their eyes? Monsieur Match, in you I salute an inveterate gambler, and I'm proud and honored to shake your hand."

"Thank you, Doctor, thank you! Thank you for those remarks dictated by friendship."

As for the Doctor, he spent his whole time this month presiding over medical conventions, making speeches to the Academy of Medicine, and quarreling with Helène. She'll drive me crazy. Our scenes increase in violence every day. She says anything that comes into her head to provoke me, forbids me to eat onions, accuses me of driving her to suicide. Apropos of onions, she's called me a sadist. I watched her rage swell up like a child's balloon . . . She also called me a monster because I refused to give her drugs. I threatened her with a fit, and she answered that I could croak as far as she was concerned, that she'd throw a sheet over my body, not out of charity but so as not to see my convulsed face, my gray tongue lolling between my lips, and my eyes bulging out of their sockets. I don't want to see the demon hyenas fling themselves on you, tearing at your carrion soul. You're a pig, a bastard, a failure, a madman, a liar . . . Quoting Shakespeare, I answered that the innocent flower grows under the thistle, and that I hid my virtues under my vices like gardeners who cover the most delicate roots with compost. This display of culture redoubled her rage. Oh, if only you'd die! If I could only get rid of you!

"All you have to do is open the door . . ."

"I won't go, you'd like that too much."

"In that case, stay then. But shut up! I hate scandal. I'm known in the building as an honest doctor, my ways are calm and my habits are regular. What will people think if they hear your crazy screaming?"

"I'm going crazy, I'm dying and all Monsieur cares about is his reputation."

"Until my dying day, my dear, I'll sacrifice everything to my reputation. It's a principle. You know that what my concierge thinks *of me* is of crucial importance *for me*. In fact, you can't imagine how much, my dear."

She sat down, resting her arms on those of the chair. She stared at me, calm now. She said: "Answer me honestly. If I was in danger of death and you could save me only at the cost of a scandal, what would you do?"

"I'd let you die. I'd be very unhappy, but I'd let you die."

"Why are you like that?"

"Because I'm dying all the time and I don't help my-self."

Alex said that he understood this perfectly. He said that if he caught syphilis, he'd rather take care of it himself than go to a doctor. He said that animals hide when they're sick. He said that to ring a doctor's bell is to lack self-respect.

It didn't matter to him. He was a rock. Who mentioned love? What was this woman to him? He closed his eyes, opened them, and she was a stranger. He has always had this strange faculty of making the world around him *alien* with a wink of his eye. At will. This was love to me, but all I had to do was close my eyes and when I opened them, this same thing had changed to hate. I loved, only to turn my love to hate—without cause. If I cultivated purity, it was so I could corrupt it. I close my living eyes on my joys and my loves . . . but look! . . . my eyelids rise on the dead white eyes of a statue. I fall asleep flesh. I wake up marble. At will, this world means love to me (or this woman; and I fall on my knees and embrace her legs, sobbing); or indifference (and I stand up, my eyes dry, dusting off my trousers).

"Monsieur Eugène?"

"Doctor?"

"You're very dear to me, and I love you with all my heart and soul. Do you think I'm joking or making fun of you?"

"No, Doctor."

"Exactly. Note! I close my eyes for two seconds; now I open them, and you're nothing to me. It would be an exaggeration to say that I don't love you anymore. No. You simply don't matter to me. That's my force, my love, I can kill you at will. To be quite accurate, I'm a child. The kind of child who adores his toy but immediately gets tired of it. Covers it with caresses and then all of a sudden breaks it and turns away. In the same way, sometimes, *the world no longer amuses me*. Helène, tell me I'm not bad—but then comes a click, a gear that slips, and you no longer amuse me."

Even then (how long ago it was!) my "absences" widened my mother's eyes. She saw my blank statue's stare resting on everything before I died of rage and madness because nothing amused me. "Where are you?" she shrieked. "Do you hear me?" She called me by my name, as though to hold me back from the edge of the abyss. "Speak to me! My child, my child!" But I was sliding away, her face fell into dust, she faded away, and my plaster eyes stared at this infinite flight of objects and faces. . . . Bubbles of saliva broke at the corners of my lips, my hands crawled toward my thighs, and, as if someone had pierced my belly with fire, suddenly I . . ."

The Doctor brought his face close to Eugène's:

"But I love you, Helène. What will happen to you? Will

you remember one day that I told you I loved you? As the lips of the judge form his sentence, mine formed the words, 'I love you,' once. But once is enough, if you remember. If, out of them *all,* you sift out these words, you'll be loved for eternity, and my hatred will break its sword against this shield. But did I say these words to you? Did you hear them?" (The Doctor's voice was harsh and vulgar here:) "Ho, ho! It's not the same thing, is it? You can't kid me, you bitch! Maybe you heard them, but I didn't say them. You're hearing things. I may be crazy but I'm not that crazy; absent-minded but not that absent-minded; stunned but still conscious!" (Turning toward Match and Alex): "You hear what she says? What she dares to say? That I swore I loved her! Get that! Listen, if those words ever came out of my mouth I'd have to be dead drunk. Dear friend, are you going to start building your lunatic sand castles again? No . . . Put these remarks down to drunkenness and my overheated blood. Forget them. And then the bitch refuses and declares her intention to 'take me literally'? To take a drunk literally? My dear, you don't have a sense of honor, your heart's barren of all pity. I should have been careful about that! I knew your heart—that rusty old safe with a creaking door . . . you'd no sooner opened that door a little, when right away you stuck in my 'confession'; but listen, my love . . . You are listening? A rat! A rat with tiny cruel eyes and a scaly tail taking advantage of this moment to slip into the safe, and you've locked it inside! You're caught now! Because the rat will eat up your pretty bird; because if you open the door he'll run away, of course, nasty rat, but the bird will take advantage of that same moment to fly away, and once again your safe will echo, empty and melancholy. I wouldn't like to be in your thieving skin. What? That stubborn mule screams she doesn't care, that she'll keep the rat *and* the bird, they'll have to get along as best they can, she says, stamping her foot. Let them eat each other if they want to!" (The Doctor siezed Eugène by the collar): "Shut up, you fool, shut up or I'll . . . You're taking advantage of my patience. You're manipulating me like a mechanical car which a child turns over to see how it works underneath! You've taken advantage of my weakness or of my old, deaf, and half-blind horse's sleep. You've broken into me like a burglar. But I'll get you out of my body; don't forget, I'm a doctor! I'll take a purge, I'll vomit, I'll clear my blood, I'll cleanse my liver with ultrasecret mineral waters. I'll give myself up to the joys of mountain climbing! What? What did I say? That I'll give myself up to the joys of mountain climbing? Fine! And I repeat it without any kind of shame: I'll crawl around on inaccessible peaks, and there I'll breathe an air so pure that it'll cleanse my lungs of all the dust your breath has blown in my face. Purity, that's what I need. I'm not pregnant with your love. No one has any right to doubt my virginity! You dropped your three words into me, but I'm going to force you to take them back. By crawling up my back and laboring my sides with spurs until I bray. Gentlemen, God is my witness that I asked nothing of her. Attached to my tether, I was calmly cropping the grass of a lonely meadow, waiting for the blessed day when my masters would send me to the slaughter-house. I was dreaming, sleeping. The tether measured off the earth for me, and it was with a little less vivacity every day that I drove away the flies by sweeping my back with indolent flicks of my tail. Actually, I'm not good for anything any more, and I think that my masters have forgotten me in this naked meadow. It is to this indifference that I owe my ability to stay alive and contemplate the evening sun setting over the sea. I'm prudent, I even avoid whinnying so as not to attract anyone's attention, and I let the children torture me without kicking them. Where, moreover, would I have found the strength to kick? I was only a very old, calm, gentle donkey, a dreaming donkey that had been badly beaten once in the old days, to make him walk faster. Now they leave me in peace. Why? Either out of forgetfulness, or so I can serve as a scapegoat for the children. When they torture the donkey, they don't do anything else.

"Accustomed to suffering as I was, their knife cuts were caresses to me. All in all, I was happy. Scribe, take note, if you please, that I was happy and asked no one for anything, not even a succulent thistle. Everyone knows that a happy creature deserves infinite respect. In ancient Egypt and in Mesopotamia they shut up happy citizens in cages, and it was forbidden to touch them, by order of the civil and military authorities. People came to visit them on Sundays and offered them peanuts, biscuits, cookies, chopped meat; and the mystery of their wisdom and of their life was admired and abundantly discussed in the schools and academies. Since . . . In short, I was living my crystal happiness, scribe, when this lady, stark naked, suddenly jumped on my back and by spurring me on and yanking at my mouth, managed to make me whinny aloud. It's your job, judges, to condemn her methods! I refuse to bray one more word in my defense. I sit on my hind quarters and lay back my ears.

"Hélène, between us, just between us, are you so proud

of your behavior? Do you dare claim I didn't warn you I might say anything at certain moments? With the stubborness of a mule and the petty Machiavellianism of a weasel, you managed to get close to me, bind me, and plunge me into a basin of glue. But I'll clean myself off, I tell you," (the Doctor made a gesture of scratching his body until it bled, scraping the skin with his nails), "I'll tear you away and you'll tremble before my new skin. Whoever saw such a thing?" (The Doctor shook Eugène more and more violently.) "You can't even say 'I love you' to someone in this country without his believing you, and, worse still, without his loving you?" (Now in the tone of the political tribunal): "Can one no longer speak merely for the pleasure of speaking? Can one no longer express one's thoughts without *thinking* them, and one's sentiments without *feeling* them? Then what have we here—a dictatorship, a tyranny, the Middle Ages, prehistoric savagery? Does it mean that if one said one would prefer to be cut to pieces rather than eat frogs, does one get cut to pieces? Is there no way of *talking* in this country?"

The Doctor vociferated at the top of his lungs, shook Eugène like a plum tree, and squeezed his neck so tight while twisting his shirt collar that our poor friend's face grew red, then purple. Luckily, our guard, alerted by the Doctor's braying, opened the door, dashed into the cell, and tore Eugène out of his executioner's hand.

"Feeling better?" he asked.

Eugène, who recovered his natural color, the Doctor, Match, and Alex gave the guard a stupefied stare. The guard turned red, blushed and backed out, swearing under his breath. It was news time. Match turned his nose to the wall and recited the bulletins.

"During an international conference held in Geneva, in which every world leader participated except for the Danish Prime Minister, it was unanimously decided to abolish freedom of the press" ("Bravo!" Eugène said) "in their respective nations. Because of this decision, the arrival of journalists and writers of all nationalities is reported in Copenhagen. President Mao Tse-Tung, who participated in this meeting, was hanged in the courtyard of a Tokyo barracks upon his return to the Far East. His death was either a crime of passion or a political execution. The celebrated ethnologist Heinsenbeck, political commentator of The New York *Times,* believes the act to have been a ritual murder." ("The less Chinamen there are, the better it is," Alex said.) "In Berlin, Dr. Strumpf, Minister of National Education, has declared there is no further question, for the moment, of raising the price of bread in occupied territories. When asked whether the massacres of the Jews will continue during the next twenty years, Dr. Strumpf answered that, to his knowledge, the cost of bread would not rise, under the worst of conditions, more than two pfennigs a kilo. In France, attacks on law and order increased throughout the nation. The highest percentages were reached during the course of the past week in Alsace, Le Vendée, Poitou, and the north of Les Cévennes. In central France, a procession of several thousand individuals, in a state of high sexual excitement and entirely naked, was dispersed as it was preparing to march on Cahors. Horace Lefébure, the coopersmith condemned to death for insulting the mayor of his village, was decapitated this morning at dawn. Before dying, he declared that he regretted nothing, and that only his lack of culture had kept him from making even more insulting remarks. The King and Queen of England have perished in a railroad accident. Along with the sovereigns, thirty-seven Englishmen met their death in the catastrophe. A certain number of particularly prolific women—the government has refused to give precise figures—have taken up arms in Mexico and Italy. Scientists at the University of Houston, Texas, have managed to graft the heads of foxes onto human bodies." ("Interesting . . ." the Doctor said).

"Following the successful experiment performed last spring in Switzerland, during the course of which the heads of lambs were grafted onto twenty-four individuals, the success of the American scientists redounds to the credit of science. Such experiments, according to Sir Peter O'Reilly, British Health Minister, will soon be widespread, and the grafting of animal heads onto human bodies can be effected on a wide scale in the months to come. Sporting news: new world records were broken yesterday at Marrakesh. The Tour de France was won by the Italian, Bolzano. The French champion, Eugène, came in third. Last minute news: Paris reports that 842,-000 individuals of both sexes were arrested during the course of the past week. Ladies and gentlemen, this ends our latest bulletins."

"So there's nothing new," Alex said.

Eugène, Match, and the Doctor answered in chorus: "Nothing new!"

"All right, kid, let's get with it," Eugène said, turning to Alex. "Tomorrow we start intensive training."

* * *

Eugène's negotiations with Sugar Ray Robinson, requiring many phone calls between New York and Paris, have finally settled a date which was to be kept secret for the moment. Judging by Alex's radiant face, the clauses of the contract must have been advantageous to him, and it is with great intensity that Eugène continued training his candidate. Every morning, Alex went through exercises that would flatten a colossus. After the training session came autocriticism and criticism sessions—one of the most original points of the method Eugène has perfected.

"Autocriticism, kid. I'm listening!"

Alex didn't conceal the pleasure he took in autocriticism. Moreover, the word "autocriticism" delighted him. This marriage of a noble word—*criticism*—and of another word which he believed of banal origin—*auto,* i.e., "car"—enchanted him. How can a boxer who indulges in autocriticism fail to be a future conqueror?

"Shall I autocriticize, Monsieur Eugène?"

"Go to it, kid."

Alex swallowed, crossed his arms:

"Well then. I'm still a little weak with my left. My right jabs in the third round seemed a little vague and didn't rattle my sparring-partner enough. And I think I got a little nervous and let down my guard for a while there, probably because I was distracted. With Robinson, that could have cost me the fight. My footwork's a little stiff. In the fifth round, after my series of hooks, I was off balance and a good uppercut might have finished me off."

"Very good," Eugène said. "And then?"

"I uncovered my liver three or four times. Unless he's blind in one eye and squints with the other, Robinson could have cut me in half. That's all. I'm through."

"All right, that's not bad."

"Did I make any other mistakes, Monsieur Eugène?"

"Your hooks are still too wide. You have to get in harder and sharper. And I don't like that chin up there like Mussolini. If Robinson catches you like that he'll knock your head off. I want to see your chin down like this, get it? Like this! Your side dodges are too wide, you look like a Negro dancing the mambo. I want quick dodges, and not all those scared contortions. Aside from that, your breathing's all right. . . . We still have a lot of work to do, kid!"

"Yes, Monsieur Eugène, but I can tell it's coming!"

Thumbs in his suspenders (that is, under his arms), a cigar (a straw) in his mouth, belly out, Eugène said:

"Listen, kid, I don't want to be hard on you. You have some bad faults, but good qualities, too. If you listen to me, if you're serious, if you remember everything I tell you, and if you do it, you'll get to be champ. As sure as my name's Eugène! I promise you. Of course, if you run around from one bar to the other, if you start drinking, and if you . . . etcetera . . . then I can't answer for anything. But if you listen to me and get what I tell you through your head, you'll be the champ."

"I'll listen to you, Monsieur Eugène!"

Today, Match said (but no one was listening to him) that his mother came and testified in his favor at his trial.

She declared that her son couldn't be a murderer. Madame, we respect your grief and we understand your affection, but the charges against your son and the proof . . . "Oh, the proof, Your Honor! You can prove anything! It's what you suffer that counts! I'm sure that my son loves me and that he's innocent."

"Where's my mother?" Match screamed.

"Here I am, my son," the Doctor said.

"Where's the Judge?"

"Here I am, Monsieur Match," Match said, continuing. "Madame, you believe your son is innocent of the murder of your husband because he loves you?"

"Yes, Your Honor," the Doctor answered. "When a son loves his mother, he's innocent of everything."

Eugène and Alex burst out laughing. Match thundered: "If the public continues to create disturbances, I shall have the courtroom cleared. You were saying, madame, that it's what one suffers that counts."

"Yes, Your Honor."

"Well, it seems your son suffered scarcely any affection for your husband."

"It was his way of loving him," the Doctor said.

"By showing him hatred?"

"It wasn't hatred."

"Ah! And what was it then?"

"I think they didn't understand each other, Your Honor."

"This 'lack of understanding' went pretty far . . . Defendant, can you tell us your feelings with regard to your stepfather? Defendant! Think of that," Match said, "he's disappeared! Defendant Match, I order you to reappear!

Oh, well, never mind, we'll go on without him . . . According to you, madame, how did your husband . . . die?"

"On his daily walk, a flower pot fell on his head from a fifth-floor window sill. He was a strong man, at the time he noticed nothing. Back at the house, he began to suffer from violent headaches, and, as a matter of fact, strong as he was, his skull was cracked. But he went to meditate in his private chapel . . ."

"Your husband possessed a private chapel?"

"Yes, Your Honor, he was a Spanish grandee."

"Go on . . ."

"So he went to meditate, took some aspirin and his headaches improved. He even ate some lemon sole, and a veal stew with carrots and fresh peas, with a good appetite. The veal stew, once the fat was removed, was his favorite dish and . . ."

"The culinary tastes of your husband are not of a nature to enlighten the Court," Match said.

"Yes they are," the Doctor said. "You must believe a wife and mother. In a case of this kind, Your Honor, *everything's* important."

"If that is so, madame, we'll hear you out."

"My husband was very fond of cannelloni, hamburgers à la Grecque—that is, broiled on a bed of laurel leaves with olive oil—and chicken with garlic; but, by far, his favorite dish was veal stew, once the fat was taken out—with carrots and fresh peas. He hated canned things. One day . . ."

"Madame, be brief!"

"Your Honor, *everything's* important!"

"All right!"

"One day, not having any fresh peas, I surreptitiously bought a can. Extra fancy! He noticed with the first mouthful, and threw the plate at my head. You can still see the scars on my face."

"They're not apparent."

"Perhaps, but I suffer from them, nonetheless."

"Was your husband so violent?"

"Your Honor, violent is the word! Now, my son detested veal stew. That night he declared: 'Damn it! Stew again!' At these words, my husband became agitated, for he believed that he was hated by anyone who didn't like lamb stew . . ."

"Veal stew, madame!"

"Sorry, Your Honor, I meant veal."

"Hey, hey! . . . Are you so sure? You're getting mixed up . . ."

"No I'm not."

"All right!"

"He grew agitated and began to insult my son. All of a sudden his headaches returned with redoubled intensity, for his skull was actually cracked. From there to believing that he was suffering on my son's account was only a step. He grew more and more agitated, and felt still worse . . . His anger fed his pain which fed his anger which etcetera, etcetera. Until the final attack. A network of tiny veins exploded in his cracked skull, and he departed this life during the weeks that followed."

"Your son never struck his stepfather?"

"Never, Your Honor. My son is a very gentle person."

"Gentle people, madame, sometimes have fits of rage

and violence . . . A single fit is enough to . . ."

"My little boy would never have *a single* fit of violence. He'll be gentle from the cradle to the grave."

"Did he never have tantrums as a child?"

"Never."

"Didn't he angrily refuse to go to church, to talk to a priest, to continue to carry out his religious duties?"

"Never, Your Honor."

"I have his testimony under my very eyes, and he admits just the contrary, madame."

"He's lied to you."

"Is he a liar?"

"Like all children; but you can believe his mother."

"Down to facts," Match said, leafing through an enormous and invisible dossier with a thumb moistened with saliva. "Down to facts, madame. At the time of these unfortunate events, were you not already . . . dead?"

"Yes, of course, Your Honor," the Doctor said.

"And in spite of that you came here to testify in your son's favor?"

"A mother never dies in the heart of her child!"

"May I ask how you happened to die?"

"Of sunstroke, Your Honor!"

"Your son didn't happen to . . . let's say . . . keep you in the sun a little bit? There have been rumors . . ."

"Lies."

"You may step down, madame."

"What are you going to do to my son?"

"You may rely upon our justice, madame."

"Thank you, Your Honor," the Doctor said, walking over to his mattress and burying his head under it.

"The session is suspended *sine die*," Match said, taking

off an invisible judge's cap. "It will resume at our discretion."

Wedged under his mattress, the Doctor groaned.

"Listen, listen, I'm going to tell you something. Come over here!"

Alex, Match, and Eugène leaned over until their ears were touching the mattress.

"Are you there?"

"Yes," the three answered.

"The real crime is to die alone. Did you hear me?"

"Yes, yes . . ." the three answered.

Our guard, during the last few days, has been rubbing his hands and winking after filling our pans. This morning, he decided to talk.

"Do you want me to tell you some news, some big news?"

"Very big?"

"Enormous!"

"Really enormous!"

"Colossal!"

"Excuse me," the Doctor said, "colossal in your eyes, monsieur, or colossal in the absolute sense?"

The guard frowned and sniffed. In the absolute sense? What sense is that? He slammed the door.

"You've made him angry, Doctor. He's a sensitive man."

"We can't be too careful. He comes in with his face all lit up and says: 'Do you want me to tell you some colossal news?' But what's to prove that this news is really colossal? Are we going to rely on this peasant?"

"We could take the risk," Eugène said.

"Let's vote," the Doctor said.

"Who's in favor? One, two, three. Who's opposed? (He raises his arm.) Three *for,* one *against.* Consequently, we agree to learn the news."

When the evening meal was distributed, the guard said: "All right, shall I tell you the news?"

"It's understood that it's extraordinary, isn't it?" the Doctor asked, filled with suspicion.

"Yes!" the guard said.

"And that it will . . ."

"Yes, that it will!" the guard interrupted.

"All right, on with it! We're listening!"

"Tomorrow," the guard said, licking his chops. "Tomorrow morning." The guard closed his mouth.

"He's playing hard to get," Alex said.

"Let him get on with it," Match said.

That evening: "This time, I'm going to tell you. You ready?"

"Yes."

"Sit down on your mattresses. Ready?"

"Yes."

"All right, boys, you may be having a companion . . . A friend . . . they're talking about some guy they're going to put in your cell! Yes! Instead of four, there may soon be five in this little nest of yours! Good night and sleep tight!"

Silence in the cell. A long, long silence. Broken by the Doctor who declared in a solemn voice:

"Gentlemen, I propose—so important is this news—

that we do not discuss it immediately after having received the shock. I propose that we meditate upon it during the course of the night, and that tomorrow morning each of us expresses his opinion and sentiments."

"Agreed!" Match, Alex, and Eugène answered.

No one has been able to sleep. Everyone was listening to the rustling of the other three mattresses. Sighs. Throats being cleared. All those night sounds that haunt the beds of couples who have quarreled and can't sleep. Anguish beat the walls of the cell with its damp bat wings. Alex turned over, turned back, sighed, belched, and emitted a series of noises that were so many appeals, so many timid attempts to provoke a nocturnal argument, but no one yielded to such incitements, and anguish changed from a bat to a toad. Crouching on the floor of the cell, it swelled up and fed on our silence and our sweat. It grew so huge that it left us scarcely any room at all. It crushed our bodies against the wall and the contact of its cold and pustular skin dried our throats. The Doctor's tongue was stuck to his palate; Alex snapped his teeth like a dog biting his fur to exterminate fleas; Eugène, as he always did when he was afraid, protected his member with both hands; Match scratched his chest. The air grew thicker. We were going to die of asphyxia, but the sun rose, seeped into the cell, pierced the toad with a lance thrust, and now we were standing, our faces livid, gray circles under our eyes. Breakfast (black bread dipped in lukewarm black water) was eaten in silence. Afterward, Alex leaped up spiritlessly, inhaled and exhaled, collapsed on his mattress; Match cupped his beautiful hands over his forehead. After reciting the news bulletins in a sepulchral voice, he lowered his head and no longer moved. The Doctor was thinking.

We were sad. Worse; in despair. We had been so happy! Why, O Lord, why must earthly happiness be more fragile than the gut of a fish line, for perch, shaken by a swordfish? Why does the furious cyclone fall upon the happy isles, tearing away the palm fronds and strewing the yellow beaches with black coconuts? Why is the gentle poodle suddenly seized with madness? Why does the flower lose its perfume and the mother her child? Why does the satyr rape the innocent virgin who then, red with blood and shame, hurls herself from the top of the cliff? Why did Helène smoke so clumsily, wetting her cigarettes with her lips, which irritated the Doctor to the point of madness.

Here, within our four walls, we had defied (what?) and introduced order! Without order, no peace! No motionless palm trees, no fruit hanging from the branches, no wake left by the boat disappearing on the horizon! We were four model boys, four good citizens who picked no quarrels and did nothing—neither good nor evil. The trouble in this world is that all our actions, all our words are rope dancers; we've discovered the solid bridge that crosses the river. Lord, why have you undermined it? We were so happy! Time didn't pass. It undulated in its place, like the wave tamed by your hand, Lord, and we were corks, borne on by the immense flood. We were riveted one to the other like the four walls of our cell—four men, four walls—and the most perfidious of drafts broke its serpent head against this barrier. Our happiness offended no one. We didn't show it to the world at large.

We hid it. We wrapped it in shadows within these four walls, and we warmed it with felt slippers. Everything was gathered together in these walls, everything was sought for, everything was found. Glory! Everything was disputed and everything was concluded! The harvest was exactly in proportion to the sowing, our water supply sufficed our deserts, we had enough words, enough eyes (four pairs), enough anxious flesh on our backs. We attained the unaccustomed space of our prison and the worm on Alex's forehead found it could lodge here, and the Doctor could have his fits here; and Eugène's beautiful eyes could search the darkness here, and Match's admirable hands could float here like lilies.

"All in all," Match, Eugène, the Doctor, and Alex concluded in chorus, "it was happiness!"

"Let us repeat in chorus once again: 'it was happiness!' "

"Gentlemen," Match said, "the discussion is open. I'd like to emphasize, in the first place, that all is perhaps not lost. First, because the stranger might not come, second, because . . ."

"Because . . ."

"Well . . . Because we're going to entertain and discuss measures which . . ."

"That's right," the Doctor said. "But we *should* discuss them in the likelihood of his arrival."

"Agreed!"

"If he comes, Monsieur Eugène, what do you suggest?"

"The question is superfluous: kill him."

"You, Monsieur Alex?"

"I agree with Monsieur Eugène!"

"You," (Match said, asking himself the question) "Monsieur Match? Persecute him! Make him a slave! And you, Doctor?"

"Drive him crazy! Patiently strip his reason from him!"

"To sum up," Match said, "we find ourselves facing three propositions: that of Monsieur Alex and Monsieur Eugène, murder; that of Monsieur Match, slavery; that of the Doctor, madness. Let us consider the advantages and disadvantages of each."

If we killed him, we wouldn't hear another thing about him and we wouldn't have to endure the sight of him, to breathe his jackal's breath, to hear his pimp's voice. He'd steal neither our room nor our air nor (Alex said) my sin from us. He wouldn't have his share of our memories. He wouldn't smell the mud in our nostrils. He wouldn't be telling us about his revolting and filthy life. We wouldn't have the nastiness of having a human being under our noses!

"If we persecuted him," Match said, "we could experiment with subtle tortures. We'd learn a lot."

"About what?"

"Ourselves."

"We have nothing to learn," the Doctor said. "That's not our purpose. On the contrary. We know everything."

"He'd shine our shoes, licking them on all fours," Match said.

"Bah!" Eugène said.

"He'd get them dirty!" Alex said.

"We could mutilate him, file down his teeth, cut off his ears."

"Bah!" the Doctor said.

"We could beat the soles of his feet until they bled, we could piss in his mouth."

The Doctor shrugged.

"We could . . . eat him!" Match said, at a loss for arguments. "One piece a day!"

"Bah!" Alex said.

"I withdraw my proposition," Match said. "It's your turn, Doctor!"

"Let's drive him crazy!"

"How!"

"Very easily. Without saying a word. We'll watch him. Constantly. Without a word, moving as little as possible, we'll stare at him all the time. In less than a week, he'll go stark raving mad and dash his brains out against the wall. I guarantee it."

"Agreed!"

He was quite a handsome blond young man. His eyes were bright blue, and his teeth strong and white. He gave each of us an adorable smile as he came in. During the eleventh night he spent with us, he tore open his veins with his teeth.

"If we'd killed him the way Monsieur Alex and Monsieur Eugène suggested, we'd have had problems," the Doctor said.

"That viper didn't suspect we'd force him to bite himself, to bite and poison himself," Match said.

Our guard, staring at the body, showed no surprise: "You guys know how to take care of yourselves!"

"We didn't touch a hair of this gentleman's head!" Alex said.

"I know," the guard said, "I was watching you. I can't pin a thing on you."

Happiness has returned between our four walls. Since the incident of the handsome young man, we've become infinitely more attentive to its *form*. It was the cherished thing we almost lost, the arm miraculously saved from gangrene. We were convalescing from our anguish. Match occasionally exploded in hysterical laughter and rubbed his hands like a horse dealer who has just driven an excellent bargain. Alex gave free rein to his genius as a jack-of-all-trades and has made (mouths wide, we admire the work of his thick fingers) out of woven straw (from the mattresses) a tiny, ravishing coffin in which, he claimed, the soul of the handsome young man was held. Eugène has recovered his sleep and his appetite. As for the Doctor, he was modest in his triumph, and spoke of his next fit with detachment. If he were to behave toward it as we did toward the handsome young man, perhaps it would not approach him. He cherished this hope. In short, the handsome young man's suicide has restored to us all— although we never really lost it—a zest for living. We strolled about, talked of one thing and another with exquisite humor, organized games and contests. Eugène having referred to the Doctor as an "eagle," we played the animal game.

The Doctor was an eagle, Match a rattlesnake, Alex— of course—a boxer (dog) and Eugène a Bengal tiger. The game consisted of imitating as closely as possible the animal of one's choice. So Alex bayed, growled, and tried to lick his nose. Eugène stamped furiously and walked around the walls of the cell on all fours; he fell down in front of Match, who was crawling about and hissing with rage while he beat the floor with his clogs to imitate (badly) the rattling of the snake's tail. Crouching on the edge of a mattress, the Doctor stretched out his neck and beat the air with his arms. Match bit Eugène, the Doctor threw himself on the snake and planted his steel talons in its neck. The dog howled, circling the three furiously intermeshed animals. But the poison took effect, and the tiger, lying on its side, was in its death agony and trembled, all four legs stiff. Its neck broken, the rattlesnake, mouth open, no longer moved. The eagle was perched on the mattress. Crouching in a corner, the dog watched him. Tiger and snake would revive only when dinner came. Another game consisted of pretending that one of us had died. The dead man, hands crossed on his chest, was laid out on a mattress. The other three watched over him, mourned him, wiped their eyes and eulogized his virtues.

Happiness, once again you are our guest. Every hour, every day, is, therefore, sweet to us, as to the honest employee during the last moments of his last day of a vacation with pay. Thus our happiness has something soft and limp about it, something melancholy, although we know it is eternal and—now—inviolable. Yesterday the Doctor laid plans for the future. He spoke of abandoning medicine and devoting himself to politics. Citizens, at the sole thought of what would become of our country should the government fall into the hands of my enemies, my heart cracks within me, my reason staggers . . . and, the Doctor said, I could have a fit (which is easy for me) on the dais. Who would then doubt my fears and my sincerity? Citizens, what is it that my adversaries desire? War! I want peace. They would starve the people when I want to feed them. Destroy the prestige of the State when I want to restore it. Brutalize our children when I want to educate them. Exterminate old men when I want to surround them with care and respect! Destroy bridges, roads, hospitals, monuments, dams when I want to build more! Capitulate to space when I want to conquer it. And if there's one point in my program on which I will not yield, it is the emancipation of women!

"Citizen candidate," Alex said, "I'd like to know if you'd let women box against men?"

"Of course, citizen!"

"That would be pretty funny to see!" Alex said, grinning.

"Citizen candidate," Eugène said, "I'd like to know if, in construction work, the right to strike would be reestablished?"

"Of course, citizen. I'd even admit the case of individual strikes!"

"Citizen candidate," Match said, "I'd like to know your opinion about the death penalty."

"I would have it suppressed every other year."

Eugène may decide to buy a garage soon. Match might go into the police force (misdemeanors). Only Alex has no intention of changing his profession. A month of our lives has thus been occupied by plans for a future which, in the past, we resolved to suppress as incompatible with the notion of happiness. But the suicide of the handsome young man had caused this fever. Oh, happiness, we shall not betray you. We shall walk on huge beaches and the wind will whip our faces and tear from our lips the thousands of words it will bear to the four corners of the earth. Seeds of our words, you will take root and grow everywhere and produce strange flowers in unexpected places, strange flowerings. "Everything we think happens," the Doctor said.

"Let's be careful," Eugène said.

"Don't worry, Monsieur Eugène," Match said, "we're powerless to control our dreams. What have you been dreaming about recently?"

"I was dancing with Jeanne. I wasn't jealous."

"And you, Doctor?"

"I've been dreaming of walking in the mountains. I also dream that I'm not asleep. I dream of endless convalescences, in which nights and days mingle in a room with walled-up windows."

"And you, Monsieur Alex?"

"I step into the ring. I take off my robe. I greet the crowd. They shout their approval. Then my opponent takes off his robe and appears in armor like knights in the old days. I think: 'That's not fair,' and I tell the referee, who answers: 'You're crazy!' I say: 'He's wearing armor, isn't he?' Then the referee says: 'Is something wrong, Alex?' Then the bell rings and the guy walks toward me, raising his iron fists. Then I tell myself: 'There's something pretty disgusting about this.' "

"And then?"

"I wake up."

"And you, Monsieur Match?"

"I'm sitting on my mother's back, watching a carnival procession that's far away, very far away down at the other end of the avenue. I watch it approaching with a hideously ugly mask coming first. I'm delighted at the thought of seeing this mask from close up, but, as it comes toward us, my mother sinks into the sidewalk that swallows her up like quicksand, and when the mask is opposite me, the crowd conceals it from me. I cry out of disappointment and because my mother has disappeared."

Since the handsome young man's suicide, our guard shows us more respect. He pours our soup for us quickly and goes out as if an intolerable odor or heat reigned in the cell. He doesn't speak a word, doesn't even raise his eyes. Have we intimidated him?

"Christ . . ." Eugène said. "If I'd known that trick of yours sooner, Doctor, lots of things wouldn't have happened."

"Which?"

"All that trouble with girls, foremen, that trouble with my wife . . ."

"Take a cat and put it in a little cage. Set this little cage inside a second larger cage. And in this larger cage put a mouse. Then watch. The mouse goes crazy," the Doctor said.

"In boxing, the Doctor's trick doesn't work," Alex said. "You can stare at the other guy all you want, it isn't enough."

"Yes it is!" the Doctor said.

"I never heard of it working."

"Do you remember your fight against the Arab?"

"Well?"

"Well, you were *there*, Monsieur Alex."

"I was there and he's dead."

"Exactly . . ." the Doctor said, gently pinching Alex's ear.

The latter pinched the Doctor's ear back, and the two stood motionless, each clinging to the other's ear. Match clapped his hands.

"Happiness? This is happiness!" he said. "A baby greedily sucking at its mother's breast, then suddenly pulling away and, with a drop of milk on its lips, collapsing into beatitude."

"Happiness? This is happiness!" Alex said: "Good pectorals and stamina."

Since the handsome young man's suicide, should I say that certain links of *gentleness* have attached us to each other? Friends, in the sense meant by citizens enjoying what is called "freedom," we may not be . . . but what *gentleness* prevails among us! Who's ever seen a more charming scene than the one formed by the Doctor and Alex pinching each other's ears, with a smile of sweetness on their lips? And how Eugène's beauty moves us! And with what care we surround Match's fragility! Our understanding is perfect. Moreover, rumors of our union have spread throughout the prison, and the other prisoners and guards don't say: "Match, Eugène, the Doctor, and Alex . . ." but "Cell X . . .". We are *one* (the cell) in *four* persons. Like God, plus one more. We're gentle, good, virtuous, transparent. We lend each other our gestures, our thoughts. There was such a degree of fusion and confusion that the Doctor asked Eugène:

"Listen, Monsieur Eugène, when's my fight with Robinson?"

"But, Doctor . . ."

"Oh, sorry! I thought I was Monsieur Alex."

Since confusions of this kind are in danger of increasing, we've decided to have a roll call every morning and evening. Alex has been put in charge of it:

"Doctor?"

"Present!"

"Take one step toward me, please, and answer: 'Here!'"

"Monsieur Eugène?"

"Here!"

"Monsieur Match?"

"Here!"

"There remains Monsieur Alex, whom I must be. Monsieur Alex? Here! The roll call's over."

Everything worked very well for about a week. But this morning:

"Doctor?"

"Here!" Match, the Doctor, and Eugène answered in unison.

"Impossible," Alex said. "I have two Doctors extra, and all I want is one. Start over again! Doctor?"

"Here!" the three answered again.

"Come on, come on now . . ." Alex said. "Be reasonable! Which of you is the real Doctor?"

"In my opinion, it's likely to be me," the Doctor said.

"We'll see about that . . ." Alex said, addressing the two others.

"What is cancer?"

Eugène and Match remained silent.

"You?"

"A virus," the Doctor said.

"Fine," Alex said, "I'll check you off as the Doctor. And I'd like you to repeat in a low voice: 'I'm the Doctor . . .' until the end of the role call, so as not to forget it."

"I'm the Doctor, I'm the Doctor, I'm the . . ." the Doctor murmured.

"Monsieur Match?"

"Here!" Match and Eugène answer together.

"Im-pos-si-ble!" Alex intoned. "I have only one Monsieur Match on my list, and one Monsieur Eugène. Now which of you is the real Monsieur Match?"

"Me," Eugène answered.

"Are you sure?"

"Yes!"

"Do you swear it?"

"I swear it."

"Fine! Then I have Monsieur Alex and Monsieur Eugène left. Since the one in charge of the role call is Monsieur Alex, I must be Monsieur Alex and, therefore, you're Monsieur Eugène."

"Right," Match said. After an hour, Match began biting his nails while his myopic, haunted eyes swept the walls of the cell. He took off a clog and carefully examined his left foot; then, his hands pressing against his huge forehead, he reflected. He said in a scarcely audible voice:

"Monsieur Alex?"

"Yes?"

"Excuse me, Monsieur Alex, but I have the distinct impression that I'm not Monsieur Eugène."

"Well, who are you then?"

"Well . . . Monsieur Match."

"In that case, would you be Monsieur Eugène, Monsieur Match?" Alex said, turning toward Eugène.

"No," Eugène said, "I'm sure I'm Monsieur Match."

"Let's check," Alex said. "Come over here both of you. Now which of you can answer this question: if you're sitting at a table of five poker players, and one player opens with a pair of jacks, if you're the second bettor with a lower pair, what do you do? One minute . . . You answer, Monsieur Match!"

Eugène opened his mouth and didn't close it again.

"You!" Alex said.

"I follow the opener," Match recited hastily, "but I'm taking a big risk. Normally, with only one pair, I would call. Of course, if someone opened after me, I raise smartly and . . ."

"That's enough!" Alex said, interrupting Match. "Signed, sealed, and delivered! You're Monsieur Match."

"I was sure of it!" Match said.

"Then I'm Eugène?" Eugène asked.

"You've got to be."

"Still . . ." Eugène said.

"Ask him a question," the Doctor suggested.

"Right!" Alex said. "Why are you in jail?"

Eugène shrugged in absolute ignorance.

"Think it over! Who did you kill?"

"I thought I tried to hang myself when I was little . . ."

"No, that memory belongs to Monsieur Match. I'm asking you the following question: Who did you kill?"

"My Helène will never love me because of my crimes and because my mother loved my little brother."

"No! No! That belongs to the Doctor!"

Eugène fluttered his eyelids.

"I offend the Lord and . . ."

"No that belongs to . . ."

"Me," Match said, snapping his fingers.

"Right! Answer the question: Who did you kill?"

"My wife?" Eugène stammered hesitantly.

"Right!"

"And what was her name?"

"Jeanne?"

"Fine, fine!

"And how did you get rid of her?"

"A bullet through the heart, and then there was a little red hole no bigger than a ten-franc piece, and I wondered how so much force and beauty could have escaped through such a little hole?"

"No, that's Guitare's death. That's my memory. How did you get rid of Jeanne?"

"I was drunk?"

"Bravo! And she was . . . ?"

"Pregnant?"

"Fine! And you kicked her in the . . . ?"

"Belly?"

"Marvelous! You're Monsieur Eugène!"

"Well . . ." Eugène said, "what if it's not true . . . Maybe I did say it, but suppose it's a lie, what about that?"

"True or false isn't the point," Alex said. "The point is, you remember it, and that's why you're Monsieur Eugène. *Verstanden?* as Guitare used to say."

"*Ja!*" Eugène answered.

Who scratches his head. Who borrows Alex's mirror-pan and looks at himself in it. Or examines his teeth. Who suddenly exclaims: "Am I Eugène?" Who calls: "Eugène? Eugène?" and cocks his head as though he were listening to a muffled echo. "I'm Eugène?" He cocked his head, one hand cupped around his ear. "I'm not Eugène?" He listened . . .

"It's damn complicated, finding out if you're who you are," he said, quite pale.

"And when you do find out . . ." the Doctor said.

"I'm sure," Alex said proudly, "I'm sure of being Alex because of the role call."

Eugène had a bad headache. He groaned. He talked. He said it was all mixed up. After all, it didn't matter to him whether he was Eugène or not, but as for swearing *for sure* . . . After all, it wasn't really, absolutely, positively sure . . . Where was the proof? All four got so mixed up . . . Yet the Doctor knew what cancer was, and I didn't. But what if I'm the real Doctor only I've forgotten, and what if he's Eugène who's remembered what I (the Doctor) taught him before I forgot? In that case, he's the one who's become the real Doctor, and, as for me, instead of being an oblivious and real doctor, wouldn't it be better for me to accept being a false Eugène, since I remember his life? Besides, I'm Match. What if I don't know how to play poker? Maybe that's because I don't want to be the gambler I used to be any more and maybe he isn't ashamed of it because he's Eugène and has never touched cards. He groaned. Match lay his hand on his shoulder.

"I'm sorry, Monsieur Eugène, but I assure you you're not me."

"You're Monsieur Match?"

Match nodded his head yes. "I am, and what proves it

is that I'm not so happy about it. If I . . ."

"Then be *me*," Eugène implored. "I, on the contrary, would be very happy being you."

"But I'm Match," Match repeated, nonplused.

"Are you really sure?"

"*Ja,* as Guitare would say," Match said ironically, "I am and I'll die of it, Monsieur Eugène."

"We'll all die of it," the Doctor said. "As a matter of fact, Monsieur Eugène, do you want to be me? If that amuses you, all we have to do is let Monsieur Alex know and it's settled. All right?"

"No," Eugène said, "I want to be Monsieur Match."

"Why?"

"Because he has a nice life."

"Do him a favor, Monsieur Match!" the Doctor said. "Be Eugène."

"I'm terribly sorry," Match said, "it's impossible."

"Why?"

"Because . . . I haven't told you everything . . ."

"Tell, then."

"I'm a homosexual."

"What do you think of that, Monsieur Eugène?" the Doctor asked.

Eugène rubbed his chin. He asked for time to think it over. The next day, he answered "here" very promptly when his name was called. Match smiled.

"How are you, Monsieur Eugène?"

"Fine."

"By the way, I'm not a homosexual. I was just testing you. If you had said: 'It doesn't matter to me! . . .' I'd have traded with you."

"Well, after all," Eugène said, "I don't care. Actually, I could even thank you for holding out. Which reminds me, what's the news today? Since I thought I was you, I didn't listen to it."

"Nothing new. Violent storms in the north, but France is primarily affected by an influx of relatively warm oceanic air from the northwest, bringing abundant clouds and brief showers."

"What season is it? Summer?"

"It's about the seventeenth of March, but the spring is particularly mild this year."

Everything returned to normal. We resumed our own names, our own skins, and each of us told his own story, his own recollections, his own thoughts. The Doctor profusely apologized, in the Japanese manner, for having been the cause of these recent incidents. He was the one, as a matter of fact, who first mistook himself for someone else, asking what date he was scheduled to fight Sugar Ray Robinson. We acknowledged his excuses but begged him—with many precautions and circumlocutions—not to begin again. Under our rough exteriors, we were still terribly fragile, and without Alex's authority what would have become of us? We were sinking into anarchy, Match said.

"Believe me, I have no intention of minimizing my error," the Doctor said, "but I'm convinced that in a certain amount of time everything would have returned to normal anyway."

It took us a good week to debate this question. Strangely enough, even Alex, who ordinarily had no interest in this kind of problem took part in the discussion. Ac-

cording to the Doctor, after a period of confusion everything would have been settled. He would have been Alex,
and then?

"Yes," Alex said, "but you wouldn't have had a chance
against Robinson!"

"I'd have had your chances, Monsieur Alex, since I'd
have been you."

"What about breathing?" Alex said. "And relaxation?
And technique?"

"They would have been yours!"

"And pectorals? And punch?"

"Yours!"

"Excuse me, Doctor, but I don't follow you. From one
day to the next, after not having a muscle in your body,
you'd suddenly be built like me?"

"Sure!"

"I'll bet you anything you wouldn't!"

"That's not the point, Monsieur Alex!"

"What *is* the point? Robinson would smash you to bits.
It would be a dishonor to my name."

"No it wouldn't: since your name would have become
mine, the dishonor would be mine."

"That's right. But Robinson . . ."

"I agree with the Doctor," Match said. "It wasn't so
much a question of exchanging our improbable futures,
Monsieur Alex, as our pasts. Actually, it was really a question of exchanging our memories, or even our crimes, or
—if you prefer—our innocence. For instance, the Doctor
would now be the murderer of Guitare d'Amour, the murderer of Mademoiselle Maridge, the murderer of Monsieur Khadi, etcetera."

"What etcetera?" Alex asked.

"He would have inherited the rest of your story."

"Listen, Monsieur Match, I have nothing to blame myself for!"

"In that case, he'd have inherited your innocence . . . Let's say: your candor."

"And then I'd have knocked off Mademoiselle Helène?"

"It would be up to you to settle that with your own conscience."

"At the start, I'd have been glad to help you," the Doctor said, "by slipping you a few unpublished hints about the case, and soon you'd have managed by yourself without any trouble."

Eugène gave his forehead a tremendous blow with his fist. It was his own way of bringing forth the spark of an idea. He's using his "lighter," Match says. Here's the idea.

"Do you mean, Doctor, that you can choose your life? Just like that?"

"Yes," the Doctor said, "you can choose *after*, not *before*."

"That's not choosing!"

"Yes it is!" Match exclaimed, launching into a tremendous lecture on the last judgment.

"You die. You appear before the Great Judge. He (Match shook out the magistrate's invisible sleeves) tells you . . . He's sitting on his throne at one end of an enormous hall whose length no human brain can fathom. You appear before him when you pass through the black steel doors, like a grain of dust. You're—so far away from him—about the size and weight of a fly's foot. Up ahead, you see Him shining in the center of a motionless flash of lightning, but the light's so dazzling that you can't make out His features. You even have to blink to keep from being blinded. By this sign, the Great Judge understands that you're a terrible criminal, since you can't look him in the face without being blinded by his Truth. (Alex smiled, transfixed, and was transformed into the child who listens to stories on long winter evenings when it is snowing outside; the Doctor had to struggle to keep from embracing him.) Only innocents don't blink in this light. Let me add, parenthetically, that ever since the Great Judge has been exercising His functions—for a long time—since the world began—it's never happened that a (let's say a "dead man") a dead man has failed to blink. Monsieur Alex, once you set foot in that hall, you can't help it; you begin trembling and sweating. Then the Great Judge says—and He has the terrible sweetness in his voice that judges have before they've judged you—he says: "Approach, dear Monsieur Alex!" What can you do? You obey. You walk toward the throne. That walk lasts eternities, but you don't notice it because you're outside time.

"Fine! Now there you are at the foot of the throne. The Great Judge says: 'Well, my dear Monsieur Alex, you're pretty much of a criminal, aren't you? Tell me a little about your life . . . Go on, I'm listening.' Oh, Monsieur Alex, that's when you have to pay attention, that's when you have to watch out, that's when you have to be very, very, very, very, very, very smart. Why? Because the Great Judge actually doesn't know a thing about you. Yes, you're actually going to tell Him everything, and He'll judge you by just what you've told him. So you have a choice between a whole lot of lives, all of which belong to you. Which one can you tell Him? If you don't find the right one—the right one, in His eyes, that's it—you're lost. Take an example. You tell Him: 'I knocked out Khadi, etcetera.' Well, now, and without knowing either why or how, you've damned yourself from head to foot. On the other hand, suppose you 'forget' the Khadi business and you tell Him how you tortured Mademoiselle Maridge, wiped out Monsieur Guitare, etcetera, and still, without knowing why or how, you're pardoned. The Great Judge laughs till He cries, listening to you. I'm taking very crude examples. But for instance, you tell Him that you sneezed one day at the dentist's and He falls into a terrible rage. On the other hand, He wriggles with joy if he hears that you smashed in the skulls of your six children with an ax after tying their mother to a chair so she wouldn't miss the show. Ah, Monsieur Alex, you've got to choose carefully!"

"With someone like that, you never can tell, can you? What would *you* tell Him, Monsieur Match?"

"I'd tell him that I hanged myself at the age of twelve, that the rope broke but gave me a terrible shock, and that I have forgotten everything since then."

"He'd condemn you," the Doctor said.

"You think so?"

"I'll bet."

"What would *you* tell Him, Doctor?"

"I have my own idea, which applies only to me; I'm terribly sorry . . ."

"Your fits? And suppose you're only a faker?"

"I wouldn't tell Him a word about that. Parenthetically, Monsieur Match, I don't like your story much, your Great Judge . . . Silly, your story's silly! You want my opinion . . . ?"

"God Himself doesn't know what mercy will inspire him on Judgment Day. 'Is *that* what my humanity was? Is that what you are, my human beings? Poor wretches!'"

"But what will He do with us? What will He make us into?"

"Statues," Alex said with a yawn.

"Oblivion," the Doctor said.

"Eternity," Match said.

"Well, if you want to play with words . . ."

And suddenly Match wondered if our prison was on the seashore, in the desert, or in the mountains. Really, Monsieur Match, you invent problems! . . . What does it matter? He wouldn't mind being in prison as long as he knew where this prison was. It tempted—he said—his imagination. By trying to guess the species of birds that cross our skylight, we tried to guess where we were but birds were rare and besides they flew very high. Thus Eugène and the Doctor argued inconclusively about a speck in the sky. A swallow, the Doctor said; a stork, Eugène said. Alex, who boasted of possessing a fox's sense of smell, sniffed several times. The air smelled of the sea, of salt and tar. He ran his tongue over his lips: at the seashore your lips get salty. Well? Alex hesitated, and to be more certain, licked his arms and legs. Match, the Doctor, and Eugène licked their hands. We hesitated to come to any decision. Alex inhaled deeply, and now it's a smell of hay that tickles his nostrils. Hay at the seashore?

"The first time I went to a whorehouse," the Doctor said, "I was sixteen or seventeen. The madame called one of her girls in and peremptorily ordered her: 'Show this gentleman your knees!' The flat-faced girl raised her skirt and revealed two enormous wrinkled knees. 'There, monsieur,' the old lady with curlers in her hair said, 'doesn't she have the most beautiful knees in the world, that little witch?' Her hands clasped, her eyes fixed, she stared at the girl's knees. I was still a virgin and I had dreamed of milky throats, smooth shoulders, alabaster thighs, and now I decided that my whole erotomaniac system had to be junked because this knowledgeable lady offered me a pair of knees to venerate. I spent a long time working out my wildly shaken eroticism all over again. For me, the idea of hay is associated with knees, for the old madame suffered from chronic sinusitis and kept sticking her nose into a bowl where some kind of brew of boiled hay was steaming. 'Excuse me, I'm inhaling,' she would say. Oh, that limp face collapsing over the bowl and turning crimson, surrounded by smelly steam! She raised her alcoholic Medusa's head and repeated in a voice broken by alternating rage and turpitude: 'Aren't those the most beautiful knees in the world?' "

"When I think of knees," Match said, "I think of church. Mine were skinny and bony. When I came out of Mass, they were striped with two long red lines, and they hurt."

"Hay and the sea don't go together," Eugène said.

We decided to make a living ladder for Match, whom Alex lifted like a feather and perched on his shoulders. What does he see when his face is up to the skylight? A wall. What color? Black. What kind of black? Soot black? Grayish black. Alex strained. At the bottom of the wall? Nothing. Between this wall and the prison? Nothing. Does he have any idea what storey we're on?

Very high. Tenth or fifteenth. Does he see any other windows like ours? Yes. Very many? Like in any prison. Does he see any birds? No. Does he hear any noises? A dog barking? Maybe . . . He can't identify it. Alex put him down.

"Well, Monsieur Match?"

"Aside from that cry, nothing."

"A human cry, or an animal cry?"

"I couldn't say. Who knows what a camel's cry sounds like?"

No one. But what made him think it could be a camel's cry? Nothing, he just happened to say that. Every day, at the same hour, Alex lifted Match up on his shoulders. If we identified the cry—which is repeated every day—we'd have some idea (however vague) of where we are. Alas! Sometimes Match thought it was the wailing of a factory siren, sometimes a woman screaming in labor (maybe our fortress is close to a maternity ward?), sometimes the barking of a sergeant maneuvering his terrorized recruits, sometimes the rumbling of a nearly extinct volcano, sometimes the trumpeting of an elephant.

Match's obsession ends as suddenly as it had begun. Why wear myself out trying to discover whether we're living in Africa, Greece, or Asia?

The Doctor had a fit. After shaking his head back and forth a few minutes, he tried to dash head down into the wall with all his might. Alex got in front of him right away and got a butt in the belly which wrung a yelp of pain from him. The Doctor drove ahead like a raging bull, and each time Alex stood in his way (to keep our friend from dashing out his brains) he got the battering ram in his belly. Terribly shaken, on the brink of fainting, Alex groaned; his eyes grew glassy; his mouth, lips sucked in, grew thin as a scar and he delivered a sharp uppercut that knocked the Doctor backward and sent him, stunned, against the opposite wall, down which he slid, head on one shoulder like a drunk, eyes closed. We picked him up and lay him out on a mattress. "Did I kill him?" Alex asked calmly.

"No," Match said, "he'll wake up in an hour or two."

"That was a nicely placed uppercut, kid," Eugène said.

"Thank you, Monsieur Eugène," Alex said.

We examined the Doctor, whose face was beginning to swell. If Alex hadn't stood between him and the wall, he would have dashed his brains out. "So," Eugène said, "when he says he's a faker, he's lying." Match shrugged. Why? Because a faker would stop before he went all the way. No. Sooner or later, a faker gets up his nerve and goes all the way.

The Doctor came to just before the evening meal, but it was impossible for him to open his mouth. He was not hungry. Instead of eyes, he had two swollen masses through which the two needles of his gaze penetrated; a trickle of blood flowed out of his nose and coagulated in a foamy mustache over his now puffy lips. Alex apologized and recited a kind of compliment that Match had taught him.

"If I hadn't intervened, Doctor, you would have cracked open your skull; therefore, circumstances obliged me to use means naturally repugnant to me outside of the ring. Please believe me that it was not with any pleasure that I resolved to knock you out, and forgive what may seem to have been brutal about my action for the sake of its effectiveness."

The breath hissing between the Doctor's lips signified: "Thank you, thank you!" The next day, his face was a deep reddish-violet, with a really black area on the left cheek, but he was brimming over with . . . Joy? No. Cheer? No, not that either. Gaiety? No. To be precise, he was brimming over with cunning. As usual, Match gave him a detailed account of how his fit occurred, which he listened to with little clucks of amazed interest, like a country girl being courted by a city slicker.

"Eyes turned up? No! . . . and you say that little drops of sweat burst out on my forehead? And I opened my mouth like a stranded fish gasping for breath? And my chin trembled? No! Yes? Really? So hard it looked like a blob of gelatin? Oh, my!"

Match described many other details, and the Doctor repeated his remarks almost word for word, like a child who knows by heart the story he has heard a hundred times, and can finish the sentences his grandfather has begun.

"And I butted my head against the wall? Against Monsieur Alex? Oh no, it *was* against the wall, but Monsieur Alex served as a shield, that's it, that's it. And I *aimed* at Monsieur Alex? No! Oh, I see . . . but of course, in a manner of speaking, I aimed my head at him. Exactly! And then Monsieur Alex hit me? Not in anger, you say. Deliberately, was that it?"

He went over to Alex and warmly shook his hand. Not at all! Yes, yes, I insist on thanking you, and I beg you to count on me if . . . Oh, no, Doctor, it was nothing, nothing at all . . . Yes, yes it was! Your behavior touches me. Alex simpered. The Doctor, his delicate hand lost in Alex's enormous fist, shook his arm, endlessly, with all his meager strength.

"Forgive me, Doctor, but I forgot one detail . . . A very important one."

"A gesture or words?" the Doctor said anxiously.

"A few words I think I made out just before the fit began. It seems to me you said . . ."

"Bah! Let's talk about something else . . ."

In the cell, the light suddenly faded. Could it be night right after we finished lunch? The blue bulb gleamed (it's on night and day, which sometimes makes Alex say: 'We're condemned to death!') and smeared our faces with violet shadows. A furious painter wiped his fingers on our foreheads, our cheeks. Eugène swore he heard a waltz. The Doctor said he had memories. He was lying on his mattress and Alex, Eugène, and Match were sitting in front of him, legs crossed tailor-fashion, on the cement floor. He had memories? Like everyone else! No, he had memories of *the future,* too. Eugène squinted in astonishment; Alex stuck his forefinger up his nose. The Doctor remembered, somehow, what he *will do.* Then you're what you might call a visionary? No, we haven't understood him properly. He's not a visionary at all, nor a clairvoyant, nor an astrologer. More exactly, if it's possible to be exact in this matter, he doesn't know if it's what he *has* done or what he *will* do that he remembers. For instance, has he killed Helène or *will* he kill her? *Has* he known her, or *will* he know her?

"Wow!" Alex exclaimed.

"That's great!" Eugène said.

Did they know that he didn't stop there, that sometimes he wondered if he already exists or if he's going to be born?

"Ho!" Alex said, as if he had received a tremendous blow on the back of his neck.

"But then, Doctor, if you're not born . . ." said Eugène, who either didn't dare or didn't know how to end his sentence.

"If I'm not born, my friends, you don't exist," the Doctor said with the gentleness of implacable evidence in his voice. His blank gaze met the eyes of his three friends, one after the other. Match drew his head between his shoulders and looked like a stuffed stork; Eugène's lips were white and dry; the kind of biceps Alex used instead of a brain made a tremendous effort.

"You don't exist . . . I'm dreaming you. My dear friends, you're only the dream of a man who's already dead, or of a man who's about to live in the future."

"That's not true . . ." Eugène stammered.

"Ah, Monsieur Eugène, the true, the false . . . That's a human presumption for you!"

"You said 'human!' " Match said.

"It's because I dream about men, that's all."

Cunning! He was cunning all right! He could anticipate them, with their big clumsy shoes, their glassy eyes, their voices, their teeth, their hair, their stone walls, their seasons, and their *lies*. He heard them thinking as if he heard the ticking of three watches. Don't challenge him! A watch stops! It breaks! Ziiiiiii! Bzzzzzz! . . .

"All I need to do, gentlemen, is to decide to stop dreaming about you and you'd disappear, dissolve; the puddle left by the storm is transformed into vapor once the sun comes out again. . . . I uncork the bottle and the ether evaporates. All I need, dear watches, is to forget to wind you up again."

"Doctor, you wouldn't do that!" Eugène said.

"Don't kid around!" Alex said.

"For pity's sake," Match said.

Above all, Ziiiiii, don't give him any orders! He'll do exactly what he feels like and don't ever forget it. Of course they could defy him. One of them, in a fit of madness, might exclaim: "Stop dreaming, Doctor! Evaporate! Break!" Bzzzzz, who would dare? If he *is* raving, what a victory! The greatest the beast has ever won! But if he's telling the *truth* . . . Oh Alex, Eugène, Match, then you're exiled from what you call life and melted into eternal darkness, eternal silence. Neither born, nor about to be born. Neither living nor dead. Nothing! Nothing! Nothing! Nothing! Not nothingness, not outside, just NOTHING.

"I said NOTHING!"

Might as well be dreamed as anything else, if they'll believe him. That's what he advised them, amicably enough. He was fond of them.

"Shall I ask you a question, Doctor?" Match asked timidly.

"I'm listening to you."

"Do I dare, Doctor?"

"Dare!"

"And you won't be angry?"

"Of course not."

"Doctor, are you sure you're dreaming us?"

"Not at all, Monsieur Match. It's just an idea of mine, nothing but an idea . . . Still, in your position, I'd be careful."

"Thank you, Doctor. May I ask you another question?"

"Go ahead . . ."

"Do you intend to dream us for much longer?"

"I'm terribly sorry, Monsieur Match, but I can't answer that."

"Why?"

"Because I'll dream you as long as it suits me, and I have no idea what whims and caprices I may have on that score."

The Doctor refused to continue this conversation. At the evening meal, he ate without a word. The next day, he was still walled up behind his silence. Match, Alex, and Eugène decided to hold an emergency council because of the gravity of the situation. A decision to defy the Doctor shouldn't be the result of sudden impulse any more than individual initiative.

"Since all three of us are concerned," Match said, "our decision must be a mutual one, and whatever it is, we should solemnly swear to stand by it. What's your opinion, Monsieur Alex?"

"My opinion," Alex said, "is that I've thought it over carefully, and in my opinion we'd better be pretty careful. After all, the Doctor's the . . . the most (Alex screwed his forefinger into his forehead) guy I know and . . ."

"So you're against defiance?"

"In my opinion, I'm against it."

"And you, Monsieur Eugène?"

"Me, I'm scared."

"Against?"

"I'm scared, you know?"

"Against?"

"Yes."

"As for me," Match said, "I'm against it because actually . . . it suits me to be dreamed. Not black, not white; not odd, not even; not true, not false—I'm just blank!"

Match explained at length the advantages of the situation, its consequences (some are important!) and the three men separated after reaching a crucial decision, which it was Monsieur Alex's responsibility to explain to the Doctor. The latter was still lying on his mattress, hands behind his head, eyes open. Alex advanced toward him with signs of infinite respect.

"Doctor, I have a decision to communicate to you."

"Go ahead!" the Doctor said without blinking.

Alex cleared his throat and, not knowing what to do with his hands, hid them behind his back.

"Doctor, we've decided that you're God."

"All right . . ."

The Doctor sighed, sat up on the mattress, and yawned noisily. He said that it was logical, quite logical.

"You'll worship me?"

Alex stammered: "We haven't discussed that yet."

"Oh, that's only a detail," the Doctor said. "Maybe it isn't even necessary, just among ourselves, to stand on ceremony."

He lay down again. He said it was logical, quite logical. He said it had to end this way. He closed his eyes.

JEAN CAU

Jean Cau was born in the Pyrenees area of France in 1925. Son of a laborer, he was educated on scholarships. In 1944 he arrived in Paris carrying a wooden suitcase. Of that time he says: "Under German occupation France was a huge prison. In 1944, with the liberation, all the doors opened. I was nineteen years old, and it was an extraordinary time."

Three years later he became Jean-Paul Sartre's secretary. He left to join the weekly "*L'Express,*" where he is a star reporter. His activities range from covering the Algerian war and French internal politics to bullfighting and other sports.